EIGHT

ALSO BY WW MORTENSEN

SLITHERS

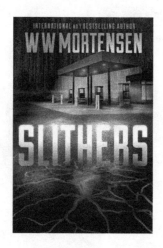

COMING SOON

THE ALPHA SPECIES

W W MORTENSEN

EIGHT

TERROR HAS A NEW SPECIES

HOUSE OF THE
SUN

ACKNOWLEDGEMENTS

For their help with this version of EIGHT, special thanks must go to Julie Sampson, Leslie Lutz, Jeroen ten Berge and Rob Siders.

For my family

PROLOGUE

The DHC-3 crawled through the darkening sky, skimming the jungle canopy. From the air, the forest was an impressive sight, an unbroken carpet of green stretching endlessly in all directions. But it was the distant horizon that had stolen the attention of Carlos Juarez as he sat at the controls of the tiny aircraft. Ahead, blackened clouds amassed, raked by lightning at the point where the jungle met the sky.

A storm was building.

Carlos shook his head. *Of all the luck.* Evening thunderstorms weren't unusual in western Amazonia, but he hated flying in bad weather.

"So much for the perfect getaway," he murmured, turning to Maria in the seat beside him. He spoke in Brazilian Portuguese, and his voice was low. "Looks bad."

For long seconds, Maria stared into the gathering veil. "Not that bad," she said, and shrugged. "I've seen worse." She turned to meet his gaze. Normally bright, her almond-coloured eyes were now dim with indifference.

Carlos disagreed about the storm but wasn't going to argue.

Below them, endless shades of green slid smoothly beneath the plane.

Changing the subject, Carlos said, "I've made arrangements for the boat to Monte Oeste. We leave tomorrow morning." As he spoke, he realised he was staring, drawn by the contours of Maria's face and the smoothness of her unblemished, deep olive skin. Her long, shiny dark hair hung in waves that stretched halfway down her back.

God, she's beautiful.

Maria must have noticed the scrutiny. "And what of your plans till then?" she asked, running her fingers through his close-cropped hair.

Carlos grinned. "And spoil the surprise? I don't think so."

Still grinning, he turned again to the view beyond the cockpit, where lightning flickered in sheets through the distant blackness like a faulty fluorescent tube.

Soon, everything will be different, he thought. *Safe.* Serious once more, he considered their escape to Monte Oeste, his mind drifting to the promise of a second chance, a new life.

He cocked his head, listening. The sound had only lasted a second—a pop, followed by a pause in the otherwise steady drone of the engine. He glanced at the instrument panel: no blinking lights or flashing gauges caught his eye. Again, he listened. The floatplane was his brother's, but he'd flown it dozens of times and knew its every tick. He was sure he'd heard something.

The engine purred comfortably. The plane pushed through the glowering sky.

"Carlos, honey—are you alright?"

Perhaps he'd imagined it after all. He smiled faintly. "Of course, everything's fine."

The words had barely left his mouth before the first drops of rain crashed hard against the cockpit glass. Carlos refocused, the incident forgotten. "Here we go." He braced himself… and flew straight into the storm's dark maw.

A rush of wind batted the aircraft, tossing it like a ship in heavy seas and jarring the tiny plane violently. Shades of dark grey and black pressed against the cockpit glass, though on all sides came flashes of brilliance as lightning sparked and flared.

"You've seen worse?" Carlos said as rain pounded the shell of the cabin. A fork of blinding white split the sky before them, and he jumped. It was close. *Too* close.

Maria chose not to reply, and—though trying to hide it, as was her penchant—was now sitting tensely upright. Carlos felt a knot of dread tighten in his stomach.

He *hated* flying in bad weather.

He turned to voice his detestation but was cut off by a deafening boom and a burst of light so bright that it came seemingly from inside the cabin.

With a sizzle, the instrument panel shut off, plunging them into darkness. Maria screamed.

The plane had been struck by lightning.

Like a school of startled fish, remnants of the flash jagged across Carlos's vision. He blinked, hearing at the same time Maria's cry of terror give way to a high-pitched wail. She was calling to him.

But there was a greater demand of his attention.

The sound he had heard only seconds earlier had come again, and this time there was no mistaking it. A pop—then silence.

The engine had died.

Without warning, the engine roared back to life, revving loudly. The instrument panel surged back as well, but it was now dotted with numerous, flashing red lights.

"Carlos, what's happening?"

Carlos stalled, taking stock. "We're losing altitude." He heard Maria's breath catch in her throat, the resolve that some mistook for coldness having all but fled her.

"Oh God…what are we going to do?"

Carlos squinted through the near-dark and found no safe place to land the stricken plane: no rivers, no clear stretch of water. To both the north and south, the ground was elevated and uneven. The shallow valley between, running west in the direction they flew, was covered in the same thick, unbroken jungle that blanketed every square mile—every square *inch*—of the visible world.

He wrestled with the controls and got minimal response. They were already too low anyway.

"We don't have a choice," he said. "We're going into the valley. If I can keep her level… the jungle might cushion the impact." He turned to Maria. There was no disguising her terror; tears welled in her wide eyes, and she gripped the instrument panel so hard her knuckles had turned white. Carlos gripped the steering yoke, his own fingers pale and trembling. "Hold on," he said redundantly.

The earth rushed up to swallow them…

The plane tore into the canopy, roaring.

Glass shattered. Metal screamed. With sickening force, Carlos was flung in his seat. The cabin alternated between light and dark like a malfunctioning strobe. Something hit him in the head, stunning him. Outside, thick branches snapped like matchsticks against all sides of the plane, filling his ears with thunder. Cutting through it all were Maria's hysterical wails. Carlos prayed her death would be painless.

But then just as everything was too fast and the noise too loud there was a release… and a sensation of slowing… and then time paused…

…before strangely, speeding up again, but gently, and it seemed the physical world was transforming, softening to deliver the plane to safety.

Carlos felt…

…a momentary sense of weightlessness….

Then, the screeching metal was no more. Everything stilled.

Carlos blinked, disoriented. Blurry veils winged across his vision like a flock of dark birds, threatening to drag him from consciousness.

"Honey? Carlos?"

The voice hauled him back to his senses, and his eyes refocused. He turned his head, pain shooting into his temples. Maria was slumped forward, her hair messed and across her face. "Are you okay?" he asked.

Maria groaned. "I… I think so."

It took a moment for the shock to clear and for Carlos to grasp that the two of them were still alive. Only then did he become aware of the seatbelt biting into his flesh, supporting the full weight of his body. They appeared to be hanging nose-down tail-up above the ground, tangled in the canopy.

Outside, the afternoon's storm-filtered light was rapidly dissolving into blackness, and an inky gloom permeated the cabin. Carlos strained to see through the windshield, but it had become a silvery maze of cracks and the plane's right wing—which had twisted across the front of the aircraft—blocked his view. With effort, he turned and glanced through the window in the door beside Maria. The glass there had shattered, affording him limited visibility. Strangely, though, and despite the lack of light, he didn't see the leaves or branches you'd expect to find in a jungle canopy.

What the…

Rain pummelled the fuselage, drumming on the De Havilland. The aircraft swayed gently. Metal groaned and strained.

And then there was another sound.

Scratching. On the outside of the cabin.

Heart pounding, Carlos was for a fleeting moment reminded of his youth, of a time when he and his brother Ramos as kids would go to the beach collecting crabs in a tin pail. The way the crabs would claw and scramble…

A scurrying across the roof echoed inside the cabin, and a dark blur streaked past the right-rear window.

A monkey?

"Carlos!" Maria cried, her voice tightening to a squeal. "Did you see that? *There's something out there!*"

More scrabbling, followed by a long silence—again, just the rain and soft creak and tick of metal. The strange sound didn't return.

"Stay quiet," Carlos whispered. Holding onto the seat, feet propped against the instrument panel, he released the clasp of his harness with a gentle click.

"*What are you doing?*"

"I'm going to look outside, get us out of here."

"*Outside?*"

Carlos climbed carefully towards the tail of the plane. His head throbbed with the effort, in keeping with the galloping pace of his heart. He tasted blood in his mouth.

Outside, the tattoo of rain continued.

At the rear of the plane, set into the wall behind the seats, was a tiny storage compartment. With a push of a button, Carlos snapped it open to expose a gleaming, chrome-plated automatic pistol. He retrieved the Colt, in the process catching sight of the palm-sized cloth bag tucked up behind the weapon. He paused to stare at the item, then abruptly closed the compartment with the bag still inside.

Working quickly, Carlos checked the .45, noting the scratching sound hadn't returned. Satisfied the Colt was fully loaded and in proper working order, he climbed back to the aircraft's battered door. Hesitating there, he braced himself and took a deep breath. Pistol in hand, he forced the door open and peered out.

Nothing could have prepared him for what lay beyond.

"*Meu Deus…*" he whispered, crossing himself.

He sensed a presence in the shattered window beside Maria. She didn't get a chance to scream. Nor did he.

Outside, the scurrying became more frantic, thunderous above the drumming rain.

UPPER REACHES OF THE RIO TEKENU, THE AMAZON BASIN
TWO YEARS LATER...

Ed Reardon glanced at his watch and cursed. Forty minutes had passed since he'd planned to break at the peak; now, standing upon it amid waist-high ferns and in the deepening shadow of the canopy, he realised he'd been kidding himself. In less than two hours it'd be dark, and by nightfall he'd hoped to be at the first marker. At this rate there seemed little chance of that, even less if he didn't keep moving.

"It's not far to the bottom," he said at last, turning to his companion as the call of a solitary woolly monkey echoed somewhere in the understorey. "I'll get a fix on our position from there."

Robert Sanchez had already removed his pack and stared intently at a hand-held GPS receiver. He looked up. "*Amigo,*" he said, his small brown eyes little more than narrow slits, "we should stop and confirm our position *now.* Once already we have strayed, and we can little afford to do so again."

Distracted, Ed listened to the monkey's cry trail off before running a hand through a mess of hair wet with rain. Sanchez was right, and he hadn't the energy to argue. Frustrated, he slumped, exhausted, against the enormous root of a kapok tree. "We're close, though, Robert," he said, pulling maps from his pocket. "I can feel it."

Sanchez said nothing as he adjusted the hood of his poncho against the drizzle. Ed did so, too. For much of the day, the downpour had been relentless, easing only in the last hour. Mostly, he'd been thankful for it. Any relief from the humidity was a godsend.

With a grunt, he slipped from his pack and made room for his friend to slide beside him. Sanchez passed Ed a cigarette before rolling one for himself, his small brown eyes as dark and impenetrable as the jungle they scanned.

Ed inhaled and relaxed a little. "I swear I don't ever want to give these up."

He let the cigarette hang from his mouth, fumbling with an old military map marked with handwritten notes. Blowing a line of smoke, he pointed to an area of the chart circled in red. "This is the place Owen told me about. As far as I can tell, we're here." He moved his finger to the right, just outside the circle.

Sanchez cross-referenced this with his own map and took GPS readings. "As I've warned you already, he's marked only a general area. It could take days to search."

"It's the centre of the circle I'm interested in. This spot here." Ed pointed enthusiastically.

Punching data into the ruggedised laptop he'd removed from his pack, Sanchez nodded in that same needle-in-a-haystack way he always did. Deep down, Ed shared his companion's concerns. In jungle like this, and lacking accurate directions, they could pass within ten feet of the site without realising it. But what choice did they have? He wouldn't be swayed, not now.

He checked the GPS, made some calculations and glanced at his watch again. "There's still enough light to reach the spot Owen has marked. If he's correct, we won't need to search."

They got to their feet, heaving their packs. Sanchez took the lead, cutting with a strength and ferocity that belied his slight frame. For the next hour the two men hacked through the green maze without a word passing between them.

Soon, they were inside the area circled on the map. They pushed on. Ed's plan was to get to the spot he'd earlier identified, take a GPS reading, then search for the first marker by spiralling outwards with foliage-penetrating, infrared binoculars.

The rain intensified, thrumming through the trees. Ed checked the time. Ninety minutes had passed since they'd checked the maps. He'd counted on another half hour of daylight, but now only a handful of the sun's rays penetrated the canopy, none of them strong.

Frustrated, Ed cursed. Time had beaten them.

We still have tomorrow, in full daylight. We'll find it then.

With that, his focus shifted to where they might break for camp. The jungle was no place to be caught—

With a suddenness that caused Ed to jump, Sanchez spun and seized him by the arm. "Look! Over there!"

Surprised by the rare show of emotion in his friend's voice—feeling it, too, in the firmness of his grip—Ed followed his companion's gaze.

Ahead, not more than a dozen yards away and covered in a thick tangle of vines and lianas rose a thick pillar of stone. Ed's heart leapt as he peered through the gloom.

The totem. *They'd found it!*

In a rush, Sanchez pulled and hacked at the clinging vegetation, nearly tripping in his haste. "It's beautiful, *amigo*! Don't you think so?"

Ed could only stare in wonder. When at last he found his voice, it was low and breathless, and he suspected most of his words inaudible. "It's real," he stammered. "I can't believe it… it's *real*…" He turned to his companion, spinning him around by the shoulders. When he spoke again, there could be no mistaking him. "My God, Robert! WE'VE FOUND IT!"

On legs that felt like jelly, Ed lunged forward, stripping away the remaining vines and running his fingers over the totem's smooth, exposed stone. It was cool and moist from the rain. "What are you doing here?" he whispered, pressing his cheek firmly against the intricate carving. "You're so far from home, aren't you?"

They set up camp only yards from the totem, finishing as the jungle swallowed the last of the light like a sated predator.

"Shall I take first watch?" Sanchez asked.

Ed sat on some deadfall at the rim of the fire pit they'd dug into the moist soil of the forest floor. He shook his head. "No, I'll do it. I'm too excited for sleep. You get some rest."

Sanchez nodded, and moved to the tent.

"You know, this is as far as he got," Ed said.

Sanchez turned, smiling. "Wake me in four hours."

Ed watched him disappear and swivelled again to the brooding jungle. Beyond the fire-glow, the totem's silhouette rose a dozen feet or more, black like the surrounding trees. A surge of adrenaline flooded his veins. Was this real? Or was it some waking vision of the dream that had possessed him for most of his adult life?

Reaching into his shirt pocket, Ed retrieved the cloth bundle he always kept on his person. Unwrapped, the stone disc seemed small and insignificant. He turned it reverently, every curve and indentation imprinted in memory. The disc was warm to the touch.

Pocketing the object, he got up, needing to relieve himself. He walked to a kapok tree several yards from the campfire. Slung over his shoulder was the Weatherby. He removed the rifle and leaned it against the tree's thick bole.

Unzipping, he looked up through the tangled branches. The rain had stopped. Finally! In all the excitement he hadn't noticed. Meagre gaps in the canopy revealed twinkling stars and a pale moon. He closed his eyes. Though the drizzle had stopped, a constant, enveloping patter came to his ears as water dripped through the leaves. The sound was familiar and would resonate long into the night, much like beautiful music. Zipping up again, he returned to the fire and reclined. For the first time in days—weeks—he felt at peace.

The hairs on his arms stood up. He wasn't alone.

Ed sat up quickly and looked past the fire, into the undergrowth.

Staring back at him, reflected in the firelight not ten feet away, were two large, round eyes.

Ed's blood ran cold in a flooding rush. Obscured by foliage, he couldn't identify the species of animal, even at such close range, but its stare was intense and calculating. His heart pounded. *A jaguar?*

Fearing to break eye contact, he fumbled blindly for the rifle.

He couldn't find it. It wasn't there.

Shit. He'd left it by the tree.

Still, it stared.

Where was the damn flashlight?

He panicked, and for the briefest of moments glanced away. Both the flashlight and rifle were right at his side—he'd been reaching too far.

When he turned back, the eyes had vanished.

Ed's heart skipped a beat. He tensed, listening for movement, twigs breaking, leaves rustling. Anything. But there was nothing. Quickly, he stood and played the beam of the flashlight across the foliage.

Something wasn't right. He couldn't see the animal, but whatever it was, it was there; he could feel it peering back at him from the darkness as he stood clearly bathed in the glow of the fire. Carefully, he put the rifle to his shoulder and aimed it into the night.

He stood like that for an age, tensed and unmoving. Finally, poor judgement got the better of him.

Slowly, he moved into the jungle.

Robert Sanchez woke with a start—and knew immediately that something was wrong.

He lay frozen, not daring to breathe.

Water dripped from above, splashing on the nylon. It had stopped raining. Besides the dripping, there was an eerie silence.

Where were the insects? The usual sounds of the forest? The forest was never this hushed.

Slowly, he sat up, reaching quietly for the insect mesh. The sound of the zip as it opened was impossibly loud.

Outside, the fire had burned low. Ed was gone.

"*Amigo,*" he called softly, not daring to raise his voice.

No answer.

He crawled from the tent and called again. Still no answer. Though he carried a flashlight, his eyes had adjusted to the darkness and he refrained from using it. He took two steps forward... and then tensed, his skin prickling.

He was being stalked.

Years ago, he had been trailed by a puma; it hadn't attacked, and indeed, he'd heard only its occasional soft footfall and caught glimpses of it through the underbrush. But it had watched him, and he'd fled its territory with it close behind. He would never forget the sensation he'd felt even before he was aware of its presence; a perception beyond the normal senses that had warned him he was in danger. The same awareness that makes the deer run before it sees the hunter.

The *exact* sensation that led him to believe there was an animal in the bushes watching his every movement.

Cautiously, he moved nearer the smouldering fire, scanning the shadows.

He expected the attack.

He knew it would come—perhaps from behind, perhaps from the bushes at either side. He hadn't figured it would come from the trees above.

The rustling of leaves alerted him to his error. He looked up as something large and dark dropped from the branches.

It was no puma.

Distantly, he heard a crack like thunder—a rifle shot—and everything went instantly black.

THE
FIND

1

It occurred to Rebecca Riley that she may have erred. The thought came as she stood hungry and exhausted with her luggage at her feet in the tiny front office of the *Edificio de Carga No 1*, a squat structure adjoining El Dorado's main passenger terminal. By then, of course, it was too late to rectify—she'd come too far to simply turn around and head home. And yet here she was, alone in a country wholly unfamiliar to her, unable to speak the language, and now, seemingly, with a serious transportation dilemma. Coming here might not have been her brightest idea.

Leaning against the counter, she fanned her face with her passport while the skinny man with the bushy black moustache shuffled through her papers again. She didn't have time for this: the thought of being stranded in such unbearable heat was bad enough, but more than that, she was on a tight schedule.

"*Ir una manera?* One way?"

"*Si, gracias,*" she said without confidence. She knew precious little Spanish.

Again, she checked her watch: an hour had passed since she'd gotten off the Avianca flight from New York. She'd been led to understand that her next flight, to Leticia in the country's south, had already been confirmed. She'd made sure to check before leaving home. The reason for the delay, then, was a mystery. After all, it was a cargo flight, and she wasn't crossing any borders.

Seconds passed as there was more shuffling.

Rebecca sighed uneasily and pushed her sunglasses back on top of her head. She knew she probably looked a fright. She felt flushed, clammy all over—the heat was never kind to someone as naturally fair as herself—and her tee-shirt clung to her, damp with sweat. She tied her black, shoulder-length hair into a ponytail and then gently massaged her temples, feeling a migraine coming on.

Having travelled little in her thirty-three years, she felt way out of her depth. She hadn't once been overseas—hadn't been *anywhere*—since moving from her homeland of Australia and basing herself in New York four years ago. She'd only decided to come down here the day before yesterday. Clearly, such trips needed a great deal more planning.

This is what you get for making rash decisions.

It wasn't the first time in the last few minutes she had so berated herself. Then again, abnormal circumstances had led her here, and she hadn't really had a choice, had she?

You could have ignored it.

No, she couldn't have. To calm her nerves, she went over it again, as she had dozens of times since Monday. That day, she'd headed into work early, taking advantage of the short and uncrowded walk from her apartment to 79th Street and Central Park West, where the columned facade of the American Museum of Natural History had cut into a grey sky. She'd diverted to the staff entrance, taking the stairs to her office and booting her computer before popping down the darkened hall to grab a coffee. The usual rituals, just like every other day.

When she'd gotten back to her desk, the email had been waiting for her—and it had stopped her cold in her tracks.

The subject field had been empty. It was the name of the sender that had caught her off-guard.

REARDON, E.

When had she last heard from Ed? A year or more?

She hadn't opened it immediately. In fact, she'd stared at the screen, running through the different scenarios that might account for him re-establishing the lines of communication. The two of them hadn't parted on great terms.

When she finally reached across the desktop to click the mouse, no imagined circumstance had come close to what awaited her.

So now here she was, after a frantic two days getting the necessary air tickets and paperwork in order. The curator and department head—her boss, who seemed to have a host of friends in high places—had no trouble getting the visa application fast-tracked on her behalf. She had some time owing and had promised to be back in two weeks. As for the International Health Certificate—requiring proof of vaccinations, particularly for yellow fever—she'd already received the various shots in preparation for next month's assignment to Caripe in Venezuela as a special guest of the *Ciudad Universitaria de Caracas*. That trip was to be her first outside of Australia or the US, and given the research was to form the basis of her upcoming dissertation had not been hastily co-ordinated. Quite the opposite: more than three months of solid planning had gone into it.

It should not have been surprising, then, that considering she'd been ready to leave last night—Tuesday evening—barely thirty-six hours after opening Ed's email, the first flaws in *this* excursion were now emerging. But she had to see this through, and that so, time was a factor.

The neatly uniformed official made a brief phone call. A moment later, another man, balding but equally presentable—and likely the first man's supervisor—emerged from a door behind the counter. The two men calmly traded sentences in Spanish. The supervisor made a second phone call and at its conclusion turned to Rebecca and asked her some questions in fluent English.

She answered them, thinking she had already gone through this. Still, it was a relief to be free of the language barrier.

At last, the supervisor smiled faintly, passing back across the counter the paperwork the first man had spent minutes shuffling through. "I must apologise, it seems there has been a… misunderstanding."

"Sorry?"

"Our freighters do not normally carry civilians out of Bogotá, and I can find no record of any arrangement."

Rebecca massaged her temple again. "I need to get on a flight today."

The supervisor nodded. "I have spoken to the captain of a flight leaving in four hours. I can get you on it but will need to charge your card. *Sí?*"

Rebecca was confused. She thought this had been sorted—no, *knew* it had—and baulked, but not for long. What difference did it make? They could get her on a flight, that was all that mattered. She passed the man her Visa.

Eventually, the supervisor motioned to the door through which he himself had entered. "Go through, please."

Wasting no more time, Rebecca thanked both officials, almost tripping to the floor in her haste to grab her bags. Beyond the door, a brightly lit passage opened straight into a fume-filled hangar. Across the tarmac sat a narrow-bodied Boeing 727-200F with the word 'Aerosucre' on the side. Beneath its belly, various boxes and crates lay ready to be heaved up to the large nose-door above the cockpit. Two men in grey, sweat-stained overalls stood amongst it all, shouting in Spanish, directing a yellow forklift.

Rebecca made her way towards them, sighing with relief, and then suddenly remembered.

Shit!

Amid the chaos of the past two days she'd forgotten she was meant to be somewhere on Saturday night. It was no big deal: just a date with a guy one of her friends was trying to set her up with. She'd forgotten to tell him she'd be out of town. A call from the hotel in Leticia would have to do, she decided. Still, she felt terrible about having to stand him up, mainly because she'd done so last weekend. She hadn't been feeling sociable and had postponed that date with some weak, last-minute excuse. She could only imagine his reaction when she told him why she couldn't make it *this* Saturday night.

Saturday morning, she'd be deep in the Amazon jungle.

2

Sandros Oliveira skimmed the surface of the river and landed the Cessna with a loud splash and a spray of water. Turning the seaplane to the bank, he nudged the narrow wooden jetty extending from its edge and alighted, heading for the reed-thatched hut at its end.

Atop vertical stilts, the small, wooden building appeared to float on the water's surface, jutting from amongst the riverbank's lush foliage. As he made for it, Oliveira's heavy black boots reverberated on the timber planking. In all, there were three jetties with enough room between them to accommodate a small boat or floatplane. Oliveira strode down the central and longest platform. Nearing the hut, he noticed the repairs to its storm-damaged roof were still unfinished. A section of thatching was yet to be replaced and the timber framework beneath was exposed to the clear, mid-morning sky. He made a mental note to attend to it just as soon as he was done with the business at hand.

Across the water, away from where he was heading, a small flock of brightly coloured parrots squawked in the trees. Insects buzzed loudly in the hot, humid air. The jungle was alive with sound.

Oliveira barely noticed, and certainly didn't care. He stared straight ahead, his eyes shaded by a pair of silver aviator sunglasses. With each hurried step, the single braid of hair he wore swung rapidly, fanning his neck above the collar of his shirt, which, unbuttoned and sleeveless, allowed a light breeze to similarly fan the sheen of sweat on his hairless, dark-skinned chest.

Shoving open the door, Oliveira strode into the hut.

Despite the sunlight spearing through the hole in the hut's roof and between the thin gaps of the slatted timber walls, it was dark inside. Oliveira lifted his sunglasses, sitting them atop the khaki headwrap tied about his forehead. With a darting glance he took in the single open room, which he confirmed to be empty save for a dozen or more wooden crates scattered across the floor. Many of the boxes were stacked haphazardly on top of one another, and several had their lids off. All of them he ignored. At the back of the room, in the corner, sat a wooden table. On top of this lay a pile of equipment, mainly the strewn innards of a disassembled radio and various bits of communications hardware. Amongst the chaos lay the object of his search. He lifted the satellite phone's handset and dialled.

The line opened, and Oliveira introduced himself to the voice at the other end. The connection was poor, and static hissed like a snake. He issued instructions.

After a brief pause, a second male voice came on the line. "Sandros?"

"I'm glad I got you," Oliveira said in Brazilian Portuguese. "I have information."

"Go on."

"There has been movement downriver," Oliveira began. "Americans, and with them a lot of equipment."

"And you've identified them?"

"No, but—"

"Then they are probably like the rest," the voice interrupted. "Oil or mining. Not unusual."

"Perhaps, but I doubt it. They are trying to keep a low profile. And they have disappeared deep into the jungle. One came in from Leticia yesterday to join them. She secured passage on a boat heading downstream: the *Tempestade*. I believe it was sent for her." Oliveira leaned forward in his chair, lowering his voice. "There is strange talk as well. They have found something."

The voice at the other end was momentarily silent. "Get to the point, Sandros."

Oliveira hesitated, and static washed down the line. "Ramos," he said at last. "It is about your brother."

3

Rebecca was dozing by the *Tempestade's* stern when the booming cry of a black howler monkey roused her. Though her cabin was below deck, it was cooler topside, which was where she had spent most of the last forty-eight hours.

In the end, the flight south to Leticia out of Bogotá had been pleasantly uneventful. She'd been happy about that. Getting to Leticia had been essential; as the gateway to the Amazon, the small border town on the triple frontier of Colombia, Peru, and Brazil was the most suitable place from which to launch the final leg of her journey. After staying the night and getting her passport stamped, she'd headed east into Brazil by privately chartered floatplane to Monte Oeste, a small village on the river where she'd been instructed to seek out an old wooden trawler owned by a friend of Ed's who would be waiting to take her downstream. Though *she* had been the one to wait—she'd done so for three hours in the blazing sun—it hadn't been a problem. That had been two days ago, and she'd been on the river ever since.

Rebecca sat up. On the other side of the net slung above her hammock, mosquitoes swarmed in their dozens, waiting for her to emerge. She supposed she might never have done so if not for a painful rumble in her stomach; as it was, she was soon up and searching for something to satisfy the pangs.

As she came around to the bow—spraying insect-repellent liberally—she heard a voice.

"They take some getting used to."

Rebecca swung around. Chad Higgins stood on the wooden rail skirting the port side of the *Tempestade*, gripping the roof above the wheelhouse. When she'd first met him, she'd been surprised. He was nothing like what she had pictured. For starters, she'd been expecting someone older; he could only have had one or two years on her and seemed altogether too fresh-faced for someone who'd spent the last decade plying the Amazon as a riverboat captain.

Chad plopped down on the deck beside her, removing the Stetson he had been wearing to reveal a mop of mousy-brown hair. He wiped his brow. He was shirtless, and his bronzed chest glistened with sweat.

Rebecca swatted at a black cloud buzzing around her head. "I can't imagine *ever* getting used to the damn things."

Chad smiled through a week's growth. "You will. That's how it works out here—The Law of Adaptation."

"Right. That's a *real* Law, is it?"

"Sure. You might even call it the Law of the Jungle."

"Survival of the Fittest?"

"Something like that."

Rebecca slapped at her arms and neck. "Well, whatever you want to call it, I hope it kicks in soon. By my reckoning already, I've donated enough blood for *two* lifetimes."

She gave herself a final coating of repellent and returned the canister to a pocket in her shorts. Night was the worst—the bloodsuckers seemed to disappear with the peaking heat. That so, relief was on its way: already, the morning was unpleasantly hot.

Rebecca glanced past the bow. Veils of mist rose slowly off the river's surface, clouding the layers of green lining both riverbanks.

She turned back to Chad. "So… who's driving?"

Chad winked, already heading for the wheelhouse. "Fear not, we're in safe hands. Got a pet monkey trained especially for the job!"

Rebecca smiled as he disappeared. "I don't suppose if he's got a moment, he could rustle up some grub? I'm starving." She had to raise her voice above the rat-a-tat-tat of the boat's engine, which, in the still morning air, sounded like the rattle of a machine-gun.

Chad called back from the wheelhouse. "There're some leftover beans and rice in the galley. If you heat them up they should be okay."

"Perfect!" Rebecca called back, already on her way. She was relieved she felt comfortable around Chad. Admittedly, the thought of being all alone with a stranger for a couple of days on a riverboat in the middle of nowhere hadn't filled her with much confidence. But Chad was apparently a trusted acquaintance of Ed's, and he'd been the perfect gentleman.

After reheating the leftovers, Rebecca headed back on deck, plate in hand. As she walked, a strand of hair fell into her eyes and she tucked it behind her ear. Since she'd decided to grow out her fringe the damn thing constantly fell astray. Now wasn't the first time she had wondered if it was worth the bother.

She took a seat at an old fold-out card-table near the bow, placing her plate down and breathing in the morning air between mouthfuls of food. Waving at a few errant flies, she looked across the water. Even after two days, she remained in awe of her surroundings. Here she was, travelling the waterways of the world's greatest river system.

They had abandoned the main stem of the river—*Rio Amazonas*, the locals had called it—for this smaller tributary yesterday afternoon, after a day of travel. While massive, there had been little to remark about the mighty river: they had stuck to the middle of it, and the coffee-coloured water had been so still and flat it had seemed static, as though it was going nowhere at all. Of course, thousands of miles downstream the river would discharge with great force into the Atlantic. She'd heard the Amazon carried as much as sixty times more water than the Nile and discharged more at its mouth than the next eight biggest rivers in the world combined, with such power that freshwater could be found 100 miles offshore. *Incredible.*

Putting down her fork, Rebecca took her phone from her pocket. She hadn't had service for almost a day now, and nothing had changed. Returning the phone to her pocket, she flipped open her laptop. Clicking on each of the twelve photographs in turn, she lingered over the images as she'd done several times already these past few days. As before, she shook her head, amazed. The pictures were no less compelling now than when she'd first viewed them in Ed's original email, and again, she felt her excitement swell. She had so many questions, and today she'd finally get some answers. She was due at Base Camp by nightfall.

Restless, she closed the attachments and powered off her laptop.

·   ·   ·

They pushed on to the sound of the chugging engine. Brown, sediment-loaded water slipped by.

It occurred to Rebecca that before leaving the main stem yesterday, they'd been passed regularly in the opposite direction by various ferries and fishing vessels. She hadn't seen any since they'd diverted down this smaller tributary.

Everywhere, greenery draped across the water, the overhanging foliage so thick it was difficult to discern the edge of the riverbank. Since yesterday, the river regularly narrowed, forcing them to travel closer to the trees. The *Tempestade* was shallow-draft, but it wasn't a small vessel—maybe fifty feet long, with a beam of about sixteen feet—and at times, the vegetation would brush against the boat. Through these slender stretches Chad had to zigzag about, carefully avoiding the floating driftwood. It was slow progress.

Rebecca pushed her empty plate away and leant back. As always, the varied hoots, squawks and chirps of a multitude of birds, animals and insects echoed across the water. To her disappointment, the wildlife remained largely hidden in the thick riverbank foliage. Still, she'd seen a troupe of brown capuchin monkeys swinging through the trees in the fading light of yesterday afternoon, and then early this morning had been treated to a pair of magnificent scarlet macaws racing majestically through the mist.

Closing her eyes, she concentrated on the layers of sound around her. The constant buzz of insects reminded her of humid summer days back in Brisbane, an undulating chorus that never ceased. This was overlaid with the less regular, though much louder and more strident calls of birds and monkeys. And beneath it all, keeping an artificial rhythm, was the unremitting chug of the boat's motor.

Yesterday, as the sun had sunk—heralded as always by silver streaks of lightning that would slither like snakes across the sky—she had also listened intently. With the dark came a whole new world of noises. Different insects, birds and frogs—the animals of the night. It struck her that at no stage could she remember Manhattan being anywhere near as noisy, yet this was a more peaceful place than any she could have dreamed of.

Her thoughts were interrupted this time by a voice: hazy, unclear. Chad was calling to her. She opened her eyes. She'd been dozing.

He cried out again. This time she heard him clearly.

"Rebecca, hold on!"

Looking up, Rebecca saw a wall of green approaching like the yawning maw of some huge, elemental beast. She burst from her seat, leaping for cover as the boat brushed against the trees of both banks. Leaves and branches scratched and clawed and snapped against the sides of the *Tempestade*, flicking up and over the roof of the wheelhouse with the high-pitched squeal of fingernails down a blackboard. Within seconds, the river widened, and the boat moved into open water.

Chad rushed from the wheelhouse. "You okay?"

Rebecca got to her feet. "Yeah, I'm fine," she said, brushing herself down.

"I figured it was going to be tight," Chad mused, lending her a hand, "but not—"

She heard nothing of the remainder of his sentence, because movement drew her attention past him, over his shoulder towards the stern. Chad turned to follow her gaze, and as he did, his face lost colour.

A small, dark shape crept slowly across the deck towards them, its movement stop-start.

"Wait here," Rebecca said, padding forward. In a few short steps she reached the tarantula… then bent and picked it up.

"Whoa…" Chad said.

Rebecca returned with the spider cradled gently in her cupped hands. Up close it was huge and surprisingly colourful. Its hair was coarse on her skin.

Chad retreated first one step, then two.

"Don't worry," Rebecca said as she came alongside him. "It's completely harmless. Generally, it's not a good idea to handle these Amazonian fellows, but I couldn't resist. I can't be sure of the exact species, but it's certainly from the family *Theraphosidae*."

"The *what* family?" Chad asked, sweating. Whether this was a result of the heat or something else wasn't clear.

"Never mind. It's beautiful, though, don't you think?"

"Are you kidding?" Chad said, averting his eyes. "I hate those things."

But Rebecca hardly heard him. "It must have been knocked from the trees as the boat brushed the riverbank."

Chad stared at her. "So… back in New York, at the museum… you're a research scientist, right?"

Again, the riverbank loomed near.

Rebecca smiled, reaching over the side of the boat and releasing the spider onto the broad leaves of an overhanging tree as the *Tempestade* passed by.

4

They motored into the early afternoon, snaking deeper upriver and farther from civilisation. They hadn't passed another vessel or seen any signs of human habitation for more than a day.

The sound of the engine cutting back a gear woke Rebecca from yet another nap. As the *Tempestade* slowed to a crawl, she peered across the bow. Jutting from the foliage ahead was the nose of what appeared to be a small, inflatable dinghy, and as they closed the gap, she saw the figure of a dark-skinned man at the stern of the vessel.

"*Oi*," he said, the Brazilian Portuguese word for hello, and Chad called back in kind. The Zodiac zoomed from the bank and drew alongside the *Tempestade*.

Rebecca peered over the rail and the man smiled at her. "My name is Robert Sanchez," he said.

After lowering the first of several wooden crates into the Zodiac, Chad turned to Rebecca. "Robert will take you from here."

Rebecca's luggage was packed and at her feet. Sanchez, standing in the Zodiac, reached up for another crate. For several minutes, the two men transferred supplies.

Everything was happening quickly now. Once Rebecca's gear was lowered, she approached Chad. "I thought you might do me a favour."

"What's that?"

"I was hoping you'd pass on my gratitude to that trained monkey of yours. Thank him for the safe trip. He's a good captain."

"First mate, actually."

Rebecca laughed, and they said their goodbyes.

"See you in eight days," Chad said.

Rebecca climbed over the rail, using the car tyres attached to the side of the *Tempestade* like rungs to lower herself. She took a seat at the bow and gave a final wave as the soft-hull inflatable sped off.

Positioned a couple of feet above the water, she was afforded a new view of her surroundings. Mostly, the stream was open and several yards wide, but occasionally the banks converged, and the Zodiac struggled to squeeze through. Part of the time they sped beneath a dark tunnel of trees, the foliage forming a dense canopy a few feet above their heads. This was clearly the reason for changing vessels. The *Tempestade* could never have negotiated such waters.

At least half an hour passed in silence before Sanchez opened his mouth for the first time. "So, *senhorita*," he called forward. "Ed tells me you work in the museum's Department of Entomology. What is your specialty?"

"Predator-prey dynamics," Rebecca said, turning back.

Sanchez nodded slowly but said nothing more. Vegetation flashed by.

After a time, Rebecca noted curiously that like her companion, the jungle, too, had fallen silent. She could no longer hear the birds and monkeys shrieking in the trees. Other than the muted drone of the motor, the only sound now was that of low, rumbling thunder. When Sanchez finally called out to her, breaking the silence, she jumped.

"Not far now, *senhorita*. Another hour."

Rebecca nodded. Thunder growled again, and something cool and wet splashed on her forearm. She looked up through the trees. Above, grey clouds had swept across the sky, claws of lightning slashing at their distended bellies.

She donned her poncho as their innards spilled earthward and became a torrent.

5

Less than an hour later—and ahead of schedule—Rebecca spotted a man standing at the treeline, barely visible through the sheeting rain and silently awaiting the Zodiac's approach. Still huddled at the front of the boat, she swept back the hood of her yellow poncho. The man smiled, waved, and held out his hand as the boat eased up to the riverbank.

"I had hoped for better weather to greet you with!" Ed said above the downpour.

Rebecca laughed as she eagerly took his hand, almost stumbling with excitement. "In this part of the world? You've got to be joking!"

Chuckling, Ed helped her ashore. He wore a poncho, too, but it was hoodless, and water streamed from his hair into deep brown eyes glistening with a level of warmth she hadn't expected. After the two of them had hugged, he asked, "How was your trip?"

Rebecca tilted her head in mock recollection. "Let me think: rain, humidity, and mosquitoes aside… a little boring really."

"Days pass slowly on the river. Hope you brought a good book."

She lifted her knapsack. "Travelling as light as possible, I'm afraid. Didn't have much time to pack, in any case."

Ed hoisted her sports bag. She had no other luggage. "Don't sweat it. We've got everything you need."

Done with the opening pleasantries, they stood for a moment in silence. Ed was the first to break it. "It's really good to see you, Bec," he said at length, his voice low. "I've missed you."

Water dripping into her eyes, Rebecca opened her mouth… then smiled faintly. "Where can I dump this?" She gestured to her luggage.

Grinning, Ed turned. "Follow me, it's not far."

Together, they started along the muddy path that climbed from the riverbank, following as it disappeared into dense undergrowth. Trailing behind, Rebecca realised her heart was racing. She'd been nervous in the lead-up to seeing Ed again, maybe more than she'd anticipated.

"I see you've finally cut that hair off," she said, pushing through water-soaked leaves. "No more ponytail."

Without turning, Ed replied, "And you're finally growing yours. I told you long hair was more your style."

The campsite was less than a minute along the trail. Five or six khaki-coloured dome-tents materialized through the foliage, scattered across a partially cleared section of forest. Two large tarpaulins were strung amid the dwellings, tied on all sides to the branches of the surrounding trees. At the edge of the artificial clearing, a couple of dark-skinned men inspected a softly humming generator. Neither looked up as Ed led Rebecca to what appeared to be the camp's main communal area: a couple of aluminium tables pushed together beneath one of the large green tarpaulins. Ducking beneath the huge sheet, Ed stopped at the first table and motioned to one of several empty chairs.

Following him under, Rebecca sat down. Her nerves had settled, allowing her to focus on her surroundings. Her first impression of the camp was positive; it seemed comfortable enough, certainly better than she'd been expecting.

Above her head, rain drummed loudly, the strong but lightweight tarpaulin sagging as the deluge gathered in a pool. Water streamed over the sides of the canvas to splash onto the muddy earth below.

Leaning away from the table, Rebecca squeezed the water from her hair. Her gaze was drawn to the adjoining worktop, where a laptop computer lay open beside a small satellite dish surrounded by various pieces of electronic and communications equipment.

Wow, a serious setup.

She supposed she shouldn't have expected anything less.

"You're looking well, Bec," Ed said, still standing. "I mean it."

Rebecca opened her mouth but stopped just shy of repaying the compliment. Now she was able to get a decent look at him, it was apparent that he, too, looked well. Perhaps a little thinner than she remembered, but healthy. He'd always been athletic and looked fit for his thirty-six years. Before she could comment, though, Ed spoke again.

"Water?" he asked, reaching into a refrigerator that stretched lengthways along the ground, obviously powered by one of several scattered generators.

"Thanks," Rebecca said as he tossed her a bottle. Her mouth was surprisingly dry, and she took two long, eager swigs before wiping her lips. "Your email came as a shock. I mean, I didn't expect you to be down here. The last I'd heard, you were in Peru, following in your grandfather's footsteps."

Ed sat opposite her. "I was—literally. I've made several trips to the Andes in the past two years, searching, like my grandfather. It was only chance that led me down here, to this place." He met her eyes. "I've found it, Bec."

"Down here? Are you sure?"

"Very sure."

"Oh my God! That's fantastic!" Rebecca said. She waited for him to fill her in, but strangely, he stared back at her silently. "Obviously, I want to hear all about it…" she prompted. "I want to see it…"

"But you've come a long way, and it's our other discovery you're *really* interested in."

Rebecca shifted in her seat. "Well, of course…"

"Hey, I don't blame you," Ed reassured her. "It's got me intrigued, too."

A voice cut across the camp.

"As sure as God made little green apples! If it isn't old Bec Riley!"

Recognising the Southern drawl, Rebecca turned with a smile. "Old? It seems you've lost none of your charm, Owen Faulkner." She stood and held her arms wide as he darted through the rain and stepped beneath the tarpaulin.

She'd first met Owen back in Australia. They'd attended the same university; he'd dated her best friend for some months. Over that time, the two of them had formed a close bond. It was Owen—years later—who had introduced her to Ed.

Now, as they embraced, Rebecca said, "I should have guessed you'd be in on this. You two are inseparable."

"What can I say?" Owen said, chuckling and pushing a pair of fashionable, thick-framed glasses up his nose. He stepped backwards. "Bec, you look fantastic."

Rebecca shrugged. "What about you? You haven't changed a bit." As always, Owen was dressed in board shorts and a Hawaiian shirt, curls of wild, blond-streaked hair protruding from under a Miami Marlins baseball cap turned backwards.

Still hasn't grown up, she thought fondly.

Equally unchanged were the boyish good looks that had made Owen a hit with the girls at university. He'd always been cute—but his tendency to nerdy eccentricity was an awkward distraction. Rebecca found this paradox endearing.

"Have you been getting any tube action lately?" she asked. Owen was a fanatic surfer.

"Unfortunately, no. I *had* hoped to get over to Sao Domingos do Capim this year, you know, and ride the pororoca."

Rebecca stared at him blankly.

"You haven't heard of it? The giant swell that sweeps up the Amazon River each year from the Atlantic?"

"No."

"I hear it's a wild ride. The Tupi called it the 'great roar' and used to surf it in their canoes."

Rebecca smiled. "Sounds like fun."

"What wave isn't? Still, you've got to watch yourself—along the way, it picks up big logs and debris. It's dangerous."

"Not to mention the piranhas!" Rebecca said, half-jokingly.

"Piranhas!" Owen said, rolling his eyes. "They're so overrated. There're a hundred things in these waters that inspire more fear."

Rebecca laughed and gave him another hug. "I've missed you, Owen. You really should get a phone."

"Bah," Owen said. "Who needs one of those?"

Rebecca shook her head. Owen's disdain for technology—and his even deeper dislike of social media—made keeping in touch near impossible. His aversion to both perplexed her. How could an anthropologist—specialising in linguistics, no less—ignore, if not embrace, evolving trends in human communication? While he understood the irony, Owen couldn't be swayed, and unsurprisingly, contact between them grew infrequent when, after university, he returned to the US, his birthplace, to accept an academic placement and finish his PhD. Years later, when Rebecca relocated to New York, she'd tracked him down. He'd introduced her to Ed soon after that.

"Okay, you two," Ed said. "Bec, there's someone I want you to meet."

Rebecca turned and caught a figure darting through the rain with a small sheet of plastic held high for protection. The woman—slim and long-limbed and dressed in a tank-top and cargo shorts—was tall, maybe six feet. She leapt a puddle of water to land lightly beneath the tarpaulin.

"Hi, I'm Jess," she puffed, smiling and holding out her hand.

Rebecca shook it and introduced herself. She was at once struck by Jess's pretty, deep blue eyes and the impossibly perfect bone structure of her face. Her smooth, tanned skin was equally flawless.

Rebecca figured the woman had to be older, but she looked all of eighteen.

"Jessy's in IT," Ed said. "She's also halfway through her masters in archaeology."

"Kind of," Jessy corrected, twirling a short ponytail of white-blond hair. "It's temporarily on hold."

"What area?" Rebecca asked.

"Meso-America, mainly the rise of towns and urbanism. Rebecca, I've heard so much about you."

Standing before Jessy, Rebecca sensed the physical contrast: herself noticeably shorter, fairer, and a brunette to boot. She leant forward conspiratorially. "Let me offer some advice—Ed never lets the truth get in the way of a good story."

Jessy smiled and tossed her a wink. "I'll have to remember that." She turned to Ed. "I hate to interrupt you guys, but Robert has asked for a hand unloading the Zodiac."

"I'll go," Owen volunteered. "I'll catch up with *you*, later," he said to Rebecca, and disappeared into the rain.

Jessy turned to follow. As she did, she tossed Ed a furtive glance, running her fingertips across his shoulder-blades before heading into the rain.

"Cute," Rebecca said when they were gone. "A little young, isn't she?"

"She's twenty-four," Ed said. "It's nothing serious."

"And she knows that? I don't remember candour being your forte."

"Don't hold back," Ed said with a smile. "Just as soon as they're finished with the supplies, you can get started. I know they'll want to see this."

"You haven't shown it to them?"

"I waited for you."

Before long, Owen and Jessy returned, this time with Sanchez. They joined Ed and Rebecca beneath the tarpaulin. At Ed's urging, Sanchez opened the refrigerator and retrieved a Ziploc bag the size of a pillow case. Its contents were dark, and condensation coated the inside. He placed it carefully on the table in front of Rebecca, then, with Owen and Jessy, moved behind her to peer over her shoulder.

Rebecca stared at the bag before pulling on some latex gloves she'd brought with her. Hands shaking, she took a deep breath and looked inside.

She was aware of what she'd find, but for a moment, her capacity to speak was lost.

6

"Wow," Rebecca sputtered eventually, hissing air through her teeth.

"That about sums it up," Ed said. "Impressive, isn't it?"

Rebecca carefully upended the bag, sliding the contents onto the table in front of her. "That's the understatement of the century," she said, as behind her Owen and Jessy gasped in unison.

"Oh my…" Jessy stammered.

It was huge.

The spider was the size of an elongated melon, the body perhaps a good foot in length. It was almost wholly black, though faint vertical stripes, flame-orange in colour, ran the course of its dorsal surface, across the carapace and abdomen. Rough, reddish grey hairs covered the body. In death, its chitinous legs had folded up beneath it, ball-like. On top of its head, directly behind the eyes, a neat hole marked the point where a single bullet had passed cleanly through its brain.

Rebecca shook her head. "This is staggering, Ed. The pictures you emailed… they don't do it justice."

Gently, she eased out a leg on either side of the spider's body, holding them apart. Extended to their full length, she estimated the span of the legs from tip to tip at more than half a metre.

Incredible.

Behind her, more murmurs of shock and disbelief, although Rebecca hardly heard them. "I've never seen a species like this... Hell, there *isn't* a species like this! This is a major find."

Her reaction seemed to please Ed. "So, what is it?" he asked. "Some kind of tarantula?"

Rebecca's heart had accelerated to an uncomfortable pace and she exhaled slowly, trying to regain her composure. "Yes and no," she said eventually. "It depends on your definition, really. I mean, these days, the word 'tarantula' tends to imply any big, hairy spider, generally your tropical variety—you know, a fist-sized body and legs spanning a dinner plate."

"I'd say this stretches the definition," Owen said breathlessly.

"Me too," Rebecca said. She'd had days to prepare for this moment and fought now to shelve her excitement, sharpen her focus. It worked, and slowly, her professional insight kicked in. With greater clarity she said, "I'll start by telling you what I know." Gently, she flipped the spider to its underside before rolling it back. "Given there's no epigynum and judging by the shape of the pedipalps—those two hooked appendages on either side of the mouth—this is a male." She turned to Sanchez. "You say this thing attacked you?"

Sanchez nodded. "We had set up camp at Site 1, a day's hike from here. I heard a noise above me, and as I looked up, it dropped from the branches."

"*Leapt*, more likely," Rebecca said.

"Sorry?"

Carefully, Rebecca rotated the arthropod so that it faced the group with its dark, lifeless stare. "See this? Like most spiders, our friend has eight eyes—four on the top of the head, on the carapace, and four on the 'face' at the front. The grouping of the eyes is consistent with a certain *kind* of spider. I'd suggest this is a member of the Salticidae family—a jumping spider."

"That's beyond creepy," Jessy said. "It *jumped* at Robert?"

"I believe so," Rebecca said. "Salticids are ambush predators. Six of their eight eyes—the two posterior lateral, the two posterior median, and the two anterior lateral—have a wide field of vision ideal for detecting movement. Once prey is identified, the large central front pair of eyes—the anterior median—lock on to the target and line up the leap."

"It saw Robert as *prey*."

"Seemingly. Unlike conventional tarantulas, which have poor eyesight, jumping spiders see very well—in fact, among the best in the invertebrate world. And they see in colour. This wasn't a case of mistaken identity."

Ed hesitated. "It watched me through the trees. Why didn't it attack *me*?"

Rebecca turned to him. "Going by what you told me earlier of the encounter, it likely switched its attention when Robert appeared. Salticids are slow, patient hunters—if necessary, they'll take an indirect route to the target, maybe lose sight of their quarry altogether. Perhaps, in stalking you, it became better positioned to attack Robert."

Jessy tensed. "So how far could something like this jump?"

"Typically, anywhere up to twenty times the spider's length," Rebecca mused. "Maybe more."

"This thing could leap thirty feet?"

"Theoretically? Perhaps."

"Shit."

Rebecca placed the spider on the table and leant back in her chair. Rain drummed loudly on the tarpaulin. "At this point, I don't have all the answers. A few things bother me—like the fact you were attacked at night. Because of their acute vision, jumping spiders are daytime hunters. On top of that, even considering the enormity of this specimen, a human is incredibly large prey. Make no mistake, salticids are recognized for their strength and ability to overcome much larger prey—but to attack such a potentially *dangerous* target… It doesn't make sense."

"What doesn't make sense is where the hell this thing *came* from," Jessy said. While clearly anxious, her voice was laced with professional curiosity. "I mean, we're all wondering it, right? This thing seems so… out of place. Like something from another era."

Owen agreed. "It makes me think of those giant scorpions and dragonflies, you know, from way back when gigantic body size was widespread. Maybe this is one of them—an ancient species that's somehow survived to the present."

Rebecca shook her head. "Those arthropods lived 300 million years ago, during the Carboniferous period. This thing isn't on the record."

"It could have been missed—some sort of previously undiscovered superspider."

Doubtful, but indulging him, Rebecca said, "It's conceivable, I guess. Spiders *were* among the few life forms to survive the Permian extinction 250 million years ago, when 95 percent of life on Earth was wiped out."

"Yes, but *how* could it have survived?" Jessy said. "There must be a reason why modern arthropods are so much smaller."

"There is," Rebecca said. "Atmospheric conditions in the Carboniferous were different. Higher levels of oxygen allowed arthropods to more efficiently oxygenate their tissues, enabling them to grow bigger. They couldn't live in our atmosphere."

Owen frowned. "We've got hard evidence here of a species that *exists*. Maybe over time, this thing's respiratory system has evolved, enabling it to live in an environment with decreased oxygen levels."

"Then why haven't other giant arthropods done the same?" Jessy asked. "Why only this species? And why only here, so isolated?"

"That's just it," Owen said. "Let's assume it *is* the only giant arthropod to have adapted. Isolation probably explains *why*."

Rebecca could see where he was heading. She'd done background reading on evolution in isolation and recalled that during the most recent ice age, the glacial advance had fragmented Amazonia from the vast expanse it is today into small, scattered pockets that had remained warm and moist while the rest of the world had turned cold. There was ample evidence to suggest that plants and animals had thrived in these isolated refuges, locked into a kind of lost world where they were free to evolve.

She turned to Owen. "You're suggesting isolation is the reason this specimen is found only here, and why it's stayed hidden from science."

Owen nodded, adding, "And like other species with a history of isolation, it evolved—*uniquely*."

"Its respiratory system—"

"Thus maintaining its size," Owen said.

Rebecca pondered this. "It's interesting speculation, but I'm still unsure. New species of spider are discovered every year and considering that much of this basin has never been explored, it's a certainty there are hundreds of species out here awaiting discovery. I'm not surprised we've found a new one—just one this *big*."

"I hear you," Jessy said. "This is straight out of a horror movie."

Owen agreed. "Well, whatever it is, we've certainly found the new title-holder of World's Biggest Spider. Anyone got the number for The Guinness Book of Records?"

His comment almost went unheard as something caught Rebecca's eye. She peered closely at the specimen, squinting at the legs curled beneath the body.

Nodding, Sanchez said, "We tried to unfurl the legs to measure the creature. One of them broke off. It's still in the bag."

Rebecca didn't respond. Turning the spider, she examined the abdomen. A shiver went down her spine.

"Bec, are you okay?" Ed asked.

Rebecca turned to Owen. "You were talking about the new titleholder? Well, it gets even better." She spun to face them all, holding the spider like it was some kind of offering. "This one's just a baby…"

7

After easing the spider from the bag, Rebecca noticed the creature was missing *two* of its eight legs. One, Sanchez had explained, had broken off after he and Ed had handled the animal. That appendage had snapped off cleanly at the base, leaving the socket empty.

She guessed that neither Robert, nor Ed, had realised that diagonally opposite, a second leg was gone. This leg, Rebecca knew, had been lost *prior* to the attack on Sanchez, because in place of it had been growing a new one.

She kicked herself for missing the significance of this, which only dawned on her when she'd flipped the specimen and observed the faint abdominal darkening.

Owen's voice echoed in her ears. "Bec! Did you hear me? It's a god-damned *baby*?"

She looked up at him and the others in turn, and hurriedly explained. "You're aware that spiders shed their exoskeletons to grow, right? Some species do this several times a year. With each moult, the old exoskeleton splits, the spider slips free, and a new shell forms with the soft new exuviae expanding and hardening like the last. The spider continues to feed and grow until a new moult is required, and the process repeats."

"So?"

"So, this process, ecdysis, may, over the course of a few moults, regenerate a lost appendage. Look at this." She gestured to the spider's half-formed limb before gently flipping the carcass. "The missing leg was regrowing. And look here, on the underside. Note the darkening? This suggests nutrients were draining from the old exuviae to be reused by a new layer forming beneath."

"It was about to moult?"

"Yes. But the thing is, while the *females* of some species moult indefinitely, for the most part, ecdysis ceases with adulthood."

"This specimen is *male*," Owen said.

Rebecca nodded. "And given its leg was regenerating—and a new moult was imminent—it can't be a *mature* animal."

"Holy shit," Owen said. It looked as though he needed a seat, and with her foot, Rebecca slid out the chair to her left. He took it. "It's a kid, and it was about to shed its skin—"

"—so it could grow even bigger," Jessy finished.

Rebecca set the spider down. "I said it was a baby—or a spiderling—and maybe that's an exaggeration. But at the very least, this is a young, immature specimen, a sub-adult at most. An adolescent."

"Christ," Owen said. "So just how big would it have grown? How big are mom and dad?"

"I don't know," Rebecca said.

The group fell into an uncomfortable silence.

"This is giving me the creeps," Jessy said, and shuddered. "I need to lie down. If anyone wants me, I'll be in my tent."

"I think I'll join you," Owen said, standing and pushing his glasses up his nose. "I mean… in my own tent, of course. A nap sounds like a good idea."

Jessy frowned, trying to make light despite her unease. "I can't say I'm not disappointed, Owen Faulkner. Rejected again."

Owen rolled his eyes and the two of them stepped into the rain, dispersing in opposite directions.

Turning to Ed, Sanchez said, "We still have problems with that generator. If you don't mind…"

"I'll join you shortly," Ed said.

Sanchez nodded and left.

Once he'd gone, Rebecca said, "Ed, I know you're not telling me the full story."

He took a seat beside her. "Sorry?"

"Come on. This is an incredible find. You know I should be getting back to the museum with this immediately, not hanging on as your guest."

"Have you thought of a name for it? I want you to get the credit."

"You found it, you should name it," Rebecca said. "But that's beside the point. I've been thinking as to why you got me down here."

Ed's brow creased. "Hang on, I didn't ask you to come. That was your call."

"You send me evidence of the most amazing specimen imaginable and expect me to sit tight? You know me, Ed. You enticed me. You left me no choice. I had to come."

"You can't be serious," Ed said. "The Rebecca Riley I know is a creature of habit—she likes to stay in control, plan ahead, give thought to consequences. How was I to know you'd up from your job and come down here? Far too risky, too impromptu."

The frank assessment momentarily silenced her.

"In any case," she said finally, "I'm bothered by something else. I mean, you're out here for a vastly different reason; something you've devoted your life to… just like your grandfather." She paused, the words hanging between them longer than she'd have liked. "My point is, now that you've found what you're looking for, I just can't buy that you've happily sat around wasting your time listening to me go on about what is, essentially, just a big, hairy spider you happened across in your travels. You could have preserved the thing and sent it to me in New York when you were through down here. Instead, you send me some enticing photos—guessing there was a good chance I'd make the trip—and wait days for me to arrive just to hear the analysis." She stared him in the eye. "So, what aren't you telling me?"

Ed reached into his breast-pocket to pull out a lighter and a pre-rolled cigarette. He lit up, and grey smoke swirled between them. "There's more, yes, but trust me, it's easier if I show you."

Rebecca opened her mouth to press for an explanation, but after searching his eyes, held back. At the best of times, Ed could be insurmountably stubborn, and his expression suggested she'd get nothing further out of him. Suddenly he appeared tired and drawn, his features weighed with more than simply a lack of sleep.

She was intrigued, but her questions could wait. Right now, she had much to do. "I need to start documenting this," she said to him. "Could you pass me that pack?"

He retrieved it, and she fished out her laptop. No larger than a small book and weighing less than a kilogram, the device was perfect for lugging into the field. Earlier, she'd noticed a couple of similarly ultra-portable PCs—all of them ruggedised, military-standard—hooked up around the camp, presumably via a LAN network.

She placed hers on the table and jutted her chin at his cigarette. "I thought you'd given up."

"Tried to," Ed replied, inhaling deeply. "But it wasn't me."

While her laptop booted, she turned and gazed into the rain. Since she'd arrived the downpour had been heavy and constant, turning the clearing into a sea of mud dotted with puddles of water laid out like a chain of tiny islands.

Ed stood. "I better check in with Robert, so I'll leave you to it. If you need anything, let me know."

"I will. Thanks."

Ed disappeared, and Rebecca was left alone at the table, her laptop in front of her and alongside it, the spider carcass.

With the sound of the rain above her and a thousand thoughts in her head, she began to type.

8

At dusk, the torrential downpour that had marked the day diminished to a light drizzle. After an early dinner of fish and rice washed down with a couple of beers—everyone was calling them *cervejas*—Rebecca decided to walk along the sodden track that only hours earlier she and Ed had followed up from the river. Her head was abuzz, and she thought a stroll might settle her down. Ed had told her over dinner they'd be heading out to Site 1—they called it S1 for short—first thing in the morning. She needed a good night's rest but feared it wouldn't come easily.

As she made her way through the rain-soaked undergrowth, frogs and crickets chirped ceaselessly around her. Before long, she was at the bank, which sloped sharply to the water's edge where the Zodiac was tethered. She stared past the vessel, across the river's glassy, untroubled surface. In the fading, faintly orange light, the water resembled a black mirror.

She hadn't heard Ed's approach and jumped when he appeared alongside her.

"Sorry, I didn't mean to startle you," he said.

"That's okay. Just a bit edgy, I guess."

"Once it gets dark, Bec, we need everyone in camp. Okay if I join you till then?"

"Be my guest."

They stood side by side in the warm but cooling air, commanding an equal share of their surroundings.

"*Megarachne Amazonas*," Rebecca said after a while.

"Sorry?"

"A name. You wanted me to think of a name. But it needs your approval—it's your discovery."

Ed pursed his lips. "I guess it has a nice ring to it. I approve."

Around them, the forest buzzed. Drops of rain skipped lightly across the river, sprinkling the surface and making soft pattering sounds. Soon, Rebecca's ears were met by a loud splashing, and she looked down to see something writhe and swirl on the river's surface. "What was that?" she said as the water stilled.

"A jacare," Ed said, "A Brazilian caiman."

"No kidding? An alligator, right?"

"Essentially, yes. Some people call them that—they're certainly related. Look!" Ed pointed at more splashing. Suddenly, the river teemed with the thrashing creatures, perhaps a dozen or more. "These are common caiman, no more than six feet long. Not much to worry about, though you don't want to get bitten."

"No, I'm sure you don't."

"Robert says he's seen anacondas catch little ones like this, crush them to death, and then swallow them whole. Can you imagine it? The ones to worry about are the Black Caiman. They grow much bigger. Twenty feet or more."

"Geez... even a giant snake would have trouble getting *that* in its mouth." Rebecca was joking but felt uneasy.

Ed assured her with a smile. "We're safe up here. But I thought I should warn you in case you wanted a dip."

"I should probably skip it."

"Might be best," Ed said. "There are things in these rivers better left alone."

"Yeah, well thanks for the reminder. But you needn't have worried. The piranhas had me scared enough."

"You've got a thing for them, haven't you?"

"A man-eating fish? Come on, you have to admit, it *is* kind of exciting."

Ed snorted in amusement. "Well, it may interest you that the most feared fish in the Amazon is not the piranha. It's actually the candiru."

Rebecca cocked her head. "It may interest *you* that I've already heard of it. It's a small catfish, only a few millimetres long, finds urine attractive.

If you're unlucky it'll follow the stream to its source and swim right up the urethra. Once there, it'll raise it spines and settle in for the long haul. Very painful."

"And impossible to remove without surgery. I've even heard of men being... *amputated.*"

Rebecca winced. "Okay. Swimming is *definitely* off the agenda."

Ed smiled, and minutes passed with the sound of a million croaking frogs and chirping insects to keep them company.

"You know, regardless of all that," Rebecca said eventually, almost breathlessly, "this place is beautiful." She turned to find Ed looking at her in an unexpected, yet familiar way. It caught her off-guard, more so when she realised the attention was not merely comforting, but welcome. "I'm really happy you found what you were looking for, Ed."

Ed opened his mouth to speak when a voice interrupted them. "Ed? Where are you?" It was Jessy. It sounded as though she was coming down the path to the river.

"I better go," Ed said. "Don't be long. Make sure your tent is zipped up, and check your sleeping bag, too. I'll see you in the morning."

"What time? I'm a heavy sleeper, remember."

Ed grinned. "You'll know," he said cryptically. With that, he started up the path. After a few steps, however, he paused and turned again to face her. "We had some good times, didn't we?"

Rebecca glanced up from the black water to return his gaze. "Yeah, we did."

Ed smiled faintly and disappeared.

Soon after, Rebecca made her own way back. By then it was dark, and almost everyone had retired for the evening. Two figures—she couldn't make out their silhouettes—sat on watch around the campfire, and hushed voices drifted on a faint breeze. She slipped quietly into her tent.

Just as she had anticipated, sleep proved elusive. The events of the day nagged at her, and when they finally quieted, she was beset by something new and unforeseen—thoughts and feelings she hadn't had in some time.

At least not since her break-up with Ed.

Rebecca did her best to push them from her mind, and at some stage during the night, she fell asleep.

9

When she opened her eyes the next morning, Rebecca understood why Ed hadn't given her a specific wake-up time. Heavy sleeper or not, she doubted there was any chance of slumbering through the cacophony of sound that erupted at first light.

Shrill screeches filled the air as a multitude of birds descended on the clearing, shrieking in the trees as if there were a jungle law against snoozing.

Rebecca sat up, rubbing the sleep from her eyes. She'd woken several times during the night, tossing and turning. With little choice, she threw on some fresh clothes and her boots and headed for the door to her tent. Drawing back the flap, she was taken by surprise at the sight to confront her.

The dark-grey clouds of the day before had gone; the rain had stopped. Glorious sunshine bathed the campsite in a soft golden glow, the surrounding trees casting cool, lengthy shadows across the ground. It was as though the jungle had been cleansed and restored, an entirely new existence spawning overnight.

Rebecca emerged, stretching and filling her lungs with a satisfying breath of air. She delighted in its freshness and felt instantly rejuvenated. Detecting the smell of coffee, she headed for the communal area beneath the tarpaulins.

Owen was sitting at the entrance to his tent, again in his Hawaiian get-up, shaking his boots upside down.

"Checking for creepy crawlies?" Rebecca asked.

Owen merely raised his eyebrows, and Rebecca continued past. The comment sat uneasily as she walked away.

In total, eight people were in occupation of Base Camp. Six would be making the trip to S1 today: Owen and herself, Jessy, Ed, and Sanchez, as well as Enrique Paulo, who she'd been introduced to last night before dinner. Two other men in Ed's employ—Martins Ribeiro and Elson Barros—would remain here at Base Camp.

Enrique stood with a tin mug in his hand, leaning against one of the aluminium tables beneath the tarpaulins.

He was young, in his early twenties at most, with a tall but boyish frame still on the verge of filling out. He was baby-faced, with gentle eyes and a thin black moustache. It seemed he was trying for a beard, but it wasn't working out. His long, braided ponytail ran almost to his waist. A small gold cross hung on a chain around his neck.

"Beautiful day, isn't it?" Rebecca said.

Enrique's English was simple, and he came across as painfully shy, particularly in the presence of herself and Jessy. Rebecca suspected he was a loner; after last night's introductions, he'd slipped away and eaten dinner by himself. Still, she got the impression he was a willing helper and a hands-on kind of guy.

"*Bom dia, senhorita.* Yes, it is beautiful. Coffee?" He was blushing.

"That would be lovely."

They made largely one-sided small talk. Suddenly, out of nowhere, Rebecca caught movement in the corner of her eye, and turned as a small animal bolted towards her from beneath the table. She ducked as it leapt high into the air... and straight onto Enrique's shoulder.

A little over a foot tall and light brown in colour, the animal had a long, curling tail and skinny limbs. The hair on its head resembled a black cowl, and its face was pale though its eyes were dark. Its small head darted left and right, and its hands waved about.

Rebecca knew the tiny—and very cute—monkey to be a Brown Capuchin. "Who's this?" she asked, relieved to see it was Enrique's pet.

Enrique fed the monkey some nuts from his hand. "*Senhorita,* this is Priscilla."

Rebecca reached up tentatively and tried to tickle Priscilla under the chin. The monkey hopped to Enrique's opposite shoulder, where it resumed eating from his hand.

"She's shy," Rebecca remarked. "With all these new people around, she was obviously in hiding last night."

Enrique laughed. "In time she will get used to you."

They spoke some more before Enrique politely excused himself and exited, sharing an apple with Priscilla as he went.

Rebecca took a sip of her coffee. It was murkier than the river had been last night, in desperate need of milk or cream. She glanced about, her search taking her to the portable refrigerator. It contained nothing to improve her coffee, but she did find the Ziploc bag tucked to one side.

Ignoring it, she took her coffee and a small sweet cake down to the river.

The sun hung low over the trees, painting a pinkish hue over their bushy green crowns and across a thin wisp of cloud that looked like a thread of cotton candy. The river was calm, cutting peacefully through the verdant greenery. Although she hadn't travelled much and had little to judge by, Rebecca found it difficult to conceive of a more breathtaking location.

The stillness broke with the sound of approaching footsteps.

"Good morning," Jessy said, drawing in beside her. She'd tied a blue scarf like a bandanna on top of her head, and a couple of blond pigtails stuck out on either side. "It's such a beautiful time of day, isn't it?"

"Dawn?" Rebecca said, and smiled. "To be honest, I'm not a 'morning' person—give me a couple of extra hours in bed any day. But yeah, I'm getting a new perspective."

They stood for several minutes, revelling in the sights and sounds, Jessy, too, sipping from a mug of black coffee. Rebecca noted with relief that this morning there seemed to be no sign of caiman in the river, although the two of them stood high on the bank and well back from the edge.

At last, Rebecca spoke up. "So, what's S2 like?" Ed had told her two sites had been uncovered, and S2 was the primary site.

Jessy rolled her eyes. "I don't know—we haven't even seen '1' yet."

Rebecca raised her eyebrows.

"It's just killing me, too," Jessy said, "knowing that Ed has made a significant archaeological find, something he wants me to see, and I'm here just hanging around twiddling my thumbs. He won't take me there, won't even tell me what they've uncovered! He avoids the subject like the plague."

"He has masterful evasive qualities."

"I think he's been waiting for you to arrive," Jessy said. Her eyes narrowed suspiciously.

"The waiting is over now."

"Finally. You know, I think Owen knows more than he's letting on, but I can't be sure."

"Those two have always been close. What do you expect we'll find out there?"

Jessy smiled. "You're familiar with his theory, aren't you?"

"Yeah, I know it."

"Well, I can only imagine. But I think it'll be big."

Rebecca got to the end of her coffee. Her immediate thought was to get a refill.

"There are more of them, aren't there?" Jessy asked.

Rebecca glanced up from her mug. "Sorry?"

"I mean, it stands to reason, doesn't it? That there are more of those... *spiders* out there. If that thing is an adolescent, it's gotta have parents. It's not just some lone freak of nature."

"You'd imagine so, yes."

"Owen told me about J'ba Fofi."

The words caught Rebecca by surprise. Of course, she knew of the Baka people, the remote African tribe who speak of a species of 'great spider', or 'J'ba Fofi', inhabiting the forests of the Congo—a species with a leg span of five feet.

"J'ba Fofi is a myth," Rebecca said.

"Are you sure?"

"Yes."

But that was a lie, wasn't it? Semantics. J'ba Fofi might not exist, but the megarachnid they had tucked away in cold storage was every bit as real as the tin mug in her hand.

"Ed says it's perfectly safe," Jessy said, "but heading out to those two sites... what do *you* think?"

Rebecca recalled the previous night's conversation, and how Ed had said he had more to show her. Her response to Jessy was measured. "In my opinion, the attack on the boys that night was a random one, a case of being in the wrong place at the wrong time. They could just as likely have been set upon by a jaguar or puma or some other wild animal. Ed's not going to put our safety at risk. So, I believe him. You shouldn't worry."

Jessy nodded, trying hard to put her faith in Rebecca's words. "I don't know why those things freak me out so much."

"They freak out a lot of people. To many, they're ugly, hairy, creepy—they *look* frightening. There's a school of thought that at some point in human evolution, spiders may have posed a genuine threat; our ancestors were likely programmed to fear them. That fear may have lodged in our psyche and been passed on through the genes. But there are other factors, too. Children's nursery rhymes, Halloween. Spiders are portrayed as creatures to fear. It's ingrained in us."

"Wait till everyone gets a load of Ed's discovery," Jessy said. A shiver seemed to ripple her neck and shoulders. "I suppose if we're leaving soon, I'd better go pack."

"Me too. I'll join you."

They returned to camp and their respective tents. As Rebecca got to hers, Sanchez appeared with a wide smile spread across his clean-shaven face.

"Good morning, *senhorita*. I trust you slept well."

"I did, thank you," Rebecca lied.

"I wanted to give you this." He passed her a broad-bladed machete. "We have chopped a good path, but the jungle is quick to reclaim."

Rebecca swept the tool through the air in front of her, appraising its grip and weight. "Just on that," she said at last. "Why don't we take a chopper out?"

Sanchez shook his head. "This time of year, the charter companies are run off their feet; at the moment, the oil and mining people have an exclusive claim on everything." He smiled. "But in any case, *senhorita*, we are a thousand miles from anywhere. No-one comes out here."

With that, he left her to gather her gear. Ed had told her to pack lightly, just the necessities. Donning her khaki Ranger cap and heaving her knapsack, she joined the others assembling beneath the tarpaulins.

The last to file in was Sanchez, with Elson and Martins in tow. The two younger men were both in their twenties, with brown eyes and short dark hair, and were today wearing khaki-coloured singlets. Elson was taller and more serious-looking, while Martins, of sturdier build, wore a perpetual smile.

Sanchez took Ed gently by the arm. "*Amigo*, I have looked at the river. There was much rain yesterday, and the water has risen. I don't believe the risk of flooding is greater, but I have warned the men to be wary. They may need to move the camp deeper."

Ed placed a calming hand on his friend's shoulder. "Whatever you think best. That's your department."

Sanchez turned and in Brazilian Portuguese issued instructions to Elson and Martins. The two parted with friendly nods goodbye.

As they disappeared, Ed gathered the remaining group. Despite being told to pack sparingly, Ed, Sanchez, and Enrique each carried an amazing amount of gear. Sanchez and Enrique both wore hunting rifles slung over their shoulders.

"Okay," Ed said, "listen up. We've got a two-day hike through some of the hottest, wettest, toughest jungle on the planet. It's vital you follow any instruction from Robert or me to the letter. By nightfall, we should be at S1. Getting out to S2—and Advance Base Camp—will take another day. Separating both sites is a deep ravine; it's passable, but dangerous, and we're going to need your A-game. All clear?"

Nods all round. Without further delay, they crossed the clearing. On the camp's north-western side, a rent in the underbrush marked the beginning of a crude path. Machetes were still required, and Ed and Sanchez did the bulk of the cutting.

Rebecca settled into a rhythm, unlike Owen, who walked directly in front of her, constantly fidgeting with the load on his back. Behind her, bringing up the rear, was Enrique, and perched behind his head, on top of his backpack, sat Priscilla. Faint, tinny strains of music flowed from the earbuds Enrique wore. She was glad that both men were preoccupied. Knowing it was going to be a long day, she was happy not to waste her energy with talk.

They moved deeper into the jungle.

As they did, Rebecca observed an aspect of her surroundings that surprised her. Rather than striking denser, tougher undergrowth—precisely what she had expected—it seemed that the more progress they made, the *easier* the going became. The forest floor was now surprisingly open.

Glancing about, it wasn't hard to determine why. Above, the canopy was so dense that almost no light filtered through. Clearly, it was difficult for trees to grow in the eternal shade below. She could only assume the reason the vegetation she'd encountered at the river's edge was so dense was because the canopy was broken.

Now, at ground level, she moved through the gloom and over a forest floor covered in leaves and dead wood. All around, massive buttress roots snaked through the soil supporting thick, bare trunks that soared without branching until they were beyond the level of the canopy. Some of the larger trees must have reached 150 feet or more.

In the spaces between their towering forms, the smaller shrubs competed for what little sunlight spilled through. Other plants like orchids and bromeliads, in their own upward scramble, had done away with roots in the soil altogether, scaling the trunks of their host trees. Above them, in the overstorey, crisscrossing vines climbed even higher.

As she stared about herself in awe, it dawned on Rebecca that she was in a kind of huge, silent battlefield, where the reward of victory was simply a place in the sun. She could almost feel the plant life jostling and scrambling and fighting for it, engaged in a war that had been fought over thousands—*millions*—of years.

In the scheme of it all, she felt small and insignificant, an intruder with no right to be there.

The day grew increasingly humid. The oppressive heat seemed to clamp over Rebecca's mouth and nose like a great hand. Her clothes dripped with sweat, and her legs felt heavy.

Enrique must have sensed her predicament and tapped her on the shoulder. "*Senhorita*, you should remove your hat, it will help you cool," he suggested. "You lose a lot of heat through the top of your head."

"Really?" Rebecca panted, "I didn't know that."

"Here, let me take your pack, until you get back your breath."

"No, I couldn't… but thank you."

"I insist. It is no trouble. I am more used to this humidity than you."

Rebecca felt guilty, but the thought of lightening the load for even a short while was irresistible. She removed her pack and passed it gratefully to Enrique. He carried it in one hand and moved ahead while Ed—who had pulled over to the side and had removed his own short-brim Bush Hat—slipped in behind her.

"He's got a crush on you," he whispered.

"Don't be silly." Rebecca nudged him with her elbow. "He's just being sweet."

They kept moving. Time passed slowly. The scenery, as it had all morning, remained unchanged, bathed in a faint green light that filtered weakly from above. When they came to an area of the forest that was different, Rebecca came to a sudden halt—just as those in front of her.

All around, and above them, strong, thick webs laced the trees in a ghostly silver-grey. Densely woven, they were tens of feet in length—it was as though giant nets had been cast across the path above their heads. The whole place had a quiet, eerie feel to it.

Rebecca knew there was nothing strange about the scene. These were ordinary spider webs, built by a common species of orb-weaver.

But no-one said a word as they eventually got going and passed beneath them.

Rebecca kept her head low, glad when they had left the huge silver nets behind.

10

They didn't stop for two hours and took their first break as they came to a large tree that had fallen across the path. It seemed as good a place to rest as any, and well overdue; by now, Rebecca was walking on legs of lead.

Off to one side, Ed and Sanchez stood deep in hushed discussion. At the flared base of a massive capirona tree, Owen and Jessy sat in silence, drinking from their canteens in great gulps. A few feet away, Enrique sat on the ground with Priscilla, his head bobbing gently to the beat of the music flowing from his earbuds.

Rebecca sat beside him, groaning with relief. "What are you listening to?" she asked, taking a sip of water. Enrique offered her the buds, and she held them to her ears.

Don't you, step on my blue suede shoes...

"The King," he said with a smile, curling his upper lip in a passable, somewhat endearing impersonation of his idol.

Rebecca smiled. "Ah... now I get it," she said, trying—again unsuccessfully—to give Priscilla a pat. "You know, you've got the same initials." She passed the earbuds back. "Elvis Presley. Enrique Paulo."

"*Si*, I realised." He grinned.

"Thanks again for helping me out back there."

"My pleasure. It is very hot today."

Rebecca took another swig just as a voice interrupted them. Sanchez waved Enrique to where he and Ed were standing.

"Please excuse me, *senhorita*," Enrique said.

Rebecca gave him the thumbs up and shimmied over to Owen, who was telling Jessy about his work with the National Indian Foundation of Brazil, FUNAI, which was the agency tasked with protecting the rights of the nation's indigenous peoples.

"Most recently I was based in the eastern Amazon, near the Pindare River, a guest of the Awa-Guaja. They're a fascinating people—the women breastfeed monkeys, you know. They *raise* them as their own children."

The rest of the story was all too familiar. As the irrepressible tide of miners, loggers, and oil companies pressed farther into the Amazon's undeveloped regions, indigenous peoples were increasingly vulnerable. Today, the Awa-Guaja people were among the most endangered on the planet.

"It's tragic," Owen said. "Up to a third of them have never been in contact with Westerners, yet we're a direct threat."

Jessy frowned. "*Never* been in contact with Westerners?"

"Yes, never—and this is a group of people we've studied for a long time. There are dozens of tribes in Amazonia whose existence we merely suspect. Imagine the impact on them."

"That's an exaggeration, right?" Jessy said. "I mean, I've heard it before… but the suggestion there are people out here who know *nothing* of the outside world seems far-fetched."

"Not at all," Owen said. "It's thought there could be as many as sixty undiscovered tribes in Amazonia."

Jessy raised her eyebrows.

"Staggering, hey?" Owen said. "We've put people on the moon, have explored other planets, and yet here are people with no written language and who hunt with bow and arrow and worship monkeys and jaguars as they have for thousands of years, living as they did back in the Stone Age. That's all they know. While we're heading to the stars, right here in our own backyard are some of our greatest secrets."

Indeed. After yesterday's discovery, Rebecca wondered what other mysteries the jungle was hiding.

"Okay," Ed said. "We need to get moving, people."

They made two more stops that day, one at noon, and another a couple of hours later. By late afternoon, Rebecca was exhausted, and not just physically. Her head throbbed, and her legs ached, but her mind, too, was tired, and her concentration wandered. Unaware of time, she hardly noticed the forest darkening around her.

Her thoughts were far away when Ed announced they'd arrived, only snapping out of her daydream when she noticed that everyone else had stopped walking. She stopped as well, and looking up, understood why no-one was speaking.

Made of stone, it towered perhaps twelve feet above the jungle floor. A tangle of vines had only recently been hacked away from it and now lay draped across it like a thin fringe of hair, apt considering that from behind the long green veil there peered a giant stone face.

It stared back at them silent and brooding, its unseeing eyes looking out from deep within the shadow of a thick browline. The forehead was tall and slightly tapered at the top. The mouth, set below a long, sharp-angled nose, was a thin, unsmiling groove that cut across a powerful and prominent jawline. Rebecca had seen that face before.

Owen began to speak. "Holy shit," he said slowly, "it can't be... it looks just like one of those..."

Rebecca interrupted, finishing the sentence for him.

"Easter Island statues," she whispered.

11

"I wasn't expecting *this*," Rebecca said as she stared up at the statue.

She summoned her knowledge of Easter Island and its famous carved-stone inhabitants. She knew it lay somewhere in the South Pacific, off the west coast of South America and east of Polynesia, and that it was covered in hundreds of unusual stone statues, the most recognisable looking much like the one in front of her. She knew also that the statues were shrouded in mystery—their reason for being there and how they got there in the first place. She'd heard weird stories of aliens and UFOs, all of which seemed ridiculous. There was a rational explanation for everything.

A handy one escaped her, though, and perhaps the rest of them, too, as they stared up at the giant brooding face.

"It's stunning, isn't it?" Ed said. He stood in front of the statue, bearing the proud look of a father showing off a newborn.

Rebecca nodded. It *was* stunning. Appraising the sculpture, she guessed it weighed upwards of eight or nine tons. How its makers could have carted it through the jungle and placed it here was beyond her.

She was opening her mouth to say so when Ed cut her off. In the blink of an eye, his expression had turned serious. "I know you've all got questions, but you'll have to save them. We need to build a fire and get the camp up and running."

Rebecca understood the reason for his urgency. All around, the jungle was slipping rapidly into a deeper gloom.

And this, S1, was the scene of the attack on Sanchez...

The statue forgotten, Rebecca turned, scanning the forest. Everything seemed as it should be.

Just the trees...

Surprised to find herself so jumpy, she loosened her pack and tossed it to the ground. While they'd been crowded around the statue, Sanchez and Enrique had slipped away, and reappeared now with a couple of large, polycarbonate crates. To one side of a shallow depression between the buttress roots of a large kapok, a pile of camouflage netting lay discarded; obviously the crates had been stashed during a previous trip. Inside the containers were several lightweight dome tents. As Sanchez and Enrique moved to start a fire, Rebecca and Owen hauled out the tents. Jessy, captivated by the statue, reluctantly joined them.

They worked quickly in the fading light. Ed, meanwhile, busied himself with a different task. Kneeling, he removed an object from Sanchez's backpack—a small but sturdy black metal box no longer or wider than a notebook computer, though almost twice as tall—and then another from Enrique's. On the front panel of each was a series of dials, switches and an LED display, and on their sides were sections of open horizontal grating like the face of a speaker. He then removed two more such units from his own pack and set all four devices on the ground in front of him.

Rebecca paused. "What are those?"

Ed lifted one of the boxes and turned it over. "Just a thought I had. It's called the UltraRid X40. Believe it or not... it's a *pest repeller.*"

Rebecca cocked an eyebrow.

"A precaution, only, I assure you," Ed said. "I arranged for them to be sent down, got Chad to deliver them. They came on the same boat as you. This particular model is used commercially in factories and warehouses to repel rodents and insects."

Moving beside him, Rebecca knelt to examine one of the boxes. "It's an ultrasonic device."

Ed nodded. "You've heard of them? Apparently, they emit a high-intensity, ultrasonic soundwave, which affects their nervous system or something."

"Many arthropods sense ultrasound via a tympanic membrane known as the 'chordotonal organ,'" Rebecca said. "A concentrated ultrasonic blast would likely cause extreme irritation."

"Right," Ed said. "Anyway, the wave is apparently inaudible to humans and most mammals, so it shouldn't bother us, or even Priscilla; at most, we might hear a soft background hum. Obviously, I haven't had a chance to run a test."

Owen had been listening to the conversation. "What about power?"

"Lithium polymer cell," Ed said, "Fully rechargeable. We've got a solar-powered recharger if we need it, though I understand the X40's power consumption is minimal."

With that, Ed stood and placed the four devices about fifty feet apart in a square around the camp. As he went he initiated a switch on each box and a corresponding green light sprang to life, followed by a gentle humming.

Once he'd finished, Ed said, "Each unit covers roughly 2,000 square feet—or 30,000 cubic feet. But I can alter the shape and dimension of their range accordingly. If they work, placed now so their fields don't overlap, we should have about 8,000 square feet of protection—about ninety feet on all sides. That includes a dozen feet or more vertically, up into the trees."

As he spoke, Ed retrieved more equipment from the storage crates, this time eight sturdy, all-weather, tripod-mounted motion-sensors. Once she finished erecting her tent, Rebecca helped him create a larger square outside the original square formed by the X40s, with sensors on each corner and in the middle of each side.

They'd constructed, essentially, an invisible, eight-foot high fence around the campsite.

"I guess we're stuck inside the perimeter?" Rebecca said.

Ed nodded. "Like the X40s, the motion detectors work on an ultrasonic system, too, so ambient light levels or the target's optical characteristics aren't an issue. Still, we don't want them set off by rain or tiny critters scurrying about in the undergrowth, so I've flicked them to 'passive'. But if something *big* crosses them, we'll know about it."

Big.

"No coverage above the sensors?" Owen said.

Ed shook his head. "Unlike the X40s, the motion detectors are line of sight only."

Rebecca had wondered about that, too, and as she studied the equipment noted there was one more feature Ed hadn't told them about. Attached to some of the tripod legs were long, vertical bars. They looked like heat lamps, but were clearly UV-emitting floodlights, or 'blacklights'. Ed had done his homework. Biologists use blacklights in the field to locate scorpions, which fluoresce under ultraviolet light. Similarly, tiny scales on the bodies of some spiders, too—particularly jumping spiders—reflect UV. If the sensors were tripped, no doubt the lamps would activate, bathing the area in ultraviolet. Clever—but was it overkill? Ed wasn't expecting any problems; he'd said so, and she herself hadn't thought there was an overt cause for alarm. But suddenly, she was hit by a flash of self-doubt: blacklights, motion sensors, ultrasonic devices—

It's better to be prepared. We're dealing with the unknown.

She put it from her mind and took a seat by the fire. With little fanfare, the last of the daylight dissipated and darkness descended, repelled only by the crackling orange flames. All around, insects chirped and buzzed. The black boxes hummed.

Sanchez prepared dinner with Owen and Enrique's assistance. Jessy returned to the statue. The stone carving, only feet away, seemed to come alive in the shifting glow of the fire, radiating not only an aura of mystery, but something more.

Rebecca turned to Ed, who was sitting with her. "I suppose now is the time to address the elephant in the room, right? *Why, Ed, is there an Easter Island statue in the middle of the Amazon jungle?*"

Of course, like the others, she already knew what had lured Ed here. She recalled that warm July night a few years back, him spilling the beans over beers at their favourite SoHo bar. He'd spoken awkwardly of the times when as a boy his grandfather on his father's side would regale him with tales of a lost city hidden deep within the jungles of South America... and of an ancient civilisation that possessed an object of strange power. Ed's grandfather had been obsessed with the topic.

Ed came from a wealthy New England family, flush with 'old money' bolstered by a property development empire. Ed's father, Henry Reardon Jnr, had gained control of the family business at a young age, taking over from his father, Henry Snr, as he had from his own father before him. Henry Snr had happily relinquished control in exchange for an early retirement. He was an avid collector, a kind-hearted yet hard-spoken man who in the years following his wife's death had found solace in scouring the globe and adding to the dozens of ancient artefacts adorning the family home.

Ed had told her there was one object of special interest to his grandfather. The artefact, a small stone disc covered in grooves and other strange markings, was rumoured to have come from an old and mysterious civilisation located in the foothills of the South American Andes.

Giddy as much with anticipation as beer, Rebecca had thought the story of the lost South American city was one she already knew, albeit in varied form, that she had heard long before she had ever made Ed's acquaintance. It went that once upon a time, several thousand years ago—in fact, at a time even before the mighty Egyptians—a great continent existed, a land that was now lost to the world, destroyed in a sudden cataclysm of erupting volcanoes and violent earthquakes and great floods that sank it without trace to the bottom of the sea.

This, Rebecca knew, was the story of Atlantis, a legendary civilisation of such wealth and technology as had never been seen before, erased in the blink of an eye. It was said that those who survived the cataclysm spread out across the world, to places ranging from the Mediterranean to Africa, India, and Central and South America, and in time founded many civilizations, the Mayan and the Incan and the Egyptian among them. Atlantis had even been linked to places like Stonehenge and the Nazca lines of Peru.

But Ed's story was not of Atlantis. What Rebecca hadn't known was that similar tales existed, rumours of *other* lost continents that, like Atlantis, now rested on the ocean floor. Atlantis was supposedly located in the Atlantic Ocean—hence its name—but Ed had alluded to a sunken, *mid-Pacific* land mass. Some referred to this continent as Mu, others T'aeva. According to legend, like the Atlanteans, the people of this continent had also fled a great cataclysm to found colonies in other parts of the world.

The lost city described to Henry Snr was supposedly one of the sites where refugees of the doomed Pacific continent had resettled.

Despite an absence of evidence, Henry Snr was fascinated with the idea that such a city might have existed. Research revealed the sixteenth century explorations of the Spanish conquistadors throughout Central and South America had been spurred by similar tales, with one story suggesting the T'aevans—who, as legend had it, could harness the power of the sun—had founded a metropolis deep in the jungle, and the secret of their power was hidden, along with mountains of gold and other treasures, within the city.

As it had to the conquistadors, the lure proved too great for Henry Snr. Before long, he embarked upon the first of several expeditions he would lead into the South American jungles in search of the colony.

Of course, Ed's father had been unimpressed—in his opinion, the whole thing was a waste of time and money. But his focus was the family business, and he didn't interfere as the bond between Ed and Henry Snr strengthened. Ed had told her the two of them would share a cup of tea or hot chocolate out in the garden, or in the library or the kitchen, and Ed's grandfather would fill his head with boy's-own stories of adventure and tales from around the world—and of course, of the lost jungle city he would one day uncover.

Years passed, so too seven attempts at finding the city, all of them unsuccessful. But Henry Snr wouldn't be swayed, and when Ed was still a boy, the family patriarch embarked on his eighth—and last—sojourn into the Amazonian rainforest.

Only a few weeks in, Henry Reardon Snr's entire expedition, suddenly and without trace, simply vanished.

What had befallen him and the dozen men who had been in his company remained forever unknown. The official explanation was that they'd become lost, run out of supplies, and had perished in the jungle, though no bodies were ever recovered.

Ed, the boy, had been distraught. At the bar that night Ed, the man, hadn't been afraid to tell her that. He'd welled with tears and waved to the bartender for two more beers. It had occurred to Rebecca that Ed had made himself a promise that fateful day. He would finish what his grandfather had started. He would prove him correct. He would prove it to his father, to himself, to anyone that doubted him. He would find the city.

Watching him talk, Rebecca had detected a deeper undercurrent, something in the way he went over certain details, the glint in his eye. She'd seen it before, even hints of it in herself.

Obsession.

She'd sought Ed's hand across the table and he'd given it to her. That night, Ed had needed to talk, and she'd been there for him. He told her about his life as a young man, about how he'd finished school with grades good enough to get him into higher studies at Boston University, where he'd enrolled in a range of subjects focusing on South American archaeology and history. He told her how he'd fallen in with some of the campus environmentalists and had become fascinated with resource exploitation and renewable energy sources. But he'd never been academically inclined, and eventually he quit his studies, to the chagrin of his father. Spurning the family legacy, Ed drifted aimlessly for a couple of years, backpacking around the world, working odd jobs. For a time, he joined Greenpeace.

At twenty-five, Ed came into a great deal of money, courtesy of his grandfather. This was what he'd been sweating on for years.

He'd had plans for his inheritance.

Ed used the money to fund his own trips to South America and the jungle foothills of the Andes in search of the elusive city and the strange object of power his grandfather had himself looked for. And in truth, the object had become his focus. He'd told Rebecca that throughout his time at university, and in the years following, the notion that an ancient civilisation could somehow harness the sun's energy had been like a seed growing in the back of his mind. His eyes had lit up when he'd said this, and then glowed preternaturally when he relayed a story suggesting the Incas themselves knew of a race with such powers and had named the city of these people 'Intihuasi'. In Quechan, the language of the Incas, Intihuasi apparently meant 'House of the Sun'.

But like those of his grandfather, Ed's trips were unsuccessful.

That mid-summer night in SoHo was not long after Ed had turned thirty-three. Rebecca had recently moved to the States after landing her new job at the museum and they'd already been on a handful of dates. Over the following months she would learn more about his obsession. She'd see, too, the undertow of doubt, anger and confusion, of frustration and impatience. But overriding all of that, she would come to recognise a fierce determination. He wasn't giving up. She admired that. And while she'd never put any faith in the stories, she'd had faith in *him*.

They had emerged from the bar in the early hours of the following morning, the sky lightening as arm in arm they walked the short distance to Ed's apartment. It was an evening Rebecca would remember with great clarity—the night she had realised, for the first time in her life, she was in love…

"Actually, Bec," Jessy said, and Rebecca spun to her, not realising Jessy had overheard her question to Ed, "it's not an Easter Island statue, or *moai*, at all—though I agree it looks like one." Turning from the statue to take a seat at the fire, Jessy said to Ed, "I believe I've cracked your theory."

"Oh?"

Jessy smiled knowingly. "Easter Island—Rapa Nui—lies 2,000 miles off the coast of South America, with its closest inhabited neighbour, another island, about 1,400 miles away. It's perhaps the most isolated of all the inhabited places in the world. While most contend the first people to settle there were Polynesians, some suggest the original inhabitants may have come from the east: South America. Local tradition, however, has it that the natives of Rapa Nui actually arrived from a long-lost, sunken land—the continent of T'aeva."

"Let me guess," Rebecca said. "Some of the refugees from the cataclysm that caused the 'lost' Pacific continent to sink fled to the jungles of South America—"

"—and others to the island of Rapa Nui," Jessy finished, "both bearing with them, in different directions, the same knowledge and culture. The arrival of strangers from the sea is a common thread in creation myths throughout the Pacific."

Rebecca turned to Ed. "So, the descendants of the original inhabitants—and refugees—of *T'aeva* were responsible for building the moai of Easter Island, and the one looming above us now."

Ed grinned. "That's what I'm proposing."

Jessy couldn't resist a smile of her own. "I'm not sure how your theory might go down with academia—"

Ed opened his mouth, perhaps to let her know what they could do with their opinions, but Rebecca cut him off. "What led you to finding it *here*?" she asked. "We're a long way from the Andes, where you originally started your search."

"I've got Owen to thank for that," Ed said.

Rebecca felt a tap on her shoulder and turned to find Owen juggling disposable trays of food. "*Bon appétit*," he said.

Famished, Rebecca gratefully took her tray and forked a portion of the MRE field ration into her mouth. It tasted like chicken. It wasn't that bad.

Ed took his own meal and patted his friend on the back. "Three months ago, Owen uncovered the last piece of the puzzle."

Owen took a seat at the fire. "Here's the thing—I didn't *do* anything. I received an anonymous package and simply passed it on to Ed."

Rebecca looked from one man to the other. As she did, something brushed her leg, and she glanced down as Priscilla leapt into her lap, almost upending her dinner.

"I told you she would get used to you!" Enrique said, laughing.

"Why, hello there, young lady," Rebecca said, steadying her tray. She gave the monkey a rigorous pat before looking back at Owen. "You were saying?"

"It's convoluted," Owen said. "But this is what we know. About eighteen months ago, while I was off in the eastern Pindare, a former colleague of mine, Irving Rosenlund, won government backing to contact a lost tribe thought to be living in the unexplored north-west. Rarely do we do this: FUNAI's policy is to demarcate these remote areas and leave the tribe alone. But Rosenlund was a glory-hound with high-level connections, and he'd managed to convince the right people there was value in such an excursion. He entered the jungle with a team of local tribespeople who would help him communicate, as neighbouring tribes usually have similar dialects. After several weeks of searching, the bastard found what he was looking for." Owen shook his head, his voice tinged with begrudging respect.

He went on. "Bearing gifts—axes, cooking implements, stuff like that—Rosenlund earned the tribe's trust. He referred to them as the Yuguruppu, and spent several months living as one of them, learning their ways, living off the land as they did."

Owen's expression darkened. "But something happened. Rosenlund went missing. How or why is a mystery—perhaps he'd offended the Yuguruppu somehow and they turned on him. No-one knows for sure. But with him went his diaries, his maps, all his research."

Rebecca frowned. "So how do you know all this?"

Owen held up a finger. "The package. Months after his disappearance, this old military map with handwritten markings shows up in my mailbox, bundled together with the tattered pages of several field diaries."

"Rosenlund's research?" Rebecca asked.

Owen nodded. "I'm guessing most of it was missing, but there were pages of handwritten notes."

"Handwritten? That's old-school," Jessy said.

"No internet, no power, remember?" Owen said. "Anyway, his notes recount an interesting story. The Yuguruppu told Rosenlund that long ago, their ancestors had encountered another tribe—a group of tall people with intimidating physiques who had come from across a great, distant river, to settle in a place that was sacred to the Yuguruppu. There, they built great huts, the likes of which the Yuguruppu had never seen. The newcomers seemed friendly, but the Yuguruppu were offended they'd built their huts on revered ground. They'd tried to stop this, but the tall people had strange and special powers which the Yuguruppu feared. In the end, it didn't matter. In settling there, the newcomers had woken the gods from their peaceful slumber. They were so outraged they banished this new tribe—and the Yuguruppu—from the sacred place."

"Gods? What kind of gods?"

"I don't know," Owen said. "Nothing about their nature or identity is revealed in Rosenlund's notes. Maybe he didn't know, or maybe that information was missing. But Rosenlund formed a theory. Understanding the Yuguruppu had no concept of the sea or the ocean, he speculated the 'great river' may have been the Pacific, and the new tribe had crossed it to settle in the Amazon basin of north-western Brazil. He wondered if the 'great huts' described by the Yuguruppu were in fact buildings."

"You mean a *city*?" Jessy asked.

Owen nodded. "He asked the Yuguruppu for its location. They trusted him enough to tell him of two places: one, a signpost that marked the borders of the new tribe's territory—they knew of others, but this was the nearest—as well as the site of the city itself."

"And Rosenlund marked this information on the map," Rebecca said.

Owen nodded. "A lost jungle city! Obviously, I thought of Ed. I knew he'd been looking much farther west, in the Peruvian lowlands, and north of there, in the Colombian lowlands, and had even searched northern Brazil near the border of Colombia and Venezuela. But he'd never ventured so far south—or so far inland. It was a long shot, but I figured he'd want a look."

"And so here we are!" Ed said excitedly. "Talk about luck!"

"After all these years, you deserved some," Rebecca said. She felt a sudden sting of tears—joy, relief and wonder all mixed together, and would have hugged him had Jessy not beaten her to it.

"And you're sure it's the right city?" Jessy asked, pulling back.

"There's no doubt," Ed said. His eyes glistened, and Rebecca sensed he, too, was on the verge of tears. "Tomorrow when we get to S2, I'll prove it."

Rebecca turned to Owen. "So, who sent you the map?"

"I have no idea," Owen shrugged, perplexed. "I had told a few people at the Foundation about Ed's search, you know, in general conversation. I presume that's the connection, but it may have gone through several sets of hands before reaching mine. Beats me how any of his research was uncovered in the first place."

Rebecca stroked Priscilla's head absently and wondered why anyone would send the information anonymously. It didn't make sense. She looked down at her lap. Priscilla had curled into a ball and fallen asleep. Her tiny chest rose and fell rhythmically as she dozed.

Ed smiled at the two of them. "I'm bushed, too. I think I'll get some shuteye myself." He glanced at Sanchez. "Three watches, three hours each."

Sanchez handed Ed the rifle as the group determined the start and finish times of each watch. Rebecca and Owen were teamed together and would take the third shift. Rebecca checked the time. It was almost eight o'clock.

Gently passing Priscilla to Enrique, Rebecca stood and said to Ed, "I guess I'll see you at the change of watch."

"Before you go," Ed said, "I need to show you something. Know how to use one of these?" He held up the rifle.

"No. Do I need to?"

"As a precaution... yes." He ran through the basics of how to load, cock, aim and fire the weapon. It was a .340 Weatherby Mark V Deluxe, complete with telescopic sight. "Magazine capacity is three, plus one in the chamber. Make sure your aim is true before you squeeze the trigger."

He passed it to her. Rebecca had never held a rifle and took it tentatively. Following his instructions, she loaded and cocked the weapon several times. Feeling no safer than before, she passed it back.

"If you have any questions, Owen knows what to do, anyway. I'll see you in a few hours." With that, he handed the rifle back to Sanchez and disappeared—into Jessy's tent.

Ah. That's why she'd counted only five tents earlier.

She headed for hers, bidding Sanchez and Enrique goodnight as she went. She could hear Owen in his tent, already snoring.

She was dead-tired and fell asleep quickly, her last waking thoughts of SoHo.

12

It seemed like only a few minutes later when Rebecca woke to the soft call of her name. It was Owen, outside the door to her tent. Groaning, she checked her watch and saw it was just after two. Struggling from her sleeping bag, she joined him at the fire.

The jungle was quiet. In the background, the ultrasonic devices hummed. A breath of wind—which, in the rainforest, was unusual—whistled though the canopy. All around, leaves rippled in gentle surging waves in the faint orange glow of the fire.

"Here, this will help," Owen said. He passed her a mug of coffee.

Still half-asleep, she took it gratefully. As she sipped, Owen dumped chunks of dead wood onto the fire, sending reddish-yellow sparks skyward. Like her, he sat on one of the now empty crates that had stored the tents and other equipment. Beside him rested the rifle that Enrique had carried from Base Camp. Next to her was Sanchez's rifle. She was surprised he'd let it out of his sight—he seemed the type of man who considered his weapon an extension of his body.

"I've been meaning to ask about Robert," she whispered. "What's the connection there? How does he know Ed, exactly?"

Owen leaned in close, keeping his own voice low. "He's only known him for a year or so, I guess. Ed had other guides, on and off, and was looking for a new one—someone who had an intimate knowledge of the jungle.

Anyway, Sanchez came recommended, a one-time soldier in the Brazilian army—Special Forces, in fact. *Grupos de Operaces Especiais*—Special Operations Group."

Rebecca raised her eyebrows. "I had a feeling he knew his stuff."

"Yeah, makes you a little more comfortable, doesn't it?"

"What about Enrique and the other men back at Base Camp?"

"Hired hands, essentially. Robert organised them. Apparently, not long before my arrival, they had trouble with one of the men— I think was his name was Cartana. I'm not sure of the specifics, but shortly after S2 was discovered, he ran out on them. Stole one of the boats one night when everyone was asleep and just disappeared."

"Really? Interesting."

Owen agreed. "More coffee?"

"Thanks."

They sipped in silence. At last, Owen said quietly, "What about Jess?"

"Hey?"

"You're trying to get a handle on everyone. You're wondering about her, aren't you?"

Rebecca shook her head. "Nothing to wonder *about*," she said. "She seems lovely. Ed's very lucky."

"They make a nice couple."

Rebecca realised he was teasing her. "Okay, tell me. How did they meet?"

Owen smiled. "Several months back, Ed had an appointment with an associate professor of archaeology from Lima's Universidad de San Martin de Porres—you know, research stuff. Anyway, this guy was heading up a dig somewhere near Cuzco in Peru. Jessy was doing some field work on that same dig, part of her undergraduate studies, I guess. They got to talking. Obviously had similar interests…"

"Obviously."

"…and now she's deferred," Owen finished. "She's a nice girl, Bec."

"I'm sure she is," Rebecca said. "Trust me, I'm happy for them."

Owen tilted his head.

"Why are you looking at me like that?"

"You still love him."

Rebecca opened her mouth to reply when a strange sound rose from deeper in the forest: a kind of abrasive clicking.

"What the hell is *that*?" Owen said. He leapt to his feet. Rebecca sprang up, too, her pulse quickening. The noise persisted, and at first, she couldn't place it, but then it seemed to draw closer and become louder, and she thought it sounded like...

Barking?

Rebecca swivelled a full 360 degrees, anxiously searching the trees, but saw nothing out of the ordinary.

Owen raised the rifle. "I can't see anythi—"

Out of nowhere, a figure appeared beside them, and Rebecca jumped. It was Sanchez. "Robert... thank goodness. *What the hell is that noise?*"

"I thought you might tell me," Sanchez said.

The sound intensified, closing in on all sides—repeating, unrelenting.

"Maybe it's the wind," Owen said.

Sanchez lifted the second rifle from its spot next to Rebecca as the sharp reverberation swelled, echoing all around and yet still closing in. The three of them shrank from it, pressing back to back. Tensed, motionless, Rebecca peered through the darkness.

Nothing but the trees...

"The motion sensors?" Sanchez asked.

"No, nothing's crossed them," Owen answered.

Rebecca shook her head. "The sensors won't help." She lifted her gaze upwards, towards the canopy. "The sound... it's coming from up there."

13

With a slow, dreadful tingle, Rebecca felt the hairs prickle on the nape of her neck.

The sound was coming from the understorey above.

How high did Ed say the X40s reached? A dozen feet or more?

"Jesus H. Christ…" Owen breathed.

Sanchez didn't panic. With slow, precise movements, he cocked his rifle and raised it.

The barking was now right upon them, sharp and loud in their ears.

Oh God…

Silence.

As suddenly as it had begun, everything fell quiet.

Dead quiet.

Except for the soft hum of the X40s and the gently crackling fire, there was no noise at all.

Nothing.

No-one moved.

Slowly, the sounds of the forest—the *normal* sounds of the forest—returned, one after another. The reverberation didn't.

All around, leaves rippled gently in the breeze. Everything returned to the way it had been only minutes before.

Owen hadn't lowered his rifle. He looked at Rebecca. "What the hell just happened?"

Rebecca was at a loss, her pulse racing. "I don't know."

"It was one of those things, those creatures," Owen said. "Christ, more than one of them by the sounds of it."

"We don't know that. We don't know what it was," Rebecca said. Her mouth was dry. "You said yourself it could have been the wind." Even to her, the words sounded weak.

Owen snorted and spun on Sanchez. "I don't understand. I thought the attack on you and Ed was a random one. I thought the trip out to S2 was safe? We need to wake Ed—wake everybody—and work out what the hell to do!"

"*Amigo*," Sanchez said, still scanning. "Listen for yourself. Whatever it was, it has gone. There is nothing out there. Not now."

Rebecca looked at both men before sweeping the trees once more. Sanchez was right. Whatever had made the sound was no longer there. She wondered if, like Owen had suggested, they should wake the others anyway, but dismissed the idea. What else could they do, other than keep watch? The group sure as hell couldn't break camp while it was still dark. She sensed Owen arriving at the same conclusion. He lowered his rifle. He was the first to take a seat, but only after several more minutes had passed. He was shaking.

Sanchez was still up with them when the sun began to rise.

14

"You said you never had any trouble, that you hadn't come across any more of those creatures," Owen said to Ed as soon as the others had woken and dragged themselves from their tents.

Ed, Jessy, and Enrique had, amazingly, slept through the incident. They were curious to hear of it now, but their questions went unanswered. No-one had seen anything. The motion-sensors hadn't been tripped. There had only been the strange sound.

Ed said, "We *haven't* had any trouble. Who knows what caused that sound? We don't even know it was a living thing—and in fact, I'm certain it wasn't. There was a decent wind last night, which probably caused the trees to scrape against each other. That would explain why you thought it was coming from all around."

Owen shook his head. "But you must have had concerns," he said. "You brought those black boxes…"

"And we brought rifles, too, for jaguar and caiman, as a *precaution*." His jaw tensed, and he pointed into the jungle. "But if there *was* something out there, the boxes did their job."

Owen opened his mouth and then closed it. Judging by his manner last night and again this morning, Rebecca concluded that Jessy had been mistaken yesterday in thinking that Owen knew more than he was letting on. He was far too edgy.

"You're spooking me," Jessy said. "Let's just pack up and get moving, hey?" She was over by the moai, camera in hand. Since waking, she'd spent the bulk of her time documenting the statue, taking video and audio notes. Rebecca sensed a shift in the younger woman's emotions: now, her eagerness to get to S2 outshone all else. To Jessy, the moai was merely an appetiser, a hint of a greater reward, and the payoff, it seemed, outweighed the risk.

For her part, Rebecca's instincts nagged her, but she chose to keep her feelings close. She packed her gear and dismantled her tent in silence.

Again, they hit the trail single-file, each of them casting a final appraising glance at the stone moai as they passed. Then they were gone, consumed by the jungle. Rebecca was lost once more in her thoughts.

They set a solid pace through the shaded forest, but their progress wasn't as swift as yesterday. The morning was again warm and humid, but today they bore extra weight in the form of the two fully laden storage crates. The equipment was needed at Advance Base Camp. Jessy, walking in front of Rebecca, suggested they carry one of the crates between them. It was a good idea, though not as easy as it sounded. Jessy seemed to stride along effortlessly, and Rebecca had to walk twice as fast as her taller companion just to keep up.

Machetes slashed, and foliage slapped against bodies. Feet stamped through the undergrowth. Above them, birds shrieked noisily, squabbling for fruit in the leafy crowns of the emergent trees.

Like the day before, the group took its first break after two hours. As it approached midday and their second break, they came to an area of denser vegetation that had them swinging their machetes with fervour. It was here that Ed halted, removing his hat and wiping the sweat from his forehead. "This is where it gets tricky," he puffed, pointing.

Rebecca followed his gaze. Only a few feet from where they stood, the forest floor fell away sharply, descending into a deep gully. She heard trickling water at the bottom, and through the thick foliage, saw a shallow stream.

"You'll be happy to learn we're almost at Advance Base Camp," Ed said. "But this is the ravine I told you about."

Sanchez removed his pack and pulled out two nylon climbing ropes, each coiled in a figure-eight.

Rebecca looked from them to Ed and then out over the ledge. "You're kidding, right? We're rappelling down?" The stream was about three or four storeys below them. The face of the ravine was almost perfectly sheer. She'd never abseiled in her life.

And she hated heights.

Near to where they stood, Sanchez chopped away the foliage and secured one of the ropes to a sturdy anchor. After testing the rig, he donned a harness and leapt backwards, falling instantly from view. By the time Rebecca peered after him, he was already at the ravine's base.

"Well… that looked easy," Owen said sarcastically.

Ed hauled the harness topside and Jessy went next. Having abseiled before, she was at the bottom in no time.

Rebecca turned to Ed, everything she'd been dreading confirmed by the look on his face. "Ed, I don't know about this. When you said there was a ravine crossing, I imagined we'd do it on foot. Isn't there another way? What if I hike along the ridge, find an easier place to descend?"

"There is no other way, Bec," Ed said, "and we haven't the time, in any case. It's perfectly safe. Even if you slip—and you won't—the safety rope will catch you. I know you hate heights, but trust me, you'll be back on the ground before you know it."

Rebecca squirmed. It was the *way* she'd find the ground that bothered her.

Owen was down next, followed by Enrique, Priscilla strapped snugly to his back. The harness appeared at the top again. Only Ed left. And her.

Shit.

There was no alternative, and Rebecca knew it. Wondering how she'd gotten herself into such a predicament—feeling somehow duped—she walked to the edge of the cliff face and mumbled another curse. "I suppose this is payback for dragging you to all those art galleries," she said, reaching for the safety gear.

Ed smiled. "That modern stuff you like was never my thing."

Slipping her legs through the two leg loops, Rebecca pulled the harness up until it was firmly around her thighs, attaching the wide nylon belt securely around her waist. She donned a snug-fitting helmet, strapping it tightly under her chin and adjusting it for comfort.

She was ready to go. Ed issued instructions, his tone calm. "Trust me, it's easy." He showed her the small, metal belaying device which attached her to the rope, and how she was to use it in controlling her descent. "Get as horizontal as you can, place your feet flat against the rock. Take it slow and you'll be fine."

After a few deep breaths, Rebecca shuffled to the edge and leant back, taking most of the weight on her legs. It felt comfortable enough, but she hadn't looked down yet. She paused, eyes closed, summoning her courage. From below, Owen and Enrique called out words of support.

Here goes.

Rebecca opened her eyes and looked down.

The ground rushed up at her, bringing with it a wave of dizziness. Ignoring it, she started her descent. Then she stopped.

Damn!

She'd gotten no more than a single step below the edge. Try as she might, she couldn't drop herself fully over the lip. "I can't do this."

"You *can*," Ed said. "The first step is the hardest, and you've already taken it. Just lean back and let the rope take your weight." He smiled. "Hell, if I can do Abstract Expressionism, you can do *this*."

"Our dates were never this dangerous. And to be honest, I think you secretly liked that stuff."

"Postmodernism, maybe."

"See, I told you!" Rebecca said with defiance, and with that she steeled herself—

—and leapt over the ledge.

The descent was slow and bumpy. She spent most of it bashing against the rock face, her heart thumping loudly in her ears. Suddenly, her feet touched something hard and she looked down.

Solid ground.

She'd made it!

Rebecca stepped out of the harness, adrenaline and relief coursing through her in equal measure.

"You did good," Sanchez whispered in her ear, patting her on the back.

"I knew you had it in you!" Ed called from above. He hauled the harness back up, and once he'd lowered their equipment, began his own descent. Minutes later, they were all gathered together in a group at the base of the wall with their gear at their feet. Sanchez recovered the rope, pulling it through the anchor which remained fixed at the top of the ravine.

Still on a high, Rebecca cast her gaze about. They were standing amid waist-high fernery on a muddy bank that stretched a few feet to the water's edge. Several medium to large-sized boulders lay strewn across the stream and in random clusters along its edge, all of them covered in slippery green moss and splotches of pale-coloured lichen.

They gathered their equipment and followed Ed beyond the boulders and into the stream proper. The clear, trickling water was only ankle-deep, and the gravelly riverbed was covered in dead brown leaves. High above their heads, the foliage joined hands in an arch. All around, thick woody vines hung in tangles that trailed down from the canopy like long, petrified snakes.

They were halfway across the shallow stream when they were assailed by hundreds of swarming mosquitoes.

"You know," Ed told them, swatting almost obliviously at the impenetrable black clouds, "this tiny stream isn't on any of the maps. We're not sure where it goes, or where it comes from. It came as a surprise when we originally stumbled across it."

Rebecca was already spraying herself with the insect repellent she kept in a pocket of her shorts. She offered it around, keeping her breathing shallow so as not to inhale the tiny insects.

They reached the opposite bank. Stepping from the stream, Rebecca felt the high she'd ridden since completing her descent rapidly deflate.

Looming before them, the rock face rose steeply out of the thick, ferny underbrush gathered at its base. Almost perfectly vertical, it was the same height as the wall they'd just come down; essentially, a mirror-image.

Rebecca groaned. "Great."

Before tackling the ascent, they decided to take a break, and perched on a large lichen-covered boulder at the edge of the stream. Enrique handed out MREs, but without much of an appetite, Rebecca snacked on a chocolate bar and some fruit from her pack. Priscilla scampered over to her, and Rebecca gave her a wedge of apple.

"You two are becoming good friends," Enrique said.

"Seems that way, doesn't it?" It was strange. She'd never owned a pet in her life and was uncertain around animals—at least anything with fewer than six or eight legs—but she was enjoying the attention.

"Hey, look!" Jessy said, her voice tinged with delight. She pointed to the canopy above.

Rebecca looked up. Several dark forms moved through the overstorey: a troop of monkeys, perhaps eight to ten. Leaves shook noisily as the dark-furred animals leapt from one branch to another.

"Woolly monkeys?" Jessy asked Ed.

"Looks like it."

They watched as the monkeys proceeded to feed above them, using their long tails to grasp branches and so keep their hands free to pluck fruit. The animals chattered incessantly between mouthfuls.

Priscilla watched them too, slightly alarmed by their appearance. She snuggled against Rebecca.

"They spend most of their lives in the trees," Enrique said. "I do not think they will come down today, but if they did, you would see them walk upright, on their hind legs like us."

The troop swung and played and fed for half an hour before retreating through the trees and disappearing.

Sanchez had spent this time preparing the equipment for the climb up the northern rock face. He'd go first, wedging camming devices into cracks in the rock and attaching carabiners through which a rope would run. Leaving the bulk of his gear behind, he began. And he made it look easy.

Rebecca could tell he'd done this before. He moved up the rock face with confidence, finding handholds with ease, gripping with his nimble fingers and pushing his body up with his legs. She suspected his military training had much to do with his speed and technique. In no time, he reached the top and hauled himself over the ledge. He disappeared, reappearing seconds later, probably after having placed on the ledge where he stood another anchor like the one he had placed on the gully's opposing side. He peered over the ledge and tossed a portion of rope down to them. "Ready!"

Nervously, Rebecca ran her gaze up the wall. The nylon rope passed through the anchor at the top. Both ends lay at her feet.

Ed looked at her and pulled her aside. "One end of the rope will be attached you, and I'll be at the bottom holding the other. If you slip, I'll take your weight until you're able to swing back to the rock face and regain your grip."

"What about you?"

"Once everyone is up, Robert will assist me from the top with a second rope."

Rebecca listened while he clarified this. "I'd like to go first."

"Are you sure?" Ed said. "You don't want to wait and see how it's done?"

"I watched Robert. Let's do this."

Ed smiled.

"You go girl," Owen said, patting her on the back.

Once more, Rebecca slipped into the harness. Ed attached the rope and checked it. "Just remember, face the rock and maintain three points of contact. Don't overstretch, and push with your legs." He spun her gently by her chin to face him. "Take it nice and slow, like you did on the way down. Don't get overconfident."

"You needn't worry about that." Despite the bravado, she was still as nervous as hell. She took a deep breath. "I can do this," she murmured.

Retying her ponytail, Rebecca stepped up to the wall, brushing aside the feathery underbrush at its base. Lifting her arms, she dug her fingers into a couple of thin cracks above her head, feeling around to ensure her grip was good.

This time there was no delay. Rebecca pushed up hard with her legs. She wobbled but felt strong. Pausing, she made certain her footholds were secure before reaching high above her head with her right hand. Again, she felt for a crack and dug in. She did the same with her left hand.

Three points of contact. Push with your legs. Don't overstretch. Oh, and don't look down.

The group cheered her on as she ascended, but she shut it out, reaching for the next handhold, the next foothold. Even when her limbs screamed with pain, she kept moving. Soon, she could hear Sanchez at the top, his voice suddenly clearer than those below, but she shut it out until the voice was so close it could no longer be dismissed.

"*Senhorita*, would you like a hand?"

She'd made it! She stole a glimpse, just briefly. Sanchez crouched at the edge of the precipice, looking down at her.

Rebecca gave him a strained smile. "No, thanks," she said, teeth gritted. "I can manage."

With a final effort she heaved herself over the ledge and rolled onto her back with a groan. Gasping for breath, she lay there as relief coursed in waves through her body. She wanted to celebrate but was too exhausted. Her limbs ached, her muscles burned, she couldn't bend her stiffened fingers. Sweat drained out of her, stung her eyes.

"You okay?" Sanchez asked, leaning over her.

"Yeah… fine… just need a moment to get my breath back…"

After a while she managed to sit up and remove the harness. She was on a narrow, lichen-covered ledge that stretched to a dense fringe of vegetation.

Free of the harness, she slumped down again and was still there when Owen's head peeked over the top of the ledge. She dragged herself into a sitting position nearby, making room so that he could lie in similar fashion, exhausted and panting. Before long, the remaining climbers were at the top, so too the equipment.

Still puffing, Rebecca said to Ed, "Now *that* was an experience."

Ed smiled and patted her on the back, and moments later, heaving their packs yet again, the six of them moved towards the green curtain and passed through it.

Back into the jungle.

Once more, they found themselves hacking at the surrounding vegetation, moving deeper along the trail Ed and Sanchez had cut the last time they'd made the journey to S2. The sound of the trickling stream behind them grew steadily fainter until it disappeared.

When she could no longer hear it, Rebecca felt oddly depressed, somehow empty at having left it behind. The change of scenery back at the stream had done her good, and the sense of achievement she had felt in conquering both sides of the ravine had revitalised her, despite the energy it had sapped. Now, heading back into the same environment as before—the thick-boled trees and their snaking buttress roots, the leaf-covered floor and its waist-high underbrush, the perpetual shade and visibility that rarely seemed to stretch more than a few feet in any direction—she felt her spirits slip away. She was tired again, and sore, and now, unusually claustrophobic as everything closed in around her. After all the hiking and hacking through the unrelenting heat and humidity, re-entering this world after emerging from the ravine felt like a regression of sorts, as though they hadn't gone anywhere at all and were somehow starting over.

She wondered how long it would take to get to S2.

In less than an hour, she had her answer.

It was strange, surreal almost.

Out of place.

All around them, steam rose eerily, as though a thick grey cloud had settled in the forest.

"This is weird," Jessy said.

Owen agreed. "It doesn't feel right, does it?"

They slowed their pace, Ed out in front, Sanchez close behind, the Weatherby now off his shoulder and in his hands. At the rear, Enrique too, held his rifle in front of him.

They moved almost blindly through the grey heat, bunched closer and quieter than normal. Occasionally, a fern frond or tree root would appear from the steamy haze as they passed, only to disappear a moment later in a swirl of grey vapour. Like before, the calls of birds and other wildlife floated from the surrounding trees, but their disembodied cries now set Rebecca on edge.

She soon realised they were walking through a depression, a shallow gully where the vapour had collected. When they started to head uphill, the vapour thinned, and visibility improved. Moments later, the cloud had disappeared altogether. She could see clearly again.

And for the second time in two days, the sight caused her to stop abruptly in her tracks.

"Welcome to S2," Ed said, breathlessly.

At first, Rebecca thought she was looking at another cloud of vapour. They stood on the lip of a huge crater within the walls of a valley fringed by low mountains, and perhaps a hundred yards down the slope lay another, smaller bowl-like depression. It appeared more vapour had collected down there—it looked like one of those satellite images from high above a hurricane—but Rebecca knew they'd left the rising steam behind. They were looking at something else entirely.

The greyness wasn't vapour at all.

By now, Owen had retrieved a pair of rubber-armoured binoculars from his pack and was staring through them. "Holy shit…" he breathed.

They were looking at a huge *web*.

15

A *gigantic* web.

Like a dense mesh of huge, silver-grey netting, it smothered the crater-like bowl. The silk must have stretched for more than a hundred yards across—weaving through the trees, cocooning the leaves and branches and thick trunks from the top of the canopy all the way to the ground. Nothing in its path was spared.

Rebecca held her hand over her mouth, too shocked to do anything but breathe.

But that wasn't all.

Within the web—*inside it*—was a huge, grey shadow.

Rebecca grabbed the binoculars from Owen, who wore them hanging limply around his neck. His mouth was agape, and the colour had drained from his face.

What Rebecca saw when she held them to her eyes defied description—defied *belief.*

Enmeshed within the web was a huge form covered in centuries of forest growth. It towered above the jungle floor.

A great, stone pyramid.

•   •   •

My God… what the hell have we stumbled on?

Rebecca lowered the binoculars, then raised them again abruptly, held by the thought for several long seconds. Her mind raced as she tried to take it all in.

No way…

A part of her was simply bursting with excitement. With *possibility*. The scientific implications of such a discovery were mind-blowing. Yet as she looked at the pyramid—she guessed well over one hundred feet or more in height and more than two hundred across the base—enshrouded as it was by jungle and the massive web, another part of her was terrified. She'd never felt such contrasting emotions all at the same time. It was exhilarating, yet troubling, too.

"Before you ask," Ed said, shattering the grip of awed silence, "there's no-one home; the place is deserted, abandoned. Whatever built that web… well, it's long gone. The joint's a ghost-town."

"Holy shit," Owen breathed. "Can you believe this? I mean, look at that, will you? *Goddamn…*"

The words were left to drift into more dumb silence before Jessy spoke, her voice flat and even. "I'm confused," she said simply as she turned to face her companions. "I didn't think they could be both."

Rebecca lowered the binoculars. "Sorry?"

Wide-eyed, Jessy looked at her. "I thought they had to be one or the other," she said. "Either a hunter *or* a web-builder. I didn't think they could be both."

It was an unexpected comment. Given Jessy's field of study, it was surprising her initial observation should be about something other than the pyramid, but Rebecca understood what she was getting at. The arachnid she had examined two days ago, the one that had attacked Sanchez, was, as she had herself determined, a jumping spider. It *hunted* its prey. Its physiology, and the way it had attacked Sanchez, had put that beyond doubt. Yet here was a web. Hunting spiders weren't web-builders.

"You're right," Rebecca said. She scanned the web. She saw no movement, no inhabitants. Ed was telling the truth—it was deserted. She turned back to Jessy, but she spoke absently now, her mind preoccupied. "While all true spiders have organs for spinning silk, generally, yes, there are two distinct types."

"However…"

"However, there are exceptions." She bit her lip, searching for an example. "There's a unique Australian spider, for instance—*Portia fimbriata*—that uses different methods to capture prey. Like the specimen back at Base Camp, it's a salticid: a jumping spider. But *Portia* is both a hunter *and* a web-builder. It can even invade and take control of the webs of other spiders; unusual, as most hunting spiders can't move very well in webs and web-builders have trouble moving in the webs of others. *Portia* can do it all, though, sometimes even stalking and killing *other* jumping spiders—"

"A real opportunist, by the sounds of it," Owen murmured.

"Indeed, and perhaps today, we've discovered another," Rebecca said. She was more focused as she looked again at Jessy. "I mean, *Portia* can do these things because it's smart, probably the *smartest* spider we know of. It uses tactics and strategy—and it can problem-solve. Couple this with the sharpest vision of any terrestrial invertebrate on the planet, and you've got a very proficient and deadly species of arachnid. Given the larger brain, and presumably greater visual awareness of *these* guys—"

Jessy interrupted. "Hang on… *these* guys?"

Rebecca nodded slowly. "Yeah, I think this is—or was—some kind of *nest.*"

"Whoa…" Owen said, "You mean like a colony? Are you serious?"

Rebecca glanced at him. "While aggregating behaviour amongst spiders is rare, yes, I think that whatever built that web down there is *social.*"

Owen blanched. "Shit. Giant spiders," he whispered. "I thought that was bad enough, but a giant *community* of giant fucking spiders? Fuck me." He whirled on Ed, removing his cap and running his fingers through his hair. "Are you sure about this, Ed? I mean—it's safe, right?"

"Trust me," Ed said, "it's okay. As I said, the place is a ghost-town. If at one time it was a nest like Bec said, it's since been abandoned. They've moved on. We haven't had any problems."

"It's just that last night—"

"Owen, there's nothing here," Ed said.

Jessy shook her head. "Ed, I can't believe you kept quiet about all of this, that you couldn't have told us about this earlier, told us what to expect!"

Defensively, Ed held up his hands. "Take another look down there! Just how, exactly, do you *describe* that?"

It was an entirely inadequate response and Ed knew it. Perhaps cornered, he shifted his pack up his shoulders and moved forward, past Jessy, oblivious to—or avoiding—the look of incredulity that had spread across her face.

"We need to get moving," he said, directing his words to all of them. "The camp isn't far, but we've got a bit to do before dark."

Rebecca flashed Jessy a puzzled look. Ed's response wasn't washing with either of them. Jessy was right: why couldn't he have told them? The two of them stood their ground as Sanchez and Enrique formed a group behind Ed. Owen could obviously sense the tension, his expression uneasy. "Ed, you're certain about this?"

"It's safe, Owen."

Owen nodded, conceding. Rebecca, though, still hadn't moved, and in truth, she was hesitating for a couple of reasons. Ed was acting cagey, but more than that, she wasn't *ready* to head to camp. Not yet. Hell, she wanted to begin her analysis, and after what she'd endured to get here—the heat, the mosquitoes, the impossibly long days of travel—the thought of having to delay it was a kick in the guts. Even more so given that finding a *colony* of these things—extinct or abandoned as it may be—had never figured in the equation. She'd known Ed had stumbled onto *something*, but not something as big as this! This would prove the greatest discovery her field had ever seen.

Rebecca was about to state her case for taking a closer look at the site, but the words never made it out.

"Come on, Bec, let's go."

It was Jessy. Tilting her head, Rebecca turned to her, but the younger woman was already on the move. Rebecca got the feeling Jessy knew Ed wasn't telling them everything, but she seemed to be hinting that now wasn't the time to pursue it.

Wavering, Rebecca glanced again at the pyramid and the huge web, weighing her options. Reluctantly, she heaved up her pack.

Without allies, an argument would get her nowhere—that much was certain. More than that, her curiosity had been piqued. She recalled how two days ago back at Base Camp Ed had acted similarly secretive when pressed about the exact nature of S2. Just as she had then, she'd let things play out.

Running the back of her hand across her forehead, Rebecca wiped at a line of sweat that had seeped into her eyes. She noticed that both her arms were caked in dirt and covered in numerous tiny scratches, the result of having pushed for hours through unaccommodating jungle foliage. *Maybe I can use the time to clean up a little*, she thought.

Accepting it was her only recourse, she joined the group, and with that they moved off, again single-file, Rebecca slotting behind Owen and Jessy, Enrique and Priscilla piling in behind her, and Ed and Sanchez out in front, leading the way, the web-enshrouded pyramid looming in their wake.

16

While not deliberate, Rebecca moved quietly, her footfalls softer than normal as the group wove through the jungle. They followed, in a clockwise direction, the lip of the large, bowl-like depression at the bottom of which lay the pyramid, the whole time keeping at least a hundred yards from the giant structure. She sensed that Owen, at least, may have been pleased by this.

Soon after they'd moved out, Enrique had tapped her on the shoulder. He'd obviously detected her disappointment at having to leave, and told her she shouldn't worry, that the view was much better from the north-western side, where they were now heading. Rebecca had smiled, eager to get to the new vantage point.

And with each passing minute, she could sense the truth in his words. As their position changed, so too did their line of sight. Stunning new angles fuelled her exhilaration. The sheer size and scale of it all was overwhelming.

She thought again about what Ed had said: that the nest was abandoned. Looking closer, she saw no activity. If the nest was occupied, then by now she should have noticed *something*. Ed was right.

She felt another tap on the shoulder. Rebecca stopped, having already spotted what Enrique had intended to point out. She gently nudged Jessy in turn. "Look." Rebecca motioned through the foliage, down towards the pyramid, to a spot a few dozen yards away.

At first, it was difficult to detect, but rising through the ferny under-growth at the extreme edge of the web was a tall, vertical mass of carved stone, for the most part smooth and intact, though chipped and broken at the very top.

A moai.

The carving was almost identical to that at S1, bearing the same deep-set eyes and postcard features Rebecca associated with the statues of Easter Island. It was only now, due to the change in vantage point, that it appeared through the thick foliage—yet even so they might still have missed it. On one side, the statue was obscured by a series of fat, silken strands, wrapping it in an unfinished cocoon. It looked as though the great stone carving was trying to escape its silken prison and had half-succeeded in doing so.

But as engaging as this was, it was obvious there was much they hadn't noticed from their original vantage point, the place where they'd first laid eyes on the pyramid. Enrique had been right. From this new position, other details came into view. Suddenly, Rebecca noticed other moai… and other buildings.

The *ruins* of buildings, anyway. Piles of collapsed and broken stone lay scattered under the forest canopy, remnants of structures jutting flim-sily skyward or lying worn and crumbled and strewn across the forest floor at the foot of the pyramid. And although the web consumed every piece, she could identify a vast amount of rubble. In fact, the longer she looked, it seemed as if the entire inner region of the bowl was simply blanketed in ruins.

The pyramid was exciting enough. But what she saw here was the phys-ical remains of a *city*. An ancient, lost city.

Intihuasi.

"I'll be damned," Owen said. He removed his glasses, cleaning them on his shirt, no doubt only to find that when he replaced them the view through their newly smudge-free lenses remained every bit as incredible. "Man—what *next*?" He glanced at Ed and shook his head. "I've gotta hand it to you, buddy, this is just… *amazing.*"

Staring ahead as though it was the first time he'd laid eyes on the scene himself, Ed whispered, "Isn't it just?"

There was a moment of silence as the newcomers took it in. Owen shifted his gaze from the ruins to Ed and then back again, shaking his head. "Man, this place, this city… it shouldn't be," he said at length. "It shouldn't *exist*, not here, not in this part of the world. The indigenous people of

Brazil and the Amazon basin—the forest people—don't build complex stone structures like this. They use wood and bone and build palm-thatched huts. Simple things built with simple materials. This is the kind of advanced architecture you might find in the jungles of Central America, or Peru. Not here."

Jessy removed her digital SLR from her pack and was now madly snapping photos. "Exactly," she said, her finger clicking away. "Geographically, the nearest civilizations capable of building something like this were probably the Incas or the Moche or the Chacapoyas, but they never penetrated this far into the lowlands."

Rebecca studied the surprisingly well-preserved pyramid. From what she could tell, the structure was square-based and stair-stepped. Each 'step'—there were nine in total—was a huge, horizontal, square-shaped platform that, in sitting on top of another, similarly shaped yet even bigger platform, helped create the impression of a huge stairway rising from the jungle floor. Unlike a regular pyramid, though, the steps didn't rise to a point, ascending instead to a flat, truncated area, as though the tip of the pyramid had been cut off. And on top of this flat, cut-off area, complete with columns and dark, empty doorways, sat a square-shaped building. At this distance it was hard to tell how big it was, yet it was perhaps the pyramid's most dominant feature and by its very nature had a way of drawing the eye.

To Rebecca, the building seemed to be a temple of some kind.

External access to the temple—if that was what it was—appeared to be gained by a set of regular-sized stairs that ran from the forest floor up the middle of the two sides of pyramid she could currently see. It was logical to assume a set ran up the other two sides as well.

"You know," Jessy said, "it looks *Mayan* to me."

Rebecca knew why that was strange. The Mayan civilization and its uniquely styled pyramids had been based not in South America at all, but throughout Central America and southern Mexico. Just what was a Mayan-like pyramid—and city—doing *here*, in this part of the world? She was aware of Ed's take on things, but still…

She felt eyes upon her and turned to find Ed watching her.

"You gotta wonder what the hell happened here," Owen said. "To the *people*, I mean. Where did they go? Where are their descendants?"

Jessy snapped more pictures. "While you're at it, where did the new residents—*the builders of that web*—come from? More to the point, *when* did they come? I think it's safe to presume they weren't present at the time the city was built."

"Maybe the city was taken from them," Enrique said. For long moments, the statement hung without reply in the hot, humid air.

"Jess," Owen said at last, his voice low. "You mentioned the pyramid appears *Mayan*." He wiped at his brow with the sleeve of his shirt. "Interestingly, the Mayans famously vanished from *their* urban centres, as you're aware. Gone, without a trace—just like that." He clicked his fingers to emphasise the point.

The longer they stood there, the less sense it all made. Rebecca wondered how the place was built, where the stone was hauled from. And why out here? Why build a city in the middle of nowhere, so far from anything, and in the bottom of a *depression*? While the pyramid towered above the jungle floor and over the lip of the smaller bowl, it was positioned in the basin's deepest point. She noted that many of the surrounding buildings were arranged around the inside of the bowl like spectators in a sports stadium; they looked *across* to the pyramid, rather than *up* to it. As it was centrally located within the city, she presumed the pyramid was a sacred hub, probably a religious centre. While unusual, the site's geographical location was most likely one of spiritual significance.

She was dragged from her thoughts when Ed cleared his throat. "There's one more thing you need to see. Follow me."

Rebecca traded glances with Owen and Jessy as Ed disappeared into the gloomy jungle ahead, Sanchez exiting with him. The steadily fading swish of machetes was the only indication the two men hadn't vanished wholly into thin air.

Rebecca wondered what could be awaiting them now and hurried to catch up. She and her companions reined in the pair, and once more the group moved around the lip of the bowl. Several minutes passed before Ed halted, holding up his hand. Everyone pressed in behind him.

"We didn't notice this at first ourselves," Ed began, "but when we did…" He paused, searching unsuccessfully for the right words. "Let's just say it's… fascinating."

Again, Owen, Jessy, and Rebecca looked at each other, confused. Rebecca turned and scanned the pyramid. She couldn't see what Ed referred to, although she did notice, spearing up through the undergrowth a short distance away, two huge moai, both at least two to three times larger than any she had yet observed. Side by side, the massive statues towered above the lip of the bowl, placed at its edge like sentinels standing to attention. She could see the upper levels of the pyramid and its central steps framed perfectly between them. She couldn't be sure, but perhaps two such moai guarded each of the pyramid's four sides.

"Can I borrow those?" Ed asked Jessy, gesturing to the pair of binoculars hanging from her neck, and as he said this Rebecca turned his way again and thought no more about the statues. Jessy passed Ed the binoculars and he lifted them to his eyes, pointing them in the direction of the pyramid, beyond the two moai. Adjusting the focus and keeping them steady, he moved aside so that Jessy could step in behind them.

"Are you going to tell us what this is about, Ed?" Rebecca asked, but Ed ignored her, and went about the same routine for Owen. Then, borrowing Robert's binoculars, he did it a third time for Rebecca.

She stared in the direction of the web, her field of vision filled with it: a kind of light, silvery greyness. Then she realised she wasn't meant to be looking *at* the web; rather, at something suspended *within* it.

A patch of smooth white, maybe… metallic?

Yes. Something metallic, tangled in the web. *Caught* in it.

That doesn't make sense, she thought. She fine-tuned the focus-knob, and gasped.

Ensnared in the silk like a hapless fly, was a small, single-engine floatplane.

THE
RAIN

17

⚡

The battered jeep bounced along the potholed road, jolting to a stop amid a billowing swirl of dust. Before it had settled, two guards in khaki-coloured uniforms emerged from the bushes, stepping up to the vehicle with submachine-guns held high. The lead guard reached for the driver's-side door just as Sandros Oliveira cut the engine and slid from behind the wheel.

Recognising him, they lowered their weapons to let him pass.

Oliveira saw Ramos Juarez not ten yards away, in the middle of the dusty track that cut a path through the dense jungle. Juarez stood with his back to him and was dressed in a white-linen suit that struck Oliveira as hardly appropriate. At the best of times, the jungle was no place for such attire. But Oliveira knew this would be of no concern to his employer. As he made his way through the dust-cloud, heading up the makeshift road, he watched unsurprised as Juarez stood unmoving, his hands clenched behind his back as he indulged in the scene of carnage before him.

Ahead, a large portion of the forest had been levelled. As Oliveira covered the last few steps to Juarez he saw a wide section of bare earth unfold before him, stretching away into the distance. At one end of it, a pile of dead, leafless tree trunks lay heaped upon each other like a mass of pale skeletons. At the other end, the cause of the destruction: three yellow, mud-smeared bulldozers. They rumbled back and forth with singular relentlessness, razing all before them.

"Sandros," Juarez said in Brazilian Portuguese, a remarkable feat given he hadn't yet turned. "On time as usual."

Oliveira stepped beside Juarez, commanding an equal share of the view. As he did, he noticed two of the machines move farther afield, their hunger not yet sated. A few dozen yards away, another huge tree was wrenched free of the ground by the third dozer, groaning in protest as it was torn from its long-held place of residence. Oliveira watched impassively as it crashed to the earth, bringing with it as it fell a host of smaller trees. It hit the ground with a thud so gigantic that underfoot the earth trembled as though in the grip of an electric current.

"Progress has been swift, Ramos," Oliveira observed, nodding. Indeed, he was pleasantly surprised by just how much headway had been made. Judging by what he'd seen already, there was every chance the new facility would be up and running as early as they had hoped, perhaps sooner. This was good news. With the recent upsurge of surveillance and crackdowns at the behest of the Americans, business had been difficult lately, and a change in operations had been forced upon them. Even their competitors had been feeling the heat: Oliveira had heard of similar facilities springing up elsewhere, in secret jungle locations hidden from prying eyes. Not that that was of any real concern to him, though. All that mattered was that affairs were running smoothly for his employer.

And Oliveira much preferred dealing with his boss when he was in a good mood.

Even so, it was apparent now that Ramos was in no frame of mind for small talk. He was still to turn and face Oliveira. "News, Sandros?" was all he said as he stared into the distance.

"I have spoken with Felipe Cartana," Oliveira answered.

Now Juarez turned to him.

Oliveira removed his silver aviator sunglasses and met Juarez with a firm yet accommodating stare. Juarez was in his mid-forties, almost a decade older than Oliveira, with relentlessly dark eyes and a strikingly handsome, though uncompromising, face. He wore his shiny, jet-black hair in a tiny, neat ponytail, unlike Oliveira's own ponytail, which was longer and braided and protruding currently from beneath a khaki headwrap.

"And?"

"He insists it is the same plane," Oliveira said. "The tail identifying number, Ramos... it matches."

For some time, Juarez didn't speak. Slowly, he turned away, staring in the direction of the dozers. An expression passed over his face, barely perceptible, though Oliveira managed to catch it: a slight clenching of teeth, a faint tightening of the muscles around the jaw at a remembered hurt Oliveira himself knew all too well.

"I'd appreciate you having a look, Sandros," Juarez said at last, softly. "Take as many men as you think appropriate." As an afterthought, he added, "Take Cartana, too."

Oliveira lowered his voice to match. "What about the Americans?"

"I don't care. Do whatever you deem necessary."

Oliveira nodded and moved to leave, but before he could, Juarez placed a strong hand on his shoulder and fixed him with a stare that stood him firm in his tracks. "Sandros, make no mistake. I want that plane located, and I want that package retrieved."

Juarez released his hold, and Oliveira retreated, heading back down the road.

18

Rebecca was stunned, silent.

Again, she raised the binoculars to stare at the mangled aircraft.

For some moments, Owen had been shaking his head. Now, he ran a hand through his wild, blond-streaked hair before replacing his Marlins cap. "Ed, seriously? You're suggesting that web, as big as it is, trapped that plane?"

Ed shrugged. "I can't say for sure, but it seems that way, don't you think? I mean, there's obviously some other explanation as to why it fell from the sky—engine failure, I suppose, as it had to get down here somehow—but in the end… well, you can see for yourself where it came to rest."

Owen obviously *could* see, and by Rebecca's reckoning, that was the problem. By all appearances, and as unlikely as it sounded, Ed was probably right. Instead of crashing into the ground after tearing its way through the forest canopy, the plane had become ensnared—*in the web*—dozens of feet above the forest floor. Now it dangled nose-down, tail-up, one wing bent around its front and across the cabin and the other, having been almost torn free altogether, trailing precariously earthward. The whole twisted wreck hung only yards from the pyramid, positioned near to its northern face and with perhaps the top third of the huge structure looming high above it.

"There's no doubt the web is holding it in place," Rebecca said. "You know, a plane like that… it's got to be a few tons at least. Can you imagine how strong the silk must be? And to absorb the momentum of an object that size, no matter how much it might have been slowed by the trees, that's something else again. The construction—the distribution of tension—must be out of this world!" She shook her head at the thought, still studying the web, which was when something else caught her eye and caused her to baulk. Double-checking, she said, "Hell... and more than that... it looks like the plane's not just *hanging* there, either."

Rebecca tried to zoom in, fumbling and squinting through her binoculars before pushing them away and turning to Ed, who had lit a cigarette. "Ed, if that web is deserted, then it was abandoned *after* the arrival of that plane. The wreckage has been partially *wrapped*."

"Wait... cocooned?" Owen said. "Like a captured insect or something?"

"Oh man..." Jessy said, swallowing hard, her perfectly tanned, unblemished features now decidedly ashen. "Please tell me they died on impact."

A finger of ice shivered down Rebecca's spine, the thought of what might have transpired simply too unpleasant to contemplate.

Jessy changed the subject. "What kind of plane do you think it is? I mean, those pontoons or whatever that are attached to the underbelly... it's a seaplane, right?"

"A floatplane, yes," Ed said, dragging on his cigarette.

Owen peered through his binoculars. "Looks like it's been there a while. Years, most likely."

"So why has no-one retrieved it?" Jessy asked. "What about its transmitter... you know... that electronic locator they use to detect downed aircraft?"

"You mean the ELT, the plane's Emergency Locator Transmitter," Ed said. "Who knows? Maybe it was destroyed in the crash. Maybe it wasn't fitted with one. They're fixed to all aircraft operating in the US, but I'm not sure of the regulations down here."

Sanchez nodded, said to Jessy, "You'd be surprised, *senhorita*, at how many aircraft have been lost out here. Most are never found. Others are abandoned. In this part of the world, flight plans are not common."

Jessy seemed confused. Ed lifted a finger to the sky and traced it over his head. "This isn't a civilian air corridor. It's likely used by traffickers."

"You mean *drug* traffickers?" Jessy said. "You're saying this is a drug plane?"

"Drugs, guns, who knows?" Ed said. "If it is a drug plane—and say it crashed due to engine failure—I'm guessing its owners wouldn't have rushed to alert the authorities. You wouldn't *want* it found, at least not by someone else. You'd simply cut your losses."

"Or search for it yourself."

"If the ELT was damaged, or not even fitted, where would you start looking?" Ed said. "You might have a general idea but without the *exact* location, out here…"

Enrique, the earbuds to his iPod dangling around his neck, nudged Rebecca gently with his elbow. "When I first saw this aircraft, it reminded me of a story my older brother told me. He said that one day many years ago, before I was even born, a plane fell from the sky only a few miles out of Manaus—my home town, and the largest town in the Amazon forest. My brother, who then was only a boy, and others, too, saw exactly where it fell, yet it took the town ten days to find it."

"Ten days, and in a heavily populated area, with dozens of witnesses," Ed said. "Jungle like this rarely gives up its secrets."

"You know," Owen said, still staring through his binoculars, "there's a series of letters and numbers stencilled on the tail assembly. I can make out most of them. It's probably an identification number."

"We should copy it down," Jessy said. "We'll pass it on to the authorities when we get back."

Ed shook his head. "Even if it *is* registered, I don't think that's a good idea. We oughtta forget we ever saw it."

As the last of the words was leaving his mouth, a great crack of thunder snapped above them. Rebecca jumped, and turned her face skyward as cool drops of rain pattered down, bouncing and pinging off the leaves. More thunder followed, but this time it rolled loudly from one horizon to the next. A storm was about to unleash.

Everyone scrambled for ponchos.

As she rifled through her gear, Rebecca said to Ed, "I'm curious about something." She gestured to the two giant moai she'd noticed earlier, within which the pyramid's large central set of foliage-covered steps was so perfectly framed. "What's the story with those two? They're much bigger than any of the others we've seen, and there's something different again about their posture…"

Jessy, who had retied the blue scarf she'd been using like a bandanna and was tucking her blond pigtails underneath it, out of the rain, added: "Yeah. They look like guards, don't they? Sentries. Ed, what do you think?"

Ed grinned. "I think you'd be more interested in what I *know*." He slipped into his poncho and pulled the hood low across his face. "I can tell you exactly what their story is."

The rain intensified, falling so forcefully Ed had to raise his voice to be heard. But he seemed pleased the subject had been broached. "Last night, I told you I could prove the city was Intihuasi." As he spoke, he slipped from the two shoulder packs that hung low at his waist, placing them on the ground. Free of them, he fished inside his shirt pocket and retrieved a tightly wrapped cloth bundle. "If you're interested in that proof, I can show you."

Rebecca looked from Jessy to Owen and shrugged. Why not? At this, Ed muttered something to Sanchez, and then handed Enrique the two packs he'd placed upon the ground. The younger man slung both over his shoulders.

"Ready?" Ed said. "It won't take long."

Minus Enrique and Sanchez, the group moved off, detouring from the path they had been traversing to one that would take them on a direct line down the slope towards the pyramid and the outer rim of the smaller bowl where the two giant moai stood guard. Ed led the way, swinging his machete. In his opposing hand was the cloth bundle, tightly gripped. This time, Rebecca brought up the tail. As she moved in behind, she glanced cautiously into the distance, scouring the pyramid and the heart of the web.

Like before, it was empty. No sign of movement—of *life*—anywhere.

A dark blur skittered past her, racing along the ground to her left.

Rebecca spun. Dead brown leaves kicked up in the blur's wake, bushes parting and springing back—

"*Espere! Parar! Pare imediatamente!*"

Yelling and cursing, Enrique rushed past Rebecca, crashing through the underbrush in pursuit of the streaking shadow.

But Priscilla was fast, off like a shot.

The monkey's attention was fixed on a pile of scattered fruit at the base of a tall, thin fig some twenty yards away. Reaching it, she proceeded to sort through the pile, glancing back with a mischievous grin at Enrique who arrived just as she found a suitable piece. She took a bite as he swept her up like a naughty child.

Rebecca turned from the commotion, smiling to herself, and ran to catch up to her three companions.

The two giant moai were bigger than she'd expected.

"Wow," Rebecca said, reaching out to stroke the cool, discoloured belly of the statue on the left. Its oversized head comprised perhaps two-thirds of the total height, while the body stretched upwards a good ten to fifteen feet. Its huge, overhanging chin jutted out so far it blocked out the rain.

Rebecca glanced up at it, noting they stood also beneath a portion of the *web*—its outermost extremities, anyway. She stepped back to take it in, wondering if anyone else was aware of the fact. High above, the silk glistened, taut and silvery, and she found herself transfixed, keen to make an even closer examination. As she considered this, droplets of rain splashed on her face, cool on her skin.

"Oh, *shit!*"

Rebecca spun. Owen started to thrash about, his arms flailing wildly, his hands slapping at his face and upper torso as though he'd been set on fire.

"*Shit!*" he cried again, "*Get them off!*"

Like her, he'd stepped back from the moai to stare up at the web. Rebecca saw the cause of his panic.

They covered his face, his shoulders, even his hair—dozens of tiny spiders each the size of a small coin. They swarmed all over him.

"Owen!" Rebecca called, running to him, "Stay calm!"

"*What the fuck?*" he screamed.

Ed and Jessy reached Owen at the same moment as Rebecca, and together they swept the tiny black bodies from their flailing companion. "They must have been washed down from above!" Rebecca said over the rain.

Owen continued to thrash, flinging them off, squashing them underfoot. Rebecca tried to calm him. Most likely, this was a batch of recently hatched spiderlings, a run-of-the-mill, and totally harmless, species. Communal webs were commonly home to squatters.

"*Jesus!*" Owen cried.

"Stand still!" Rebecca said. Within moments, the last of the spiders—and several insects—were gone. Rebecca drew Owen's attention to her own shoulder and an alien-looking insect that she proceeded to calmly remove. "The sudden downpour must have dislodged them. It's okay now."

But Owen was still spinning, brushing at himself.

His antics caused Ed to smile. "Come on, buddy." He flicked a couple of critters off his own person. "You've seen stuff like this before. Nothing to worry about."

"You're kidding, right?" Owen said, clearly unimpressed by the relaxed manner of his companions. Only when he was convinced the last of the creatures had been displaced did he refit his hood, yet still he was agitated. "*Nothing to worry about?* You didn't have them crawling in your hair!"

Rebecca, Ed, and Jessy had a discreet chuckle before returning their attention to the two giant moai. Ed untied the cloth bundle he'd earlier retrieved from his shirt pocket.

Sulking and grumbling away in the background, Owen continued to fidget, not caring that his efforts were lost on them. "Is there anyone who'd appreciate a bucketful of spiders tipped over their head? No, I don't think so. Jeez."

Ed removed the stone disc and held it up. It had been a while since Rebecca had laid eyes on it, even though she'd studied it dozens of times before. Circular and greyish-clay in colour, the relic was roughly the size of a man's palm, flat on one side, with the other curving out half an inch or so. Charcoal-coloured spiralling grooves marked its smooth, almost polished surface. Ed's grandfather had obtained the artefact from a private collector in Copenhagen, before later gifting it to Ed. This was the object that had originally spawned his—and in turn Ed's—obsession with Intihuasi.

Ed held it now in the direction of the moai. As he did, Rebecca's gaze was guided to a small indentation she hadn't seen earlier, a flat and otherwise unremarkable circular recess pressed into the statue's chest, sitting about five feet above the ground. The groove was the size of a drink-coaster, and as Ed held the disc before him, Rebecca sighed in realisation.

"*Esperar! Priscilla!*"

Priscilla was at it again. Like before, Enrique ran after her, bolting now in circles and figure-eights.

"She's giving him a hard time this afternoon," Jessy commented.

"Perhaps it's the 'terrible twos," Owen mused.

Rebecca wasn't as flippant. As she watched, the game of cat-and-mouse took Priscilla and Enrique farther afield than earlier, closer to the lip of the bowl. Enrique stooped as he ran, arms outstretched.

Rebecca was overcome by a sudden unease. She glanced back at the pyramid, the web. Again, deserted. A ghost-town, just like Ed had described. She turned back to Enrique, watched as he bent down to lift Priscilla from where she had finally paused, again to eat.

Something didn't feel right.

Priscilla clambered onto Enrique's arm, another piece of fruit in her tiny hands. She skipped up to his shoulder and resumed eating.

Something was wrong.

"Okay," Ed said, attempting to swing the attention back his way. He held out the stone disc. "Watch this."

But Rebecca ignored him, her eyes fixed solely on Enrique. Seemingly unaware, Ed moved the disc anyway, tracking it towards the recess in the moai's chest.

Enrique looked up, caught Rebecca's gaze, smiled.

For Rebecca, everything moved in slow-motion.

Get out of there.

She swivelled from Enrique to Ed, and then back again.

Enrique. Get out of there.

The stone disc was only an inch away from the indentation. Rebecca opened her mouth. She had to warn him, had to warn Enrique.

Ed smiled, looked back at Owen and Jessy. "Showtime," he said, still grinning.

And then… all hell broke loose.

19

Enrique met Rebecca's gaze a split-second before the forest floor behind him exploded upwards.

In that moment, and though he wouldn't have understood why, he must have seen her eyes go wide.

Rebecca had no chance of warning him. It happened fast. She could only look on, horrified.

Something huge had launched itself with terrifying, blinding speed from a hole in the ground behind Enrique's feet—a hole that a moment before hadn't existed. It was big enough for the dark, blurred shape to squeeze most of the way out—and the thing hit Enrique hard. Under its weight, Enrique pitched forward, shrieking as the creature grasped him by the haunches and in the same, practised movement pulled him forcefully downwards, slamming him face-first into the ground.

In that horrifying split-second, Rebecca got a good look at what it was. Pivoting in response to Enrique's cry, Jessy must have too, and she screamed.

Astride Enrique's back, horrible legs twitching and flailing as it tried to subdue its prey, was a spider more than a yard wide.

Enrique bucked violently beneath it, tried to shake it from his back, his eyes wide with terror, but it was too strong, too fast. Long before any of them could move to help, it was over.

With a great, violent tug, the creature dragged Enrique screaming into the hole in the earth. He was gone in the blink of an eye, his cries suddenly muffled and lost.

Then there was nothing.

Enrique had vanished; so too the spider, and the hole itself.

There was only the forest floor again.

New screams erupted. Male voices shouted. Rebecca, tears in her eyes, could only stand in disbelief, rooted to the spot. Though she could no longer see it, she knew that the hole Enrique had been dragged into was still there, had been there all along, but was now, as then, simply covered—*cleverly disguised*—by a flap of earth.

A *trapdoor*.

They had to get out of there.

"*Oh shit!*" Jessy said.

Staggering, Rebecca followed Jessy's gaze and through a mist of tears stared straight into two big, glassy black orbs.

Eyes.

The anterior median eyes of a huge spider.

Its dark, hair-covered body was almost perfectly camouflaged against the kapok it clung to—Rebecca was vaguely aware of pale green and brown stripes running across its dorsal surface, heightening the concealment. But she could see it well enough, and it stared straight at her. She froze, her gaze locked with the creature.

It's studying me.

The creature's dark, monkey-like face remained still, tufts of whitish hair framing eyes from behind which burned an intense alertness. The lifeless specimen back at Base Camp was one thing; this was altogether different...

It's sizing me up. It sees me as prey.

Suddenly, Rebecca was aware of more eyes upon her—to the left, another set, and another on the ground not far from that.

There were three of them.

Three that she could *see*...

All were huge—the size of large dogs—their forelegs lifting in aggressive threat-poses...

Time stopped. Rebecca knew she had to run, because at any moment these creatures would pounce. But she couldn't. She couldn't make her legs move. A flush of panic washed over her. Why wouldn't her legs move? Yet in the back of her mind somewhere, she already knew the answer. Even so, she couldn't believe it.

She stared again at the first spider. Once more, their gazes locked.

The megarachnid pounced, its strong back legs propelling it through the air towards her.

In a sense, it was strangely compelling. Rebecca watched as the creature arced her way, twisting gracefully in the air from its vertical hold on the tree so that at the peak of its leap, and on its descent toward her, she could see its soft, smooth underside, delicately exposed. She noticed, too, how its legs were spread wide, poised to embrace her.

She stood her ground, waited for it to come.

She was hit hard.

20

The impact didn't come from the direction Rebecca was expecting.

A split-second before the pouncing spider had finished its descent, something else had leapt across from the side, from somewhere to her right, hitting her and snatching her from the creature's embrace.

It slammed into her, collecting her around the waist, the collision sending her flying sideways through the air.

She hadn't seen this new attack coming but had a flashing thought of the two arachnids she'd noticed just before the first spider had leapt.

They were hunting as a pack.

The first spider had held her in its gaze long enough for one of the others to take her by surprise…

Rebecca hit the ground hard, she and her attacker falling together in a painful heap. She grunted as the wind was knocked from her lungs, her back driving against something solid and unyielding. Immediately, she twisted into a sitting position with her attacker still attached around her waist. Feeling its weight, she kicked out, punching and thrashing with all her strength. Then she heard a voice, a male voice, screaming her name, and realised she hadn't been hit by a spider at all, but by Ed.

Ed!

Ed had pushed her out of the path of the arachnid that had leapt for her. They'd tumbled sideways together, a tangle of limbs. Now, they found themselves tightly wedged at the base of a massive tree, jammed between two huge, flaring roots that soared higher than Rebecca's head and fanned out like great blades on either side of her body. Rebecca was pressed up against the main trunk, Ed lying on top of her, facing her. He moved to stand, got to his knees…

"*Ed… the spiders!*" Rebecca shouted, but even as the words left her mouth the first of the creatures leapt flailing onto Ed's back, slamming him down on her. A second huge shape followed instantly. Rebecca let out a terrified scream. Ed's face was now pressed flat against hers, and the two spiders, twitching and jostling for position upon his back, were themselves only inches away. She could see the lightning blur of their legs above him, could hear them scratching against the tree. Ed folded his arms protectively around her. For some reason, the creatures seemed to be ignoring him, trying to get at *her*, their frenzied efforts hampered by Ed's body and the flares of the buttress roots to either side. She couldn't understand why they were so intent on her. As their efforts became more frantic, the noise of their legs scraping and ripping at the tree increased, amplified by the buttress roots around her.

Fangs flashed, terrifyingly long, only inches away.

They couldn't get at her.

As though accepting this, both creatures abruptly changed strategy, striking instead at the next best target.

Rebecca could only watch in horror as the two arachnids sank their venomous mouthparts hard and fast into Ed's back.

Together—and repeatedly.

21

Jessy sprinted, foliage slapping at her face, clawing at her clothing.

Shit…

She'd seen the spider leap for Rebecca. She'd been aware of at least two more, one of which had pounced at *her*. She'd turned and fled, unaware if her companions had done likewise. She wondered if she was still being pursued but was too terrified to stop; it sounded as though something was tearing through the undergrowth behind her.

Having strayed from the path, her bearings were shot. Underfoot, leaves and twigs crunched loudly—despite the rain the ground remained hard and uneven and her boots had to fight for purchase, her ankles straining with each impact—but then alarmingly her next step was into mid-air and she was tumbling through space, plummeting through nothingness. Suddenly, the ground reappeared. She hit it hard, and a lightning bolt of pain shot through her, and she rolled, bouncing downhill, now alternating between the air and the earth, over and over. The underbrush ripped and flayed at her skin and she squeezed shut her eyes until finally, mercifully, she rolled no more.

Breathless, Jessy came to rest facedown at the base of the steep embankment. She lay there unmoving until a fiery agony in her left leg flared, urging her to roll over and crane her head. The limb was a mess of blood.

Oh God…

Another throb of pain. She averted her gaze and stared skyward through slitted eyes. She could see nothing but waist-high ferns. Birds called overhead, and rain pattered on fronds, and then dimly, a male voice drifted through the trees. It seemed a long way off. She didn't have the strength to answer.

Where was her pursuer?

Heart in her mouth, she tried to get up, knew she faced certain death if she didn't get moving. But she couldn't muster the strength. Her head fell back to the ground.

The last thing she knew before she blacked out was a sudden rustling in the bushes to her right.

22

Rebecca had seen the shadow fall across her less than a second before the two spiders disappeared from her vision. Until then she'd watched helplessly as the creatures struck at Ed not once but several times with blinding speed, finally leaving their fangs embedded in his back to pump more venom into him. He had lain on top of her, eyes shut, selflessly absorbing their wrath. Rebecca tried to strike at them, but her arms were pinned.

Then there was the shadow and they were gone. In all the chaos Rebecca thought the creatures may have fled, but then realised that wasn't the case. She heaved upwards. Expecting the worst, she was surprised when Ed moved with her and stood, seemingly uninjured.

"*Ed?*" She spun him around—

—to find his shredded backpack in tatters, its shattered contents spilling to the ground and coated in a viscous, watery-grey liquid.

The spiders' fangs hadn't penetrated.

He was okay. She threw her arms around him, tears in her eyes.

They shared a quick hug, then separated, and Rebecca cast a lightning-glimpse at the surrounding trees. There appeared to be no further threat. She shot a grateful glance at Sanchez who stood a few feet away, his machete blade stained with a long, dark smudge. Lying at his feet were the bodies of the two megarachnids—one of them in two separate, grisly pieces, the other intact but with a great rend down its length and its contracted legs curled into its abdomen.

The shadow had been Sanchez. He'd saved them, but there was no time to rejoice.

"Where's Jess?" Ed said, spinning about.

"Owen's gone too…" Rebecca said.

Sanchez turned and disappeared soundlessly into the brush.

Trailing Robert, Rebecca burst through the bushes with Ed to find Jessy sprawled semiconscious amongst the leaf litter, Owen kneeling over her.

"Jess!" Ed said, surging down the embankment. At the bottom, he fell to his knees and cradled her head in his hands.

Jessy moaned, her eyes fluttering open. "Are they gone?" she groaned.

"The spiders? Yeah, they're gone," Ed said. Again, Jessy's eyes fell shut.

Owen turned to Ed, then Rebecca. "I'm sorry for taking off… it's just that I saw the third creature leap towards us. I didn't look back… I have no idea what happened to it, how far it chased us." Owen told them he'd trailed Jessy the whole way, catching glimpses of her through the trees. Then she'd dropped from view. Pointing to Jessy's leg, he whispered, "I think it's broken."

Clearly Sanchez had concluded likewise. Having already collected two sticks to use as splints, he knelt beside Jessy and gently roused her. Then, searching his pocket, he removed a small, plastic bag, and passed her something from inside it. "Here, chew this. You'll feel better."

Jessy struggled to focus. "What is it?"

"Coca leaf."

Jessy chewed obediently and seemed to calm. Rebecca knelt beside Sanchez, elevating Jessy's leg while Sanchez applied the splints. Fortunately, the bone hadn't pierced the skin; the blood was the result of superficial cuts. Sanchez attended to these, too, as well as a nasty bump to the back of Jessy's head. "You'll be okay," he assured her as he got up. He nodded to Rebecca, suggesting they give Ed and Jessy some breathing-space.

With Owen in tow, Rebecca followed Sanchez out of earshot.

"Fuck me," Owen blurted in a low voice. "What the hell just happened?"

Rebecca shook her head. No longer able to contain them, she let the tears flow freely. "Dear God… poor Enrique."

"I thought Ed said the place was *deserted*? A ghost-town!" Owen said. "Bec, what was that thing *doing*? First, they're jumping, then they're building webs, and now they're coming out of the ground!"

Rebecca looked up and blinked, trying to piece her thoughts together. "I don't know."

Owen grasped her by the shoulders. "Hey, come on! I don't mean to be insensitive, but we need you. Are we *safe* here?"

"I saw three of them back there," Rebecca said. "Robert killed two. I don't know what happened to the third."

"I thought it chased us. Surely it didn't follow us this far?"

"I don't know," Rebecca said again. "Perhaps it lost you, pursued you to the limit of its territory and gave up. *I don't know.*"

"*Amigo,*" Sanchez said, scanning the trees, "I believe we are safe for now." He turned to them. "Ms Baxter's break is bad, and she's concussed. We must get her to hospital."

Owen nodded, heaving a breath and adjusting his Marlins cap.

Rebecca, too, tried to compose herself. "Let's get on the sat-phone to Base Camp right away."

At that moment, Ed pushed through the ferns. He shook his head. "Enrique was carrying my shoulder pack when we went down to the moai."

"What?" Rebecca said. "You mean the phone was in *there*? You're not serious…"

Ed nodded.

Owen spun on him. "Ed, you said it was safe to be here! What the hell just happened?"

Rebecca put her face in her hands, panic rising in her. "Ed, please tell me you've got a PLB." She removed her hands and held her breath. Personal Locator Beacons worked like EPIRBs, emitting a distress signal relayed by satellite to a rescue centre.

Ed frowned, tossing her an orange-coloured device the size of a cell phone. The unit was sticky to the touch and punctured with ragged holes.

"It was in my backpack," Ed said. "Like everything else, it's destroyed."

Rebecca dropped the PLB to the ground and wiped her hands on her shorts. "You carry only one?"

"Enrique had one."

Rebecca looked from Ed to Sanchez, and then back again. An uncomfortable weight settled in her stomach. "So, what's our situation, then?"

"Fucked," Owen murmured.

"Let's stay calm," Ed said.

The weight in Rebecca's gut grew heavier. "Let's get this in perspective. I've got a cell phone back at base camp—I left it there because I haven't had service for days. I brought my laptop but without the sat-phone, we can't connect to anything." She turned to Sanchez. "What about the radio? We could try Base Camp with that."

"We are long out of range, *senhorita*."

"Someone else might hear us."

Sanchez shook his head. "They would need to be within a few miles, and on the right frequency. It is unlikely. We are in pretty deep here."

"You're not fucking joking," Owen murmured.

Ed held up his hands. "As I said, let's stay calm, okay? I think we should go back and conduct a search of the area where Enrique was... taken. Maybe something was dropped, left behind."

"Are you kidding?" Owen said. "There could be dozens of them there now! They could be all over the place!"

Sanchez replied bluntly, "*Amigo,* we have no way of getting in contact with Base Camp, or anyone else. What would you suggest?"

"Have we got *anything* we can use?" Rebecca asked.

"Signal flares," Sanchez answered.

Owen rolled his eyes. "What good are *they*? There's no commercial traffic here, and as for private aircraft... outside of the plane caught in that web, we've seen nothing."

"Which is why, despite the risk, the search makes sense," Ed said. "If it proves fruitless, we'll return to Base Camp. There's another sat-phone there, we'll call for a floatplane—it'll be faster than calling in the *Tempestade*. It'll have to land in the main river, but we can use the Zodiac to rush out and meet it."

"Aren't you forgetting something?" Owen said. "How the hell do we *get* her back to Base Camp? She can't walk!"

"We carry her out by stretcher."

"*What?*" Owen blurted. "It's almost two days back to Base Camp, and that's for the able-bodied! You can double that if we have to carry her. And what about the ravine? This is crazy."

Rebecca rubbed her brow. "Getting angry won't solve anything, Owen."

"What do you suggest, then, Bec?"

Rebecca turned to Sanchez. "What about a helicopter? Two of us could head back to Base Camp and call from there—we've got the GPS coordinates; the chopper could be sent to this exact location. The other two could sit tight with Jessy and wait for it." It sounded like a good plan, but then she recalled what Sanchez had said to her before departing Base Camp yesterday. "But of course, we're in too deep for a chopper to get to us."

Sanchez cocked his head. "Maybe for civilian or privately chartered aircraft, *senhorita*. But a long-range search-and-rescue team, perhaps the military… it's a possibility."

Ed looked at Sanchez and nodded. "I think it's our best option."

Sanchez seemed to agree. "I will go. But alone. I am much quicker than any of you and will get there fastest. I will send the chopper."

"Hang on," Owen said. "What if you fall and break a leg like Jessy, or get bitten by a snake, or worse still, one of those creatures comes after you? If you don't make it, for any reason, the rest of us are as good as dead!"

"Then join me," Sanchez said. "One of us will see it done."

Rebecca nodded. "I think it's the best we can do. You two head back to Base Camp, call in a chopper. Ed and I will stay here and look after Jessy."

"Not here," Ed said. "We've got another camp, remember? But first things first—let's get back and conduct that search."

23

"That's it. That's it there," Rebecca said. She was lying prone in the under-growth with her elbows propped up and a pair of binoculars to her eyes. On either side of her, Owen and Sanchez lay in similar fashion. All around them, broad, spreading ferns rose skyward. It was still raining.

"This is crazy," Owen said. "Why can't either of you see that?"

They'd relocated Jessy to Advance Base Camp—the S2 campsite—on a triangular stretcher: three long sticks with the camouflage-netting from the crates they'd brought from S1 strung tautly between them. Ed had stayed with her while the remainder of the group had returned here—the lip of the large bowl that looked down on the spot where Enrique had been taken—to determine if anything had been left behind and could be salvaged. It didn't appear so.

"Are you sure that's it?" Sanchez said.

"Not entirely," Rebecca answered. "Usually there's a trigger mechanism: silken trip-lines, sometimes a silken mat or a root or stick or something with a thread attached. Brushing the trigger will set off the alarm and alert the spider in its burrow that prey is approaching, like a fisherman feeling a bite on the line with his finger. But finding either the trigger or the door is notoriously difficult—disguise is the whole point—and right now, I can't see anything out of the ordinary. But from memory, I think that's the spot."

"We're not going anywhere near it," Owen said. "I can't see the trigger, *or* the door. Let's check it once more with the binoculars and get out of here."

Sanchez agreed, and scanned again. "I do not see anything. Do you?" he asked Rebecca.

Through her binoculars, Rebecca scoured the area around the trapdoor. She shifted her view to the right, towards the two giant moai. In the end, Ed hadn't managed to slip the stone disc into the recess; the sudden attack had prevented him. To her at least, the relationship of the disc and the indentation remained a mystery. "No," she said, "Nothing at all."

"Okay then, let's go," Owen said. "They could be back at any moment. We didn't see them arrive the first time until it was too late. Robert?"

Sanchez nodded. "There is nothing here. We shall go."

The bushes ahead of them shivered, their leaves rustling.

A flash of brown launched into Rebecca's field of vision, too close for the binoculars to focus. Reflexively she threw them to the ground, rolling off her stomach and crossing her arms defensively in front of her face.

Priscilla leapt straight into them with a frightened cry.

Rebecca let out her own involuntary yelp before clutching the tiny monkey to her breast. "Oh, you gave me a fright," she panted. She stroked Priscilla's head, shielding her tightly. "The poor thing's shaking like a leaf."

Without further comment, they got to their feet and retreated to Advance Base Camp as noiselessly as they were able.

24

By the time Owen and Sanchez were ready to leave camp, the forest had grown dark, the sun sinking from behind blackened clouds in a spreading pool of orange. They would travel light, taking with them one of the Weatherby rifles, a tent, and a few basic provisions. Ed had insisted they also take an X40. A single unit weighed no more than a couple of pounds and offered 2,000 square feet of cover—ample for their requirements.

They'd fixed the remaining three devices in a triangle around the campsite, surrounded by the eight motion sensors.

Rebecca helped Owen into his pack, lifting it while he slipped his arms through the straps. The plan was simple: double-time it to S1, catch a couple of hours sleep there beside the moai and then aim to get into Base Camp by mid-afternoon the following day. Unfortunately, this meant crossing the ravine not only in heavy rain—the downpour had yet to relent—but in the dark as well. After two days of hard slog, it would test them physically and mentally, and Owen had wondered aloud if he was up to it. But what choice did they have?

Conversely, Rebecca, Ed, and Jessy would have plenty of time to rest and recuperate, although they faced a different plight. While a helicopter might be dispatched as early as tomorrow afternoon, with no means of communication, they could only sweat on its arrival, eyes peeled, and fingers crossed. The fate of their two companions was entirely out of their control, and only time would tell if Owen and Sanchez had made it.

The two men gathered the last of their equipment, including the necessary climbing gear, and prepared to say their goodbyes. They paid Jessy a visit first. Since the group's arrival at Advance Base Camp less than two hours ago, she'd been resting. They beelined through the rain to the other side of the clearing and Jessy's khaki-coloured dome tent.

Sanchez had discovered the clearing that now housed Advance Base Camp back when he and Ed had first found the city. Although not as generously set-up as Base Camp, it had almost everything they'd need. The site—which, for the next 24 hours would serve as refuge to half the group—was situated some two hundred yards or more from the city, tucked well out of view. The small, natural and elevated clearing was dominated by the remnants of one of the biggest trees Rebecca had ever seen. Once upon a time, the thing must have been enormous, wider at its base than the length of a bus and towering well beyond the canopy. Now, though, all that was left of the once-proud giant was a woody outer shell, comprised of a mass of parasitic strangler vines that had consumed its massive girth like a kind of organic armour and starved it to death. The tree itself had long since rotted away, the remaining 'skin' a lasting tribute.

They had dubbed this hollow core the 'cave', for obvious reasons. It was so big—and now, thanks to two well-placed tarpaulins, dry—that it served not only as a storage area for their supplies and equipment, but as a plot for their tents as well. They'd been able to set up two of the compact, dome-shaped dwellings side by side within it, with ample room to spare.

The clearing itself was fully screened by the thick canopy above. On all sides, the ground fell away steeply, so that their camp was ringed by a natural, looping moat. This ensured adequate runoff for the teeming rain. Around the edge of this moat, the motion sensors had been set.

At the clearing's southern end—right at the cave's entrance—a large tarpaulin had been tied off to the surrounding trees as further protection from the rain. It sheltered a small, lightweight but sturdy aluminium table, a couple of chairs, and, powered by small, stand-alone generators, several high-intensity LED lights that bathed the area in a stark artificial glow.

As Owen and Sanchez disappeared into Jessy's tent, Rebecca saw Ed standing by the fire pit, staring vacantly ahead. "You okay?"

They'd dug the fire pit into the soft, damp soil, lining its rim with logs and shielding it from the elements with a tarpaulin pegged to the ground and angled upwards about forty-five degrees.

Ed poked the fire with a stick, another tarpaulin above his head. "It's all falling apart, you know."

"What do you mean?"

"This isn't how it was meant to turn out. Once the rescue team sees this place, it'll be a circus. Others will come. I didn't need this, Bec, not now."

"*You* didn't need this?" Rebecca leaned into him, straining to keep her voice low. "You're kidding me, right? Forgive me if I don't sympathise, but you have no right to feel sorry for yourself! Enrique's *dead*, for Christ sake! You've got to live with that, we all do. And now Jessy's hurt. We have to get her back, and that's all there is to it—*whatever* the consequences here. Right now, your only concern should be with her."

Ed bristled. "What the hell do you take me for? I'm *devastated* about Enrique. And Jess? I hate seeing her in pain. But for now, we've done all we can. We're getting help. But the rest of it? You're wrong, Bec. I've earned the right to feel this way. This is my project. This is my *life*."

Rebecca softened, but she wasn't swayed. "What do you want, then? You've found the city. You've fulfilled your grandfather's dream, your own dream. Who cares if others come? What more do you want out of this?"

He frowned at her, tilting his head. "You have to ask?"

At that moment Owen and Sanchez emerged from Jessy's tent and exited the cave.

"You're *mad*, Ed," Rebecca said hurriedly, suddenly understanding. She lowered her voice even further. "It can't be done. It's not worth the risk. *You won't make it*." She looked at him, eyes narrowed. Owen and Sanchez were almost upon them. Ed made to move, but Rebecca held him back. "Don't make this harder on Jessy."

"Okay, then. We're off," Owen announced, he and Sanchez drawing up beside them. Rebecca tore her gaze from Ed and gathered Owen in a hug. "Be careful, won't you?"

They were ready to go. Sanchez retrieved a foil-covered tube from his pack, tore it open, and removed a long cylinder. He bent it in half, and the chemlight sprang to life, glowing a bright, luminescent blue that would last for the next twelve hours. He clipped it onto his backpack. The plan was for Owen to trail the light through the forest while Sanchez—aided by a pair of head-mounted night-vision goggles, or NVGs—guided them back.

"Stay safe," Ed said. Handshakes gave way to more hugs.

"We'll be seeing you," Owen said.

Without wasting another moment, Owen and Sanchez disappeared into the gloomy surrounds.

Rebecca watched their backs and hoped desperately there was truth in Owen's words.

25

When they were gone, Rebecca spun on Ed.

He held up his hands. "Don't waste your breath."

Rebecca scowled. "I'm going to check on Jessy." She charged through the rain. Ed followed her to the tent.

"Knock-knock," Rebecca said, waiting for Jessy to invite her in before drawing aside the flap.

Jessy sat up. She looked terrible; scratches consumed her face, and her hair and clothes were messed and muddied.

"How are you feeling?" Rebecca asked.

"I've seen better days. Got a killer headache, too."

Kneeling beside her, Rebecca retrieved aspirin from the First-Aid kit. She wished they had stronger painkillers.

Jessy washed down the tablets with a gulp of water. "To tell you the truth," she said, her expression turning sad, "I can't stop thinking about poor Enrique. What happened… it was awful. I hope it was… *quick*."

"It was," Rebecca lied. She knew there was every chance it wasn't, and her falsehood now was as much for herself as anyone.

Ed pressed in and sat down in the tent's cramped confines. He took Jessy's hand and stroked it.

Jessy smiled at him. "What about Priscilla?" she asked Rebecca.

"Shaken, but she'll be okay. She's sleeping out on the table."

Jessy seemed happy to hear it, but it wasn't long before her smile dissolved. She turned to Ed, concern etched in her face. "I heard Robert speaking to you earlier. About the campsite. Among other things, he said it was 'defensible'. That was his exact word. Tell me, Ed, and be honest. The last time you were here, did you have any… *problems*? Are you expecting those things to come after us?"

Ed lowered his gaze. "Jess, we thought the site was deserted. Hell… as horrible as it was, the incident back there was isolated. Prior to our arrival this afternoon we'd spent several days here without seeing anything, without any problem at all. Trust me. Those things don't know we're here."

Rebecca watched Ed before turning calmly to Jessy. "I'm sure Robert was just being cautious. He's ex-military. He likes to be prepared."

Jessy didn't seem convinced. "I've been thinking. You know, when it happened, they appeared together, as a pack. Those 'jumpers', they attacked you guys as a team. The third chased Owen and I, and we either lost it, *or* it gave up for some reason, simply chased us from its territory." She clasped her hands together, her expression intense. "But given how smart you say they are, and that they have exceptional vision, I don't believe we *lost* it. So why, then, did it turn back? We know they co-ordinate their attacks, so I think it turned back to *regroup*. I think it was alerting others to come search for us."

Ed reached again for Jessy's hand, and when he spoke, it was in the soft manner of a parent whose child complained of nightmares. "Try not to worry yourself, Jess. If they had regrouped, wouldn't they have found us by now? If there are more of them out there, I'm sure they've already forgotten about us."

Jessy sighed. "But that's my point! *How* can you be sure? If we're talking about an active nest, we're not safe here at all! Think about it. The one that got Enrique… that wasn't a jumping spider. It was a trapdoor spider. I'm thinking these things are more like *ants*, and they've all got a different job within the colony. And, maybe like ants, they warn each other when under attack, or when there's large prey that needs to be subdued. Ants do everything in numbers—that's their strength. When that thing in the ground attacked Enrique, the 'jumpers' were instantly alerted, maybe to assist or to protect the colony from attack. *Just like ants.* And, like ants, sooner or later, whether they remember us or not, they'll send out scouts to find food. *That's* what I'm trying to tell you."

Jessy's words hung in silence.

Eventually, Rebecca spoke. "If they do inhabit that web—which now seems a safe bet—then yes, it'll be an organised community. Social spiders *do* exist. But I'm not sure about the comparison with an ant colony and a division of labour. Social spiders don't have a caste system like ants or bees. What you're describing is unheard of."

"What, like their *size*, you mean?" Jessy remarked, her voice dripping with sarcasm.

"I guess we can't be sure of anything," Rebecca conceded, biting her lip.

Jessy pressed. "The one in the ground was different to the others. Heavier of body. It wasn't a jumper."

Rebecca nodded. "Then we've only got two possibilities."

"And they are?"

"The first is that you're right, and this is a single, eusocial species, with a caste system and a division of labour. Caste polymorphism would account for variations in body shape and size."

"And the second possibility?"

"The second is that there are two *different* species living and working together in symbiosis. The spiderlings that fell on Owen were most likely 'squatters'—a separate, regular-sized species living in the host web unnoticed. Perhaps the 'jumpers' live side by side with the 'trapdoors', tolerant of each other."

Jessy screwed up her face, scoffing at the notion of two or more different and *gigantic-sized* species living interdependently.

Rebecca was inclined to agree with her. "Whatever scenario, I guess it doesn't change our situation any. What does, however, is the point you made a moment ago, about scouts searching for food. Most social spiders live in the tropics because their food source—insects, namely—is in plentiful supply most of the year. Given their size, these guys would need a lot to sustain them, certainly more than just insects. I'm guessing birds and monkeys and larger animals would be on the menu; virtually anything that might blunder into the web."

"Or anything they could *hunt*."

Rebecca nodded. "By travelling farther afield than the web's confines, they'd avail themselves of larger and more varied prey." Rebecca turned to Ed. "Whether they remember us or not is beside the point. Jessy could be right. In order to gather the enormous amount of food required, maybe they do send out scouts, converging when something's been located. Maybe they will, by chance, come searching, and in numbers."

Jessy seemed relieved to be taken seriously.

Ed, however, drew a sharp breath. "Look, all this speculation… it isn't doing us any good. We've got the motion sensors and the X40s. The chopper will be here tomorrow. Jess, you need to rest."

Rebecca nodded, figuring it was better not to burden Jess further. "Why don't I fix us something to eat?" She moved outside to the sound of heavy rain. She didn't go far, venturing no farther than the cave's entrance and the tarpaulin set up with the LED lights.

Priscilla was curled up asleep on the table, her tiny chest rising and falling. The poor thing had only been able to find rest in the full glare of the lights. Rebecca tried not to disturb her, though she did briefly stroke the little monkey's head. With her other hand she waved at a cloud of mosquitoes; unfortunately, the lights had attracted swarms of insects. Not daring to turn them off, she reached into her pocket for the repellent.

Ed emerged from Jessy's tent some time later.

"Good timing," Rebecca said. "This is ready to go." She'd heated MREs. As Ed came to lend a hand, she paused to look up at him. "It's why you asked me here, isn't it?"

"Sorry?"

"Why you got me to come down here. To help you get in there. Into the pyramid."

Ed glanced over his shoulder and spoke low. "I thought we'd discussed this already. I never asked you to come, I just sent you the material."

"You wanted my opinion."

"Of course! You're the expert."

"An expert, who could help you get inside."

Ed shook his head and sighed. "You don't get it, do you? Fate, in the unlikeliest of coincidences, had delivered me an opportunity. Yeah, I wanted you to see this place—because I owed you."

"Owed me?"

Again, Ed glanced over his shoulder before leading her several more steps from the cave's entrance. He took her gently by the arms, just above the elbows. "Bec, you kept me going. You encouraged me, urged me on, gave me the strength and support to keep at it when I was ready to give up. I wanted to show you what came of your sacrifices. I wanted you to feel justified, and that it wasn't all just a waste of time."

Rebecca exhaled softly, dismissively. "A waste of time? You're being melodramatic, and I don't deserve this kind of credit."

"Yes, you do." He pulled her closer, his eyes welling with gratitude, and suddenly, something more. "You're more responsible for me finding this place—realising my dream—than you can ever imagine."

She fell into his gaze, and he leaned into her. For a moment she hesitated there, her body close against his. Then she lowered her eyes and eased away. "I don't know if I can bear that responsibility," she said. "I don't know if I can handle knowing I'd given you the strength to keep looking, to find this place… and then didn't *stop* you from going in there. Because if you do, Ed, you won't make it out alive."

She raised her eyes. He said nothing in reply and looked away. For an eternity, they stood unspeaking.

"Had you planned for me to accompany you?" Rebecca said eventually.

Ed looked back, his expression changing as though a switch had been flicked. "I never intended that," he said, shaking his head. "And especially not now. If I'd known the nest was active, I would never have brought you here."

For some time, Rebecca remained silent, unsure of what to say. At last she said quietly, "Have you any thoughts about how it can be done?"

"Yes."

That was the end of it. After delivering Jessy's meal, they talked some more, out by the fire, but Rebecca chose not to pursue the subject. She didn't need to. What she needed was time to think. Eventually she stood, her mind tired and heavy, and announced she'd try and rest. As she headed for her tent, she nervously scanned the trees.

If the three of them survived the night, she'd make damn sure that tomorrow, Ed got on the chopper with them.

26

Rain teemed down.

Even above the downpour—and before they had reached the edge of the darkened ravine—Sanchez said to Owen, "Hear that?"

Running water—a lot of it, and loud. Shocked, Owen stepped up to the ledge. Murky water rushed through the gorge below. Not a torrent, but more voluminous than the ankle-deep stream they'd crossed around noon that same day.

"I am not surprised," Sanchez said. "A dry wadi can become a river overnight. Flash flooding is common out here." As he spoke, he shrugged his pack, removing the harness and two coils of nylon climbing rope.

"Is that wise?" Owen questioned above the rain. "I mean, crossing it now, in the dark? The water's rising. It's too dangerous."

Sanchez didn't look up. "We have no choice, *amigo*. We must get across, and the sooner the better. Come daylight, it will be impassable."

Owen drew a calming breath. Sanchez was right. If they left it too long, they'd miss their window.

Securing the rope, Sanchez backed to the ledge and dropped over it.

Owen called after him. "Just for the record, I still think this is crazy!" He walked to the ledge and peered over, but the shadows had already swallowed his companion.

The process was the same as earlier in the day. Owen retrieved the harness and helmet with a second rope, raising the items before lowering the backpacks and remaining gear to the bottom.

While Sanchez held the first rope—still anchored to the top—Owen descended. The NVGs weren't suited for such a close-range task, so he worked without them, the beam of his headlamp illuminating the wet rock in front of him.

With Sanchez's direction, he was soon at the bottom.

The first thing he noticed as his feet touched the ground was the lack of standing room at the base of the ravine wall. Barely two feet separated the wall and the water's edge—already, water lapped at his toes—and with every moment the thin patch of mud and rock grew steadily narrower. Owen was amazed the stream had risen so quickly, but he didn't stand gawking for long. They were committed now, and the clock was ticking.

Sanchez anchored a rope for the crossing. While he worked, Owen glanced restlessly about. Rain slashed through the beam of his headlamp. On all sides, fern fronds rose to their waists.

"I want to apologise," Owen said above the downpour.

"For what?"

"For my behaviour this afternoon. I was short with the others, and particularly you. I didn't handle things very well. I'm sorry."

Sanchez continued to work but looked up briefly. "Not at all," he said, and resumed his task. Owen guessed that was the end of it. He was glad.

Sanchez wedged a camming device into the rock wall, fed a rope through it, and then fixed one end of the rope to the harness. He glanced at Owen. "Remove your socks, keep them dry. Put your boots on without them for the walk across. We'll towel our feet on the other side."

Owen did as he was told and removed his footwear. "What about caiman?" he asked, scanning the rushing black water.

Sanchez didn't answer. Owen baulked, wondering in what way he should take his companion's silence, but was unable to question him further. Already, Sanchez had waded into the dark stream. Assaulted by rain, he pushed against the flow of water, the rope trailing from his harness, back through the camming device. The other end of the rope spooled from Sanchez's hands, so that it ran in a loop behind him, taut above the surface.

Slowly and cautiously, Sanchez pushed through, and soon enough, he was across. At no time did the water rise higher than a few inches above his waist.

My turn, Owen thought.

Clambering up the opposite bank, Sanchez fixed both ends of the rope to a tree, the loop running two feet above the stream's roiling black surface. Using the second rope, Owen retrieved the harness and helmet, which Sanchez had attached to the first rope with a carabiner so that he could pull them above the water. Once their equipment had been ferried over, Owen slipped into the safety gear.

Okay, don't think about caiman. He hooked the carabiner to the chest-high guide-rope and plunged his foot beneath the stream's obsidian surface. *Just get across.*

He felt his way along. As he pushed forward, black water sped by, pulling at his waist, rain drumming loudly on the hood of his poncho. Above it, he could hear Sanchez calling out words of encouragement. Before long, he had reached the stream's midpoint.

This isn't so bad, he thought, and stumbled.

Owen's feet sped out from under him and he hit the water hard. Falling beneath the surface, the churning torrent roaring in his ears, he realised he hadn't drawn a breath and panicked, but then suddenly he was topside again, feeling the harsh pull of the rope. Stationary now, he lay parallel to the streambed, water crashing past him on either side.

The safety rope had saved him! Thank Christ.

The speed with which he'd been upended was astonishing, as though the flow had been awaiting his lapse in concentration. If not for the rope and harness, he would have been swept to his death.

He coughed water. He had to get to his feet. The stream thundered past his ears, yet still he could hear Sanchez calling to him. With effort, he found the bed underfoot and forced himself up. Straightening, he steadied himself on the rope and swivelled, regaining his bearings. Somehow, his glasses were still in place. Through droplets of water he sighted the waving figure of Sanchez and headed for it.

There were no more stumbles, and soon, still spluttering water, he was across.

"Are you okay, *amigo*?" Sanchez said.

"Yeah, thanks." Owen coughed, feeling more embarrassed than anything.

"I was hoping it wasn't a caiman," Sanchez remarked, helping him from the harness. Owen looked at him, unsure if he was joking. Sanchez gave nothing away.

They dried their feet, pressed up against the ravine wall. After towelling their boots, they slipped back into their dry socks before beginning the third, final, and most difficult phase of the ravine crossing.

The ascent.

Sanchez retrieved the ropes, drawing them through the anchor.

Owen had been dreading the ascent. Difficult enough in broad daylight, it'd be even more dangerous in the dark, pounded by rain.

Still, they had to keep moving. The stream continued to swell.

Sanchez fitted his headlamp and began.

He moved carefully, paying the slippery rock face due respect. In the faint light of the full moon that seeped from behind the blanketing clouds, the wet rock glistened, rising into the night like a sparkling wall of silver. Gripping the trailing safety rope from below, Owen watched Sanchez wedge camming devices into the wall and fasten the rope with carabiners.

As his companion drew fluidly away, his black silhouette dark against the rock, Owen was overcome by a creeping dread. He looked about himself but saw no reason for alarm. Cursing his jumpiness, he released one hand from the rope to wipe the rain from his glasses. It was difficult to see through their splotched lenses. Behind him, the water continued to rise, lapping now at his heels. He swivelled, looking to the side, back over his shoulder again. In these parts, you should never stand close to the water's edge. He recalled what Sanchez had said about caiman and pressed as close as he could to the wall. Soon, the water would be as high as his ankles...

He heard a splash and just behind him, on the surface of the stream, a long, dark shape cruised by...

...*just a log*...

He shook his head, cursing again, and ran his gaze up the rock face. Sanchez was three-quarters up and almost gone from sight. Owen's uneasiness grew, and he felt a mild stab of fear. He realised he was being irrational, but suddenly wanted to be free of the ravine, and quickly. Again, he glanced up at Sanchez, but this time in desperation.

If anything happens to Robert, I'm in big trouble.

The rain pelted down.

Get me out of here…

Above him, Sanchez reached the top and heaved himself over the ledge. Owen watched him disappear.

And felt the hairs prickle on the nape of his neck.

He spun about, looked around, twisted back the other way.

Nothing.

He knew he was acting foolishly, but at that moment, standing there gripping the rope at the bottom of the ravine with the suffocating blackness clamping down, worming in through his pores, Owen felt more alone, more isolated, than ever in his life, as though he was the only person left on the planet. He might well have been.

The water rose higher. It crawled up past his ankles, up his shins.

The night was so dark.

Sanchez hadn't reappeared.

Something's happened to him. What do I do now?

At the top of the rock face, Sanchez's head appeared in silhouette, beyond the ledge. "Ready, *amigo*? Let's go!"

The words instantly dispelled Owen's growing hysteria and he snapped back with a jolt. He needed no further urging.

After the packs and equipment had been raised, Owen headed up. Anxious to escape the ravine, he commenced eagerly, and the next half hour was a blur. He was barely cognisant of the ascent.

The next thing he knew, a pair of small but strong hands clutched at him from above, hauling him over the ledge.

Owen fell flat on his back.

Exhausted, he stole a moment to catch his breath, the rain falling around him. Below, the water had reached the wall, beginning its own creeping journey up the rock face.

Now they were permanently cut off from their companions—by foot at least. The helicopter was their only hope.

"That," Sanchez said, "is something I would not attempt again."

Owen sat up, panting, unable to read his companion's expression in the darkness. But despite it, for some reason, he broke into a laugh, and Sanchez returned it. "It *was* a stupid thing to do, wasn't it?" Owen chuckled.

They continued laughing for some moments, before Sanchez stood, patting Owen on the back. "Are you ready, *amigo*, to tackle the next stage?"

Owen nodded and got to his feet. His boots made a squishing sound. His socks were saturated.

"Here," Sanchez said, retrieving a dry pair from his pack.

Owen thanked him and slipped them on.

They headed back onto the trail that led to S1, Owen tracking once more the glowing blue chemlight. He was dead-tired, but Sanchez's selfless gesture in giving him his spare pair of dry socks, coupled with the laugh they had shared, boosted his morale. Suddenly, he felt more at ease with his often-humourless companion.

Owen shifted his pack up his shoulders and forced his leaden legs forward. His body ached to its core, and he desperately craved sleep. But he refused to complain. He wouldn't let anyone down, not now. And anyway, the sooner they got to S1, the sooner he could rest—even if only for a short time.

And for now, that was all he could think about.

27

Rebecca had been sleeping deeply when the nightmare jarred her awake. She sat up, her heart pounding like a hammer in her chest. She wiped at her forehead, ran a hand through her sweat-soaked hair.

Already, the horrible vision was withdrawing like a rat absconding into shadow. She could have let it go, but instead, she grabbed it by the tail and dragged it back into her mind's eye.

I need to know.

Now, she replayed the dream clearly, and was gripped once more with dread.

Just like the first time, it came from above, over the top of the motion sensors; slowly, almost mechanically, on a single thread of silk flowing smoothly from its abdomen. Its legs, splayed wide in a starburst, were deathly still as it slid noiselessly to the ground, its forward pair of appendages reaching for it. At their tips were retractable claws like those of a cat—climbing claws—and they flexed and sheathed. Velvet-like hairs, dark and bristling, ran the length of the jointed limbs. As the creature lowered itself, Rebecca knew that its eight glassy, black orbs, glinting in the meagre moonlight, saw all.

Saw *her.*

Halfway now between the canopy and the ground, the creature's silhouette, on the other side of the tent's flimsy nylon ceiling, was unmistakable. It remained so still it was as though someone lowered on a fishing line a giant Halloween toy, though Rebecca knew it was anything but.

She knew, and yet she couldn't move. Not a muscle. Every one of them had turned to stone, rooting her to the spot. She tried to sit up but had no feeling in her limbs. Desperately, she tried to work the muscles around her jaw and call out to Ed and Jessy, tried to scream, yet her mouth wouldn't work. Then suddenly there were legs reaching for the tent, reaching for her, and inevitably the dark shape was no longer the frightening yet inert, toy-like apparition but a horrible blur of motion as it ripped wildly, madly at the nylon, claws out, tearing it to shreds…

Rebecca almost screamed for real.

She shut the dream from her mind, took a moment to chase it away and clear her head. She glanced up. Of course, the tent's nylon ceiling was still intact. No threat lurked beyond it. In fact, several feet above, a tarpaulin had been strung across a section of the cave's hollow core to protect the interior from the elements. Impossible to see through.

"Shit."

Rebecca tried to compose herself.

She wasn't perturbed by the dream. It was more than that. Earlier today, when the huge spider had pounced for her, she'd suspected that something had been amiss but in the heat of the moment, she'd dismissed it.

It wasn't easy to do that now.

Surely not…

There was an obvious explanation, of course; the only thing that made sense. While desperate to refuse it, there seemed no denying it.

"Shit," she said again, but this time the word was born of an increasing, inescapable dread. "This can't be happening."

28

When Rebecca drew herself from the tent a few minutes later, Ed was loung-
ing by the fire, the Weatherby against his leg. He seemed surprised to see
her.

"Can't sleep?" he asked, straightening. It was just after midnight, and
they had agreed she should rest until three.

"Not a wink." It was the second time tonight she'd lied, but a discussion
about her dream wasn't an option. She took a seat beside him. "I guess I
should have taken first watch, seeing as I was up and all."

"Nah, I wouldn't be able to sleep either."

Trying to divert her thoughts, Rebecca sipped from her canteen. "I
wonder how the boys are faring?"

Ed checked his watch. "By now, they'll be long past the ravine. With
luck, they should be coming up to S1."

Rebecca bit her lip, fixed her sweat-dampened hair into a messy ponytail. "Speaking of which, I'm bothered by something."

"What? About S1?"

"Yeah, something that came up in our conversation with Jess before
dinner. She reminded me of what I said to Owen this afternoon, about why
the spider that chased him and her just seemed to give up and disappear.
Jess suggested it might've been to summon reinforcements; I'd thought it'd

simply pursued us to the limit of its territory and abandoned the chase. But neither explanation considers one vital fact."

"What's that?"

"The original attack on Sanchez and yourself at S1. Why was that jumper so far from the nest?"

"Scouting for food?"

"Maybe. But S1 is more than half a day's hike from here—too far to haul back captured prey. And in any case, the specimen was an adolescent. It wouldn't have the strength."

"I agree. It doesn't make sense."

"We can presume there's no relationship between these creatures and the people who built Intihuasi. There's no indication of spider worship, no statues in their honour. So, what's the connection? Why the concentration here? And why the attack at S1?"

"I've wondered about that," Ed said. "You'd assume they wouldn't range from here, to the *exact* spot where the moai stands, so far away. Not even by chance. There's gotta be an explanation."

"There's only one that makes sense," Rebecca said, fixing him with a grim stare. "Something we missed at S1. Something we didn't notice."

Ed leaned forward.

"Somewhere near Site 1," Rebecca said at length, "there must be a second nest."

29

The eyes were the first thing Sanchez noticed, peering through the gloom as though a giant had roused from its slumber. As he drew nearer, the night-vision goggles discarded and the beam of his flashlight cutting through the night, the rest of the pale stone face emerged ghostlike from the dark.

The moai.

"Thank the stars," Owen said with a sigh, flopping at the base of the statue as though his legs had turned to jelly.

Sanchez was equally grateful to have arrived at S1 but said nothing. He activated the X40 and turned his attention to building a fire.

"I'll look after the tent," Owen said, "just gimme a moment."

Sanchez knew how to build a fire in the wet. Soon, he had growing flames. "I know it is late, but I'm hungry. Want something to eat?" He searched his pack for food, then realised Owen hadn't replied.

He spun. Owen was asleep, mouth ajar, snoring softly. He hadn't re-moved his pack and lay on top of it like a turtle on its back. Noting he was wrapped tightly in his poncho and protected from the rain, Sanchez let him doze.

Heating his ration, he looked about. The statue loomed over him, as dark and brooding as the night before and no less spectacular. He wondered about its secrets.

The rain didn't relent. Sanchez figured he'd have to get up shortly and erect the tent, but for the moment he sat quietly.

Despite the downpour, the buzz of insects echoed loudly on all sides. It was a good sign. Everything seemed normal, as it should be.

He wondered, briefly, if it would stay that way.

Sanchez forked a mouthful of chicken and hunkered against the rain.

When he heard the noise an hour or so later, it sounded distant, other-worldly, and he realised he'd been dangerously close to sleep. Sanchez sat bolt upright, his gaze boring through the murk. He'd been trained to manage sleep-deprivation and berated himself for the transgression.

Even so, few people could have detected the sound: a sharp crack, like a twig snapping.

Sanchez listened. Over the drum of rain, he discerned the hum of the X40, the chirping of insects, and the rhythm of Owen's snoring. Other than that, he heard nothing.

Regardless, his finger crept to the trigger of the Weatherby. He recalled the night he'd been attacked here, and then the strange barking sound last night. He raised the rifle and lowered the NVGs over his eyes. As though slipping beneath the surface of a pool, he entered a world marked by contrasting shades of green.

For minutes, he waited like that, unmoving, save for his head which he craned slowly about, scanning. He couldn't see anything out of the ordinary.

Just the trees.

The noise didn't come again. There was every chance he'd misheard: he was fatigued, had managed only a couple of hours sleep over two days. Maybe his weary mind was playing tricks. Maybe this was his body's way of waking him up.

Maybe.

There was no point waking Owen. He couldn't risk any sudden movements, and he was too alert for sleep now, anyway.

Rifle in hand, Sanchez kept the goggles trained on the jungle, curled against the rain, knowing that as tired as he was, he'd have to see out the night awake.

30

Rebecca was loading supplies into her knapsack when Ed stirred and woke.

It was just after dawn, and still raining. Ed had fallen asleep two hours ago, out by the fire, which had burned low. Though it had been her watch—and still was—he'd offered to stay up with her. When he'd drifted off, she'd let him doze undisturbed.

Now, he sat up in his chair. "What are you doing?"

Rebecca finished stuffing her equipment and zipped shut her pack. "Waiting for you to get up," she said, slipping the straps over her shoulders. "I'm heading down to the north-western vantage point to observe the nest. I want to make sure the three of us aren't sitting ducks. Jessy's still asleep."

Ed stood, shaking his head. "I can't allow that, it's too dangerous. We shouldn't separate."

Rebecca ignored him. She'd come to her decision not long after the dream last night. She had to do this, and by herself. Hell, *for* herself. She needed to know.

She grabbed her machete off the table. "It's not up for discussion, Ed." With her spare hand she gave Priscilla a quick pat. The monkey, still asleep, curled up tighter. Rebecca looked back up at Ed. "I won't be long. Stay here and keep watch."

And with that, she left.

.   .   .

She was surprised it took him an hour to come for her.

She heard footsteps, and then behind her the bushes trembled and burst open. Ed pushed through.

Rebecca was sitting on the ground, binoculars in hand, exactly where she'd told him she'd be: the north-western vantage point, the place where yesterday they'd halted to check out the plane. It had the best view of the city and the web. "You left Jess by herself?" Rebecca asked.

Ed seemed short of breath, must have double-timed it down here. "When she woke up and I told her you'd taken off, she insisted I come and bring you back—she wouldn't hear of you being out here by yourself. She has the Weatherby, but I can't leave her on her own for long."

Rebecca suddenly felt awkward. "Yes, of course, I understand. Listen, Ed, I'm sorry I ambushed you before, but I had my reasons." She thought about yesterday's attack and the dream last night, and before she knew it words were tumbling from her mouth. "I never told you what led me down this path, did I?"

"The path from camp?"

"No," Rebecca said, and almost smiled. "My career path."

The expression of worry that had marked Ed's face melted into a look of piqued interest. Wary of time, he ducked beneath the rudimentary 'blind' she'd created using the leftover camouflage netting and sat beside her. "Led you to it? No, you never did."

Rebecca cleared her throat. "One day when I was about five or six years old, my father piled myself and my two older brothers into the car and headed to my grandma's place. About a month earlier, granddad had passed following a long battle with emphysema, and for some time prior, grandma's health had been deteriorating, too. Granddad's death seemed to exacerbate it, and the family decided she should she go to a home, get the care she needed. It was sad for everyone. The house would be put on the market. It was in an older, inner-city suburb back home in Brisbane, full of little timber homes and frangipani trees in every second garden. I guess it was spring, because the aroma of those flowers was thick in the air."

Rebecca went on. "Anyway, Dad was cleaning out the garage. My brothers were outside tearing around like madmen, so I joined Dad and started sticking my nose into everything. The garage was big and full of junk, dusty old furniture, cardboard boxes, all that kind of stuff. Sitting on top of a bag full of clothes was an old hat of Grandma's; I think it was a pillbox. Anyway, it was all covered in dust, but pink and intricate and beautiful, and I put it on. There was an old pedestal mirror in the corner—it was grimy and when I spread my hand across it the dirt and dust just smeared more—but I could see my reflection well enough and standing there looking at myself in Grandma's hat with my long, charcoal locks of hair right down to my waist, I thought I was the prettiest girl in the world. Then my father called out, wanting me to go back outside or something, and I hurriedly removed the hat. That's when I noticed the huge spider. And I mean *huge*."

Rebecca paused reflectively. "*Holconia immanis*. A Huntsman. Anyway, it was sitting right on top of my head—had been in the hat. I froze, couldn't move, couldn't do anything, and instead of scurrying off quickly like it should have, the thing crawled slowly through my hair, down the side of my face. It was *tangled* in my hair, and by then my brothers were at the door pointing and laughing. That's all they did—they laughed. And I still couldn't move. It was horrible."

"That's terrible, just awful. You poor thing."

"As of that day I was terrified of spiders. Not just scared of them; I developed a disorder. By the time I hit my teens it was crippling."

"You're kidding!"

"At its height, the fear was so great I couldn't go to bed at night if my parents hadn't checked the room first. Eventually they took me to a specialist, a psychologist. Slowly, I was taught to face my fear. The spider was gradually demystified. I was exposed to it, became familiar with it. With time, the phobia disappeared. In fact, an opposing effect took hold. Miraculously, not only was my fear of spiders cured, it was replaced by a fascination that ultimately evolved, I guess, into an *obsession*. And so here I am today, doing the job I do."

"Bec… I don't know what to say. That's one hell of a story."

"There's an interesting footnote, too," Rebecca said. "While the fear of spiders is gone, to this day, I still get ice-cold shivers at the faintest whiff of frangipani. Funny how stuff like that stays with you. And you know, after the experience in the garage I got mum to cut off all my hair. I hated long hair for as long as I could remember and never grew it back, not even in high school." Pausing, she lifted her ponytail. "This is the longest it's been since that very day."

"Hell," Ed said. "I wish I hadn't teased you about growing it."

"You weren't to know."

"I don't understand why you never shared this before."

Rebecca shifted restlessly. She looked down to the web and then back again. "You know, I've seen some activity in the city. I've worked out a few things."

Ed frowned at the change of subject but went with it. "And?"

"Firstly, it's definitely an active colony. And I think Jessy was right with her 'division of labour' theory. You need to look hard, and be patient, but I've seen several individuals this morning, attending to the web—removing debris, repairing sections damaged by the rain. By all appearances, they're 'workers', confined to duties *within* the web."

"They don't leave it?"

"I don't think so. While I imagine they'd attend to prey caught in the silk, the jumpers—or the hunters, or whatever you want to call them—likely do all the work outside the web, ranging out from the nest."

"What about that one yesterday, in the ground?" Ed said.

"I'd expect them to be more opportunistic. If anything, they might play a kind of guard role. In any case, I think all of them reside together as a group, and not only within the web, but the city itself. *Within the pyramid.*"

Ed looked at her. "The pyramid? What makes you say that?"

"For starters, there are workers out and about today. Where were they yesterday? And anyway, doesn't it make perfect sense?"

"I guess it would explain why we thought the place was deserted," Ed said.

Rebecca nodded. "And not just that. They're hard to spot, too. I'm fairly certain they're able to alter their colour and blend with their surroundings."

"What… like a chameleon?"

"Yes, or like an octopus," Rebecca said. "Octopi can merge perfectly with the background, by virtue of light-reflective cells known as chromatophores. The striations of colour on the backs of the jumpers—the hunters—that attacked us were different to those of the specimen at Base Camp. We *noticed* three spiders yesterday, but they were camouflaged, they blended with the trees. Today, those in web, the workers, are the colour of silk."

Ed fidgeted. Rebecca saw him glance at her laptop, which was closed to conserve the battery. Sitting on top of it was a cylindrical vial. She picked it up, raised it to the light. "A sample of the venom from yesterday's attack," she said, studying the viscous, grey liquid. "It was all through the remains of your pack. Unfortunately, I don't have the equipment to put it through a proper analysis, but I'll take it home with me, run some tests when I get back. I was wondering what type it was."

"Type?"

"What class of venom: neurotoxic, necrotic, maybe a combination."

Ed took the vial from her hand and gazed into it. "What about tarantula venom? They're big spiders. Maybe the type and toxicity are similar."

"You could be right. Tarantulas aren't seriously venomous—not to humans, anyway. Their bite might make you sick, but you won't die. While this stuff *might* be deadly, there's a chance it's relatively harmless."

"Interesting."

Rebecca nodded. "Most highly venomous creatures are small. Larger creatures don't *need* a powerful toxin, because they're able to subdue their prey by force. These guys, while formidable, also live socially, so they'd need to keep their food fresh, bringing it back for others to feed. That the hunters appear to return to the nest would seem to support this." She stared at the vial. "Most likely this is a slow-acting neurotoxin."

Ed nodded. "So, rather than kill their prey outright, they paralyse them and bring them back to the nest—*alive*—for all to feed?"

"Probably, yes. Spiders can't eat solid food, so they'd vomit up digestive fluid, pumping the victim's wounds full of it until their insides are like soup. Then they'd imbibe the juices as though drinking from a straw—" Rebecca stopped herself, catching the sudden pained expression on Ed's face. Berating herself for her insensitivity, she changed the subject. "You should get back to Jess. I want to hang around a while. I'm safe here and can see everything that's going on. I'll join you shortly."

Ed stood. He wasn't happy but seemed less opposed to the idea than before. "Promise me you'll keep your eyes peeled and head back at the first sign of anything unusual. I mean it, Bec."

"I will. Promise."

With that he moved to leave, but hesitated, weighed with conflict. "I want you to know, I really missed you. I never realised how much until I saw you get off that boat three days ago."

The words caught Rebecca off-guard. "I missed you too, Ed," she said eventually. "Seeing you again has brought back some incredible memories."

"I made a mistake, Bec, you know that. I should have tried harder. Tried to make it work, tried to make *us* work."

"Ed…"

"I mean it."

"It's all in the past now."

Ed nodded. He again turned to leave but then stopped and faced her once more. "Ever wonder what might have been? Maybe this is a second chance of sorts. There's gotta be a reason why we've found ourselves here, now, together."

"I know why I'm here," Rebecca said, and smiled.

Ed smiled too, headed off again, but then turned on his heel once more.

"What now?"

"Hey, don't get snippy."

"*Snippy*?"

"I just wanted to leave this." Ed reached into a pocket in his shorts, retrieved a small black object that looked like a cell phone with a stub antenna. He tossed it to her. "If you need anything, let me know."

Rebecca caught the device, a comm radio. "Thanks," she said, placing it on the ground beside her. "Will do."

She turned back to the pyramid just as Ed himself turned—this time for good—and headed briskly back to camp.

31

The riverboat crept between drooping trees, winding through the narrow waterway to the staccato chug of the engine.

Sounds like it's goddamned choking to death, Felipe Cartana thought. Of course, it wasn't. That was how it always sounded.

He looked from the bow, back to the stern. In tow behind, bobbing in the wash of the larger boat, was a much smaller, newer, and faster watercraft. The Zodiac could seat twelve and was equipped with a 150-horsepower petrol motor, along with a much quieter electric one.

Including the driver, there were nine men on the boat. Most were either sleeping or cleaning weapons. Not Oliveira, who stood with his booted left foot upon the stern rail, watching the trailing Zodiac. Flicking the stub of his cigarette into the river, he headed up to the bow, towards Cartana. As he approached, Cartana, sitting in front of the wheelhouse, folded the tattered map and placed the GPS receiver on the deck beside him.

"How far now?" Oliveira asked in Brazilian Portuguese. As always, his eyes were hidden behind silver aviator sunglasses.

Cartana caught his own, admittedly rodent-like, features in the lenses of Oliveira's glasses. He looked away to squint into the distance. "Not far," he said simply. He ran thin fingers through his dark, oily hair, which he had neatly slicked back. "It won't be long."

Oliveira turned on his heel and disappeared. Cartana noted his queries were becoming more frequent. He sensed Oliveira's growing impatience and wondered if this would shortly give way to anger. He hoped it wouldn't.

Cartana turned forward again, still squinting.

Ahead, the river forked unexpectedly.

Strange. The main stem, the one they were following, headed off to the left, but to his surprise there was another, narrower stem branching right. He consulted the map but couldn't find this smaller stream. The river constantly changed its course, but still…

He was hit by a thought and mulled it over.

There's been a lot of rain in the last twenty-four hours…

He pursed his lips.

I wonder…

He turned again to the map. He had the precise co-ordinates of their *ultimate* destination, had circled the area on the chart in red. But the site wasn't accessible by boat, and to get there they had to go via an initial destination, one that itself could only be reached in the Zodiac. They would hike inland from this location to reach their goal. If they continued their present course down the main stem, they would get to the first destination sometime this afternoon. Of course, they'd have to deal with some cursory resistance and most likely stay overnight, which meant they'd make a fresh start on foot in the morning. From there, the trek to the main site would take two days.

Cartana traced his finger along the map, running it from their current position to the circled area. He bit his lip. Though it wasn't on the map, if the fork ahead led to where he thought it might—if his hunch was correct—then there was every chance they'd reach the circled location by nightfall, cutting *two days* from their journey.

It was a gamble. Making mistakes had repercussions. He bit his lip so hard it started to bleed.

The fork loomed. They were right upon it.

Shit.

"Turn here!" he cried, calling back to the driver in the wheelhouse. He swallowed hard, ran a sweaty hand through his dark, greasy hair. "Take the right fork."

32

It was several hours later when Rebecca heard Ed emerge from the under-brush behind her. At that moment, she realised she was in the exact position he'd left her in earlier. She was surprised at how fast the time had flown.

Ed stepped beneath the blind and sat next to her. "I can't stay long," he said. "I brought you this. I thought you might be hungry."

He passed her an MRE. Even though she'd packed food, she hadn't had a break all day. "Thank you!" Rebecca said, famished. She tucked into it, noting he'd also brought one of the X40s. It was operating; she could hear it humming.

While she ate, Ed lifted the binoculars to gaze down at the pyramid.

After a time, her mouth full, she said, "You know, Ed, I've been think-ing. You're right about people coming here. They will, and it won't be for the sideshow." Rather than sympathetic to the concerns he'd expressed to her last night, she was excited, enthusiastic. Furiously chewing—as though she hadn't eaten in days—she nodded in the direction of the web, and the pyramid at its heart. "The potential for science and industry… it's mind-boggling. They'll swarm over this."

"Uh-huh."

Rebecca washed the food down with water from her canteen be-fore taking another huge bite. "Did you know the giant orb weaver's silk is sixty times stronger than stainless steel? It's also much lighter and can stretch almost half its length without breaking—you could tow a jumbo with a strand half the thickness of your little finger! It's long been the view we might one day use spider silk as a building material: bullet-proof vests, aerospace components. Future spacecraft might be made of the stuff! The problem, however, is in *harvesting* the silk. Handling huge quantities of spiders isn't workable. For one, they'd cannibalise each other. But this species is communal and produces incredibly strong silk in massive amounts. Hell, Ed, a discovery like this is going to make *everything* possible."

Ed looked at her as though hoping she wouldn't give herself indigestion. "You think that's enough to cause them to come?" he said, snuffing a laugh. "You don't know the half of it."

Rebecca swallowed, took no more bites, and Ed smiled knowingly.

"What I was trying to show you yesterday," he said. He nodded down the slope at the two huge moai standing like twin guards at attention. "It's difficult to explain. I'm a little unsure myself."

"You know we can't go back down there, not after what happened."

"I know."

Still, Rebeca was intrigued. Observing the colony at this distance, up here in the blind, hadn't been an issue—she'd felt none of the effects or anxieties she'd feared she might. But now she was seized by the same motivation that had gripped her following the dream last night; an overwhelming urge to confront herself and confirm she was still capable. "How many times have you been down there?" she asked. "Before the rest of us arrived?"

"Several, at least."

Silence.

Ed looked at her. "If you want to, I'll take you down and show you. It'll be quick."

"We shouldn't," Rebecca said, shaking her head.

She realised she'd picked up the X40.

"It'll be quick," Ed reiterated. "Trust me, this is something you've got to see."

Moved by a force beyond her control and better judgement, Rebecca stood. Together, they exited the blind, and tentatively, Ed led her down the slope. Rebecca cradled the softly humming X40 to her breast.

They followed the same route as the day before, each with the quiet, watchful stride of one negotiating a minefield. All the while, in between keeping an eye on the path ahead of them and the trees all around them, Rebecca studied the web. She couldn't see any workers.

They were halfway down when, despite their caution, Rebecca's unease heightened.

This is crazy. Turn back.

As if sensing her doubts, Ed took her hand and squeezed it. Rebecca allowed herself to be towed. A moment later, they drew up in front of the left-hand moai.

"This is what I was trying to show you," Ed said, his voice low. They were in the same spot they'd been standing just prior to the attack on Enrique. In Ed's right hand was the stone disc, which he'd already unwrapped.

There was no hint of the previous day's fanfare. Carefully rotating the disc, Ed lined it up with the round indentation that was set into the middle of the moai's broad chest.

Then, as Rebecca watched, he clicked it snugly into place…

…nothing.

Seconds passed. Rebecca looked at Ed, confused, when from deep within the earth—right under their feet—a low growl rose like a roll of thunder. It built in intensity, and suddenly the ground beneath them began to vibrate as though gripped by a mild earthquake. The tremor grew in power and Rebecca had to concentrate on keeping her balance.

"That's not all," Ed said above the rumble as she turned to him incredulously. He nodded up at the moai. "Watch."

By now, the statue, too, had begun to quiver, and there was a sound like crackling electricity all around them. The quality of the air itself seemed to change, and the hairs on Rebecca's arms and the back of her neck stood on end. But what happened next caused her jaw to drop, and she wondered if she was seeing things.

Something was happening to the statue.

It had begun to…

…*shimmer*…

No, I'm imagining it, Rebecca thought. *It can't be…*

And then, incredibly, as if to rebuke any doubts she might still have entertained, the giant moai heaved upwards…

Rising off the ground.

No way…

"The effect is even greater when the sun isn't blocked by clouds," Ed told her above the rumbling.

Rebecca couldn't believe her eyes. The moai appeared to be floating—only by an inch or two, if that—but it also seemed different, somehow detached or removed... *untethered*. She wondered what that meant. Untethered from what, exactly? She had an urge to stretch out and touch it, but sensed she wouldn't be able to... *reach* it?

"What the hell is this?" she said.

Ed removed the disc. It came out reluctantly, as though caught in a vacuum. As it did, the shaking incrementally decreased, and the statue shimmered faster, flickering. Then the pressure of the air shifted, popped, and suddenly the crackling sound was no more, and the statue was miraculously back in place... had, she thought, returned, or *reattached*.

Rebecca looked at him, eyes wide, stunned.

Ed glanced at the web before taking her by the hand again. "Come on." He led her back up the slope, speaking as they went. "I don't know what it is exactly," he whispered. He didn't look back. "But I think you just witnessed some kind of *repulsive energy*, something within the Earth that interacts with the disc and the statue."

"Repulsive energy?"

Ed turned, looked her squarely in the eye. "Gravitational repulsion," he said simply. "Antigravity."

33

Rebecca had to move fast to keep up with Ed, mindful of noise. She glanced over her shoulder. It didn't appear the colony had been roused, or that they were being pursued.

Only when they had reached the blind did Ed stop. He cast an eye along their route. Seemingly satisfied they'd gotten away undetected, he turned to her, the stone disc back in his pocket. "I know what you're thinking," he said, a little breathless. "And I agree. The concept sounds way out. But I've done some digging, and it's not as far-fetched as you think."

Rebecca turned from the web. "Antigravity. UFO stuff, right? Next you'll be telling me aliens built the pyramid."

Ed hesitated. "No, not quite. But you saw for yourself, right?"

That much was true.

Ed's eyes lit up. "Look, there're some strange ideas out there, but the subject's not the reserve of crackpots and cultists; it's the subject of *science*. The idea that gravity and its effects can be reduced through technology is nothing new. I mean, both the US and Britain are involved in antigravity research. NASA and Boeing have programs. Canada, France, Japan, China, Russia—they're all investigating this. Big money is being thrown around."

Rebecca felt oddly removed, but he had her attention. "Go on."

"But what if there was a *naturally occurring* force in opposition to gravity, undiscovered by science? Einstein theorised the four natural forces—strong and weak nuclear, electromagnetic, gravitational—might be explained as part of the one fundamental, interconnected force. This is the Unified Field Theory, a kind of 'theory of everything' to define all aspects of the universe within one framework. He couldn't prove it, but what if he was on to something? What if all the *known* forces are connected, and within this framework, there are other *unknown* forces, immeasurable by today's standards? What if there is a yin to gravity's yang?"

Rebecca pursed her lips. "I don't know…"

"We know the universe is expanding at an accelerated rate. Something is pushing the galaxies away from each other. Science suggests there's an inherent force in the universe, a form of antigravity, originating in space, responsible for this expansion. It's called 'Dark Energy.'"

"I don't know…"

"Okay, well how about this?" Ed was electrified, humming along now. "You're familiar with my theory about the city, right? That it was built by an ancient people able to harness the power of the sun. What if this power, whatever it is, gave the T'aevans the ability to move huge objects? Look at the city. Where did all the stone come from? How did they move it through such thick vegetation?"

"I did wonder that."

"I know you've been wondering about the city's location, too, and why it was built out here, in the huge bowl. I believe the people of Intihuasi were *attracted* here. This place is a vortex, a convergence of the energy—the *force*—we witnessed in action moments ago."

Rebecca drew a deep breath. "You're suggesting the T'aevans were attracted here because, for whatever reason, this area is most in tune with their 'power'?"

"Yes. It's been suggested ancient peoples have been attracted to various sites around the world, possibly drawn by an energy they could somehow sense. We've seen Native Americans—and Australian Aboriginals—embroiled in legal fights over sacred land later discovered to be rich in uranium. Perhaps they sensed the natural radioactivity?"

Rebecca frowned. "Okay, let's assume there's a repulsive force undiscovered by science but known, somehow, to these people. How does it work, exactly? How does one tap into it?" She shook her head. "What's the connection between the disc, the moai, and the sun? How do they fit into the equation?"

"I don't know exactly," Ed said. "But some scientists theorise antigravity technology might be achieved through a yet-to-be discovered connection between electric and magnetic forces. We know the Earth's magnetic field extends far into space, effectively connecting with the Sun's atmosphere. Solar flares affect this field, causing geomagnetic disturbances on our planet: power surges, blackouts, disruptions in radio, television, or satellite communications, navigational problems. But more than that, these 'gusts' of solar wind change the chemical make-up of our atmosphere and create electrical fields. The effects are more pronounced at the northern and southern poles of the planet, where more of this solar wind gets through in places known as 'cusps'. What if there are other places, like these cusps? That bowl down there might be the site of some geomagnetic and electrical irregularity exacerbated by the Sun itself, a place where the *repulsive force* is most effective."

"*Uh-huh,*" Rebecca said, not sure if she was following. "What about the disc, then? What's the story with that?"

Ed took the stone disc out of his pocket. "Admittedly, the disc has shown nothing out of the ordinary in any of our tests. It seems to be an average—though intricately carved and polished—piece of stone. If there's a field here encouraging some kind of repulsive force, it's obvious that certain stones interact with it. Complete the circuit. Maybe this disc exudes something we're not familiar with."

"I guess it's possible."

"It's not so far-fetched. Lodestones, pieces of magnetite used as magnets, were once thought to be magical. Likewise, maybe this disc, or the statues themselves, or both, are imbued with a force immeasurable by today's standards, one the T'aevans were aware of. Some metals, for instance, when hit with light, can create electricity. This is called a photoelectric effect. Maybe there's a similar effect happening here with these stones, fuelled by the Sun's energy. Science tells us magnetic fields *push* things that have been charged by static electricity."

"*Uh-huh,*" Rebecca said again.

Ed looked at her. "Most of it I don't understand myself. Of course, there are other *less* scientific theories out there."

"Here come the UFOs."

"Not quite. But there have been strange goings on at ancient megalithic sites around the world—sites like Stonehenge, for example—and some suggest these places, which number literally in the hundreds, were built deliberately in alignment with invisible energy lines within the earth.

'Ley lines' are the hypothetical straight lines of energy that some say connect these prehistoric sites across the globe."

"Strange goings on?"

"Visions, unexplained healing. And more significantly, *levitation*." He hurried on. "And there are legends, too, that tell of the Atlanteans having flying aircraft—*gravity-defying* aircraft."

"It's never been *just* about the city, for you, has it?"

Ed nodded, smiling excitedly. "This is it, Bec. Just think about it: the power to move huge objects using a free, clean, naturally occurring and re- newable source of energy! We're not just talking about moving *stone*—we've only seen the tip of the iceberg. I mean, once we learn to harness it, who knows what this power can do?" He grabbed her by the shoulders, his eyes wide and intoxicated with promise. "Hell, forget the implications for science. This could revolutionise everyday life, make for a better world! Imagine gravity-defying cars and planes! Being no longer dependent on fossil fuels! Imagine the impact on greenhouse gas emissions and global warming! This could mean a cleaner, more efficient world!" He was nearly jumping out of his skin, and it took him a moment to calm. "Look, I know it's a leap. Quite a leap, in fact. And out here, outside the city, it's all speculation. The legend of Intihuasi suggests the true secret of its power lies *within* the pyramid."

Rebecca said nothing.

Ed raised his eyebrows, imploring her to say something, anything. "So, what do you think?"

For some time, Rebecca maintained her silence. At last, she cleared her throat and drew a sharp breath. "What I think, Ed, is that I've never heard such an expansive collection of 'maybes' and 'what-ifs' in my entire life." She looked away, off in the direction of the city, before turning back to him. "What I also think, is that you're right."

34

Rebecca shook her head. "I mean—and I can't believe I'm saying this—in a way it makes sense, doesn't it? Something's going on, I saw it myself. And something attracted the T'aevans to that huge depression in the ground. What's more, something attracted the *new* inhabitants, too. The spiders." She felt giddy at the thought of it all. "You mentioned that indigenous peoples have been drawn to sites rich in uranium, which is naturally radioactive, and we know what exposure to radiation or radioactive materials can do, how it can cause genetic damage, birth defects. Aren't there even theories purporting electromagnetic rays cause cellular mutation? What if there is something in there, within that bowl, that exudes high levels of radiation? That might explain the *size* of the spiders, mightn't it?"

In the distance, they heard the first guttural stirrings of an afternoon storm. Ed turned to Rebecca. "I don't know. I choose to believe the energy's safe and clean. But trust me, something *is* in there, and I want to find out what."

With that he turned back to the pyramid and fell into a thoughtful silence. Rebecca checked her watch, surprised it was almost four o'clock. If everything had gone to plan, Owen and Sanchez might have called for the chopper already. Still giddy, she made for her gear, readying to leave, but paused and glanced at Ed. "When the chopper gets here, you're getting on it with the rest of us. Just so you know."

Jolted from his reverie, Ed looked mildly surprised. "You don't think I'd let you go alone, do you?" He tossed his head in the direction of the camp. "No need to worry. I'll be taking the chopper back, and when I know Jessy's okay, when she's settled in safe and sound, I'll return—with a plan, and more equipment."

"We'll see about that," Rebecca said, unable to prevent her upper lip from curling into a half-smile.

Ed grinned, too. "I better head back and check on Jess."

Rebecca nodded, and turned to scan the pyramid. "It seems quiet down there… it doesn't look like we stirred anything up. I might stay a little longer."

Ed nodded. "If I need you, I'll call on the radio. But don't be long. When that chopper gets here, we're *all* getting on it. We're not leaving anyone behind."

35

The chopper wasn't on its way just yet.

Sanchez had hoped for swifter progress. Maybe it was the weather, or fatigue. Most likely it was both. In any case, they were behind schedule.

This morning, when the sun had first begun to rise, obscured once more by dark, grey clouds, the jungle had been slow to lighten. Still, Sanchez had been relieved to see the first rays break the canopy. Though uneventful, it had been a long night.

Owen had woken with those rays, having slept straight through. Sanchez had expected criticism, and he'd gotten it: Owen had been mortified he hadn't taken a watch. The debate had been short-lived, however, and in minutes they'd broken camp, Sanchez eager to push on and confident there was every chance they'd get to Base Camp by mid-afternoon as anticipated. *That*, Owen had been happy about. Now, though, it didn't appear they'd be getting in before nightfall.

Sanchez thought briefly of the others. He hoped they were safe. He thought, too, about the chopper. Now, the rescue crew would have to work in darkness. More than that, a storm was brewing.

He hoisted his pack, adjusted its weight upon his shoulders, and pushed himself even harder, Owen right behind him.

They were almost there. Two more hours would do it.

36

The Zodiac entered the ravine under cover of the approaching storm, its motor cut and silent. Half a mile back, they'd switched to the quieter electric motor before shutting it off, too, hoping to retain the element of surprise.

Not that they should have been concerned, Cartana mused. No-one was around to hear them, and anyway, the rain and rising waters masked their passage. Still, the eight of them dipped their paddles silently, pushing the craft through the gorge.

Cartana pressed closer to the edge of his seat. He could barely contain his excitement—or his *relief*. The gamble had paid off. The fork in the river had brought them exactly where he had hoped. This was the place.

From his position at the front of the boat, he scanned the ravine walls. *There.*

He put up his hand and balled it into a fist. "Stop. This is it."

Cartana had made sure they'd brought with them the necessary climbing gear. As the boat bumped against the wall, bobbing in the chop of the swollen stream, he reached for the rock face, searching for a suitable spot to secure the vessel.

Oliveira was beside him. "Are you sure this is the place?"

"Yes, this is it." Cartana ran his eyes up the wall. "Look." He pointed to the small ring of metal—a carabiner—dangling from the camming device wedged into one of the many cracks above.

In no time, the eight of them had scaled the wall. Crowded with the others on the narrow rock ledge, Cartana looked skyward. At most, they were an hour from their destination, but the fast-approaching night would likely beat them. No matter. Adequate light remained, and besides, they were now two days ahead of schedule, all thanks to him—

An angry flash of lightning pierced the trees and Cartana jumped. He wasn't surprised by his edginess. Although the approaching dark was of little concern, the storm was another story. Lightning flashed again, and thunder too, rumbling like a livid god woken from a deep sleep.

They may have been ahead of schedule, but they still needed to make haste.

The eight of them moved out swiftly, hunched and silent, and disappeared into the jungle at the ravine's edge.

A long, ragged peal of thunder caused Rebecca to push the binoculars from her eyes. She cocked her head, listening.

More thunder, and a flash of lightning, too.

She glanced at her watch. Ed had left her an hour ago and she'd returned to the blind to resume her observations. Now it was almost dark, and though he hadn't called, he was no doubt expecting her back.

She wondered about the chopper, where it was.

Another crack of thunder.

For the past hour, the storm had been building, but now sounded ominous. The drizzle of the last few hours had grown heavier, too.

Okay, time to go.

She wasn't keen on being caught out here in the middle of a raging thunderstorm.

She grabbed her gear, stuffed it into her pack, and turned briskly towards camp, another crack of thunder clapping loudly on her heels.

As she disappeared, she wasn't aware of the eyes—eight in total, in four rows of two—that had been watching her the entire time from a hiding place high in the canopy.

37

The two hours passed quickly. Sanchez breathed a sigh of relief.

They were less than a hundred yards from the clearing that housed the team's Base Camp, and with night almost wholly upon them and the eternal rumble of thunder above, it couldn't have come sooner. He and Owen pushed their exhausted legs even faster, stumbling through the rain and the last few feet of undergrowth. Effectively twenty-four hours after they'd left the others, and on little or no sleep, they had prevailed.

Sanchez broke into a jog, but only yards from the clearing, staggered to a halt.

The sound of rushing water rose above the thunder and rain.

Not good.

The alarm bells had sounded a couple of miles out, when neither Elson nor Martins had answered his radio calls. He'd dismissed it as bad reception, or that the two men hadn't heard the radio above the storm.

With Owen in tow, Sanchez burst into the clearing as a loud clap of thunder broke overhead. He drew up quickly, his legs suddenly shot through with weakness. Owen fell to his knees.

Base Camp was gone.

.   .   .

Simply... *gone.*

The water had since receded and lapped now at the far edge of the clearing, but it had taken almost everything in the camp with it: generators, tables and chairs, tents... *and all their electronic and communications equipment.*

Gazing in disbelief, the two men moved through the fading light into the middle of the clearing. Debris lay everywhere—wedged against tree roots, stuck high in branches—all of it waterlogged and draped in mud and vegetation, no doubt damaged beyond repair.

Sanchez shook his head. "I told them to move it deeper."

"Robert... look."

Sanchez turned. Owen motioned to a tangle of partly submerged tree roots. Wedged in there by the floodwaters was a bundle of rags.

No. Not rags.

They ran across the clearing, sloshing through puddles of ankle-high water. Sanchez reached into the muck and with a grunt pulled the body from the mass of roots. It flopped limply in his hands.

The head was missing.

"Holy shit..." Owen said.

"I think it's Elson."

The corpse was otherwise intact, although its arms and legs were broken and twisted at grotesque angles. There was also a puncture wound to the chest—to the left of, and just above, the heart.

"Floodwaters could not have done this," Sanchez said, pointing to the injury. "And the head has been *hacked* off."

Owen glanced away, swallowing a few times to compose himself.

"I think he died before the river rose," Sanchez said, easing the body back into the water lapping the base of the tree. "It would explain why they didn't move the camp." He gazed about. "But where is Martins?"

"I've heard of this before," Owen said ominously. "Explorers, anthropologists, FUNAI agents—literally hundreds of people over the years, their bodies found mutilated. Some with their heads missing..."

Sanchez looked up at him as Owen glanced at the surrounding treeline, scanning. He seemed agitated, on edge.

Sanchez eyeballed him. "What is it, *amigo?*"

But Owen had fallen silent, his face paling. "Don't move," he whispered. "We're being watched."

·   ·   ·

Sanchez froze.

Thunder boomed.

"Keep talking," Owen said. "Act normal. We're being *observed*."

"By what?"

"Actually, by *whom*. Behind you, in the trees about twenty yards away—a young indigenous man. He's standing there, looking at us."

Sanchez glanced again at Elson, at his punctured chest, the ragged stump of his neck…

Slowly, he moved his hand up to his shoulder, to the rifle.

Damn. Anxious to rid himself of their weight, he'd left the rifle, and his pack, by a tree when they'd first entered the clearing.

"What does he want?" Sanchez whispered.

"I don't know, but we're about to find out. He's coming over."

Slowly, Sanchez turned.

"Stay calm," Owen said. "No sudden movements."

The man was short. He was also entirely naked, except for a thin cord around his waist. Sanchez guessed from his boyish but stocky frame he was in his late teens, early twenties. Crouching, he crept towards them, his bare feet skipping lightly over the forest floor. He was incredibly quiet. In one hand, he carried a tall, thin bow, in the other, several arrows. Sanchez noted his jet-black hair was cropped in a ring around his head and shaved at the top, as though he were wearing a crown of thorns. His intensely dark eyes were encircled with red and black dye, his arms banded with red paint.

The young man stopped about twenty feet away. Sanchez and Owen stood their ground, returning his gaze.

Perhaps confused by the sight of such unusually pale skin, the man's focus was on Owen.

"He hasn't seen people like us before," Owen murmured. "He's curious."

"He killed Elson."

"We don't know that."

The young man kept staring. He didn't appear threatened by them, nor was he threatening in his stance.

"Can you talk to him?" Sanchez asked.

Owen cleared his throat. "I can try." He offered a few stuttered words, perhaps in varying dialects. Sanchez didn't give it much chance; while tribal languages could be similar, he guessed the group to which this person belonged was far removed from any Owen had dealt with.

Even so, the man cocked his head as though he might have understood. If he did, he said nothing.

Owen turned to Sanchez and shrugged.

Straightening, the man spun to face the trees from which he had emerged and made a short, high-pitched whooping noise. Sanchez tensed and followed the man's gaze to the treeline but saw nothing of note. He glanced back at Elson's decapitated body, then to his backpack and the rifle resting against the tree.

Owen read his thoughts. "No, don't."

"I can reach it," Sanchez said.

"No. Leave it." Owen nodded at the treeline. Several shapes emerged from the gloom, other tribesmen stepping quietly from the trees into the clearing. There were five or six of them—all males, and all with arrows drawn back in their bows.

The young man pointed at Sanchez and Owen and waved them towards the treeline.

"He wants us to go with them," Owen said.

"We're not going anywhere."

Agitated, the young man whooped and waved again.

"We don't have a choice," Owen murmured as another man approached and shoved each of them in the back.

Sanchez bristled.

"Best we cooperate," Owen said.

Sanchez glanced at the men, and then the rifle.

You'll never make it. Not now.

He relented, and let Owen lead them across the clearing. The tribesmen fell in beside them, nudging each other excitedly.

Numb with disbelief, Sanchez thought of their companions at S2, and Jessy in particular. Elson, and presumably Martins, were dead. The sat-phone was lost to the floodwaters. There was no way of contacting the chopper, no way of mounting a rescue. And now they'd lost the rifle, too.

The young man jabbed him hard in the ribs, back the way they'd come.

Not good.

Together, he and Owen followed their captors into the dense undergrowth, disappearing as night and the storm proper swept in to swallow them all.

38

Back in camp, Rebecca adjusted the hood of her poncho as another streaking flash scorched the clearing. A moment ago, the sky had opened, disgorging torrential rain. Overhead, thunder boomed. Rebecca wondered if the heavens were being torn asunder.

"What about the boys?" she said to Ed above the din. "What happened to the chopper?"

Ed ignored her and dashed across the clearing, double-checking the motion detectors and the X40s, which they'd set in a triangle with the cave at its centre. Running back to the tarpaulin, he tightened the corner ropes.

Rebecca repeated her question. "Ed? What about the chopper?"

"It'll be here," he called above the rain.

Rebecca shook the water from her poncho. Priscilla, who'd been hiding under the table, leapt into her arms. Rebecca hugged her, at the same time frowning at Ed. He obviously harboured the same doubts as her.

Rain pelted down. Rebecca decided she wasn't finished. "I was thinking—"

The sound rose in the distance, sudden and jarring, and Rebecca jumped. Reflexively, she cocked her head, listening, but knew instantly it was the same terrible noise from two nights ago at S1. She froze.

Selenocosmia crassipes.

The words swam up from her subconscious and into focus. She'd drawn the initial comparison yesterday morning, but uncertain, had kept it to herself. Its common name was the *Whistling Spider*, a large, ferocious-looking species of Australian tarantula, so named because it would scrape its pedipalps—the two hand-like appendages on either side of its mouth—across its fangs and mouthparts, producing a loud and menacing whistling, or *barking*, sound. It was used as a warning. This sound—and that of two nights ago—was similar.

Not similar. The same.

They're coming again...

"Ed!?" Jessy called from her tent.

Ed bolted for the cave, snatching up the rifle as he went. "Bec, come on!"

Rebecca moved to follow, but for some reason, couldn't lift her feet.

No. Not now.

The barking intensified, rising from all directions, clearer now than the waves of thunder pounding overhead. Rain poured down. Lightning flashed.

Please no...

Rebecca's heart thumped, and a shot of adrenaline flooded her veins.

Was it possible?

It had to be. She'd felt the first stirrings yesterday, then again in the dream last night. There could be no other explanation. After all these years, after all her treatment, even despite what had become her career, her life's work.

Once more, she was the helpless child staring in the mirror with her brothers standing there laughing at her.

No... please, no...

Then something tripped the motion detectors and blacklight flooded the clearing.

Somehow, Rebecca tore herself away, or so she thought. In fact, halfway to the cave, Ed had turned back and seized her by the arm, and suddenly she was inside the huge hollow tree with Priscilla grasped terrified to her chest and Ed and Jessy beside her.

"*What's happening?!*" Jessy cried.

Rebecca gazed through the cave mouth and into the clearing. Every UV lamp had triggered, throwing waves of dark violet, and overhead, lightning sparked and flashed like a strobe. With each burst of illumination, she saw more spiders—they clung to the trees, perched in branches, crouched like springs upon the ground, all washed in blacklight and fluorescing like so many ghosts in the darkness. They didn't move so much as swell with every flash, appearing out of nowhere, barking.

How could we be so stupid? We were never safe here. Why didn't we get out when we had the chance?

At least a dozen of the creatures, each the size of a large dog, circled them like a pack. More crept out of the 'moat' that ringed the clearing, up and over the rise, gripping the trunks of the trees with their glowing, pale blue legs, watching, then disappearing with the next flash only to reappear elsewhere. They were positioning themselves, swarming, increasing their numbers…

Why weren't they being driven off by the X40s?

More now, and with each flash of lightning, more again, surrounding them. Two dozen, maybe three.

What were they waiting for?

Jessy was hysterical. Ed raised the rifle—not that it would be enough.

Out of the corner of her eye, Rebecca saw the first creature leap in their direction, sailing across the clearing. It was joined instantly by another, and then a third. They were airborne quickly—together, as a group, their horrible shapes soaring through a flash of lightning.

Ed didn't get to squeeze the trigger.

39

An explosion of automatic gunfire ripped Rebecca from her stupor. In the leafy confines of the clearing, the sound was deafening.

She dived for cover and Ed and Jessy hit the ground with her. Protecting her ears from the onslaught, Rebecca looked up to glimpse spiders being torn apart, legs and bodies shredded—brief images starkly illuminated by strobe-like bursts of lightning and multiple muzzle flashes.

What the hell?

Lightning flashed again. An instant of darkness followed. Four, five… no, six muzzle flashes erupted out of it, maybe more, coming from all sides now.

Rebecca kept her hands pressed against her ears, and so did Ed and Jessy, all of them splayed low, away from the withering assault.

It was over quickly, and an eerie hush fell. Even the thunder seemed to hesitate. For a moment, there was only the rain.

Rebecca's ears rang.

"What just happened?" Jessy whispered, terrified.

Cautiously, they raised their heads…

The clearing was empty of spiders and gunmen alike.

Not fully empty.

All about, the still-fluorescing body parts of what must have been two dozen megarachnids lay scattered and sprawled—legs, carapaces, chelicerae—all oozing dark, gooey fluid. Rebecca scanned for movement and noticed several legs retracting into shattered bodies, but nothing else.

No living creatures.

Not one.

She could hardly believe her eyes. The devastating assault had shred and splintered the surrounding vegetation. Some of the smaller trees had split down the centre and crashed to the earth, others had been severed in half. Most had limbs amputated. Leaves and branches lay ripped and strewn across the forest floor.

As she was taking this in, mouth agape, a group of shadowy figures came slowly into view.

"Okay," a heavily accented voice boomed in English. Its owner, one of the figures and presumably the leader, held aloft and at arm's length the ruined body of a superspider. "Who will tell me what in God's name this is?"

40

He was draped in a poncho, hood drawn low in the pummelling rain, face obscured by shadow. For all the disgust he showed the oozing carcass held out in front of him, it might well have been a severed human head. He flung it to the muddy earth and wiped his hand as two more figures, similarly dressed and guns up, drew in like wraiths from the trees on either side. They flanked him, joining the three already in his company.

Rebecca's mind reeled. In total, six figures—all with raised weapons, all in silhouette.

"Come out, please. Do not be afraid."

Ed and Rebecca held their ground. Jessy had crawled to the entrance of her tent, craning to see.

"We've got an injured person in here," Ed said. "Her leg is broken."

A pause, then, "Come out, so we can talk. This rain is too loud."

Ed and Rebecca traded glances.

"Please. We mean you no harm."

Again, Ed and Rebecca exchanged an alarmed glance. "What choice do we have?" Rebecca whispered, passing Priscilla to Jessy before moving towards the cave's exit.

A gentle peal of thunder rolled overhead. The storm was easing.

"Who are you?" Ed asked as he and Rebecca stepped warily from the cave. He still held the rifle and raised it slightly. The barrel got no higher than a few inches before a shadow fell across them.

"Please, *senhor*. Nothing stupid."

Another of the gunmen had sneaked up behind them and pressed the muzzle of his weapon into Ed's side. Rebecca sensed yet another man step in behind her. That made eight of them. "We don't want any trouble," she said, raising her hands as Ed relinquished the rifle.

"Good, neither do we. Where is the other?"

Ed eyed their weapons. "As I said, she's injured. She can't walk."

The leader gestured to the man behind Rebecca, who peered cautiously into the cave. "There is only the three of you?"

"Yes. Who are you?" Ed said. "What do you want from us?"

The man at the mouth of the cave threw a nod to the leader, who then turned to the rest of his men and proceeded to issue instructions in Brazilian Portuguese. Four of the men fanned to opposing edges of the clearing. One remained, whispering to the leader.

"There should be eight of you," the leader said, turning to Ed. "Where are the others?"

Ed straightened. "How the hell could you know that? *Just who the hell are you—*"

"They're dead," Rebecca interjected. "All of them. Killed by those things." She nodded at one of the carcasses.

There was a moment of silence, the leader seeming to ponder her words. The X40s hummed in the background. Eventually, the man spoke again. His English was good. "What say we talk tomorrow, then? I'm sure your ordeal was exhausting." He turned to walk off but then stopped and pointed distastefully at the carcass he'd hurled to the ground. "You can tell me about those in the morning."

Dipping his head, he turned for the edge of the clearing.

Ed's expression darkened. "Hang on a minute—"

"*Senhor*? *Senhorita*?" The man who had previously poked Ed with his gun motioned to the cave.

Ed ignored him. "Hey!" he said above the rain, calling out to the leader. "You can't come marching in here—"

"Ed, leave it." Rebecca took him by the arm. "Let's go."

The gunman poked Ed again with his weapon, an AK-74 Kalashnikov assault rifle. Ed held up his hands. "Okay, okay."

They moved to the cave, past the table and chairs, Ed and Rebecca out in front, the two gunmen behind, herding them along. Rebecca ducked in the entrance, and Ed followed. The men took stance at the cave's mouth.

Jessy clutched Priscilla as Rebecca and Ed clambered in beside her. "Ed?" Her voice trembled. "What's going on?"

Rebecca closed the flap but didn't zip it. "Who the hell are these people?" she whispered to Ed.

Ed took Jessy's hand. "I don't know," he answered both women. He turned to Rebecca, his voice low. "They look and hold themselves like soldiers, but I doubt they're regular army. Paramilitaries or guerrillas more like it. '*Ratos de agua*', perhaps."

"What?"

"'Water Rats'. River pirates."

"How did they know there were eight of us?" Rebecca asked. "And how the hell did they *find* us?"

Ed shook his head and frowned, leaning over to peer through the tent's entrance. "I have no idea," he said. "But whoever they are, if they wanted us dead, they wouldn't have put us in here with two guards outside." He leant back. "No doubt they want something from us."

"What should we do?" Jessy asked. She had the bloodless, confused look of a driver whose car had just been hit unexpectedly from behind.

"I guess we sit tight," Ed said. "It's all we *can* do."

"Sit tight?" Jessy said. "What about the chopper? What if it comes tonight, as planned?"

Again, Ed shook his head. "I don't know."

Rebecca could hear activity outside, and voices too, but couldn't make out what was being said; the gunmen kept their tones low and had reverted to Portuguese. Occasionally, the words were followed by footsteps sloshing busily through puddles. Those sounds faded until only the drumming of rain on the tarpaulins remained.

Eventually, Rebecca said, "There is *one* explanation. It makes sense, after all."

Thunder rumbled, and even though it was distant now, Priscilla, shaken, broke free of Jessy's embrace and darted to Rebecca, who scooped her up.

As the tiny monkey snuggled in, Ed turned to Rebecca. "What are you thinking?"

Rebecca leaned forward, shifting Priscilla's weight like a mother juggling a small child. "I'm thinking," she said, "that maybe we've just met the owners of that plane."

41

Owen stumbled over a tree root and picked himself up.

For more than two hours he and Sanchez were forced along the trail, three tribesmen in front and three behind, their pace brisk. Weighed with fatigue, Owen barely kept up, but then Sanchez also seemed to struggle, probably as amazed as he at the speed of their barefoot captors. The men glided effortlessly, melting through the trees.

The rain had eased, and the forest was otherwise quiet. Sanchez had fallen quiet, too. Owen sensed he was angry about having walked into an ambush and was secretly planning their next course of action. What that might be, he didn't know, but he was certain they wouldn't simply run off impulsively. Their abductors were too fast and agile; they'd have to wait for the right moment.

He wondered where they were being taken.

At last, Sanchez broke the silence, nodding ahead. "Up there."

Owen followed his companion's gaze. Through breaks in the canopy, rising over the treetops, leapt orange sparks.

A fire.

On cue, the tempo of their march increased. Moments later they entered a small clearing. At its centre burned a fire that sent a single plume of smoke snaking skyward. Around the fire, set in a ring, were five or six thatched huts. Owen thought he could see the tops of half a dozen more in the dense foliage beyond.

They'd arrived at their destination.

At first, the village seemed deserted. Then, slowly, with the same curious manner displayed earlier by the leader of their captors, a young boy appeared. He emerged from behind one of the domed huts, followed quietly by an even younger girl. Men and women appeared, too, until from out of nowhere at least two dozen people had assembled in the clearing to stare back at them.

Exhausted, dirty, their clothes ripped and soaked, Owen and Sanchez could only return their gazes. As the crowd looked on, the young leader directed them to one of the huts and forced them inside, slamming shut a rudimentary door behind him as he left. There, in the darkness, Owen slumped to the floor, drained and weak. Sanchez stayed on his feet.

"Did you see them?" Owen murmured, hearing a level of excitement in his voice that belied his fatigue. "See the way they were looking at us? They haven't seen people like us before. This is amazing. And this settlement—it's a large one, all things considered. I counted at least a dozen huts."

Sanchez scanned the walls. Through thin gaps seeped faint orange firelight, and as Owen's eyes adjusted, he saw a determined expression on his companion's face. "I know what you're thinking," Owen said. "But we don't know who killed Elson, or what happened to Martins. It might not have been them."

Sanchez continued his search for weaknesses. "They have brought us here against our will."

"We were trespassing. They're defending their territory. We can't jump to conclusions."

"We can't leave anything to chance, either."

Sanchez sounded mentally drained, but his words rang true. Crossing paths with a rare Amazonian tribe was exciting, but the gravity of their predicament couldn't be ignored. They were captives, and to look past that, to defend their detainment or seek justification for it, was naïve, even reckless.

Outside, voices rose excitedly. Owen imagined the young men were recounting tales of their recent foray.

"Should we make a run for it now, then?" Owen said. The dwelling was little more than leaves and thatching; breaking out wouldn't be difficult.

"Are up to it?" Sanchez asked.

Owen considered this. Despite having had more sleep, he wasn't as fit as Sanchez and was probably even more exhausted than his companion. "Maybe. But if they come after us, at the speed they move, they'll catch us quickly. And there could be reprisals."

Sanchez agreed. "Let's rest and regain our strength a little, maybe wait for them to drop their guard. We'll make a break in a couple of hours."

Owen nodded, but then a thought flashed into his mind. "And what then? Return to Base Camp? It's decimated."

"Base Camp is our only option," Sanchez said. "Maybe we can salvage something. If not, there is always the Zodiac. We can use that to summon help." He looked at Owen, lowered his voice. "*Amigo,* if we can get out of here, we can still send that chopper."

42

It was too cramped in the small tent for the three of them—four, counting Priscilla—so Rebecca took her in her arms and retired to her own. They seemed safe enough for the moment and had agreed they should rest while they had the chance. It was easier said than done. Like the others, Rebecca was exhausted, but still full of adrenaline.

Restless, she lay on her back and stared at the tent's ceiling, unsure how to feel.

They wouldn't have survived the night if these people hadn't arrived when they had—hell, they wouldn't have lived through the next *minute*—but what it spelt now was a mystery. She, Ed, and Jessy were captives, that much was certain, but if these men were drug runners or gun runners or some rebel or paramilitary group, why keep the three of them alive? What's more, where was the chopper? She was worried about Owen and Sanchez.

She had other, more personal concerns, too, but tried to suppress them. She got the feeling—*thank God*—that the door that had cracked open to invite the fears of her childhood had been slammed fully shut by the sudden gunfire.

You can't be certain of that, Bec.

No, I can't.

And what if, while it was open, something came through?

She silenced the thought and tried to calm herself.

The single upside—if there was one—was the irony that there were now eight, heavily armed men outside, not just keeping watch on *them*, but on their surroundings, too.

Rebecca closed her eyes. The evening's events—and the questions—played over in her mind.

She tried to sleep.

43

Owen had just closed his own eyes when he heard a noise outside.

It came again; a low shuffling, then a voice, and he sat up—

—just as the door to the hut exploded inward. Half a dozen tribesmen burst inside. Owen lurched to his feet but tripped in the confusion and fell. Sanchez was already up and fighting—Owen saw him knock two men to the ground with swift kicks—but his resistance was short-lived. Lightning fast, four more attackers converged on Sanchez, clubbing him furiously with their fists and raining blows upon his head. Sanchez stopped struggling and fell limp. When his assailants cleared away, lifting Sanchez and binding him with lengths of vine, blood poured from great gashes in his forehead and dripped down his chin.

The remainder of the tribesmen—eyes wide and full of intense energy—turned on Owen. He submitted.

This is bad.

They'd been caught hopelessly off-guard, and Owen felt a flush of panic. Clearly, they'd made a terrible misjudgement and should have run when they'd had the chance.

Hurried and excitable, the men hauled Owen to his feet, strapped his arms to his sides and wrapped strips of vine around his torso. Like Sanchez, only his legs were left unrestrained. Several hands pushed him towards the door. Sanchez, still dazed from the attack, staggered in front. The men supported most of his weight.

It was drizzling outside, and the night sky was unusually dark. The two of them were ushered to the fire.

It seemed the entire tribe had reassembled around the blaze—men, women, children—all whooping and yelling, their expectant faces glowing red in the firelight. They parted as Owen and Sanchez approached.

Only one of them held his ground as they neared. He stood in front of the fire, in silhouette, awaiting them silently. He took shape as they pushed through the throng, and Owen gasped.

In that moment, looking upon the figure, it all came together.

Earlier, he'd been mistaken in thinking he was the first Caucasian these people had encountered. Now, he knew exactly who they were. This was the lost tribe Rosenlund had discovered.

The Yuguruppu.

It all made sense. Owen knew from the notes Rosenlund had copied into his field diary that the Yuguruppu worshipped certain gods who resided in a sacred part of the jungle. These gods had been awakened by a 'foreign tribe' that had settled in the sacred place and built within it a great city. In failing to repel the foreigners, the Yuguruppu had displeased the gods and were banished from the sacred place. Rosenlund's notes hadn't revealed the nature of these deities, maybe because the Yuguruppu, wary of another foreigner, had kept this secret.

Owen, however, could guess the gods' identity.

As they came to a halt in front of the fire, Owen looked up at the shaman in front of him.

On his head was an elaborate headdress, in the shape of a giant spider.

Owen's mind raced. Religious veneration of spiders was common amongst primitive societies on almost every continent, and he was aware of tribes in the Amazon who considered spiders sacred. But he knew, too, that the creatures worshipped by the Yuguruppu were of a type no other culture could have possibly imagined.

Sanchez murmured through blood-caked lips. "What's the story with this guy?"

The shaman approached Owen and paused to appraise him. He was an old man, small of frame, with dark, wise eyes and a wrinkled, inquisitive face. If not for the frightening adornment atop his head, he would have seemed amiable. Owen stiffened as the old man stooped, drawing the grotesque face and eyes of the spider level with his own. Glinting red in the firelight, the eight glassy orbs bored into him, and for a moment, returning their gaze, Owen was convinced the shaman had lowered himself purely to allow the thing atop his head a decent look. Of course, he was being ridiculous. The headdress was no more than carved wood, the eyes no more than polished stones, the eight disproportionate legs that sprang from its bloated and blackened abdomen—stretching halfway down the shaman's back and shoulders—no more than strips of thickened tree bark.

Yet still…

Owen shivered. "I don't know, but I've got a feeling we're not going to like it."

The shaman undertook a similar appraisal of Sanchez before pushing past and raising his voice to the assembled crowd.

"What is he saying?" Sanchez asked.

Owen shook his head. "I've no idea. I'm not familiar with the dialect. A tribe of this size usually has its own."

They kept their voices low. Around them, spurred by the shaman's hoarse, melodic tones, the tribespeople began to whoop and dance and chant wildly. In all the excitement, they seemed to forget about Owen and Sanchez.

"What do we do, just stand here?" Owen said.

"We should have fled earlier. Maybe we should do so now, take our chances."

But Owen knew there was no hope of success. They were surrounded by three or four dozen people in the full glow of the fire. The Yuguruppu might presently be ignoring them, but clearly, he and Sanchez were the guests of honour.

No chance of leaving unnoticed.

The Yuguruppu continued their frenzied dance, the ceremony working its way into full swing. Owen wondered how long it would go for… and what awaited them at its end.

It would be several hours before he'd find out.

44

To her surprise, Rebecca obviously *had*, at some stage during the night, drifted off to sleep. She realised this when Ed's voice came suddenly to her ears, rousing her from another troubling dream. She sat up with a startled jolt.

Priscilla, also startled, leapt into her arms.

It was just after first light. Rebecca checked her watch and figured she must have dozed for almost four hours, still in her clothes and boots. The tent was steamy, and she felt clammy. Ed's voice came again, and Rebecca unzipped the flap to find him outside, urging her to follow.

Apprehensively, she peered out of the cave, and the events of the previous night came back with a rush.

The guards were still there. The rain had stopped, too, and Rebecca saw through gaps in the canopy a glorious, clear blue sky. It was just as humid outside the tent, and strangely, smoke hung in the air. The moderate fire of the night before had been replaced by a bonfire, the men feeding it with armfuls of shredded tree limbs and assorted arachnid parts. Minus several trees, the clearing looked almost normal.

She got a few stares from the men. All of them had discarded their ponchos, mostly in favour of fatigues or black or khaki singlets. Like Ed had said last night, they obviously weren't regular army. This morning, they looked more like a band of militia.

She slipped into Ed's tent, Priscilla in her arms. "Ed, what's this about?"

Jessy, who was awake, smiled faintly in greeting. Ed had reapplied her dressings.

"I should have known," Ed said.

"Known what?"

"Known what this was about. I couldn't sleep, so an hour ago I demanded to speak with the leader."

Rebecca raised her eyebrows. "And?"

"Firstly, we're safe for the moment. You were right, Bec, they're connected to that plane, but I don't think these guys are the owners. The leader's name is Sandros Oliveira. I think he and his men are working on the owner's behalf."

"What do they want?"

"Oliveira insists they're not interested in us, and if we behave ourselves, do exactly what he says, he'll let us go. I'm sure he won't help us out of here, but he'll leave us to our fate. He claims they'll be gone by nightfall."

"If only we could believe that," Rebecca said.

"Well," Ed said, "He seems reasonable, and I've made arrangements that might give us reason to. I've cut us a deal."

Jessy shot Ed a worried glance. "Cut us a deal? And what did you mean when you said you should have known what this was about?"

A sense of foreboding had overcome Rebecca, too. "Ed, how did they find us here? How did they find that plane?"

Ed answered slowly. "They found it, because they had a guide who had been here before. Felipe Cartana."

Rebecca tilted her head. The name was familiar.

"Cartana worked for me," Ed said, "and was with us on the return trip here after Robert and I found this place. He helped transport the first batch of equipment."

Rebecca nodded. "I remember now. Owen told me the other night. He disappeared suddenly in one of the Zodiacs not long after you got here, didn't he? You're saying he's returned?"

Ed nodded. "I saw him out there when the guards took me to Oliveira. He spotted me and scurried into the jungle." Ed snorted and shook his head. "When he ran out on us, Robert and I thought he'd lost it, panicked when he saw what was here. Robert was pissed—after all, he'd hired the men, they were his responsibility. Now Cartana was gone and we'd lost a Zodiac, too.

Anyway, we assumed we'd never see him or the boat again. Clearly, Cartana recognised the plane and led these men back here."

"He works for them?" Rebecca asked.

"Directly? Who knows? We didn't exactly ask for CVs. Maybe he's couriered for them in the past."

"You think they're drug runners?" Jessy asked.

"Most likely. Drugs, and guns too. Out here, the two go hand in hand. Commonly, the locals are dragged into the network. And here's the thing: recently, our government, and the governments of several South American countries cracked down on unregistered private flights, at the same time escalating the number of anti-drug surveillance flights. Harassed from the sky, the drug cartels moved their processing plants deep into the jungle, coercing villagers and indigenous people into moving the drugs on foot through the forest, away from prying eyes. Maybe these people had such a hold over Cartana that he was too scared *not* to say anything. Or maybe he thought he'd be in line for a big reward."

"So, again," Rebecca said, "what do they want from *us*?"

"They want something from inside that plane," Ed said. "From us specifically, they want information, expertise."

"Cartana saw what they were up against," Jessy said.

Ed nodded. "I think these guys had been monitoring our movements from Monte Oeste; mine, with all the ferrying back and forth of equipment, then probably both you girls, and Owen too, as each of us arrived and took trips downriver in the *Tempestade*. Not surprising—they'd be cautious of foreigners so far off the tourist track and must have been curious."

"And when Cartana contacted them, they put it all together," Rebecca said.

"Right. And so now they're here with a bunch of experts at their disposal, presuming we'd know exactly how to deal with the situation. And if we were preparing to go in anyway—"

Jessy flinched. "Hang on. Preparing to go in *anyway*?"

Ed didn't miss a beat. "I had to make a deal, Jess. It was our only chance."

The colour drained from Jessy's face. "What kind of deal?" Her voice cracked before rising. "You don't mean you offered to go in there, after that plane?"

"I had no choice, Jess. What could I have said?"

She paused, her eyes full of stunned incredulity. "*No*, Ed, that's what you could have said! What the hell were you thinking?!" Jessy's voice climbed with every word, teetering out of control.

"Jess…" Ed said.

"No, Ed! This is insane! You'll never make it! The plane's stuck in the *middle* of that web, surrounded by those… *things*. You're out of your mind! It's suicide!" Tears had welled in her eyes and began to roll down her cheeks.

Rebecca put a hand on Jessy's knee and squeezed gently. "Ed. What's inside the plane?"

"They didn't exactly say. A package of some sort, I think. If I can get it for them, they'll leave us alone. Oliveira promised me that."

"*Bullshit!*" Jessy said. "You're simply going to take him on his word? Even if you *were* able to get this package, you think they won't just kill us the moment you hand it over? Why leave witnesses?"

Ed sighed. "Maybe you're right. Who knows if we can trust them? But had I refused, we'd be no better off. I've bought us time, if nothing else." His voice had risen, and he lowered it again. "This is the only way, and it's gotta be me. They think I'm the scientist, the expert. That's what I told them. I said they should send me if they wanted the job done."

The sense of finality in his tone seemed insurmountable. Jessy dropped her gaze and her head fell. Rebecca's mind spun as she tried to comprehend the mess in which they'd found themselves. For the moment ignoring the lie Ed had told Oliveira about his profession, she asked, "How will you get in there?"

Ed said, "They've brought ropes, harnesses, grappling hooks. Hell, they've even brought a flamethrower or two. I figure my best chance is to somehow get in over the top—maybe make my way in from this side, through the canopy. I can burn through the web and use the grappling hook to lower myself to the plane from above."

Jessy shook her head. "Over the *top* of the web? It rises all the way into the canopy!"

"It's the only way, Jess. I can't get in at ground level."

By the look on her face, Jessy couldn't believe her ears. "Ed, *please*. Let's think this through. Let *them* go in! We can direct them—relay instructions from out here, over the radio."

Ed shook his head. "No, Jess. I've made a deal. As I said, they don't need us otherwise. I have to go in, and it has to be over the top. There's no other way."

He wouldn't be swayed. Jessy must have understood that and began to sob again, burying her head in Ed's chest. He held her.

It was always going to come to this, Rebecca thought. *This is exactly what he wanted.*

She looked at Ed sadly, wondering about his version of events, curious as to how many falsehoods lay within it.

"There's no other way," Ed reiterated, mouthing it silently to Rebecca as he stroked Jessy's hair, her head still against his chest.

Rebecca closed her eyes. After a time, she looked at him again and spoke quietly. "No, there is another."

45

Ed looked confused. "Sorry?"

Rebecca shook her head. "Jessy's right. You can't go in over the top. But there's another way."

Jessy straightened. "What do you mean?"

Rebecca held up a hand to stop her before she got her hopes up. "I can't promise it's safer. And Ed, if I thought I could talk you out of this, I would. But I'm going to help you so there's a chance of you returning. That said… there's good reason you can't go over the top."

Ed's eyes narrowed. "And that is?"

"Because of the nature of the web, and the silk it's made from."

"You're saying I can't get through it?"

"You need to understand what you're dealing with," Rebecca said. "Spider silk has more than a single purpose; there're eight different varieties. Some silks are used for constructing webs, others for lining nests or burrows, others for forming egg sacs. The different silks are manufactured by different glands." She paused to take a breath, the enormity of his risk washing over her like a flood. "I studied the site for a long time yesterday, and I can tell you there's no access over the top. You won't get past that kind of silk."

Ed frowned and looked over his shoulder, through the tent flap. He turned back. "So, what are you suggesting?"

"Here's the thing. Just like silk, there are many kinds of webs—designs vary greatly from family to family, species to species. This one is a 'space web'—a three-dimensional structure different to your more common, two-dimensional 'orb web', you know, the type in your garden that looks like a cartwheel."

Ed glanced again at the tent flap, as though concerned the guards would overhear.

Rebecca lowered her voice. "Picture this: we've got that great depression in the ground out there, and sitting inside it is the pyramid, a portion of which is sticking above the bowl's rim. Entwined about it is the web. At first glance, the web seems random, unstructured. But it's not. Rising from the lip of the bowl and high into the canopy is a dome-like 'lid' of silk."

"A *lid*?"

Rebecca nodded. "This lid runs through the canopy and down the other side, encapsulating the pyramid. Hundreds of silken support lines—scaffolding, essentially—run horizontally from the dome and extend into the forest above and beyond the bowl."

"Like the threads attached to the two giant moai," Ed reasoned.

"Exactly," Rebecca said. "They're not there to capture anything, they're simply a means of support. You've also got these very same threads running towards the centre as well, attached to the pyramid, and others running vertically into the canopy. The dome itself is the catching-surface, the place where prey gets stuck. The scaffolding suspends it in place. Flying prey might hit the support threads and get knocked onto the catching-surface, but they need to hit *that*—the dome—to become properly entangled."

Rebecca made sure she still had him before clearing her throat to continue. "The dome is a network of interconnected 'sheet webs', woven together like patchwork. They're extremely sticky. Simply put, anything that hits them gets stuck. Running a few feet beneath this outer layer—think of the different layers of an onion—is an internal dome called a 'barrier web'. This is constructed much the same as the outer sheets, but it's dry."

"Dry?"

"Non-adhesive," Rebecca said. "Ever wondered why spiders don't get stuck in their own webs? Partly, it's because they have these areas of dry, non-sticky silk. The barrier web is a communal layer through which all the spiders in the colony can move, grabbing prey entangled on the outer catching-surface and dragging it through."

"Uh-huh," Ed said.

"Where the *plane* is entangled—a third of the way down the pyramid's northern face—is an area I suspect was once the dome's *former* ceiling. It's a horizontal, trampoline-like sheet web. The spiders have built over the top of this sheet to form the current ceiling. Maybe they did this because the plane caused irreparable damage when it crashed into the original sheet." Rebecca shrugged. "In any case, you're confronted by this: moving down from the canopy, you have the top sheet of the dome—the current roof or ceiling—then a few feet beneath that, the communal barrier web. A few feet beneath that, is the *old* ceiling—the old capture-sheet which was once the top of the dome, where the plane is entangled. Then, beneath *that*, is most likely another barrier web extending to the ground and the base of the pyramid."

Ed wiped at his brow. Rebecca realised she was also sweating. It was warm in the tent with all of them crowded in there.

"I can guess where you're going with this," Ed said. "To get to the plane, I've got to get past the outer *adhesive* layer and into the inner *non-adhesive* layer, the barrier web, so I can move around like the spiders, right? But that's the problem, isn't it? How do I do that? How exactly do I get in there, past the outer layer? Burn it with the flamethrower?"

Rebecca shook her head. "You might be able to burn through the catching-sheet, but you'd attract a lot of attention."

Ed frowned. "So, you're telling me I can't go *through* it, and I can't go over the *top* of it. What exactly, am I to do?"

Rebecca looked at him. "Simple," she said. "You go underneath it."

46

"*Underneath* it?"

Rebecca nodded. "I said to you earlier I thought the colony's central communal area is likely located within the pyramid itself. It makes sense: they'll have built themselves 'retreats'—sheltered chambers, galleries, places to rest and hide—and I can't see any of that in the visible regions of the web."

"Sounds like an ant nest," Jessy said.

Rebecca nodded. "Ant colonies have numerous chambers—nurseries, places where food is stored, even gathering places for workers, all connected by passageways. Many of the non-territorial species of social spider build large-scale nests with similar traits." Rebecca eyed Ed. "I know how to access the nest and *avoid* the web entirely. I can get you underneath it."

"The trapdoor," Ed said slowly.

"Right," Rebecca said. "Most trapdoor spiders have a burrow—a tunnel—leading down from their door, and several other tunnels or escape routes branching off it. It stands to reason that the individual we saw yesterday would have access to the nest."

Ed smiled. "A tunnel that leads *under* the web and into the communal area."

"I'm guessing right into the pyramid itself."

Jessy's face drained of colour. "And you're suggesting he goes in there—through the trapdoor and into the pyramid—via that tunnel? Into the nest? That's *worse* than going over the top! The heart of the nest?!"

"I'm hoping he'll find another tunnel, one that circumvents the heart and leads up into the area at the base of the pyramid. If he can get there, he'll find himself in the lower barrier web—the one beneath the plane."

"The non-adhesive web…" Ed said.

"Non-adhesive, and not as dense. The outer capture-sheets are built to absorb a lot of energy: big, fast prey. Their radii are more numerous, far thicker and stronger. But the barrier web isn't designed to catch prey, so you should be able to move through it. Mind you, when I say move, you won't be able to climb up through the strands."

"Let me guess—no leverage."

Rebecca nodded. "That's why prey can't free themselves once ensnared. You'll be able to pass through the web at ground level, but you'll have to use the surrounding trees and vegetation to climb up higher. I'm guessing you can use the steps on the pyramid's northern face to position yourself across from the plane and fire the grappling hook from there."

"Right," Ed said. "But didn't you say the plane is entangled in the old capture-sheet? That'll stop me from getting inside, right?"

"Technically, yes," Rebecca said, "but here's the thing: unlike most orb webs, which are rebuilt every day, the space web is a permanent structure and rarely requires renewal. While this is convenient, there's a downside. Sticky silk eventually loses its adhesiveness. I suspect the stickiness of the old capture-sheet will be minimal, due to its age. The spiders won't have renewed that layer of silk, because they simply built a new layer of sticky silk *above* it."

Ed smiled. "And the silk the plane's wrapped in? What about that?"

"A different variety again," Rebecca said. "Spiders cocoon their catch with *swathing-silk*. For whatever reason, these spiders swathed the plane. It won't be a problem, though. You'll be able to penetrate the swathing-silk easily enough. It's non-sticky. Try slicing it with the machete but burn it if you have to."

Jessy shook her head vehemently, visibly distressed by the whole scenario. "No. *No!* That sounds okay in theory, but he'll draw too much attention. They'll be attracted to his movements. They'll sense him and converge long before he can get near the plane."

Rebecca disagreed. "Not necessarily," she said. She looked at Jessy, bit her lip. "Not if he goes while they're asleep."

Jessy frowned.

"You've heard of 'circadian rhythm'?" Rebecca said.

"The twenty-four-hour biological cycle of activity and inactivity," Jessy said. "Most organisms obey it to some degree."

Rebecca nodded. "Spiders are no exception. While we're not sure if they 'sleep' in the true sense, they certainly go through a daily interval of rest marked by a drop in metabolic rate. Having seen this species in action, I believe they're nocturnal."

Jessy shook her head. "What about the attack on Enrique? That was during the day."

"It might merely have been an attack of opportunity," Rebecca mused. "Or they could be crepuscular: active during twilight. It was late afternoon when they attacked. Every other encounter has been at night. I'm not saying they don't have the capacity to be active during the day—after all, most spiders with good vision are—but the evidence points more to daylight hours being the time they shut down. There wasn't much activity in the web yesterday; a skeleton crew was on call, but even those members stayed huddled and unmoving for much of the time. Meanwhile, the rest of the colony was nowhere to be seen. Logic suggests they'd retreated into the heart of the nest. It also suggests that if Ed can get in while it's still light, while most of the colony is *inside* the nest resting, his chance of success will be improved."

Ed straightened. "That's good enough. I go in today—underneath, through the trapdoor." He moved to leave but made it no farther than the tent's entrance. "One problem, though. What about the spider that's guarding it?"

47

Rebecca crouched in the low-lying fernery a few dozen feet from where Enrique had been attacked. Flanked by four of Oliveira's men, she lowered her binoculars and glanced at Ed.

From his position in front of the blind, Ed tossed her a discreet wink and turned to Oliveira on his other side. "There should be a trigger mechanism—silken trip-lines, sometimes a silken mat or a root or stick with a thread attached."

He looked back at her, and Rebecca gave him an almost imperceptible nod. So far, he'd played his role to perfection, delivering the lines she'd fed him earlier with ease.

Juggling Priscilla, who had wanted to stick close, Rebecca shifted her gaze to Oliveira. She hadn't gotten a good look at him last night, but when she'd laid eyes on him this morning—poncho discarded, fatigues tucked into military boots, sleeves ripped from a faded khaki shirt and not an ounce of fat on his muscular frame—she realised he was young, at most a year or two older than her. He wasn't as aggressive or impulsive as she'd anticipated, either. Like Ed had said, he seemed reasonable.

He also seemed impressed by Ed's plan. Fortunately, he'd agreed that the sooner Ed got going, the better. He'd mobilised his men and the group had moved down here, seven of them in total. Jessy, tent-bound, had stayed behind with two minders. Cartana, who was keeping well out of Ed's sight, had stayed, too.

Looking at Oliveira now, Rebecca dared to hope that maybe Ed was right, that once they'd gotten what they wanted, these men would leave as promised and she, Ed, and Jessy would somehow get out of here. Still, she was wary. While Oliveira was calm and deliberate, his eyes were impossible to read because they were hidden always behind a pair of silver aviator sunglasses. And as willingly as he had listened, beneath the surface flowed a disquieting undercurrent that suggested it was imperative Ed uphold his end of the bargain.

Which meant getting to the plane.

So they'd amassed down here to search for the trapdoor. Oliveira had proposed his men accompany Ed, but Ed had convinced him of the importance of going alone. Fewer people, less noise. Likely aware Ed wouldn't try anything stupid while the girls were hostage, Oliveira had agreed, but he wasn't the type to leave anything to chance. The four guards who'd escorted them here were heavily armed.

Rebecca scanned the group. The men struck her as clones of Oliveira—of similar age, lean and fit, with dark skin and long, messy hair. Despite some rough edges, they seemed alert, disciplined. They rarely spoke and moved with military precision.

The one who strayed from the mould was Oliveira's second-in-command, De Sousa. He had an entirely shaved head and stood at more than six feet tall. His height, barrel chest and tree-trunk arms made his companions look weak in comparison. Rebecca found his behaviour unsettling. More than once she'd felt his gaze, and when she looked, he'd be grinning.

After the first time, she kept her distance.

"The trapdoor won't be obvious, nor the trigger," Ed said, maintaining the subterfuge.

Rebecca turned to his voice. She had to give Ed credit. He was convincing, and Oliveira seemed to be buying it.

She'd told him earlier that the door would be disguised to blend with the forest floor. Even so, she figured their chances of finding it were high—now that the rain had passed, shafts of sunlight broke in several places upon the leaf-covered ground, and visibility was above average.

"There," Ed said, pointing. A fine mat of silken trip-lines fanned out in a circle several feet in diameter. At its centre was a bare patch of earth.

The trapdoor.

"There's one of them behind that door," Ed said. "Two of its forelegs will be pressed against the lid, ready to swing it open. Other legs will be caressing the silken trip-lines, waiting for prey." He swallowed hard. "We saw it the day before yesterday. It's big. Damn big. And fast, too. For all intents and purposes, it's a sentry."

The door was more than a yard across. Judging by the look on Oliveira's face, Rebecca guessed that had he not witnessed last night's attack, he would have scoffed at Ed's claims.

Eventually, Oliveira said, "So, how do we get it out? Knock?"

"We need to lure it out, and kill it," Rebecca said.

Oliveira smirked, wiping at a line of sweat that had eased from beneath his khaki headwrap. "And what, *senhorita*, should we use as bait?"

A shadow fell across Rebecca and suddenly Priscilla was torn from her grasp.

"HEY! What the hell are you doing?" Rebecca cried, standing and lunging for Priscilla as De Sousa backed away with the monkey in both hands, at arm's length out in front of him. Priscilla shrieked and flailed in his grip.

"Stop it! You're hurting her!" Rebecca screamed, and charged at him.

De Sousa leapt easily out of reach. "Bait," he said, grinning.

"NO!" Rebecca yelled, pouncing again, but this time one of the other men caught her wrists and twisted them behind her back.

"Ow!" Rebecca cried.

"Hey! Take it easy!" Ed said to the man and moved towards him. A second man grasped him from behind, halting him. A third stepped in, weapon raised.

Ed turned to Oliveira. "There must be another way."

Oliveira ignored him and jutted his chin at De Sousa, who proceeded on a path to the trapdoor.

"No!" Rebecca kicked out at her captor, connecting with a muscled leg. As she struggled, the grip tightened on her wrists until she couldn't feel her hands. "You're animals! *A bunch of fucking animals!*"

"Let her go!" Ed said, also struggling.

A short distance from the trapdoor, De Sousa moved beneath a large capirona, using it as cover. Held in front of him, Priscilla squirmed, but she was tiring.

"Please… stop him!" Rebecca said tearfully, spinning on Oliveira, who said something in Portuguese to the man holding her wrists. She felt a release and not knowing what else to do, rushed into Ed's arms as he too was freed.

Oliveira issued further instructions to the man who had intercepted Ed, and then turned to Rebecca. "Do not fear. Luis never misses."

Checking the mag of his weapon and punching it back in, Luis smiled crookedly. He was missing a front tooth.

"What are you doing?" Rebecca asked, and as the words left her mouth De Sousa snapped his arms outwards and launched Priscilla towards the trapdoor.

"No!"

Priscilla landed awkwardly a couple of feet beyond the silken mat. Shakily, she got to her feet and glanced about, dazed but unhurt. De Sousa had tied a thin rope around her neck.

Ed turned urgently to Oliveira. "The last time the sentry burst out other guards—other spiders—came for us."

For a time, Priscilla seemed confused and stared blankly ahead. De Sousa jerked the rope and pulled her closer. By now, Luis had moved down the slope and had set himself against a tree, the rifle trained on the trapdoor. Spurred into action by De Sousa's tugging, Priscilla started moving. Her ordeal seemingly forgotten, she picked over the ground for things to eat. She found a fallen piece of fruit, put it to her mouth, and paused. Then she took another step forward, onto the mat, and Rebecca jerked her head away, unable to look.

Nothing happened.

Rebecca turned back.

"Why does it not take the bait?" Oliveira whispered.

And then it did.

It was every bit as terrifying as two days ago. In a blur, the ground exploded upwards, the sentry—all legs and bared fangs—launching itself from the wide hole beneath.

Luis was equal to the task.

By the time Rebecca had even registered gunfire, the sentry was slumped dead at the tunnel entrance, its legs retracting into a ball.

Rebecca ran for the trapdoor. Ed went with her and grasped a leg of the shattered sentry before the carcass could slide back into the hole. At the same time Rebecca scooped Priscilla into her arms.

Somehow—*thank God*—Priscilla was still alive, but she screeched in pain. In the split-second before Luis's bullets had found their mark, the spider had dug its fangs into her left haunch, leaving two nasty-looking punctures. Priscilla thrashed as though on fire. Rebecca flew into action, discarding the rope around Priscilla's neck and tending the wound. As she wrapped the limb with a piece of her own shirt, she noted Priscilla wasn't exhibiting the usual signs of envenomation. Not yet, anyway. Toxins had varying effects on animals; cats and dogs, for instance, were largely unaffected by the bite of the Australian funnel-web spider, a species deadly to humans *and* monkeys. Sometimes, too, a bite could be 'dry'. In this case, the spider probably hadn't had time to inject its venom. Still, she'd monitor Priscilla closely.

"Poor monkey," De Sousa said with a cruel, taunting laugh. He loomed over Rebecca. "Too bad for her, eh?"

Rebecca leapt to her feet and slapped De Sousa's face.

De Sousa's grin dissolved, and he raised a fist, wide-eyed in fury. Ed leapt in front of him.

"Enough!" Oliveira commanded.

"Disgusting," one of the other men said, seemingly oblivious to the confrontation. He was studying the carcass of the spider, clearly stunned by the size of it even though half its dorsal area had been blown away. "I hope that's the only one down there."

It took another command from Oliveira, this time in Portuguese, for De Sousa to yield. Eyeballing Ed, the big man chuckled and lowered his fist. Before backing away, he blew Rebecca a kiss, licking at the blood running from a gouge in his cheek opened by one of her nails. Rebecca turned away, repulsed.

Ed turned away, too, and went back to the burrow. He held back the lid of the trapdoor and shone his flashlight down the hole. It was silk-lined and incredibly dark. For a few feet, the burrow descended vertically, bending upwards after that to perhaps run parallel with the forest floor. It led off in the direction of the pyramid and seemed wide enough to squeeze through.

Luis crouched and touched a finger lightly to the silk. "Not sticky," he observed.

"It's just for waterproofing," Ed told him.

Rebecca finished bandaging Priscilla's wound. The poor thing had calmed, perhaps in shock. Rebecca stood, clutching her to her chest as she would a frightened child. As she did, she glanced at the carcass on the ground a few feet away. One of the men poked it with a stick. Even at this distance, Rebecca could see it was different to the original specimen Ed had discovered: the body shape, eye pattern and legs were inconsistent with those of a jumping spider.

Oliveira searched the surrounding trees. "No others? Why is it different this time?"

Ed was wary. "I don't know. Perhaps we killed the sentry before it had time to alert them."

Rebecca, too, was starting to feel uneasy. Ed's point was valid, but there was every chance the spiders communicated via pheromones, signalling each other by scent. If so…

Oliveira read her thoughts. "Perhaps we killed it in time," he said, "or perhaps they are yet to come." He ushered Ed to the hole with his now-drawn pistol. "Hurry. Get going before they do."

48

The ceremony continued without pause through the night, relenting at dawn when the shaman, bathed in sweat, raised his arms and called it to a halt. Exhausted, Owen had long-since fallen to his knees, drifting in and out of sleep at the foot of the fire as the Yuguruppu danced tirelessly around them. He didn't think Sanchez had slept but couldn't be sure. At one stage, Owen had told him his theory as to who these people were. Otherwise, they'd hardly talked.

At the conclusion of the ceremony, they were dragged to the edge of the clearing. The shaman, still wearing his headdress, led them into the jungle depths with the entire tribe forming a long column through the trees behind.

They're going to kill us now, Owen thought grimly.

Everything had become a blur. Owen's sleep-deprived mind was foggy. He was hungry and thirsty, and his arms ached from being tied for hours at his side. His mud-caked legs—bloodied by the foliage—could hardly perform the job asked of them.

He wondered why Ed hadn't encountered this tribe earlier. Why now? Base Camp had been set up for weeks with no sign of trouble. Perhaps Ed's arrival hadn't initially been noticed, or maybe the Yuguruppu had been biding their time. Perhaps after the team had left for S1, members of the tribe had ambushed Elson and Martins, had tried to capture them as they had he and Sanchez, but it went wrong—maybe the two of them had fought back—and they were killed, Martins' body washed away by the floodwaters.

They entered a small clearing. The shaman took stance at its centre and Owen and Sanchez were brought before him. As Owen shuffled into position, he glanced down.

Close to where they stood was a large hole in the earth, maybe twenty feet in diameter. He hadn't noticed it at first, mainly because it was covered by a massive flap of leaves and twigs that had been woven together and placed there to disguise it. Rising from the pit to emerge from beneath the cover were long, silvery tendrils that snaked across the forest floor like great tree roots.

Spider silk.

Owen's breath caught in his throat. He was looking at the entrance to a nest.

With Sanchez beside him, Owen stared at the covered pit. He thought of recent events at S1: the attack by the juvenile spider, and the mysterious barking sound. When they had been captured by the Yuguruppu the previous evening, they had exited Base Camp in the direction Owen and Sanchez had just come from, heading *back* in the direction of S1. Was S1 near this nest? Had they returned that far?

His thoughts dissolved as the crowd behind them parted. He turned as two men approached, carrying between them a domed object about four feet in width and wrapped in broad green leaves held firmly in place by a thin vine strung around the outside. The men placed the object at the shaman's feet and leapt away.

"What is *that*?" Sanchez whispered.

The shaman whooped, and to the crowd's encouragement, danced in circles around the object, stooping occasionally to slap it with his hands. Finally, he produced a stone knife and with a single stroke cut away the vine. The leaves fell, revealing a cage-like basket. Owen took an involuntary step backwards.

Inside the basket, bathed in morning sunlight, was a very large and angry jumper.

The creature was the size of a large dog. It raised its forelegs menacingly, the classic threat-pose of an agitated, aggressive spider. Venom glistened at the tips of its three-inch fangs, hanging in swinging threads.

The crowd hooted with excitement, but the cries were tempered now with awe. *Respect.*

"This isn't good," Owen said. A wave of nausea washed over him.

Out of the crowd came another man who passed the shaman a long stick with a bowl-like attachment at one end. The old man raised the staff to more whooping, then used it to prod the spider through the bars of the basket. The spider jumped and kicked angrily at the pole, causing the basket to rock from side to side.

"He's provoking it," Sanchez said. "I thought they revered these things?"

With lightning speed, the spider seized the shaft and with a swift, downward strike sank its ample fangs deep into the bowl.

Owen's stomach churned. "He's milking it."

Two more tribesmen moved in with sticks of their own, flanking the basket and poking the jumper to draw it away from the bowl. The spider released its hold and spun to face them, rattling its cage. Blood-red stripes running the length of the creature's dorsal surface seemed to reflect its rage.

The shaman withdrew the bowl, and to the delight of the crowd raised it to the air. As he did, Owen felt the sharp jab of a spear tip in the side. Two Yuguruppu forced him towards the old man.

Owen resisted. "Robert…" he said, turning to Sanchez. He dug his heels in but was pushed forward.

Please, no…

Owen's bottom lip quivered. The hot drum of panic hit his chest, and suddenly the air felt thicker, harder to pull into his lungs.

He was about to die… and there was nothing he could do to stop it.

Sanchez sprang forward, rushing the shaman, but the blow came fast and hard.

Thunder reverberated through his skull, and Sanchez saw stars. The world tilted crazily, and then something cold and wet pressed against his cheek. He realised he'd crashed facedown into the mud. Blinking hard, he fought to stay conscious, only dimly aware he'd been struck but lucid enough to know that if he blacked out, he was dead.

He bit down on his tongue. Hard.

It had the desired effect. Instantly, his mouth flooded with the coppery taste of blood, pain searing through him like a bolt and forcing him back to his senses. His vision cleared. He got to his knees, expecting a second strike.

No additional blow came, and he stood unsteadily, at which point hands grasped him and held him firm. Warmth trickled down his neck and across his shoulders. Through the dizziness he saw the bowl already lifted to Owen's lips. Owen struggled, but his arms were still bound, and the men who held him in place jerked his head back by the hair. Pinching his nose shut, they forced him to drink. Sanchez could do nothing but watch helplessly.

Owen fell into the hands of his captors and another series of cheers and whoops swelled from the crowd.

Sanchez hadn't noticed that in the meantime, the pit cover had been removed. It only came to his attention when the two men holding Owen dragged him to the gaping hole.

Stepping up to the rim, they tipped him forward. Owen teetered, and then to the frenzied hoots of the crowd fell soundlessly into the void.

Below, a dull thump echoed.

Sanchez's eyes fell shut. He was certain that Owen had been dead before he'd even hit the ground.

It was his turn next. Sanchez's mind raced.

More hands clutched his shoulders, pushing him forward. The tribe pressed into a tight circle around him. The chanting that had begun when Owen had been thrown into the pit swelled as the crowd's anticipation grew.

The shaman moved towards him, bowl in hand. If he was forced to drink from it, he was as good as dead. Spiders used venom to kill, or to stop their victims struggling while they fed. If not fatal, the toxin would at best paralyse him—and by then it would be too late.

He looked left and right, felt the grip of his guards.

He had no choice.

Sanchez moved fast, throwing his weight hard against the Yuguruppun to his left, the one standing nearest the pit.

Together, the two of them tumbled sideways into its gaping maw.

49

Standing by the trapdoor, Rebecca watched as Ed tested the night-vision goggles. They were a snug fit. He was ready to go.

While Oliveira had for obvious reasons refused Ed a gun, he'd consented to the Brazilian-designed FH-9 flamethrower now strapped to Ed's back. While not a large unit—gun-like in appearance, it was sleek and compact with a short, barrel-like nozzle—the three underslung, fuel-storing cylinder tanks were bulky and awkward. It'd be tight, but Rebecca was confident he could squeeze it into the tunnel.

Ed had also been equipped with a very modern-looking grappling hook. Black and tubular and attached to fifty-feet of high-tensile nylon rope, the gas-propelled hook bore collapsible blades that opened upon firing. He'd strapped that device to his outer right thigh. To his left, he'd belted a machete in a long black sheath.

Webbing pouches in a harness around Ed's chest and waist stored the remainder of his equipment. Despite their apparent ineffectiveness the night before, Rebecca had urged him to take an X40. They'd worked at S1 the night they'd heard the barking sound. He carried one in a chest-pouch but would trigger it only if threatened—any unnecessary vibrations would alert them to his presence, and the intent was to elude attention.

Ed tested his comm radio, in a pouch up near his neck. It worked. He turned to Rebecca. "See you shortly."

"Just be careful, okay? Promise me that."

Ed nodded.

"Remember, move lightly and take it slowly," Rebecca whispered. "When you get into the barrier web, make sure you avoid the signal-threads. And if anything goes wrong…"

"It won't." Ed moved to the burrow and hesitated. Turning back to her, he opened his mouth to speak, but said nothing. He wore the same expression she'd seen yesterday when they were together in the blind, as well as three nights ago down by the river. On those occasions she'd dismissed it as no more than the knowing gaze of a past lover. Of course, it was more than that, and she wondered how strong and deep it ran, how genuine it was. She sensed Ed intended to kiss her and decided she wouldn't stop him.

"I'm sorry I got you into this," Ed said.

"Ed…"

Instead of moving closer, he smiled faintly. "Look after Jess, will you? Keep an eye out."

Rebecca nodded. "Of course."

She was aware he'd said his goodbyes to Jessy this morning, before they'd come down here to search for the trapdoor. He'd been in there a while. Watching him now, all suited up and ready to go—her own confused feelings swirling inside her—she wondered how Jessy had handled it. She was suddenly beset by a deep sadness. But for whom—Jessy, Ed, or herself— she couldn't be certain.

"I'll be back before you know it," Ed said. "All of this will be over soon."

Rebecca managed a smile. "Get going, will you?"

They helped Ed into the hole, headfirst, two of the men holding his feet, two more the trapdoor while Ed wriggled in on his stomach. He seemed to fit okay. Rebecca watched as they lowered him. His feet disappeared beneath the rim. Then all four men moved back, and the flap of earth sprang shut.

Just like that, Ed was gone.

THE
NEST

50

Darkness swallowed Sanchez as he fell into the pit.

He and his guard landed in a heavy tangle of limbs, the young tribes-man yelping in pain. The floor of the pit was hard, and Sanchez, too, grunted as the wind was driven from his lungs.

The impact caused the two men to untangle, and they bounced and rolled away from each other. In the confusion, Sanchez lost sight of his startled minder, the younger man disappearing into deep gloom. The Yu-guruppu, it seemed, had immediately replaced the cover, snuffing out the light. Sanchez wondered why the tribe had so hastily sacrificed one of their own…

He refocused, looking urgently about. It was impossible to tell how far they'd fallen—it was too dark. Mind racing, Sanchez got to his feet. His plan hadn't extended beyond leaping into the hole. Hurriedly, he worked on the cords binding his torso. He'd been subtly slackening them ever since he and Owen had been led from the hut. He'd made reasonable progress. Now, he could feel them loosening further. *Nearly there.*

As he laboured, his eyes adjusted to his surroundings. Faint chutes of light filtered through imperfections in the cover above, offering limited visibility.

Sprawled face down a few feet from where he stood was Owen.

Before Sanchez could move to him, the attack came. The young tribes-man sprang from the darkness, slipping the shaft of his spear up and over Sanchez's head, down to his throat so that it was horizontal to the ground. Sanchez was yet to free his arms and couldn't block the move. The young tribesman pulled backwards, choking him with the spear, and Sanchez felt his windpipe collapsing.

He flung his head back savagely.

He connected with the Yuguruppun's nose, shattering it, and they fell backwards together, the young man taking Sanchez's full weight upon him. The wind exploded from his adversary, but still the tribesman main-tained the choke-hold as he lay sprawled beneath him. Sanchez struggled for breath. At the edge of his vision, stars appeared, followed by a spreading pool of darkness, and he was about to pass into that darkness when out of it appeared a form. It stood fleetingly above them, and then there was a dull thud and a release and oxygen whooshed into Sanchez's lungs. He rolled away, spluttering, gasping.

Owen!

Still gasping, Sanchez struggled to all fours. The slap of two bodies con-necting and wrestling gave way to a muffled thump and a cry of pain.

He had to get to his feet. Turning his head, still trying to draw breath, he saw Owen out of the corner of his eye. Again, his companion was sprawled on the ground, although this time he was on his back and clutching his ab-domen. Beside him lay the discarded spear. The young Yuguruppun was gone.

Sanchez leapt to his feet. The cords binding his body had almost come free, having barely withstood the previous assault. With a final burst of strength, he broke them apart, shaking them to the ground and spinning to face the attack he suspected was coming. He'd barely brought himself around before the young man hit him full-charge in a tackle around the waist. Only the unyielding wall of the pit brought them to a halt. With a loud crack the two of them bounced off it, crashing once more to the ground. Dazed, Sanchez was the quicker to his feet, but only just. The young man was draw-ing himself upright when Sanchez lunged, looping his right arm around his opponent's neck. In the process, his right knee slammed into the man's face. Reaching his left arm over the top of the tribesman, Sanchez grasped him by the thin cord around his waist and drove him backwards, picking up speed with every step. Just shy of the wall he released the headlock.

The Yuguruppun slammed into the wall at full speed.

Sanchez had expected a devastating impact. It never came. Instead, his opponent fell soundlessly into the rock, as though it had relented to absorb his momentum.

Blood gushed from the young man's shattered nose. He was out cold. He was also *stuck* up against the wall, fully supported in an upright position.

Sanchez realised he hadn't thrown his opponent into a wall at all. The Yuguruppun had become ensnared in a *web* stretching from the floor of the pit to the point where it met the cover above. Three of the surrounding walls were solid rock, covered in non-sticky silk. But behind the fourth, was nothing.

Nothing but a huge, dark hole.

You're kidding me.

The pit wasn't man-made. It seemed to be the entrance to an underground cave system, and the curtain of sticky silk forming the fourth wall was some sort of door, probably placed there to keep intruders out.

Sanchez spun from the bloodied Yuguruppun. He had to work fast.

He knelt over Owen, who moaned softly, and saw why his companion had been clutching his abdomen. The tip of the tribesman's spear had sliced through the cords binding his torso and had entered Owen's body to the right of the navel. It looked bad. Owen's right arm had come free of his bindings, and he'd been stemming the blood with his hand. Sanchez wrested away the last of the vines and placed his own hand on the wound. With his free hand, he tore a strip from his shirt to use as a bandage. Maintaining pressure, he tied the dressing firmly. It wasn't perfect, but it would hold.

Owen continued to moan. Sanchez wished he had water to give him. Standing, he thought about how he'd get the two of them out of there. As he did, the hairs on the back of his neck prickled.

Sanchez turned to find the young Yuguruppun had disappeared.

Spinning, Sanchez searched for his adversary.

A gaping hole had appeared in the web where the Yuguruppun had been just moments ago. Beyond it was a deep blackness.

The young man was nowhere to be seen.

Without taking his eyes from the silken rent, Sanchez stooped to retrieve the spear and once more scanned the pit. Nothing.

Cautiously, spear in both hands, its tip forward, he stepped towards the hole. Braced and alert, he listened for his opponent's footsteps, assuming he was trying to outmanoeuvre him. He heard nothing.

Sanchez crept forward. Three feet to the hole.

Ahead, something stirred. He sensed it shifting in the darkness beyond the hole in the silk. He froze and heard a shuffling sound, then more silence. Stepping closer, Sanchez strained through the gloom. He stepped up to the silk, drawing level with it.

Sanchez stuck his head through the hole and peered into the darkness beyond.

All along, he'd presumed the Yuguruppun had regained consciousness, freeing himself from the silk and retreating into the shadows. He'd been wrong. The young man hadn't done that at all.

He'd been *removed* from the web.

The barking noise—low, almost a growl—came as the attack burst from the blackness.

Sanchez brought the spear up as glistening fangs filled his vision. Leaping through the hole, the jumper hit him in the chest with stunning force. Sanchez tumbled backwards as its forelegs gripped him by the shoulders, the huge arachnid firmly atop him as he struck the ground.

The spear was all that separated them. Sanchez held the shaft horizontally across himself like the Yuguruppun had earlier. The creature locked its dark, curved fangs around the stick, clicking and hissing only inches away, venom spraying from their tips. On either side of the animal's mouth, its two hand-like pedipalps waved in the air, clawing, brushing at his face. Long, spindly legs pummelled him. The thing tried to press down, using its weight to overpower him. Sanchez didn't dare strike back for fear of losing his grip on the spear. It was all he could do to keep the creature at bay.

A second jumper appeared beside him, landing with a padded thud a couple of feet to his left.

Sanchez met its gaze. Eight glassy black orbs peered back at him, sizing him up.

The second jumper reared, lifting its body off the ground to expose the stiff shield of its sternum in a menacing threat-pose. Raised skyward, its legs were not unlike the arms of the shaman when he had beseeched the crowd.

The creature struck swiftly with its fangs.

Pain seared through Sanchez's left shoulder, arcing through his arm as if he'd been stabbed by red-hot pokers. He cried out, unable to prevent the scream as the frenzied jumper removed the grooved teeth and reared again.

Somehow, he still had the spear, which held the first jumper at bay. He instinctively heaved upwards, rolling left in the one motion.

The first jumper, still stubbornly attached, rolled with him… *right into the path of the second.*

It was enough to unbalance the rearing, second jumper and cause it to scamper backwards. Momentarily, the two spiders became entwined, legs flailing. Attempting to disentangle itself, the first jumper released its hold on Sanchez. It was all he needed. He was on his feet in a flash, spear in hand. He spun to face them, his back now to the web.

Both creatures were already in the air.

Reflexively, Sanchez jerked his body sideways and ducked.

The first of the spiders clipped him with two of its legs as it passed, attempting to change its trajectory mid-leap to match the movement of its target. Sanchez felt it whoosh past his face, its velvety soft hairs caressing his cheek as it slipped by.

The second jumper had taken a lower angle to that of its companion, aiming for his torso while the other had aimed for his head. Because Sanchez had ducked, it now came directly at his face, legs spread in a starburst, its soft underbelly rushing into his vision.

The spider leapt onto the tip of Sanchez's spear, impaling itself in the centre of its plate-like chest. Momentum sent the creature coursing down the spear, the shaft passing effortlessly through the soft, yielding flesh.

It's not slowing down…

Alarmed, Sanchez watched as the spider, legs spread, continued down the spear towards him. The shaft disappeared before his eyes. His left hand, gripping the weapon, disappeared with it… *right into the creature's abdomen.*

Still, it slid. An inch from Sanchez's face, it stopped—and all eight legs closed around his head and shoulders.

Impossibly, the creature tried to draw him nearer. Its strength was immense. With his left hand still trapped inside its body, the right pinned by the smothering hug of its enclosed legs, Sanchez strained to pull his head backwards and away. The creature's jaw-like mouthparts moved feverishly, the two unsheathed fangs clicking, spraying venom an inch from the tip of his nose. Still, it pulled, the stench overpowering, faintly fishy and sweet. He gagged.

Sanchez released the spear from his left hand. Ignoring the wound to his shoulder, he thrust up his arm, fingers outstretched. The creature's insides parted to allow him passage, wet and foul and acrid, and his eyes stung.

Whether or not the organ he finally located was its heart, or its brain, Sanchez couldn't be sure. Whatever it was, it was large enough to grab. It felt warm. Gripping it fiercely, Sanchez tore his hand out.

The spider shuddered violently, its legs releasing him and twitching madly as though gripped by an electric current. A geyser of foul-smelling liquid sprayed across Sanchez's chest and face.

The creature was dead.

He flung the whole oozing mess—spear and skewered prize included—to the floor, spinning to face the other jumper…

…and almost smiled.

When it had leapt for him, clipping him on the way, it had continued into the remains of the web. It was now *stuck* in the silk, its efforts to free itself serving only to trap it further.

Relief washed over Sanchez. He was lucky the creature hadn't leapt straight through the hole and had instead struck the surrounding strands. But he didn't hesitate. The jumper was still alive, and if it managed to escape…

He rushed back to where he'd tossed the spear. With his boot on the carcass of the first spider, he slid the weapon free and spun back to the trapped jumper. The creature continued to struggle, unable to get leverage, although two of its legs had indeed writhed free.

Raising the spear, Sanchez stepped up to his defeated adversary. The jumper, sensing him, stopped moving.

Sanchez peered at the creature, trapped helplessly in the web, and shivered with revulsion. He raised the spear.

Without warning, the spider brushed its free rear legs over the back of its abdomen. It was quick. A stream of fine hairs puffed out like the spores of a fungus, hitting Sanchez square in the face. The pain was immediate and intense, as though he'd been set afire. In reflex, he jerked the spear tip upwards, into the spider's brain, killing it instantly. It fell limp in the web, dark ichor spilling to the ground.

Dropping the spear, Sanchez stumbled backwards, his vision blurring. Clawing at his face, he pulled at the stinging hairs and flung them away. The burning endured, however, and it was some time before it eased. With it, his vision improved, but remained watery.

He was processing this turn of events when the sharp throb in his left shoulder intensified. He looked at the bite—the two neat puncture holes with their spreading pools of crimson—and bandaged it with what was left of his shirt. He ensured the injury was tightly compressed—if he'd been injected with venom, it was vital he slow the flow of toxins to his heart.

He returned to Owen, who was semiconscious, and checked his abdominal wound. The bandage seemed to be working, but he required urgent medical attention.

Through tear-filled eyes, Sanchez looked up. The pit-cover was still in place. Beyond it he could hear the tribe chanting and whooping, in the throes of some sort of victory ceremony. Even if his vision improved and he managed to climb the pit wall with his injured shoulder, somehow dragging Owen up with him, they'd never escape the throng.

Sanchez pulled Owen to his feet, each man grunting in pain. With his companion draped over his good shoulder, he decided upon the only available course of action.

Eyes stinging, Sanchez headed through the hole, into the darkness.

Into the nest.

51

Rebecca was in the blind, alone. Behind the netting, two guards stood quietly.

She glanced at her watch. Forty minutes had passed since Ed had entered the burrow, thirty since he'd last reported in. She was getting worried. Where was he?

She scratched her right arm. This morning a lesion had risen there, probably an infected mosquito bite. She was surprised and concerned her carefully maintained defences had been breached, and clearly more than once; other sores dotted her body, too. But the welt high on her forearm was the problem—the itch was maddening. Raised like a rash, it seemed to be getting worse by the minute. A pinprick of blood and pus had pooled at its head and she wiped it away.

She did her best to ignore it and lifted the binoculars to her eyes. Realistically, she didn't think Ed would be exiting the tunnel just yet, but in the absence of radio contact, she had an overwhelming need to locate him visually.

Since he'd entered the burrow, Rebecca had been left largely to her own devices—ignored by Oliveira, though always shadowed by two of his men. Following Ed's first report, Oliveira had disappeared. Where to, she had no idea. For the most part, she had kept her vigil here, though minutes ago she'd returned to camp to check on Jessy and bring her up to speed. Jessy had seemed distant and removed, erecting a wall, perhaps, against the inevitable threat of bad news.

Without warning, Oliveira appeared behind her and Rebecca jumped. He crouched beside her as the comm radio on the ground between them hissed to life.

A wash of static, then Ed's voice: *"You there? I've made it. I'm out of the burrow."*

Rebecca's heart leapt. She snatched up the radio. Minutes ago, she'd tried to raise Ed herself, but had gotten static. She'd figured the burrow had been interfering with the signal; either that, or Ed had switched off the radio for the remainder of the journey.

"Ed, we're here," she said. "What do you see?"

A pause.

"Not much. Without the flares and the goggles, nothing at all. It's pitch-black in here." Ed carried infrared flares—virtually invisible to the human eye, but able to increase the brightness and range of the NVGs, which needed minimal light to function.

"I'm currently standing…"—static—*"…cross-tunnel of some sort… a T-junction. The burrow opened straight into it. This new tunnel runs roughly north-south. And you know…"*—more static—*"…it might even be man-made. It seems to be lined with silk, like the burrow… stale smell."*

The signal wavered and then cut out altogether before coming back. The reception was poor. Several of Ed's words were lost.

"…otherwise, all's quiet." More interference, then: *"Any suggestions… direction?"*

"North is where the plane is," Rebecca said.

"North it is, then. The air seems a little fresher… I'm heading uphill…"

"Ed, I think we should maintain radio silence where possible. Just keep us informed."

"Okay, will do. Speak to you soon, then. Out."

The radio went dead.

Rebecca returned the handset to the ground and scratched her arm again.

"So far, so good," Oliveira said without turning, lighting a cigarette and taking a long draw.

Staring at the pyramid, Rebecca said nothing.

After a while, Oliveira said, "You have been wondering about the people I work for. It is understandable. I imagine you have been wondering about me, too, and the kind of person I am."

"I've already worked it out," Rebecca answered coldly.

Oliveira exhaled a line of grey smoke.

"What's so important about that package?" Rebecca said. "That you'd come all the way out here for it?"

Oliveira inhaled. "It is the property of my employer. He would like it returned."

As always, his eyes remained hidden behind the reflective lenses of his aviators, but Rebecca noticed his jaw clench, and got the distinct impression there was a more personal reason for him being here.

They fell into a long silence. Eventually, Oliveira said, "So what brings *you* here?"

Rebecca opened her mouth to reply but didn't. The sore on her arm was bleeding again, the itch intensifying. It was almost as though…

She felt herself blanch.

Something was writhing beneath her skin.

"What the hell?" she shrieked. "There's something in there!"

Oliveira took her wrist and examined the sore. "Yes, there is."

"*What is it?*" Rebecca cried, withdrawing her arm in panic.

Oliveira took it back. "Here, give me your hand."

"Why? What are you going to do?"

Calling in Portuguese, Oliveira summoned Luis, who approached and smiled at Rebecca, revealing once more his missing front tooth. He knelt beside her as Oliveira blew a mouthful of smoke from his cigarette into the swollen, pus-filled wound.

"What are you doing?" Rebecca said, her alarm growing.

Ignoring her, Oliveira muttered to Luis as the second man took her arm. Oliveira blew more smoke, and Luis proceeded to massage the site of the bleeding boil, carefully manipulating the surrounding skin before squeezing his fingers together quickly and hard.

Rebecca yelped in surprise and revulsion as a tiny worm shot out of her arm, landing on the ground at least two feet away.

Oliveira lunged for it. White, and about an inch long, the thing wriggled between his fingers.

"That was *in* me?" Rebecca said, bile rising in her throat. "What the hell is it?"

"The boro, *senhorita*. Botfly larvae."

"What?"

Oliveira smiled at her and held the larvae out for closer examination. "Days ago, this fellow's mother, a tiny fly, caught a mosquito and laid her eggs on it. Upon release, that mosquito fed on you. At least one of the eggs fell on you and later hatched, and this fellow burrowed into your skin. Once fully grown, it would have emerged through its breathing hole—the hole in your skin we squeezed it from." Oliveira threw it to the ground and squashed it beneath his boot. "We have all had them. Disgusting, eh? But nothing of concern."

Rebecca swallowed a few times, trying to regain her composure. Disgusting didn't cut it.

Luis smiled. "There will be more. You will adapt." With that, he got up and left.

Rebecca swallowed again. "Great," she murmured, reminded of something Chad had said to her a lifetime ago. What had he called it? The Law of Adaptation?

Rebecca glanced at the bleeding welt. It needed antiseptic cream. On the ground beside her, Priscilla rested peacefully. She gave her a pat and wondered if all mammals were prone to such violation.

Oliveira stood to leave, drawing on his cigarette. "Luis is the best at removing the boro. When you find your next, we shall call for him again." He chuckled and flicked the cigarette stub away.

"Great," Rebecca repeated as he left. "Just great."

Only minutes later, a cry cut across the north-western vantage point—sudden, abrupt. It came from one of Oliveira's men, stationed near the trapdoor. He'd been ordered there to keep watch on the web and get a visual on Ed as he emerged from the tunnel. He'd spotted something.

Rebecca stood and raised the binoculars, thoughts of the boro mercifully forgotten. Something moved at the foot of the pyramid's northern face and she reached for the radio as it crackled to life.

"Bec. You there? I'm out of the tunnel."

"I'm here. We've got a visual on you. No trouble getting out?"

"*None at all. We were right about circumventing the nest, but I didn't think it would be this easy. The cross-tunnel brought me here—it went up in a continual straight line.*"

"Nothing branched off it? No other tunnels leading elsewhere?"

"*None that I noticed. The passage is definitely man-made—constructed by the people who built this city, unlike the burrow, which was obviously dug out by the spiders. Not sure of the tunnel's exact purpose, or what might have been waiting in the other direction, but then maybe that's best. Anyway, it's led me to a kind of square at the front of the pyramid, which is where you can see me now. I think it's a courtyard or a plaza or something.*"

Oliveira stepped in beside Rebecca. "How's the silk?" she asked Ed. "Can you move through it?"

"*Yeah. I'm in a barrier web. There's silk everywhere, covering everything, though it's not sticky and I can move freely. The threads aren't dense.*"

Rebecca scanned the web. She couldn't see any workers. "Can you see any… residents?"

"*Negative. This place is Snoozeville. This is gonna be easier than we thought.*"

Oliveira snatched the radio from Rebecca's hands. "What about the plane?"

"*I can see the plane above me. The northern staircase is off to my right. I'm heading for it now. I'll have that package before you know it.*"

Despite everything running perfectly to plan—or perhaps *because* of that—Rebecca felt a shortness of breath. Something wasn't right. She thought about the spiders' ability to alter their colour and match their surroundings.

Oliveira must have read her mind. "Do not be complacent, *amigo*," he advised Ed. "You know those things are there somewhere, eh? You should be careful."

"*Don't worry about me. I'll be in touch soon. Out.*"

As Rebecca watched, Ed picked his way across the plaza, through the barrier web. The large central staircase lay not more than forty feet from where he had emerged from the tunnel, rising to the pyramid's truncated peak. Every few steps, Ed would pause to disentangle a clinging thread of silk, but none appeared to be hampering him seriously. He reached the staircase and began his ascent. Rebecca noted he was much smaller in comparison to his surroundings than she'd expected, ant-like against the towering back-drop of the huge pyramid. The great stone staircase also seemed to rise at a steeper angle than she'd initially conceived. Seeing Ed there put everything into perspective.

The staircase must have been in good condition, not overly worn by time or the elements or greatly hindered by silk or vegetation, because Ed climbed the northern face surely. Occasionally he would pause to use his machete, but otherwise his ascent was fluid.

There remained no sign of any workers attending to or guarding the web. They were there somewhere. Rebecca kept an eye out for movement, ready to warn Ed. She gripped the binoculars fiercely.

Ed was halfway up when, for the first time, Rebecca dared to believe their plan might work. At this rate, Ed would be at the plane in a matter of minutes. She wondered what he was feeling right now. With all that had happened, she'd overlooked the momentous nature of the occasion: Ed was inside *Intihuasi*, climbing its centrepiece, up close and personal with the object of his—and his grandfather's—lifelong search. He must have been bursting with excitement. Rebecca wished she could have seen his face.

Two-thirds of the way to the top of the pyramid, Ed drew level with the plane, which was hanging nose-down, tail-up in the old capture-sheet. He climbed several more steps before turning away from the pyramid to face it. He removed the grappling hook from his thigh.

Oliveira leaned forward with his binoculars. "This is it," he murmured breathlessly.

Without fanfare, Ed aimed and fired the hook. It shot across the narrow chasm separating the plane and the pyramid, soaring towards the aircraft with the nylon rope spooling in loops behind it. The shot hit home. Ed secured his end into a crack in the stone steps with a rock-climbing anchor.

His voice came over the radio. *"Okay, let's get this show on the road."* In the distance, he turned and waved. *"See you soon."*

52

Ed faced the pyramid. He stood a few steps below the rope and reached up to grasp it. Already, he'd discarded the cumbersome flamethrower. Heaving up his legs, he hooked his ankles over the tightly drawn line. To make for an easier crossing, he'd fired *down* to the plane. He'd worry about the more difficult return trip later.

Hand over hand Ed pulled himself backwards, down to the plane.

The plane's left wing had been sheared almost clear by the crash and dangled earthward by a thread, but the hook had looped over the plane's right wing, which was bent around the front of the aircraft like an arm held protectively against the sun's glare. When Ed reached it, he was level with the aircraft's nose, the lowest point of the plane proper. Hence, and about forty feet of aircraft rose straight up above him. He noted it was a single-engine De Havilland. Through the swathing-silk that tightly bound the fuselage, he saw red stripes running laterally from head to tail on an otherwise plain white exterior. In places, he saw splashes of rust.

Ed swung himself around, stretched up and grasped the wing's edge. The metal had been warmed by the sun but was cool enough to touch. Once he was sure of his grip, he let go of the rope with his feet.

The aircraft dipped, adjusting to his weight. Metal groaned and creaked above him.

"Hold. Please," he murmured, not daring to move, waiting with his elbows hooked over the top of the wing for the swaying to subside. In moments all was still again.

Ed considered his next move. He had to act quickly. His perch was precarious: he couldn't find purchase with his boots on the wing's sheer surface, so his arms bore the brunt of his weight. Initially, he'd planned to climb over the wing and in through the windshield, but now he saw there wasn't enough room to squeeze between the wing and the nose. He'd have to climb several feet higher and enter through the door. He was in luck: it already looked to be open, though he'd have to cut through a layer of swathing-silk.

Ed heaved himself up and threw his right leg over the wing.

Again, the plane dipped. This time, the drop was more dramatic, the aircraft twisting clockwise.

"Shit!" Ed's heart thumped as metal groaned once more in protest. *Make this quick*, he told himself.

He reached for the windshield's riveted edge, holding on with the tips of his fingers and pushing on the wing with his right leg. He lifted his left leg and stood, both feet on the edge of the wing, his chest pressed flat against the roof of the plane. He paused to catch his breath. At no stage did he look down. He was sweating profusely, adrenaline surging through his veins.

Almost there.

He unsheathed his machete and shimmied left. Arriving at the roof's edge, he reached beneath the fold of the wing to slice at the silk wrapping the plane's exterior. The old fibres came away effortlessly, exposing the open doorway beneath, only partially obscured by the aileron. Sheathing the machete, Ed climbed over the twisted wing and in the one fluid movement swung feet-first through the open hole.

He was inside the plane.

Oliveira had told him to look for a small compartment at the rear of the plane, behind the seats.

Crouching, Ed moved beyond the threshold, forward of the front seats and into the cockpit proper. He perched on the aircraft's instrument panel.

"My God," he whispered, glancing about. "What the hell happened here?"

Everything was covered in silk: the seats, the cockpit instruments, the floor, the ceiling. The entire cabin.

Beneath him—he was careful to avoid it—the windshield had shivered into a maze of silver cracks. The passenger-side window was shattered. All around, faint smears of dried blood covered the seats and controls and walls like splatters of rust, grisly evidence of a horror Ed cared not to think about. There was no trace, however, of the pilot's remains, or those of his passengers, if he'd been carrying any.

They'd been removed.

The hairs rose on the nape of his neck and Ed turned, shutting the door behind him. For the moment ignoring Oliveira's instructions, he looked down to the instrument panel beneath his feet. He tried the radio, but of course it was dead. He looked for the plane's inbuilt EPIRB. He couldn't find it, but given the instruments beneath his feet were clearly useless—smashed, rusted, without power—what good would it have been anyway?

He clambered over the seats and headed up to the rear of the plane. Again, the aircraft swayed, and around him the metal moaned and complained. He paused in the cramped confines, waiting for the aircraft to settle before continuing his climb. He wondered how much strength remained in the old capture-sheet, and how long he had before the wreck was purged and sent plummeting.

The rear of the plane lay ten or twelve feet aft of the cockpit. Ed grabbed at the walls, pulling himself up. As he ascended, strands of old silk clung to him as though he was being wrapped in a sheet of dirty, rotted lace. He ignored it. Above him, at the very rear and jutting from the wall, was a mounting bracket, together with what looked to be a fixed antenna of some sort. He seized the bracket for support and heaved himself higher, noting this was the brace to which the ELT—Emergency Locator Transmitter—would normally be attached. No ELT had been fitted.

With his spare hand, Ed stretched up for the handle to the storage compartment and turned it. The door swung outwards.

The package was there.

It was just as Oliveira had said it would be: tucked behind one of several small, netted pouches used for securing cargo. Still hanging by one arm, Ed reached for it with the hand that had opened the compartment. The cloth bag was palm-sized and squarish, bound like a Christmas present with a black leather cord. Curious as to its contents, he squeezed it, and it yielded. Fearing it was breakable, he didn't test it further—the first squeeze had felt like he'd been grinding something together, maybe several things.

He considered opening the bag for a look but couldn't untie the knot with one hand.

Instead, he secured the bag in a webbing pouch at his waist and reached up for the radio at his neck. "Bec, Oliveira. I've got the package."

Static. No response.

He tried again but the result was the same. He'd give it another go on the outside.

Moving swiftly but carefully, Ed climbed back to the door. Despite his caution, the plane rocked more with every step, and he worried his luck was draining with the passing seconds.

Back at the door, he noticed something he'd missed upon entry. The object was jammed up in front of the seats where the pilot's pedals met the floor. He grabbed it and stashed it into his pack before turning back to the door. Opening it a crack, he peered out. No spiders. He pushed it all the way open and stepped onto the door's narrow metal edge.

As he reached again for the radio, he realised what he'd achieved. He had the package. All he had to do was shimmy back to the pyramid, descend the steps, and get back into the tunnel. "Mission accomplished. I've got the package, and I'm—"

"ED! FOR CHRIST'S SAKE! GET BACK... THE PLANE! GET OUT OF THERE NOW! GO!"

What...?

A soft, padded thud echoed from somewhere up above, and the plane lurched beneath Ed's feet. He thrust out a hand, clutching the edge of the door to maintain his balance.

With dread, he turned and looked up to the tail of the plane.

The creature sitting there was huge—maybe four feet across its jointed, spindly legs. Along the length of its body ran pale grey stripes of different shades, blending it with the surrounding silk. The second creature, he noticed, was just as big, but positioned in the web itself, higher than the first and off to Ed's right as he faced the tail.

He sensed the third behind him, on the other side of the gap separating the plane and the pyramid, crouched on the stone steps he'd earlier ascended.

Ed drew a sharp breath. The barking sound, low, threatening, reverberated around him. He closed his eyes.

The megarachnids came at him swiftly, from three different directions at once.

53

NO!!!

Rebecca fell to her knees, both the radio and binoculars slipping from her grasp. "Ed!" she cried. Sobbing, she dropped her head into her hands, barely aware of the sudden blur of motion that was Oliveira as he quickly exited the blind. She heard him bark orders and mobilise his men, but hardly noticed as they swung into action around her.

Why hadn't Ed responded? She'd been screaming into the radio for an eternity, trying to warn him. She and Oliveira had plainly seen the three spiders making their way through the web, converging on the plane. Having to watch Ed exit, unknowingly stalked, and then unable to do anything about it, was devastating.

What had gone wrong?

Her mind whirled. Obviously, the spiders had seen him, perhaps detected movement and had left their retreats to investigate. They'd responded as a group, swiftly positioning themselves for a deadly ambush.

If only Ed had heard her and gone back inside, he might have stood a chance.

In the end, the speed of the attack had been frightening.

Rather than jump—the workers seemed capable of small hops only—they had skittered through the barrier web, bridging the distance to the plane in seconds. As such—and perhaps mercifully—it was over quickly. Ed didn't seem to resist, but then, all Rebecca could see was a blur, a darkened mass as the spiders set upon him. She may have turned away. The next thing she knew, they were bundling his limp, motionless form—cocooned in swathing-silk—through the barrier web and down to the base of the pyramid.

Then they'd disappeared.

Rebecca lurched forward and vomited where she knelt.

"*Por favor, senhorita,* on your feet." It was Luis.

Rebecca shrugged his proffered hand. "Don't touch me!" Hot tears streamed down her face.

"I have orders to return you to camp. You must come with me."

"What? That's what *Senhor Oliveira* wants? This is *his* fault! He can go and get fucked for all I care. In fact, why don't you go tell him that!"

Oliveira must have been close. He appeared suddenly, dismissing Luis and turning on her. "You are coming back to camp now," he hissed. "I will not ask again."

"Or what? What will you do? This is *your* fault! It's your fault those things got him, your fault he was in there in the first place! If it wasn't for you, he'd be okay. It'd *all* be okay, you asshole!" Rebecca leapt to her feet and sprang forward, swiping at him with her fist.

Oliveira caught her wrist mid-swing. "You really believe that, *senhorita*? I did not think you that dull." He released her, and Rebecca winced, clutching at her arm. She looked at him, confused.

Oliveira exhaled tersely. "I could hardly have stopped him," he said. "He came to *me* with the plan, insisting he enter the city and try for the plane. I knew it was folly but agreed; I needed to gauge their reaction. I was surprised he got as far as he did."

Rebecca straightened, eyes narrowing. *It was Ed's idea?* "So, you used him as bait? You knew this would happen?"

"I knew less than you, *senhorita*," Oliveira said knowingly. "Despite your conviction, your friend was not coerced into anything. It would have been foolish to squander his enthusiasm."

Rebecca slumped, almost falling to the ground again. Oliveira was telling the truth. It wasn't a stretch to accept that Ed had exaggerated the terms of his meeting with the leader; she'd already harboured doubts about his story. And plane or no plane, he'd always intended to enter the city. She could never have stopped him, even with Jessy's assistance. This was always how it would end.

"So, what will you do with us now?" Rebecca asked. "Ed said he had the package. Now it's lost for good. It's over."

Oliveira smirked. "*Senhorita*, I do not know what you take me for. Your friend's capture was a scenario I had anticipated. All is not lost." He leaned out of the blind and called to the only one of his men yet to return to camp, a lightly built soldier standing guard by the trapdoor.

"Asensi!"

The man named Asensi, who had been staring into a small handheld device that looked like a cell phone, nodded and rattled off something in Portuguese.

Oliveira turned back to Rebecca. "I had a tracking device inserted into the webbing vest worn by your friend, in the event this should come to pass. I knew it was the last item he would likely misplace in there. If, like he claims, he has the package, then wherever he goes, it goes too. And we will follow."

"You're going in after him?"

"Him, the package—yes, but this time we will do it right, *senhorita*. You are coming with us."

Rebecca hesitated, hoping she'd misheard. "Sorry? What makes you think I'd be of use... in *there*?"

Oliveira shook his head. "Once again, you believe me a fool. You must, or you wouldn't persist with the charade. I know who you are, what your profession is. Do you believe that I mistook *him* for the expert? As I said, I let him in, so I could learn more about what I was up against. From the beginning, I saw in his eyes what he wanted. And I saw it in yours, too."

Rebecca was unsure how to respond.

"We are wasting time," Oliveira said. "I require your expertise. I know that part of you is curious—and even more of you *hopeful*—so enough talk. If those creatures are nocturnal, like you say, then the light is precious." He looked at her humourlessly, his tone impatient. "Now, as I said, we are returning to camp, and we are going now. We leave for the nest in thirty minutes."

54

⚡

"He's gone, isn't he?" Jessy said. It seemed less a question than a statement of resignation.

For a moment, Rebecca couldn't look the younger woman in the eye. "I'm sorry," she said at last.

Jessy shook her head angrily. "It was always going to turn out this way. I said so. Didn't I tell you both? He's a bastard for putting us through this."

"We could never have stopped him. You know that."

Jessy snorted. "That doesn't change anything, does it?" Her eyes were red-rimmed, and her hands shook. Rebecca could tell she was devastated, but the wall she'd put up earlier—the defence she'd erected against this very outcome—held firm.

"I don't want to get your hopes up," Rebecca said, "but there's still a chance."

"What?"

"Oliveira is taking a group of men inside. He wants me to go with them as a guide. There's a transponder fixed to Ed's vest, and Oliveira intends to follow the signal. He might still be alive."

"Alive? *How*?"

"They took him inside the nest—paralysed, likely unconscious, but alive, I'm sure of it. I suspect the venom of the workers, or the web spiders, is less potent than that of the jumpers, because they use the web to tire and subdue their prey. Being so large they're also very strong, so they don't require a powerful toxin. When Priscilla was bitten, she showed no ill-effect, and generally primates are similarly affected. It gives us hope, however small."

"You said the bite on Priscilla might have been 'dry', because of how quickly it happened—that she probably didn't *get* envenomed. We can't hope for the same."

Rebecca drew a sharp breath. "It's our *only* hope."

There was a long pause. Eventually, Jessy said, "So how do you feel about going in?"

"Sorry?"

"You don't want to, do you?"

"I have to. I've got no choice."

"I can tell something's wrong."

As recently as a few hours ago, Rebecca would have shrugged off the comment and told Jessy everything was fine. Now, a part of her no longer wished to maintain the deception—not after everything that had happened. She opened her mouth, but hesitated. *We don't have time for this.*

Thinking better of it, she moved to leave, but Jessy reached out and clasped her hand. She could have pulled away, but something held her back, something other than Jessy's hand, and suddenly, tears stung her eyes. Again, her mouth opened, and then she heard a voice that surely wasn't hers. "You're right, something *is* wrong."

"Are you worried about what you'll find in there?"

"Yes, but it's more complicated than that. I'm not sure I can do this."

Jessy frowned, not quite comprehending. "But you're the most qualified of all of us. If anyone can do it…"

"You don't understand," Rebecca said, and again, she readied to leave, but didn't. "I don't know how, or why, but when those spiders attacked the day before yesterday, and then again last night, I froze, both times."

"All of us were scared. It's understandable…"

"No—I had a panic attack." The words came now in a rush, spilling, unstoppable, and as they did, a wave of intense relief washed over her. She realised that subconsciously at least, she'd craved this all along, had yearned for the subject to be openly confronted. But even as she felt a glorious weight lifting from her shoulders, in counterbalance remained a troubling uncertainty.

It's out of the bag. You need to face it.

She looked at Jessy. "When I was a kid, I suffered a crippling fear of spiders."

Jessy's eyes widened. "What?"

"With treatment, I overcame it. But last night… something triggered. My heart raced. I couldn't breathe. All the classic signs, just like when I was a child. It was as if the disorder hadn't disappeared but had simply lain dormant, just below the surface…"

Stunned, Jessy squeezed Rebecca's hand.

"I don't know if I can physically do this," Rebecca said. "I'm afraid that once inside, I'll freeze again. I'm afraid that if I come face to face with one of them, it might be worse than it was two days ago, and last night. What if it fully takes hold of me? I'll be no good to anyone. In fact, I'll be a liability—to myself, to Ed. *That's* what I'm worried about."

For a moment, Jessy seemed lost for words. "Bec, I'm astounded," she said eventually. "I can't imagine what you went through as a child, or what you're going through now."

"I'm sorry to have dumped this on you."

Jessy squeezed Rebecca's hand firmly. "Bec, you're confused and angry, because this fear is casting a shadow over all you've become, and you're blaming yourself for somehow letting it in. It's understandable." She shook her head gently. "But this isn't your fault. This isn't something you can control. You haven't done anything wrong. Once you get inside the pyramid, you'll do what you need to do. You'll overcome this. You'll get the job done."

"I don't know."

"Bec… you'll do it for *Ed*." She paused and then said softly, "He still loves you."

Rebecca had been looking down at her lap, but at Jessy's last words her gaze snapped up. "What are you talking about?"

"I can tell. You mean a lot to him."

Rebecca shook her head. "There's been a lot of water under the bridge, Jess. He might love me as a friend, but what we had is finished now. We're mates. That's it." Rebecca picked at a stray thread on her sleeve, unwilling to look Jessy in the eye. She wasn't being entirely truthful, but couldn't be certain of her own feelings, let alone Ed's. She suddenly felt ashamed she'd allowed Jessy to comfort her when, given the circumstances, it should have been the other way around. Hurriedly, she said, "I get the feeling you mean more to Ed than either of you realises. Once this is over, you'll both know it. Just wait and see."

Jessy's eyes warmed at the comment, as though she'd been craving acknowledgement for some time. Rebecca felt a rush of guilt. She hoped she hadn't spoken out of line.

"Don't tease me," Jessy warned playfully, but she was beaming, and beneath the smile was the most genuine look of promise Rebecca had seen in as long as she could remember. It was so affecting it sparked something in her. She came to a realisation: it was clear, crystallised, focused.

None of this matters—Ed's feelings, yours, Jessy's—none of it. You have one objective and one only.

Rebecca straightened. "I'll get him back, Jess."

Jessy just kept smiling.

Rebecca took a gulp of water from her canteen before unzipping the First-Aid kit. She felt buoyed by a fresh infusion of purpose. "How's the leg?"

"Sore and itchy." Jessy shook her head. "I just need to get out of this goddamned tent. The sooner I do that, the better."

Rebecca smiled faintly and passed her some aspirin. The dressing on Jessy's leg needed no immediate attention, so she checked Priscilla's wound and changed her bandages. Thankfully, the bleeding had stopped. The lacerations mightn't have been as deep as she'd thought.

Once she'd finished, she dabbed antiseptic cream on her own sores, then lifted Priscilla and clutched her to her chest. "You've been so good, haven't you, young lady?" She turned to Jessy. "Look after this girl, won't you? She shouldn't be a problem—she'll nap most of the time. You may need to change the dressing. Oh, and she likes a slice of apple every now and then. It's her favourite."

Jessy smiled. "Don't you worry about us—we might be a couple of invalids, but we'll look out for each other." She tossed her head at Priscilla. "You've taken quite a shine to her, Bec, for someone who's never owned so much as a goldfish."

Rebecca smiled too and patted Priscilla gently on the head. The tiny monkey hobbled up to her shoulder and settled in with her arms around Rebecca's neck.

Soon enough, Jessy's mood turned grave again. "It's been almost two days now since the boys left. Something bad has happened."

"We don't know that," Rebecca said. "Robert knows what he's doing. Ed said the rain would have held them up. And the chopper… who knows how long it'd take to get one out here? It could take days to mount a proper rescue."

Jessy's voice sank almost to a whisper. "Chopper or no chopper, you realise we need to be out of here by nightfall."

Rebecca nodded.

"You have to be quick, Bec. You need to get in and out—*fast*. We both know they're coming again, and we both know it'll be worse this time. There won't be any second chances, no last-minute rescues. If you're not back before dark—"

"I'll be back before dark, don't you worry. And then the three of us will find some way out of here. You, me, and Ed—together."

"Do you really think he's alive?"

"Yeah, I do."

Jessy offered Rebecca some last-minute advice, explaining in general terms the potential layout of the pyramid and what could be expected.

They hugged warmly. After all they'd endured, Rebecca sensed a bond forming between them. She was glad for it. "You hang in there, okay? I'll be back."

Jessy held up a hand in goodbye. "I'm counting on it."

55

Rebecca stepped from the cave's entrance deep in thought, Jessy's warning about being back by dark resounding ominously in her head.

Jessy was right, of course—Rebecca had reached the same conclusion. The spiders were aware of them, no doubt, and the intensity of the encounters had escalated over the previous two evenings. Should she and Jessy be caught out here again, the consequences would be dire. They couldn't take that chance.

No matter what, they had to be gone by nightfall.

She was so deep in thought she failed to notice that the two guards normally posted in front of the cave had disappeared. She also missed the large figure approaching from the other side of the cave's entrance.

"Well, well, well," De Sousa said, catching her as they collided. "I knew you'd come running into my arms."

Rebecca struggled in his grip. "Let go of me!"

De Sousa covered her mouth with one huge hand, muffling her cries. His other hand cuffed both of her wrists, his fingers like clamps.

"Easy," he said, his voice low. He glanced about as though ensuring they were alone, and Rebecca wondered if De Sousa himself had dismissed the guards. Yanking her sideways, he pulled her around the side of the huge dead tree that was the cave. *Out of sight.*

A wave of panic overcame her, and she thrashed. But De Sousa was far too strong. She tried to scream, but he clamped his hand even harder across her mouth.

"Shh!" De Sousa pulled her near. "What is wrong? I do not mean you any harm."

Rebecca flailed, but she was like a child in the hands of a giant. De Sousa didn't seem to notice her exertions.

Again, he glanced about. "Come now, *moca*," he said, "I am not that bad. We simply got off—how do you say—on the wrong foot. I did not intend injury to your pet. Let us make up and start over."

Rebecca kicked out hard, catching him in the groin with her right foot. Reflexively, De Sousa released her.

Immediately realising his error, De Sousa lunged, but before he could grab her again, she was out of reach, beating a hasty retreat through the bushes.

He didn't come after her but called out as she ran. "*Moca,* if I cannot have *you*, then maybe I can find someone more accommodating?"

Rebecca ran across the clearing, her skin crawling. De Sousa didn't follow, and she paused to compose herself. Looking up, she saw Oliveira and Asensi enter the campsite from the path that led to the north-western vantage point. She ran to them.

"*I need to speak with you*," she said to Oliveira, shaking so badly her teeth clattered. "*Alone*."

Asensi grinned at Oliveira, who returned the smile before dismissing him. When Asensi had gone, Rebecca stepped in close. No-one else was within earshot. "De Sousa. Is he going in with us?"

"What?"

"De Sousa—is he entering the pyramid, or staying behind? He's staying, isn't he? I can tell. Well, just now the psycho attacked me, and threatened to harm Jessy. He knows he can do it, too, while we're in there, in the nest, without you around—"

"Listen to me—"

"No! *You* listen to *me*! I'll do whatever you need in there, assist however I can, but I need to know that asshole is under control! If he's not, and we get out of there alive and I find out he's hurt her in any way, I'll make sure you regret it. I want your word on this, or you can forget about me going inside. *Do we have an agreement?*"

Oliveira paused. "*Senhorita*, she will be safe. You have my word."

"Good," Rebecca said, still shaking. She turned to leave, but Oliveira seized her arm. Leaning close, he lifted his sunglasses for the first time to reveal a pair of ice-blue eyes, startling and unusual for his complexion. They bored into her, their intensity as arresting and irresistible as his grip on her arm. He spoke in a low, controlled manner, so low it was almost a whisper. She had to strain to hear him.

"You have my word, as promised," he said. "But trust me, if you believe yourself in a position again that you would strike deals or make demands of me, I will take you myself and feed you to those things in that web down there. This is not a game, and I am not one to be toyed with. Remember who is in charge, and do not forget it, or it is you who will regret it. Now, *senhorita*, do *we* have an agreement?"

It wasn't the reaction she'd expected. Until that moment, she'd thought Oliveira reasonable, approachable, even decent. But now it hit her with crystal-clear intensity, and she couldn't believe she'd been so foolish. She'd lost sight of her standing in all of this. What had she been thinking? These people weren't to be taken lightly, much less dictated to. Oliveira and his men were criminals. Who knew what they were capable of, what they might do, especially if pushed? They followed no rules outside of their own, and that she'd bargain on anything to the contrary was absurd. She and Jessy were prisoners. She had to remember that. In fact, at the end of all this, if Oliveira didn't finish them off outright, he'd at best leave them here, on their own, no doubt to die alone in the jungle.

If there was *any* chance of getting out of this alive, she had to play it smarter.

Rebecca nodded, and Oliveira released her. "We leave in ten. Be ready."

She couldn't help herself and took off at a run, overcome with emotion. As she fled, she noticed De Sousa, who had obviously been watching the conversation, grinning at her.

"Be seeing you soon," he laughed as she disappeared, tears in her eyes.

56

Exactly ten minutes later, Rebecca stood at the trapdoor as Ed had less than two and a half hours previously, ready to enter the burrow. It was just after noon.

She'd pulled herself together, sternly reminding herself of what she had to do. She'd had a cry—a quick one—but that was it. She had to remove all emotion and steel herself for the task at hand. If Oliveira was going to use *her* to get into the nest, she'd use *him* in kind, to help her get to Ed. That was all she wanted, all she was focused on. The incidents with both men, even the conversation with Jessy, had brought her clarity.

In total, four men would accompany her inside: Oliveira, Luis, Asensi, and another younger man by the name of Costa. As she had feared, De Sousa would stay behind with the two men guarding Jessy. Since their arrival last night, Cartana had seemingly gone to ground. He'd stay, too.

Rebecca had wondered about having four men watch a single woman with a broken leg. Most likely, Oliveira wanted enough firepower to repel another attack. And for reasons of stealth, he probably wanted to enter the nest with limited numbers. It made sense. Maybe he'd even done the right thing by Jessy, too. Rebecca had noted how De Sousa had defied at least one order from Oliveira—the initial command to back down following the altercation involving her and Ed this morning—so maybe there was tension between the two she wasn't privy to. Maybe Oliveira *had* secretly ordered someone to keep watch on De Sousa, just as she had urged. She hoped that was the case. Still, the thought of leaving Jessy and Priscilla alone, especially with Jessy in such a helpless state, didn't sit comfortably. She'd urged Jessy to be vigilant, but there was little more she could do. Now, she had to focus on her own concerns.

Gathered around the trapdoor, Oliveira's men checked their weapons for the umpteenth time, boasting about what they would do if they should encounter any of the arachnids. Despite their bravado, Rebecca sensed they were uneasy.

She stepped next to Oliveira and nodded towards the device in Asensi's hand. "Will that work underground?"

Oliveira nodded. "It is military hardware, high-powered, designed for this kind of work. We can track the signal via satellite. Once we lose line of sight with the sky, we'll lose that reading, but the spread spectrum digital radio signal will kick in. The device also has an internal proximity detector. Not as accurate, perhaps only to within thirty yards, but adequate for the job."

"Good," Rebecca said. "I need to stress again the importance of keeping quiet. Five people will make noise. Too much, and they'll come for us. If they do sense us, they'll probably call for assistance, might tap the walls of the nest like ants to warn others of encroaching enemies. Or they might give off some sort of chemical signal, an alarm pheromone. Either way, if we're discovered, they'll swarm, they'll come in numbers. We need to be prepared."

"We will be." Oliveira motioned with his weapon, calling for Asensi to enter the burrow.

Rebecca stepped to the entrance and cut him off. With a deep breath, she said to Oliveira, "If it's all right with you, I'd like to go first."

Oliveira eyed her suspiciously.

"I need to," Rebecca said. "Please, trust me."

"As soon as we exit, I want Asensi on point."

Rebecca nodded, thanking him and moving to the trapdoor. "Could you leave the lid open? I want some light to filter down."

Kneeling slowly, Rebecca stared at the dark hole stretching into nothingness. She didn't like guns but wished to God she had one now. She felt clammy. Beads of sweat formed on her forehead, stung her eyes. "Boy, it's hot in there."

You're stalling. Get going. You can do this.

But she found it hard to move. Her heartrate increased. It was happening again, just as she had feared.

No…

She sensed movement behind her: Oliveira stepping impatiently to the hole.

JUST DO IT!

"Grab my ankles," she said to Luis, who was beside her. She leant forward and took a deep breath. Her heart pounded.

Ducking headfirst, she squeezed into the burrow.

She was in.

Oh God…

It was a tight fit, wider in girth than her shoulders, but only just. It was incredibly dark and smelled earthy, dank. Non-sticky silk lined the burrow's narrow circumference. Luis held her feet, supporting her weight so she could manoeuvre fully inside.

"Okay," she said. Her voice sounded muffled. "I'm in. You can let go."

Rebecca pushed, sliding down to where the tunnel bent parallel with the forest floor. There was barely enough room to move; her arms were pressed up beneath her chest, her upper body just off the ground. So restricted, she had grave doubts as to whether she'd be able to propel herself along. How had Ed managed it, and with all his gear on?

An image of the sentry dragging Enrique backwards through the tight space hit her with full force.

She pushed it from her mind.

Ahead, it was pitch-black, her body blocking the light from above. Rebecca slid the NVGs over her eyes and activated the IR illuminator. The burrow came into focus, shaded in green. Without delay, she pulled forward, her forearms and elbows taking the strain. To her surprise, she moved. She repeated the process and inched deeper, wriggling forward on her belly. She felt like a caterpillar burrowing into the earth.

Before long, she heard the others clambering in behind her. She shuffled forward, making room. Soon the entire group was inside, the four men joining her in a bizarre conga-line.

No turning back, she thought.

Don't get distracted. Just keep moving.

But even that wasn't easy. Her lungs laboured, as though the air had turned to syrup. The humidity pawed at her face like an invisible hand. Rebecca pulled forward. Already, her arms hurt.

The first stab of claustrophobia came only minutes later. At first, it wasn't overt, more a vague, smothery feeling. Then, slowly, everything closed in around her, the burrow shrinking before her eyes. She blinked, steadied her breathing.

Deal with it.

She kept moving.

But it got worse, and with it came something else, something that tingled her spine and nearly made her cry out in fear.

It was only an image, coming for her in her mind's eye, but it was terrifyingly real. Fangs bared, forelegs raised, it scurried up the tunnel towards her, not once, but several times, playing in her head like film running in an endless loop.

Gotta get a grip…

Despite the heat, Rebecca shivered, and wriggled deeper into the burrow.

57

Light struggled through the dark—faint, but he sensed its reddish hue through his eyelids and felt its warmth on his skin.

Gradually, his eyes opened, but only to slits. They were heavy and sore, and the thin ray of sunlight that had fallen directly on his face and roused him was painfully bright. Beyond it, he could feel a heavy blanket of darkness.

Avoiding the light, squinting through the gloom, he turned his head. It hurt to do so, and he shut his eyes again as a wave of nausea washed over him. When the feeling had passed, he opened his eyes once more, but this time he kept his head still, waiting for his vision to adjust. While it did, other senses kicked in like systems in a computer booting up, and his nostrils flared. The air, dank and stale, was laced with a smell that was difficult to place: thick, heavy, animal-like. It was hard to breathe.

He was sitting. His legs were spread wide, and his arms were raised above his head. He couldn't budge any of them and figured they were bound somehow, though he couldn't crane his neck to see what by. A tingling sensation thrummed through his body, as though the blood flow to his extremities had been blocked and they'd fallen asleep. He tried to stand but couldn't move.

His eyes adjusted. Was he in a room of some kind? There were shapes around him, but they were formless, unidentifiable.

What is this place? What am I doing here?

He felt as though he'd woken from a deep sleep. Maybe a coma. Maybe he'd been out for days.

He shifted his gaze. Motes of dust swirled through the beam of light, which he followed to the dusty, stone floor. Framed by the light was an object—a backpack—and scattered along the ground, disgorged in a trail, were its innards: flares, a radio, something unrecognisable.

He willed his hand towards them and felt some movement in his bindings, but the effort drained him, and he slumped forward.

He decided to summon the strength for another attempt, and as he did—out of nowhere and for no apparent reason—an image formed hazily in his mind's eye: a woman's face, a beautiful, dark-haired woman with green eyes. She was smiling at him, but then suddenly her eyes grew wide—

A shuffling sound nearby, something brushing lightly against the stone. It was near, and large. Too large, he knew, for a scurrying rat.

He peered into the murk, and when the sound came again, the darkness itself shifted before him, a black shadow moving in his direction, and now he could make it out.

It was no rat.

The creature was monstrous, more than a yard across, closer to two, and it crept towards him purposefully, hypnotically almost, its legs rising and falling in perfect synchronicity. He tried to cry out, scream, but couldn't—his mouth was dry and parched—and as he searched the area desperately, he saw something else, too. Just off to the right of the advancing spider, stuck up against the wall, off the ground, floating in a sea of silk. He hadn't seen it earlier, before his eyes had adjusted.

A jaguar.

Frozen in time, it was curled into a ball—claws bared, jaws wide open in what might have been a soundless roar of defiance… or an agonised cry of fear.

They had killed a jaguar…

As he watched, horrified, a spider the size of a man's fist crawled unhurried out of the animal's open mouth, as though deliberately mocking the once-proud beast. Slowly, it moved back over the cat's face…

…to join the rest of the writhing mass of spiders—*baby* spiders each the size of a saucer—crawling over its body.

The jaguar was covered in a mass of feeding, baby spiders.

Again, he struggled, realising his fate. He too was caught in a web, bound and restrained like the jaguar.

The huge spider was by now almost upon him, just a few yards away. She rotated on the spot so that her abdomen faced him. He knew it was a she, because over the rear of her body crawled *dozens* of spiderlings.

Her babies.

She wasn't the threat—*they* were.

Just like those consuming the jaguar they were by normal standards large, each the size of a regular tarantula, with abdomens resembling—and at least as big as—a kiwi fruit.

And there were so many. They scrambled over each other, such an incredible mass of them it looked as though they were erupting from somewhere within the female, pouring and spewing across the floor as though she was giving birth to an endless wave.

They came at him.

Panicking, trying desperately to escape, he pulled his right arm free of the web. Yet with no strength to keep it vertical, it fell straight to the floor, hard.

He felt something beneath his fingertips.

…the spiderlings came, skittered across the floor towards him like an unrolling black carpet…

He moved his fingers. His hand had hit down on an object resting on the ground. Subconsciously, he realised there was something he had to do with it. Eyes focused on the advancing spiders, barely registering his own actions, he worked quickly. His stiffened fingers fumbled, but at last he managed to lift the switch. Hand shaking, he slid it right, pushing forward the breaking tab.

A beeping sound came to his ears, indicating the device was now operational.

He'd turned it on.

For whatever reason, he knew that was what he had to do, was what he was *meant* to do, and he'd done it. He'd initiated the device.

With that, he slumped forward, his energy at last depleted, and closed his eyes.

The spiderlings came at him like a horrible black wave.

58

Sanchez couldn't see a thing. It wasn't that his eyes, still burning from the volley of stinging hairs, had betrayed him. It was simply because the cave running off the pit was utterly devoid of light. The meagre amount that had filtered through the pit-cover had dissipated long ago, and now, he couldn't see his hand in front of his face.

This was madness.

He had no idea how long he'd persisted, stumbling along blindly with Owen over his shoulder, but he had to turn back. Earlier, with no other recourse left him, the plan to venture in here had seemed viable. His only other option had been to climb the pit wall, somehow getting Owen up with him and then evading the frenzied Yuguruppu whom he could still hear celebrating above. With an injured shoulder he'd thought it impossible, but what choice did he have now? To continue was pointless. And suicidal.

He considered again the lighter in his pocket. It was almost empty. He'd intended on saving what little there was but moving blindly meant he'd eventually blunder into a web, or another of the jumpers would leap through the blackness to attack. Either event would be deadly; he didn't possess the energy to escape or resist.

As unrealistic as it sounded, he had to return to the pit and climb out.

He was turning around when his dragging feet hit something on the ground, and Sanchez stumbled and fell to the cave floor. Owen crashed down with him, moaning with the impact.

"Sorry, *amigo*," Sanchez said, untangling. He grimaced and put a hand to his injured left shoulder as a bolt of fiery pain seared through it.

He did his best to ignore it. What had he tripped over?

He reached into the darkness, groping the object at his feet. It felt like…

Sanchez scrambled for the lighter, deciding that *now* he could spare a small amount of fuel…

The tiny flame leapt to life, and Sanchez saw immediately the object that had caused him to stumble.

A knapsack.

What the hell? He lifted it, strands of silk that had affixed it to the cave floor coming away like pizza-cheese. It was black, compact, and made of good-quality nylon. And it was heavy.

Baffled, Sanchez reached for the opening, unzipped the pack, and up-ended it. A flood of objects fell through the light onto the ground: a bloated, yellowed notepad, pencil in the spine; a pair of reading glasses in a hard case; a small steel can with no label, coated in rust; a beige-coloured cloth cap, heavily sweat-stained, with a flap of material at the back to protect the wearer's neck from the sun.

Sanchez frowned.

There were a few other items, most of them blackened and unidentifiable and covered in mould, perhaps foodstuffs of some kind, their damaged packaging having exposed the contents to the air. He rummaged through them, ensuring there was nothing he'd missed.

There was still weight in the pack, something else inside it.

Sanchez felt around, found a zippered pouch at the front, and undid it. He reached in and pulled out the item, holding it close to the light.

A shiny, metallic canister.

He shook it, and liquid sloshed about. It was a hip flask, silver-plated judging by the tarnished exterior. He noticed an inscription engraved on the front and wiped away the dust to read it.

I. R.

A LITTLE SOMETHING SURE TO HOLD YOUR SINGLE MALT AS DEARLY AS YOU!

CONGRATULATIONS AND BEST WISHES ON YOUR NEW POSTING

FROM ALL THE FACULTY AND STAFF

DEPARTMENT OF SOCIAL ANTHROPOLOGY

UNIVERSITY OF CAMBRIDGE

IT WON'T BE THE SAME WITHOUT YOU!

Unbelievable!

Sanchez recognised the initials. The flask—and knapsack—was the property of *Irving Rosenlund*, Owen's former colleague at FUNAI. This was incredible! It was one of Rosenlund's field diaries that had mysteriously come into Owen's possession, along with the old hand-marked military map he and Ed had followed to S1. But Rosenlund had mysteriously disappeared and was presumed dead.

It was now obvious what had transpired. Rosenlund had been sacrificed—just like he and Owen had been. Maybe he'd offended the Yuguruppu and they'd reacted violently, catching him by surprise. It would explain why he still had his knapsack with him.

Sanchez felt a pang of empathy but didn't linger. He refilled the pack and slung it, and then unscrewed the cap of the flask. He took a whiff. Scotch Whiskey? He swigged, grimacing, and offered some to Owen, but was careful to preserve a small amount. From the knapsack, he retrieved the cap and tore off the flap of material, binding it firmly around the spear. He doused it with the whiskey.

Perfect!

Sanchez took the lighter and touched the flame to the alcohol-soaked rag. It took hold with a *whump*, sending out a sphere of light much larger than that afforded by the lighter.

He wished immediately it hadn't.

Sanchez hadn't thought he'd see much of anything—certainly hadn't been prepared for the sight that *did* come to him, and any celebratory thoughts he may have had were cut dramatically short.

He spun with the torch, a sliver of ice coursing down his spine, the hairs on his neck prickling instantly.

Surrounding him on all sides—staring back at him with their cold, dark eyes—were *dozens* of jumpers.

They leered at the edge of the light, a horde of arachnid faces. Gazing, watching.

Row upon row, some no more than a few feet away, above him, beside him, behind him, clinging to the web lining the ceiling, and both walls of the cave.

They were everywhere.

Sanchez waited for death, hoped it would come quickly.

But the spiders didn't move. They simply stared.

What were they waiting for?

Then, he realised.

You're kidding me…

They weren't alive.

Dead? All of them?

No. Not dead. Something else.

Slowly, Sanchez raised the torch.

Exoskeletons. Not *spiders*, but the old, rigid *skins* of spiders.

He released a breath. These were the casings routinely shed by young-sters or adolescents as they grew larger. He moved eye to eye with the closest specimen, amazed at how intact it was, how well it had maintained its shape and form. In every way, it was an exact duplicate of its former possessor.

He cast the torch about.

The skins weren't placed in a pattern. They looked random, discarded. Maybe the creatures came here to shed in safety.

As his heartbeat returned to normal, he looked closer at his surround-ings. He saw other things, objects on the ground in scattered piles, and in the web, too. Most he couldn't identify, but some, he realised, were bones. Animal bones, hundreds of them.

The cavern was a dumping ground. The spiders discarded their waste here. He was encouraged. If he was right, the cavern should be a long way from the heart of the nest.

Even so, the old skins hadn't yet decomposed. They were fresh. Obvi-ously, the arachnids came here regularly.

Sanchez scanned the gloom. Now that he had light, he didn't need to return to the pit and could stick with his original plan. On the far side of the cavern, at the edge of the light, he discerned the faint outline of an exit opening into more blackness.

Heaving Owen, he made for it, passing through the gallery of faces staring back at him with their blank, lifeless eyes.

59

It was little wonder it had taken Ed so long to emerge from the burrow—it seemed endless. Rebecca saw by the luminous hands of her watch that it was near on one o'clock. Ed had emerged after forty minutes. Rebecca's group had been at it for just over fifty, and still, there was no end in sight.

We must be close.

Thankfully, much of the journey had been downhill. In fact, the angle of the descent had been surprisingly acute. No doubt, they had been moving with the contour of the bowl, working their way down the steep depression and beneath the web. Only recently had the burrow levelled out again. She was sure they were now somewhere beneath the pyramid.

Behind her, the sound of the others inching along echoed in her ears, reverberating in the burrow's narrow confines. She hoped it wasn't enough to cause an investigation. The vision of the sentry still haunted her, and the thought of the real thing…

She checked her watch again. It wouldn't be long.

60

Jessy lay staring at the tent's ceiling, Priscilla curled up in a ball and sleeping soundly beside her.

She couldn't quiet her mind, couldn't stop thinking about all that had happened. Mainly, she couldn't stop thinking about Ed and what had happened to *him*. God, why? Not knowing if she should start grieving, or perhaps dare hope for his return, was more than she could bear. She missed him desperately, felt painfully alone.

This can't be real…

About half an hour ago, it had fallen unusually quiet outside, but suddenly, voices drifted to her from the cave's entrance. Someone was speaking with the two guards out front, but she couldn't make out the words. Footsteps followed—two pairs retreating into the distance. After a moment of silence, a rustling sound disturbed the air not two feet away, on the other side of the tent flap.

Jessy sat upright.

Oh no…

Despite the heat, she'd pulled the zip down tight, but now it crawled slowly, inexorably, upwards.

"Who's there?" She tried to sound calm. Surreptitiously, she reached her hand around to slip it under the duffel bag she'd been using as a pillow.

De Sousa stuck his head inside the tent. "Just checking, *moca*, I did not mean to alarm you." He grinned at her. "So, how are you? Anything I can do?"

Beneath the duffel bag, Jessy's fingers slipped around the scissors from the First-Aid kit that Rebecca had earlier sneaked into her tent. "No, thank you." Her throat was dry.

With only his head inside the tent, De Sousa looked her up and down, appraising her. "I disagree, *moca*. I am sure there is *something* I can do." His grin widened, and he made to enter.

Jessy was about to pull the scissors when a voice cut loud and clear through the afternoon heat. De Sousa paused, turned to it. He seemed annoyed. For the moment, Jessy's hand remained hidden.

The voice came again, in Portuguese. Closer now. Just outside the tent.

The muscles around De Sousa's jaw tightened. "I'll be back, *moca*. Don't go anywhere."

He contemplated her again, laughed, and then backed from the tent and disappeared.

Jessy didn't move. Her heart raced at a million miles an hour. Not far from the tent, De Sousa and another of the men—Cartana, perhaps—spoke in rapid fire Portuguese. She didn't think the guards had returned.

She waited, listening, not moving a muscle until she heard the pair retreat, still in conversation. She then lunged for the zip and pulled it down hard.

Her hands shook, and her eyes stung with tears. *Shit!* She had to get out of here. *Now*. She looked about. Could she move with one leg in a splint? She had to. She'd take her chances in the jungle.

She made for the door… but was too late.

The guards returned, talking and laughing, the acrid smell of cigarette smoke wafting into the tent.

No!

What now? Seconds became minutes. De Sousa didn't return, but her terror grew.

He'll come back eventually. I need to get out of here.

The guards fell silent. Jessy decided to peek outside. Maybe she could sneak past them, create a diversion of some kind. She reached for the zip.

A succession of strange sounds made her jump, and she jerked her hand away sharply.

Quick, dull popping sounds, maybe four in total, just outside the cave's entrance. Half a second later, louder sounds: something hitting the ground?

What the hell?

Jessy stilled, her hand an inch from the zip.

"Hello?" she called cautiously, immediately wishing she'd kept her mouth shut. She got no answer in any case, just the insects chirping in the heat. A couple of birds flew into the clearing, shrieking noisily, and faded into the distance.

Hesitantly, Jessy reached for the zip and raised it quietly, peering beyond the cave's wide entrance.

Both guards were there, out the front, as expected. But neither was standing, and they weren't napping, either.

One of the bodies lay pressed against the flared base of the cave: she could see half of it—the left arm, the left leg—protruding into the dead tree's entrance. Next to it, sprawled on its back like a discarded doll, lay the other body. She could see that in its entirety.

Jessy raised a hand to her mouth. "Oh my God." Her heart skipped a beat, and she ducked back behind the tent flap. The two guards were *dead*. How? De Sousa?

Her thoughts galloped. After a moment, she stuck her head out for another look.

She missed him on the first pass: he was almost imperceptible against the dark foliage. It was only as his voice called across the clearing that she refocused and picked him out.

"*Pare imediatamente! Qual é o seu nome?*"

It wasn't De Sousa.

He was about twenty feet away, on one knee, dressed in jungle fatigues, face streaked in broken shades of black, brown and green, perfectly camouflaged with the surrounding vegetation.

Motionless, he looked directly at her, the barrel of his weapon trained at the bridge of her nose.

Jessy froze, her gaze sweeping the length of the weapon to the figure's own head, and the unique, round, flat cap, olive-green in colour, sitting atop it. A flash at the front of it bore some sort of crest or emblem, yellow in colour.

She knew who wore such a distinctive garment.

Raising her hands, palms out, Jessy said, "Wait, don't shoot! I'm American!"

She understood the meaning of a green beret.

The US Army Special Forces soldier slowly lowered his weapon, looking her up and down before turning his head into the clearing.

"Captain!" he called across it. "I think you better get over here."

61

They'd reached the end of the burrow. Its dark outline—an oval on its side—lay just ahead, maybe fifteen feet away.

Rebecca slowed and drew herself up quietly. She inched her head into the cross-tunnel beyond.

As Ed had suggested, the tunnel was indeed man-made. Unlike the earthen burrow, it was constructed of large, stone bricks cobbled together. It looked high enough for her to stand. It, too, was lined in non-sticky silk.

Rebecca looked left and right. Both directions extended into deeper blackness, disappearing beyond the range of her goggles' IR illuminator. It was deathly quiet.

Gripping the edge of the opening, Rebecca slid awkwardly into the tunnel. Jumping to her feet, she checked both ways again before brushing herself off. It was a relief to be free of the hole and standing once more, although her legs felt like jelly. She pumped them to get the circulation going before helping the others from the burrow.

"You got a reading?" she whispered to Asensi, the first to exit behind her. A foul smell, like stagnant water, hung in the air, thick and suffocating. It was hard to breathe, let alone speak.

Striking an infrared flare, Asensi consulted the receiver in his other hand. "Faint, but *si*, this way." He pointed off *through* the tunnel wall, in a south-easterly direction.

Soon, the rest of them had exited, too. "We've got a signal," Rebecca said to Oliveira. "As we thought, we need to go south. Down there." She jutted her chin to the right. The floor sloped away gently, downhill and out of sight. The impenetrable blackness beyond was unsettling, foreboding. Once again, Rebecca felt a chill pass through her, despite the humidity.

Ignoring her, Oliveira touched a hand lightly to the wall. After inspecting it closely he knelt and cast his gaze along the floor in both directions.

"This tunnel must have been constructed at the same time as the pyramid," Rebecca told him quietly. "Jess thinks it's an access passage, probably to a subterranean chamber—"

"Something has recently been through here," Oliveira interrupted, raising an index finger to his lips. "Here… look at these drag marks." He stood, facing south before moving past her, waving to his men.

Rebecca glanced to where he had indicated, searching the barely visible scuff marks in the dust at her feet. As she did, Oliveira whispered back to her without turning. "We should get moving, *senhorita*. South, as you say."

Already, Asensi had moved to point. While he would lead from the front, Luis, who was carrying the second FH-9 flamethrower, would bring up the rear.

Rebecca didn't have to be told twice. Obediently, she slotted in behind Asensi as Oliveira addressed the group. "From now on," he whispered, "we keep the talk to a minimum. Single file, nice and easy, no sound." He nodded at Asensi, who set off. As Rebecca moved to join him, Oliveira caught her by the arm, halting her. "Best you keep your eyes peeled, too, *senhorita*. They are about—I can feel it."

He released her, urging her forward, and with his words ringing ominously in her ears, Rebecca turned without comment and followed Asensi deeper into the blackness.

62

It seemed to Jessy that Captain John T. Aronsohn was the kind of guy who liked to do things by the book.

She could tell by the way he held himself, the way he talked. He had a habit, she noted, of punctuating his sentences to pause thoughtfully over his words, and she doubted he ever said anything without weighing it in line with standard procedure. Not that she had an issue with that—in fact, she was over the moon about it. He was obviously level-headed, in control.

And his actions had most likely saved her life.

Jessy guessed the Green Beret leader was only marginally older than her—thirty, tops—but he seemed mature beyond his years. Of average height, he was lean and broad-shouldered, with close-cropped, dark brown hair. Although masked by camouflage make-up, his face was scarred, the skin pock-marked, though it didn't detract from his appearance, and she found him quite good-looking. She was even more taken by his eyes: dark and knowing, *understanding*. His was an experienced, worldly face, in contrast to that of the young soldier who'd found her.

When she'd followed Sergeant McGinley's fresh-faced gaze into the clearing, Jessy had been amazed to find up to a dozen soldiers staring back at her. Aronsohn had signalled for his men to establish a perimeter, and upon learning of her injury, called for a medic. She'd been brought gently from the tent to a chair beneath the tarpaulin where the medic had knelt to attend her leg—redressing it, injecting her with painkillers and antibiotics and God knew what else. It seemed only when Aronsohn had felt secure had he spoken to her directly, crouching beside the medic and giving her his name and rank before questioning who she was, and what she was doing here.

Beaming, Jessy had introduced herself, but not before embracing Aronsohn tightly. "Thank God you came! I'm surprised you found us though. I guess Robert must have given you the co-ordinates—"

Aronsohn held up a hand. "Ma'am—just a second. What say we back it up a little—start over, nice and slow."

Jessy frowned. "Sorry?"

Aronsohn paused again, cleared his throat. "Ma'am, I'm not sure who you think we are, but there's obviously been a misunderstanding. We weren't looking specifically for *you* at all. To be honest… we had no idea you were here."

Jessy hesitated, perplexed. "Then just what *are* you doing here?"

Aronsohn glanced across the clearing and back again. "I'm not at liberty to divulge that, but I *can* say there's an operation in this area." He asked her once more why *she* was here, but Jessy's attention was drawn away as two of Aronsohn's men came in to remove the poncho-covered bodies of the guards still lying on the ground in front of the cave.

"How many did you see?" She nodded at the dead men. "What about the others?"

"The others?"

"The other two. There are two more of them."

Aronsohn narrowed his eyes and with a series of quick hand signals waved his second-in-command to the edge of the clearing. "Wit, secure it," he mouthed.

"And there's four more," Jessy informed him, "with two of my friends, inside the pyramid."

At that, Aronsohn froze. Slowly, he turned back to her. "*What pyramid?*"

63

Rebecca thought it strange.

There'd been no junctions or cross-tunnels, no chambers or passage-ways feeding off the main shaft—nothing at all. She recalled how Ed had said there was nothing on the way up, either, just the one, long passageway.

Why was that?

They'd been following the foul-smelling, stone-hewn tunnel for several minutes now. It was impossible to tell how deep they were beneath the pyramid. Not that it mattered. Asensi, with no option, had continued to lead them deeper, having long-since put away the receiver in favour of his Kalashnikov.

Fortunately, the weapon hadn't been needed. Despite Oliveira's warning, they hadn't encountered any spiders, or noticed any other burrows. But Rebecca wasn't complacent. The tunnel itself wasn't part of the nest proper. That lay ahead. This was just a means of access. Getting carried away with what was a relatively easy entry would be premature at best.

They kept moving, silently following the passageway deeper.

64

⚡

Jessy waited for Aronsohn to find the right words. When he had, they passed his lips as little more than a breathless mutter.

Of the twelve-man team, half were still searching for De Sousa and Cartana. Two had stayed behind to guard the camp. The remaining three had accompanied Jessy and Aronsohn to the north-western vantage point, two of them transporting Jessy on a stretcher between them.

And while it was the pyramid they had come to investigate, Jessy guessed it wasn't the sight of *it* that had them so awestruck, more the huge web surrounding it.

"*Jesus H. Christ,*" McGinley said. "*What the fuck?*"

It was the first time since the attack the day before yesterday that Jessy had herself laid eyes on the pyramid. No spiders were apparent. Had any of the creatures been moving about, she guessed the soldiers would have reacted with even greater incredulity.

Scanning the structure, she was overcome with a sudden rush of longing for Ed. It was so overwhelming she would have burst into tears had a rustling sound behind her not severed her thoughts. She spun as one of the soldiers surged from the bushes: Wittenberg, Aronsohn's second-in-command. He was a tall man, thin-faced and whippet-like.

"*Holy shit…*" he said, his gaze on the web.

Aronsohn turned to him, but Wittenberg said nothing more, standing there with his mouth ajar. "*Wit!*"

Wittenberg blinked. "Sorry, sir. It's just that…"

"Tell me about it."

The younger soldier refocused, shaking his head like a boxer in a daze. "Captain, we couldn't find anyone. Not a trace. If there were men out there, they're gone now."

Jessy baulked, a cold dread running through her. "Captain—"

"Keep searching," Aronsohn said to Wittenberg, who nodded and disappeared. Turning to Jessy, his expression softened. "Don't worry, we'll find them. In the meantime—"

"Sir—I've got confirmation." The young, dark-skinned soldier was Harper, one of the men who had accompanied them down here. He was kneeling on the ground a few feet away, in front of the blind, punching commands into a ruggedised laptop. He turned to them with a satisfied grin. "406 MHz beacon, 5-watt signal. That's it, all right."

Jessy hesitated. *Signal? What did he mean by that? Was there a signal coming from inside the pyramid?*

Aronsohn's expression remained indifferent as he turned to Harper. "Keep on it. Find out what you can. And while you're at it, jump back on the horn—get us an update on that medevac." Harper nodded as Aronsohn turned back to Jessy. "Okay, ma'am, I think it's time we got you out of here, hey? We're bringing in a chopper, so we can get you to a hospital." He seemed more urgent now, and glanced again at both the pyramid, and the huge web. "But as I was about to say a moment ago, *in the meantime,* I think you and I need to have a chat."

It didn't take long to get him up to speed. Throughout the briefing Aronsohn sat quietly on the buttress root of a large kapok, listening without any show of emotion.

Now, at the end of it, he leant back and ran his hand across his forehead to catch the sweat. "Quite a story," he said. His manner was less formal than before.

Jessy nodded. She was surprised at how readily he could accept it.

"And your two friends are in there as we speak? Inside the pyramid?"

"We can't leave without them."

"No, I don't intend to. What about the other pair—the two who returned to Base Camp?"

"I don't know what's happened to them, or how to contact them."

"We'll work something out."

After a long pause, Jessy said, "So why did you kill those men?" She leant closer. "And what was Harper talking about? He said there was a signal."

For a moment, it seemed Aronsohn hadn't heard her, but at last he opened his mouth, his tone official again. "I can't tell you the specifics. What I *can* say is we were on the trail of people known to us. We were following them when we detected something else, a distress signal. We detoured, tracked it to this vicinity, only to pick up the trail heading into your camp, which is why we ended up there first, rather than here. Now we know the signal we were following is coming from inside that pyramid. Your friends, I presume."

Jessy could only assume so, too, but wasn't sure if the presence of a distress signal was good news or bad. She was also confused as to *how* a signal could have been sent in the first place.

She looked at Aronsohn, remembering Ed's comment about the US government clamping down on the thriving cocaine trade by actively harassing drug traffickers from the sky. She presumed the CIA, DEA, or maybe the Air Force or State Department were tasked with this. Ed had said that as a result, the drug cartels had been forced to alter their modes of operation, and so now, increasingly unable to smuggle contraband through the air, had resorted to carting it through the jungle, on foot. It stood to reason that to counter this, the US would need to alter its methods too, pursuing smugglers through the jungle, on foot. A counter-narcotics team would be ideal for such an operation. And why not? Who the hell knew what kind of covert ops were undertaken without public knowledge? It wouldn't have surprised her to learn that Aronsohn and his men were one such team, tasked with hunting down traffickers.

Yet if that were true, Aronsohn hadn't originally been hunting *Oliveira*, given he'd said they had 'detoured' to follow the distress signal. Furthermore, he'd had no idea of how many men had been guarding the camp. That they had killed the two guards seemed to indicate the mere presence of an armed and unauthorised force out here in the middle of nowhere was all Aronsohn required for a 'shoot-first-ask-questions-later' course of action. Again, who the hell knew *what* happened out in the real world?

Whatever the case, Jessy figured Aronsohn was unlikely to confirm her suspicions. She didn't pursue it further.

"One other thing," she said to him. "We think they're nocturnal, perhaps active in early twilight. That doesn't leave us much time."

"We'll make do," was all Aronsohn said in reply. He got up to leave, patting her on the knee. "I don't want you to worry anymore, okay? You're safe now. We'll have a chopper here in a couple of hours. Then we'll get you and your friends out of here."

With that, he smiled and disappeared. Jessy stared after him, and suddenly, she couldn't *help* but worry.

Had he even heard her, listened to what she had said? She glanced at her watch.

A couple of hours?

In a couple of hours, it'd be dark.

65

Several dozen yards beyond the opening Sanchez had found on the other side of the cavern, the passageway split in two.

He paused, hoisting Owen with his good arm, his left holding the torch before him.

Which way now?

He tried to focus. The two natural tunnels looked identical, and like everything down here, both were silk-lined. Sanchez hesitated. The last thing he wanted was to delve deeper into the caves—he needed a way *out*. But there was no telling which of the two options, if either, would get him there, and presumably, at least one would take him closer to the heart of the nest.

This was a problem.

Sanchez squinted and directed the torch down both shafts. His head swam, and his vision blurred. The venom surging through his bloodstream made it difficult to concentrate. Moments ago, he'd stopped to catch his breath and had popped coca leaves into his mouth to pep himself up. They'd had some effect, but he still felt light-headed.

Come on. Keep it together.

He heard something and spun the torch back to the tunnel on his right.

There! It came again, a faint breath of wind...

Sanchez watched as again, the torch flickered.

His hopes rising, he drew the flame back in the opposite direction, seeking a similar reaction from the passageway on the left. There was none.

Sanchez went right.

66

A couple of hours, Jessy thought.

This is going to be close.

She'd decided she'd be better off awaiting the chopper in more comfortable surroundings and had moved back to camp. She rested now in front of the cave with Priscilla clutched to her chest, patting her absently, deep in thought.

While overjoyed at their impending rescue, she was at the same time worried. Aronsohn had promised to help Rebecca, but he hadn't told Jessy how.

She had to get Rebecca a message.

"I need to lie down," Jessy called out to the two soldiers who had been tasked with guarding the camp. Declining an offer of assistance, she let Priscilla jump down and scamper ahead before making her way to the cave mouth on the crutches the medic had crafted from sturdy branches. She'd appreciated the kind gesture, welcoming the new-found freedom, however limited. Now, at least, she could get up and stretch whenever she wanted. And as the painkillers had already kicked in, she could move without discomfort.

Jessy arrived at the cave mouth and paused there in the shadows. Hidden from view, she gave the soldiers time to conclude she was in her tent as claimed. Re-emerging, she hobbled as fast and as quietly as she was able, circumnavigating the huge tree. The corpses of the two dead guards were there, having been dragged out of sight.

Though she was herself out of view, Jessy worked quickly. The bodies—each of them draped in a khaki poncho—lay side by side amongst waist-high fernery. Jessy parted the vegetation, bending awkwardly and lifting the nearest poncho with one of her crutches. Controlling her repulsion, she reached under and patted the dead man's clothing. Just as she had hoped, the object was hidden inside one of his pockets, and she took it and slipped it into her shorts before sneaking back to her tent. She was certain she hadn't been seen.

Jessy presumed the comm radio would be set to the right frequency. Still, she had no intention of using it just yet. Rebecca wasn't carrying a radio herself, and so getting a message to her meant alerting Oliveira to the fact he'd lost the camp. His reaction to that, she was certain, wouldn't be favourable. More than that, Aronsohn would be monitoring all channels as a matter of procedure. *He* wouldn't be happy if she tipped off the enemy.

Which meant for now, it was better to keep her cards close. Rebecca needed time to find Ed, and time to get out. Ultimately, Aronsohn could deal with Oliveira and his men. But now, if needed, and when the moment was right, she could get a message through.

Hurry, Bec, find him. And get the hell out of there.

The radio remained in Jessy's pocket. And she waited.

67

Deep beneath the pyramid, Rebecca glanced at the luminous hands of her watch.

"How far do you think this goes?" Oliveira whispered, as if reading her mind.

"I wish I knew," Rebecca answered.

For the last few minutes she'd focused solely on the tunnel ahead, and the deeper they went, the deeper her unease. She checked her watch again. Had heading down here been the right decision? Maybe they should have gone to the surface and found another way in. If the tunnel didn't get them to the central nest, they were in trouble.

With no obvious end to the passageway and no proof of where they were going, it was hard not to feel anxious. If they were lost down here in the darkness when the spiders woke…

She considered voicing this to Oliveira when in front of her, Asensi stopped dead in his tracks.

Stumbling, Rebecca pulled up sharply.

What the hell?

Then out of nowhere, she heard it, too.

·   ·   ·

De Sousa smiled.

He was sure the girl couldn't have known she'd been watched through a pair of binoculars from the bushes some forty or fifty feet away. More than that, she couldn't have guessed, either, that in the opposing hand of her observer, pressed to his lips, was a comm radio of his very own.

De Sousa had seen her search the bodies of his comrades.

Again, he smiled, lowering the radio and sweeping his gaze past the cave to take in the campsite. He counted nine, perhaps ten soldiers. Beside him, Cartana crouched low in the undergrowth, out of sight.

De Sousa scanned the cave's entrance. Since acquiring the radio, the girl hadn't re-emerged. She was probably resting. De Sousa adjusted the focus for a sharper view, but the cave was too dark.

Both he and Cartana had been returning from the north-western vantage point loaded up with the equipment Oliveira wanted brought back to camp, when the soldiers had appeared out of nowhere. De Sousa had seen his comrades gunned down and had retreated with Cartana into the bushes. He was confident the two of them hadn't been detected. When the soldiers had later come looking, he and Cartana had withdrawn to hide amongst the vegetation. Having crept closer again, De Sousa sensed the soldiers had scaled down their search and consolidated the camp.

He pondered this latest turn. There was no getting back into the clearing—the soldiers were stationed all around it. He could likely take a few of them out, but not all of them.

He lowered the binoculars and put the radio to his lips.

He'd already switched to the other channel. This way, the woman couldn't eavesdrop on the conversation.

Still eyeing the cave, De Sousa keyed the talk button.

Rebecca heard a low buzz.

At first, she had to strain to catch it, but then its intensity grew. Definitely a humming sound, low in pitch. As quickly as it rose, it faded and disappeared. Seconds later it returned, this time accompanied by a faint but obvious vibration underfoot.

Asensi looked at Rebecca.

"What is *that*?" she mouthed at him as the hum diminished and throbbed back.

Ahead, nothing but blackness.

Asensi frowned, muttering in Portuguese as Oliveira stepped up beside them. Clearly, he could hear it too, though he remained stone-faced. Another pulse, and more trembling.

The noise, whatever it was, sounded close. *Felt* close. Rebecca couldn't shake the feeling that somehow, it felt unnatural too. That unnerved her even more. The sound didn't seem to be coming from a living source. Mechanical, maybe?

"What about the signal?" Oliveira said to Asensi.

From where she stood, Rebecca could read the receiver in Asensi's hands. She peered at the screen just as the glowing blip they'd been tracking vanished. Rebecca felt a rush of panic, but almost instantly the blip reappeared. Clearly, the signal was diminishing with each pulse of the strange humming sound, reappearing between pulses. The sound was causing interference, but they could still track the transponder.

Asensi gave the thumbs-up, and with that, Oliveira waved them down the tunnel, towards the source of the noise.

Rebecca fell into step behind Asensi. Despite her recent fears the tunnel mightn't grant them access to the nest, there was little doubt it was leading them *somewhere*—heart of the nest or otherwise. Obviously, there was a specific reason for the tunnel's construction; like the pyramid itself, it had a purpose.

And now, whatever that might be, they were about to find out.

68

De Sousa keyed his radio and sneered.

Like before, a wash of static hissed loudly in his ear, and he jerked the handset away. He couldn't understand—they shouldn't be out of range. Something was interrupting the signal.

Snarling, he raised the binoculars to spy on the soldiers. Soon enough, another idea came to him.

De Sousa smiled. He switched off the radio and pocketed it.

"Come," he grunted at Cartana, mindful to keep his voice low. Dragging the smaller man up by the collar—but hunching down, doubled at the waist—he nudged him in the back. "Move."

They slipped away soundlessly, disappearing into the undergrowth, and again, De Sousa grinned to himself.

No. They weren't finished yet.

Not by a long shot.

Almost there.

Rebecca figured they were close to the source of the strange hum—it was now at its loudest, and the accompanying vibrations thrummed in her bones. The phenomenon played havoc with the transponder signal, causing it to drop in and out, although just now the reading had bounced back strong. The device was near.

Which meant so too was Ed.

Ahead, the silk-lined tunnel levelled out, veering left, to the east. Cautiously, Asensi led them on, his assault rifle now in one hand and the receiver in the other. In silence, the group rounded a bend to find that just beyond it, the shaft terminated. Finally, they'd reached the end of the passageway.

And when they saw it, to the last of them, their eyes went wide.

No way...

They emerged from the tunnel slowly, mouths agape, into a large, natural cavern perhaps a hundred feet in diameter.

Torn into the middle of the low-lying ceiling was a great, gaping hole, above which rose a huge, silk-lined and funnel-shaped shaft that disappeared into deep blackness. But as amazing as this was, it was nothing compared to what lay directly *beneath* the huge funnel, half-buried in the floor of the cavern.

Though desperate to reject the thoughts tumbling through her mind, there seemed no denying the truth; Rebecca knew precisely what she was looking at.

This place wasn't the heart they'd been searching for, and probably had nothing to do with the nest at all. But it was clearly the reason for the tunnel's existence. The reason, perhaps, for the entire city's existence.

And unsurprisingly, it was nothing short of spectacular.

69

"So, you believe her?"

Wesley 'Bull' Harper raised his eyes from the laptop as McGinley circled the blind to stand beside him. He shrugged. "Yeah, s'pose I do." He tossed his head in the direction of the pyramid. "What else could explain that shit?"

The ginger-haired McGinley stared where Bull had indicated, captivated by the ruined city and the huge web strung about it. He shook his head. "I guess so. But *goddamn*—just look at it, will you? *Jesus*." He turned back to Harper. "Just what do you suppose it's all doing out here? I mean, you got that great big structure, in the middle of nowhere and all—that seems strange enough, don't it? But then you got that freakin' web! What is *that* about? Just looking at it gives me the creeps."

"You always were a mommy's-boy."

"Fuck you, asshole."

Bull chuckled, caressing the M16 beside him. "Man, there ain't nothin' out there old Bully-Boy can't handle."

"Yeah, well handle this, motherfucker." McGinley patted his own weapon as if it were an extension of his manhood.

Harper rocked his head in laughter.

McGinley did, too, before the younger soldier turned serious again. "Why do you think the Captain sent us on this wild-goose chase, anyway?

Off huntin' some signal? You ask me, whoever set it off is already dead, man. History. If that woman is right about them things, there ain't nobody in there alive. God only knows why you'd ditch the mission for this shit—" McGinley paused mid-sentence as he realised Aronsohn had appeared beside him. "Sorry, Captain, I—"

"Please, speak freely, Sergeant."

McGinley cleared his throat. "Well, sir, I was just wondering, is all. Wondering why we went off mission."

Aronsohn raised his binoculars to stare at the pyramid. "We're still on mission. We've simply taken a detour. Anything else on your mind?"

"Well, yeah, sir, I guess there is."

Without looking up from the screen of the laptop, Harper bit back a chuckle.

McGinley didn't seem to notice. "I was also wondering, sir, what's inside there, you know? Why those people would even think of goin' in a place like that—you'd need some helluva reason, right?" He paused, and when he spoke again his voice was lower, more serious. "And so then, it got me wonderin' also, what we ourselves mightta just walked into."

Aronsohn slowly spun from the pyramid, lowering the binoculars to face his young charge. "You know, Mac," he said, nodding, "I've been wondering that myself."

70

Astonishing.

Rebecca guessed the object stretched six or seven yards across. It was difficult to be certain of its exact dimensions, because not all of it was exposed above the floor of the cavern. Most of it lay buried in the ground.

As far as she could tell, the object was a solid sphere. Every few seconds, the thing would glow a brilliant, glaring orange, humming and quivering and causing the ground to vibrate before fading and plunging the cavern into complete darkness. Over and over it would do this like a huge, slow-beating heart.

Chemlight in hand, Rebecca moved deeper into the chamber, trance-like, unable to believe her eyes, unable to speak. The men, equally mute, struck flares and tossed them about.

The sphere seemed to be made of a smooth, dark alloy. Rebecca deduced this between pulses, when she could look at the orb directly. In places, clusters of opaque rods towered from its exterior in uneven formations, some several feet high and resembling random growths of crystal. Like the sphere itself, the rods blazed orange with each pulse.

The growths were peculiar, but stranger still were the bursts of energy leaping spasmodically from the orb's surface. They looked like erupting solar flares, but were reminiscent, also, of forking lightning. Like sizzling electricity, they crackled in the air before dissipating.

No-one uttered a word.

Rebecca crossed to the opposing side of the cavern, moving closer to the sphere and climbing the raised mound of earth that had been pushed up around it. The object radiated warmth, and her skin tingled pleasantly.

She glanced up at Oliveira and the rest of his men. All of them stood staring in amazement.

Her initial shock started to ease, but her curiosity grew. The scientist in her wanted answers. Rebecca continued circling the object, and then stopped and crouched before it.

And that was when, without warning, the ground beneath her feet opened and Rebecca fell through the floor of the cavern and disappeared.

"*Senhorita*... are you okay?"

Rebecca lifted her head, shielding her face as a large clump of dirt rained from above. Luis peered through the hole that had just swallowed her, arms outstretched.

Rebecca got gingerly to her feet and brushed herself off. She'd fallen about ten feet, landing heavily and turning her ankle. It hurt, but the injury wasn't serious.

"Are you okay, *senhorita*?" Luis repeated.

"Yeah, I'm good."

"I will lower a rope. What do you see down there?"

Rebecca slipped her NVGs over her eyes. She stood on a narrow earthen ledge, no more than two feet wide, below which was a seven-foot drop—

—to the floor of what appeared to be a large, subterranean cave.

Wow...

The natural cavern opened wide before her and disappeared beyond view. She'd fallen straight through its ceiling.

And as large as it was, it was covered entirely in silk.

Rebecca swivelled on the spot. A few feet to her right was a curtain of thick, dangling roots. Through it she could see a portion of the sphere's underside, partially exposed to the cavern below. Somehow, and despite the continual, rhythmic shuddering, the sphere remained firmly lodged between the two levels, stuck between the chamber above and the cavern below.

Rebecca glanced from the sphere to the cavern and back again.

Something caught her eye.

Directly beneath the sphere's exposed belly, on the cavern floor, lay several elongated rods—the same opaque crystals that protruded from the sphere in clusters—only these had been sheared clear of the object and had dropped to the ground.

Unsurprisingly, they didn't glow like the rest. They just lay there unattached, broken, lifeless.

And then, just like that, it came to her. Clear as anything.

She knew.

Knew what all this was about. Knew about the sphere, the arachnids, Intihuasi… *everything*. It was all connected, coming to her in a single moment of clarity, a mind-blowing revelation almost too difficult to grasp. But somehow, Rebecca knew she was right.

And it scared her witless.

Suddenly, the rope Luis had promised dropped through the hole. The end of it landed at her feet with a soft thud.

With a final, nervous glance at the cavern, Rebecca seized the rope and climbed as fast as she was able.

71

"You… felt it too, then?"

The sound of Owen's voice made Sanchez jump, and he drew to an abrupt halt in the middle of the dark passage. "What… the breeze at the fork back there? You felt that?" He hadn't realised Owen had regained consciousness. "You must be getting better."

Owen coughed. "…I guess so."

Sanchez paused, thrusting the torch ahead and behind before leaning against the tunnel wall. "Well, I am pleased to have you back, *amigo*."

Owen smiled faintly. "So, how're we doing?"

"Could be better," Sanchez said with a shrug. "But our situation is looking up. There must be an opening at the end of this passage, something that leads outside, through which that breeze is passing. Find that, and we have our exit." As he spoke, he caught Owen staring at the bloody punctures in his left shoulder. "One of them got a shot on me. I'll live."

"Good to hear," Owen said. He grimaced and clutched at his abdomen.

Sanchez lowered the torch. Owen's once-bright Hawaiian shirt was ripped, dirty, and drenched in an alarming amount of blood. He checked Owen's wound. While there had been some leakage, the dressing had stemmed the flow. The bleeding was under control. He straightened.

Owen craned his head about. "What is this place, anyway?"

"Some sort of natural cave system."

"It seems big."

"It's part of the nest."

Owen shook his head. "Fuck this, man. You know, the second we get out of here, out of this goddamned *jungle*, the first thing I'm gonna do is pack up my shit and move back into the biggest goddamned city I can find. I'm done with this."

Sanchez gave a half-smile. "The first thing? I thought you'd be hitting the surf."

"Okay then. The *second* thing I'm gonna do…" Owen coughed again. "What about you?"

"Sleep, for about two days straight."

Owen chuckled, clearly relishing the thought, and Sanchez patted his companion on the back. "I am sure we will both get our wish, *amigo*, but we should save our energy for now, eh?" He glanced dizzily at the silk-lined tunnel before them, stretching into the blackness. "We are almost done here, but we may yet need our strength."

72

Rebecca emerged from the hole, lifted by Luis and Costa.

"You hurt?" Oliveira asked.

"No," she answered, scrambling to her feet. She was certain her twisted ankle wouldn't be a hindrance.

"Good." Oliveira nodded at the sphere as it intensified, the air crackling with electricity. "So, what in God's name do you suppose this is?"

Rebecca brushed herself off and looked urgently about. "You wouldn't believe me if I told you. What's the latest with that signal?"

Oliveira looked at her. "Asensi's on it. If there is something you should tell me—"

"No, there's nothing. We need to find Ed and get out of here."

Asensi, who had been studying the small receiver in his hand, nodded at Oliveira and pointed to the funnel torn into the cavern's ceiling. The signal was coming from the level above. It was too dark to see what lay up there, beyond the funnel, but Rebecca presumed it was the pyramid's interior. By her reckoning, the chamber housing the sphere was essentially a subterranean vault, and the pyramid had been built over the top of it. The signal, therefore, was coming from somewhere within the pyramid itself.

Clearly sensing her desire to get moving—and perhaps reminded of the reason they were here—Oliveira snapped his fingers at his men and gestured to the hole in the ceiling.

Rebecca followed his gaze.

Time to climb the funnel.

The hole torn into the ceiling above their heads was eight or nine yards across. From this opening, the sloping sides of the funnel rose through dirt and rock for about forty feet, widening like a cone to a much broader opening above. The sides of the funnel were covered in silk.

Aiming high, Luis fired his grappling hook into the funnel, and it soared up and over the funnel's upper lip, where it found purchase. The rope trailed down the slope. The men hoisted Asensi into the hole and he hauled himself up the incline, his hands straining on the knotted nylon.

"This heat is incredible," Asensi said.

Oliveira urged him on. "Just climb."

Reaching the top, Asensi pulled himself over the ledge and disappeared.

Oliveira called up to him. "What do you see?"

No answer.

Rebecca glanced nervously at Oliveira, who turned and cupped his hands to his mouth. Slightly louder this time, he said, "*Asensi! WHAT DO YOU SEE?*"

Finally, Asensi's voice floated down to them, but it sounded distant, soft, as though he daren't raise it higher than a whisper.

"I do not know, Sandros," he said, clearly on edge. "It... it is hard to describe."

73

Rebecca was third up, behind Costa, and like him, saw what had so stunned Asensi.

"Oh my…" she whispered. "*We've got to find Ed. Now.*"

As suspected, they were inside the pyramid.

The huge, domed chamber was cloaked in darkness, the high-point of the ceiling easily out of range of the NVGs. At the edges, however, where the ceiling was closer to the ground, it was possible to infer the dome's dimensions, and *that* was what had startled Rebecca.

It was huge, like an inverted version of the silken funnel from which they'd just emerged, though on a far greater scale. Above them, gargantuan sheets of dry-silk swept to the edges of the chamber like the canopy above a bed, the web emanating from an unseen, central point high above them. Rebecca was reminded of the interior of a huge circus tent.

It was deathly quiet. In fact, it felt deserted.

Oliveira was the last of them to reach the top. He crossed himself. "*Meu Deus…*"

Rebecca turned from him and drew a ragged, heaving breath. The chamber smelled thickly pungent. The air was still and heavy with moisture.

Oliveira spun, called softly to his men. "He is in here somewhere. Find him. *Quietly.*"

As Oliveira's men dispersed, Rebecca panned her head about. The room was circular at the base. She noted absently how the huge bricks of the stone floor extended from the chamber's curved wall right up to the funnel mouth they'd just exited. The funnel itself hadn't been disturbed—the floor had been placed deliberately around it. As she'd guessed, the people of Intihuasi had been aware of the object in the chamber below them—

Rebecca tensed. A peculiar sensation slid over her—not dissimilar to the smothery claustrophobia that had overcome her in the burrow earlier—and her skin crawled. The feeling seemed almost tangible, as though something was tugging at her... urging her. Not physically, more a suggestion or an insistence, maybe a kind of vague, mental intrusion, but she felt compelled to—

"*Senhorita...!*"

Rebecca snapped out of it, sensed... a release. She glanced at Oliveira, who beckoned her. Disoriented, she moved to cross the floor, but as she did, something squished beneath her foot, almost causing her to slip. She lifted her boot. It was covered in a slimy, wet substance. She noticed more of the stuff on the floor around her—

Guanates.

Excrement.

"What the—"

A hand shot from nowhere to clamp over Rebecca's open mouth.

"Shh," Oliveira whispered, pulling her close. He spoke directly in her ear, his voice low, barely audible. "This is the heart of the nest, is it not?"

Rebecca nodded, thinking it to be, but...

"Then why have they not yet come for us, eh?" Oliveira asked. Slowly, he released her, pistol now in hand, head craning about. "It is too quiet. And just then, it was as though—"

"*Sandros!*" It was Asensi, on the far side of the chamber, gesturing vigorously. Before him stood the shadowy outline of a narrow doorway, unhindered by silk. "Come! This is the way!"

Oliveira pulled Rebecca forward, weapon tightly gripped.

Rebecca was still unscrambling her thoughts. "Just then—what were you about to say?" she asked Oliveira.

"Forget it," he whispered. "Let us get out of here."

.   .   .

Beyond the opening was a set of stone steps which they took to with haste, desperate to leave the chamber behind. Rebecca scaled them unsteadily, still bothered by Oliveira's words, still reeling from all she'd seen and felt. Oliveira was right: where were the spiders? Why hadn't they attacked? And just now… had something been inside her *head*?

Rebecca spun, half-sensing a gaze upon her. Other than Oliveira and his men, trailing behind, she saw nothing.

Get it together…

She shook her head and kept moving. They had to find Ed, and they were closer now than ever. Focusing on her feet and the steps before her, Rebecca climbed quickly, urgently, following Asensi, who in turn followed the signal. Seemingly, Ed had been removed to a section *adjoining* the central nest, which wasn't surprising. There'd be multiple chambers in a colony like this, all with different uses.

The stairs ended. At the top was a narrow landing. Off to the left, a silk-enshrouded passageway rose into deeper blackness. To the right was an open doorway.

Asensi stopped before the opening, receiver in hand. Enthusiastically, he turned, nodding. "This is it. He's in here."

They'd found him!

Unable to control herself, her heart pounding in anticipation, Rebecca pushed to the front earnestly, past Asensi—

—only to be quickly driven back.

The stench was horrendous.

"Oh, God…" she said and gagged, recoiling. "*No…*"

She knew the smell, and immediately, her hopes of finding Ed alive dissolved.

It was the smell of death, and the room reeked of it.

No…

Tears clouded her eyes and Rebecca wavered where she stood as Asensi and Costa—covering their noses with the backs of their free hands—moved past her, cracking chemlights. Preparing for the worst, she removed her NVGs as a soft, phosphorescent glow bloomed around her.

The light didn't reveal the source of the stench. What she *did* see, however, momentarily threw her.

The room, heavily enshrouded in silk, was large and rectangular, its sides running for about twenty feet, the rear wall perhaps thirty.

The floor-space within was filled with gold.

The trove shone through drapes of silk and centuries of dust, glittering in the light—mounds of jewellery, bowls, ceremonial masks, and tiny statuettes shaped like moai. Some of the items were inlaid with jade and silver and other precious gems and metals. It must have been worth a fortune.

The legends were true…

Like excited children, Luis and Costa rushed for the nearest cache and began stuffing their packs.

Oliveira didn't stop them. Hand to his nose, he said, "*Asensi?*"

"Yes, Sandros, the signal—over there."

But Rebecca had already sighted the slumped, motionless form through the silk, sitting on the ground beyond one of the far mounds of treasure.

Ed…

She burst into a run, tears streaming down her cheeks.

Ed's arms and legs were splayed apart, each stretched to their limit and firmly secured with silk. His torso was cocooned, and so too was his face, as though he'd been mummified.

Falling to her knees beside him, Rebecca pulled at the silk, her heart drumming so hard she feared it would burst from her chest.

God… please let him be okay…

She tore at the strands on his face, exposing his eyes and nose. He didn't react. He was pale, bloodless.

Lifeless.

Please, no…

Finally, she managed to free one of his arms and take hold of his wrist. Her hands uncontrollably.

There was a pulse.

Faint, but a pulse! Rebecca's heart leapt.

Yes!

"*Ed!*" She didn't mean to raise her voice but couldn't help herself. Madly, she tore again at the silk.

Oliveira shoved her aside, sending her sprawling. From the ground, Rebecca shot him a bewildered glance.

Oliveira seized Ed by the shoulders and shook him. "What did you see in there?"

"What the hell are you doing?" Rebecca cried, rising.

Oliveira ignored her and moved to within an inch of Ed's unresponsive visage. "What was inside the plane? *Tell me what you saw!*"

Oliveira had lost it. Rebecca sprang to her haunches and leapt at him, hands outstretched. "Leave him alone!" She pushed Oliveira as he had her, but he was like a slab of granite and the hit had little physical effect. Regardless, he released Ed, and did so without retaliation.

Blinking slowly, Oliveira stood and glanced over his shoulder. Dropping beside Ed, wrapping him in a hug, Rebecca was sufficiently shocked by Oliveira's strange behaviour to turn and follow his gaze. Behind them, Luis, Asensi and Costa were still stuffing their packs, and Oliveira's gaze shot past the men, to the right of the open doorway through which they'd entered. There, a large stone disc with raised teeth around its edge—much like a cog—sat flush against the wall in semi-darkness. Rebecca presumed the disc to be a door of some kind. Beneath it, set into the floor, was a line of grooves: clearly, a track over which it could slide.

Suddenly, Rebecca felt uncomfortable with her back to the opening, as Oliveira seemed to be.

"Asensi, Luis," Oliveira said, jutting his chin at the door. As the two men moved to slide the large disc into place, sealing the room, Oliveira turned back to Rebecca. "The package—has he got it?"

"Please—help me get him out."

Together, they worked to pull Ed free of the silk. At last he fell forward limply, collapsing into Rebecca's chest. She caught him, and he moaned softly.

Trembling, Rebecca whispered, "Ed, it's me. *I'm here.*" She was crying freely again, unable to rein in the surging waves of relief and elation. It was all she could do but hold him.

She wanted desperately for him to return the embrace.

Like before, Oliveira was impatient. While Rebecca continued to rock Ed in a close hug, Oliveira wrenched at the remnants of swathing-silk and rifled through the pouches of Ed's vest. Soon enough he seized upon an object and straightened, prize in hand.

For an instant, Oliveira stood there, silently contemplating the small cloth bundle, weighing it in his hands. Rebecca saw through watery eyes that the package was a bag of some kind, folded over on itself, the drawstring wound tightly top to bottom, and then back laterally. For a moment, even she was taken by it, drawn by its mystery, and she opened her mouth, a thousand questions on her lips.

Asensi's voice interrupted her. "Listen! Hear that?"

She turned with the rest of the group. One of the others said, "What?"

"That sound."

A hush fell over the room, and Rebecca soon heard the sound for herself, jarringly out of place.

Beeping.

A high-pitched, beeping sound: faint, intermittent… and *electronic*.

Oliveira grasped Rebecca by the arm. "Come."

Rebecca winced. "What?" She still clung to Ed—who remained barely conscious and unaware—but Oliveira urged her to stand.

"*Come*," he said again.

Rebecca resisted, but Oliveira was too strong. He tightened his grip, causing her to grimace, and she had no option but to ease Ed gently against the wall and comply. As soon as she was back on her feet, Oliveira shoved her forward and ordered the group to hunt for the source of the sound. Reluctantly, Rebecca snatched up one of the green-glowing chemlights and used it to disperse the last of the shadows.

Almost immediately, a voice called out: "Over here!"

Hesitant to stray far from Ed, Rebecca turned to the voice, her gaze drawn to a mound of bowls and cups in one of the room's silk-enshrouded rear corners. There she saw Luis, and in front of him, an opening previously out of range of the chemlights.

A low doorway.

"Here… I need more light," Luis said. He held the chemlight before him and brushed back a thin veil of silk. "Looks like there's another room back here… the sound is coming from in there." He moved to squeeze through the opening, but Oliveira caught him by the arm.

"No," Oliveira said, and jutted his chin at Ed. "I am not finished with him. I need him awake."

Obediently, Luis crossed the floor to where Ed was slumped. Rebecca felt Oliveira's hand on her wrist.

This time she didn't resist. Glancing at Ed one last time, she stooped as Oliveira dragged her through the low doorway.

.   .   .

The stench was worse back here.

Rebecca had grown used to it, but now it hit her again, harder than before. She gagged and covered her nose and mouth with her shirt, but there was no escaping it. The smell seemed to *worm* its way in through her pores, burrowing into her body.

Again, more chemlights. Repelled, the darkness took residence beyond the glow like a vile, watchful beast. Rebecca noted this new chamber was smaller than the room from which they'd come—different in shape, too. For one, the ceiling was much lower, and the opposite wall was angled slightly. But the space was just as silk-enshrouded.

The beeping sound was close.

Trailing Oliveira, Rebecca stepped cautiously into the mass of fibrous threads, anxious at what she might find. Her muscles trembled with foreboding, the chemlight shaking in her hand. She wanted to return to Ed.

Directly in front of her, towards the ceiling, weak sunlight speared through a crack in the sloping rear wall, tree roots prying the stone apart like searching fingers. Rebecca guessed the room was at one of the far edges of the pyramid—

She stopped as something squelched softly underfoot.

Slowly, she lifted her boot, but it wasn't what she'd been expecting. The boot came away with a soft sucking sound, a red, gooey substance hanging in strands from the heel. Repulsed, Rebecca wiped it against the floor, at the same time kneeling for a closer look at the large sticky puddle beneath her feet, a good square metre in size. It looked like…

There was something else.

Tiny. Gold. Rebecca poked her finger at it.

A cross: a tiny, gold crucifix.

She knew what that meant, and with her breath catching sharply in her throat, she turned to her right, holding the chemlight before her as the sound of buzzing flies came to her ears.

He was virtually unrecognizable.

Though still vaguely human in shape, the corpse was little more than a desiccated, bloodied husk. As Rebecca brought the chemlight to bear, a cloud of flies dispersed into the air, some disappearing through the crack in the stone wall above. She waved the rest away, biting back bile at the sight of the fat, white maggots squirming over the corpse's exterior. While disfigured beyond recognition, Rebecca knew by the presence of the gold cross whose body it was. Sobbing, she looked down at what was left of Enrique, almost entirely consumed within the surrounding folds of silk.

Dear God, what a terrible way to go.

Except for that which had seeped out around him, Enrique had been sucked dry. His skin had become little more than a loose bag for his bones.

Rebecca pressed the back of her hand to her mouth. Regaining control, she inspected the corpse more closely, noting there were more than just the one or two wounds she would have expected: Enrique was covered in *hundreds* of tiny puncture marks…

A sudden crash beside her cut through the stillness. Turning, she saw Oliveira's boot stamping down upon a hard-plastic object the size of a GPS receiver.

A personal locator beacon—that was what had been beeping! Concerned only with Enrique, Rebecca hadn't noticed it sitting on the ground beside her, framed by the square of light from the crack above. Enrique must have activated the device sometime prior to his death.

Now, it had been deactivated.

Rebecca said nothing. Why Oliveira had destroyed the PLB was obvious, and hardly surprising. He didn't want attention.

"We should get out of here," she said, standing.

But suddenly Oliveira was holding firm. Rebecca followed his gaze—

—and understood why.

Throughout the room, immersed in the sea of silk and only now brought into stark, hideous contrast by the artificial glow of their combined chemlights, were the corpses of a host of other victims, all in varying states of decay, many, like Enrique, covered in maggots.

Rebecca's stomach rolled at the gruesome sight. As far as she could tell, they were all *animal* corpses, but even so, a chill swept through her. She and Oliveira were surrounded by death, a blunt reminder of the inherent threat of this place.

It seemed to spark Oliveira into action, and he seized her. "Let us chat, eh?" His eyes flared with that dangerous look that had manifested in their confrontation just prior to entering the burrow. His tone was equally intimidating. "Time for answers, okay?"

Rebecca squirmed in his grip. "Sorry?"

Oliveira pulled her close. "I want to know everything: about them, about that object buried in the cavern below. You know more than you let on, and I want to know what it is. *Compreender*?"

"I don't understand—"

"*You know something*," Oliveira hissed, tightening his grip.

Whimpering, Rebecca said, "I've got a theory."

"Tell me!"

Rebecca was confused. Now that Oliveira had what he'd come for—the package, whatever the hell it was—why wasn't his sole focus on getting out? Escaping? Why was he delaying his exit? And why was he keeping her so close? With the package in hand, her position was at best precarious, maybe even redundant. But Oliveira's manner, though alarming, was intriguing. He had wanted Ed conscious. Why?

Whatever the reason, time was an issue; outside, night was fast approaching, and they needed to get moving. But she knew Oliveira wouldn't relent, not until he had his answers.

"All right," she said. "But not here… this smell…"

Oliveira pulled her to the doorway. As they went, Rebecca stooped and seized a hard-rubber case of aerial mini-flares from the ground beside Enrique's spilled pack. Somewhat surprisingly, Oliveira didn't stop her.

As she was ushered from the room, Rebecca stole a final glance at Enrique, the young man she'd known all too briefly, then crossed herself and pocketed the tiny gold crucifix she'd snatched at the same time she'd picked up the flares. She muttered a quick prayer for him, then ducked through the doorway.

74

They returned to the first room to find Luis hunched over Ed. "He is waking," he said, beckoning them over.

Rebecca squirmed from Oliveira's grip and rushed to Ed's side. He was indeed rousing: soft murmurs escaped his lips and his head lolled about. Rebecca steadied it in her hands. "*Ed!*"

Ed's eyes cracked open, struggling to focus. "*B... Bec?*" he moaned, his head as floppy as that of a new-born baby. "*Man... do I... feel like shit... or what?*"

Once again, Rebecca felt a sting of tears, but this time she was beaming. She threw her arms around him. "Take it from me, you *look* a damn sight worse." She kissed him, almost laughing as relief coursed through her.

Free of his silken bonds, Ed tried to return the hug and force a half-smile of his own, but the effort was too great and again, his eyes fell shut as he faded from consciousness.

"Ed!"

Oliveira crouched beside her. He shook Ed, who didn't respond. "Wake him again," he said to Luis. He stood and once more lifted Rebecca by the arm. "Let us talk."

His strength was frightening, and Rebecca felt as though she'd been caught in the current of a raging river. Oliveira manhandled her to one of the room's distant corners. Out of earshot, he spun her by the shoulders. "Talk!"

His demeanour was unsettling. "It's just a theory," Rebecca blurted.

"I want to hear it."

But she didn't know where to begin. She was confused, reeling with all that had happened. What's more—now faced with it—she couldn't help but feel her theory was pure absurdity. Her mind raced. She didn't want to incite Oliveira further by giving him useless, irrelevant information.

Oliveira shook her. "Tell me what you know and start at the beginning."

Rebecca nodded. "All right." She took a deep breath, running the back of her hand across her sweat-drenched forehead before clearing her throat. "When I arrived three days ago, Ed had this specimen—one of the spiders. He'd killed it in an attack on him and one of his men a few weeks back. I'd never seen anything like it and could only presume it was a survivor from another era, maybe an example of a prehistoric species unknown to science that had evolved in isolation to gigantic proportions and endured to the present. But something didn't fit. Then, when I saw that object in that chamber, well, suddenly, it did." Rebecca paused, steeling herself before blurting, "What if these things didn't evolve here, as I first thought?"

Oliveira's eyes narrowed. "Did not evolve in this jungle?"

"No. On this *planet*."

"What?"

Rebecca looked at him and swallowed hard, struggling to verbalise her thoughts. "What if they aren't indigenous to this planet at all? What if these spiders… are *alien?*"

As always, Oliveira's expression was stern, humourless. Even so, had the circumstances been less pressing, Rebecca was sure her revelation would have caused him to laugh.

"You are not serious," Oliveira said.

Rebecca nodded. "Trust me—I find this harder to stomach than you. But you wanted to know what I thought, and I'm telling you."

Oliveira was wary. "Continue."

"You saw that sphere down there with your own eyes. Where do you think it came from? How did it get there? More pressingly, *what the hell is it?* Seems to me it isn't local, and that doesn't leave many possibilities. When I was in that chamber and the cavern below, I had a thought about the boro."

Oliveira frowned. "What?"

"The boro, the botfly larva," Rebecca said. "What if that thing in the chamber below is some sort of... probe, an unmanned, extraterrestrial craft of some kind?"

"How is that related to the boro?"

"Hear me out. Imagine this thing's mission is to rove indiscriminately throughout the universe, recording, amassing data, or more specifically, sent to individual planets, like we send probes to the Moon, or to Mars, in search of life, or to collect samples. What if, in doing so, it picked up something in its travels, deliberately or otherwise? A specimen or contaminant of some form. An *egg*." She paused. "That's when I thought of the boro. Remember what you told me? You said the botfly would catch a live mosquito, attach an egg to it, and release it again unharmed. The mosquito would go and feed as normal, at which point the egg would hatch and the botfly larvae would burrow into the skin of the victim, to itself feed and grow within."

"That sphere down there, the probe, is the egg-carrying mosquito."

"Exactly," Rebecca said. "Hundreds, perhaps even thousands of years ago, the probe is redirected to Earth to continue its mission, to collect *more* samples. Or perhaps something happens to it—maybe it was damaged somehow—and it's pushed off course and comes here by accident. Out of control, it plunges at tremendous speed and impacts with our planet, the force of the collision so great it causes a huge crater—the deep bowl now housing this pyramid—but also causing the probe to drill its course farther downwards, beneath the surface. Ultimately it comes to rest deep within the ground but teetering above a deep and extensive network of caves beneath. Engineered by technology beyond our comprehension, the probe survives the impact, but is damaged. Something *else* survives the crash too, something that had been inside the probe, protected by it. Something alive. And that living specimen, or contaminant, or whatever it is, hatches—or simply escapes the damaged probe—and is released into the caves, where it takes up residence. Years, maybe decades, pass. On the surface, the jungle reclaims the crater, while the organism retreats into its new home beneath."

"Like the boro larvae."

"Yes, exactly. Meanwhile, the new people—the city-builders—arrive here. From where, it doesn't matter. They're attracted to something emanating from within the crater, to the power perhaps radiating or leaking from the damaged probe. They build their city, harnessing an energy or force already known to them but in existence here to a strength never seen before.

298 · WW MORTENSEN

Perhaps the leaking probe is interacting with a pre-existing, geomagnetic anomaly, amplifying the effect." She paused as a new thought came to her. "Hell, maybe the probe crashed here, or was attracted or even *directed* to this very spot, specifically because of its relationship to that anomaly." She recalled Ed's theory about the area being a convergence of energy, a vortex of some kind. Perhaps the probe's presence was less accident than design. "Anyway, the layout of the chamber downstairs proves these people were aware of the object. Perhaps they revered it, considered it a gift from their gods. Either way, thinking this to be a sacred place, they build the pyramid on top of the sphere, all the while unaware of what has made its home in the bowels beneath. Yet ultimately, they somehow arouse the creatures, *agitate* them, and the species that had lived or even lain dormant for so long beneath them returns—and takes over."

Oliveira seemed sceptical. "But how could such an organism go unnoticed? And why were they not awakened when the city was built?"

"Who knows how extensive the caves are?" Rebecca said. "They might be huge. I remember hearing about this cave system in the US… Mammoth Cave, I think. It has a network of passages upwards of 400 miles in length, stretching over two mountain ranges! Perhaps the organism had retreated far away, *miles* away, only returning, for whatever reason, decades later." Rebecca thought about the attack on Ed and Sanchez at S1, and how, as a result, she had assumed there was a second nest nearby. Now she didn't think so. No doubt these caves extended deep underground, maybe as far back as S1. And if that was the case—if they were talking about a single huge nest—then it might extend for *tens* of miles.

The thought sent a shiver down her spine.

She recalled the story Owen told them about the Yuguruppu's reverence for the crater site, and that their gods lived there long before the builders of Intihuasi had arrived from across the sea. Could the spiders have been their gods?

"Okay," Oliveira said. "Let us assume the sphere is a probe of some kind, and these things are extraterrestrial. Why *spiders*?"

"Why not? Arthropods—insects, arachnids—are the most successful life-forms to have inhabited *this* planet. They're by far the most numerous and have spread into virtually every environment. They're extremely adaptable. Jointed legs are the best means of traversing all forms of terrain, underwater included. If there is life out there, in other parts of the universe, wouldn't it develop as arthropods have, seeing as though they're the success story of our own planet? The formula works. It's more plausible that an advanced form of life should develop in this manner than in any other way—"

Rebecca paused. Oliveira seemed distracted, removing his Beretta 92F from its holster on his hip. As she watched, he ejected the magazine and checked it over.

"So... that's it," she said to him slowly, eyes glued to the gun. "That's my theory. The spiders are an accidentally introduced species, brought here from somewhere else, by that object down in the chamber."

She was trembling. *This is it.* He has the package and all the information he needs. He has no use for us anymore. Her lower lip quivered. "What now?" she stammered.

Oliveira looked back up at her, reinserting the mag with a swift, sharp smack. "What now?" He pulled back on the slide. "Fortunately for you, *senhorita*, I have requirements of you yet, so *now*, we get your friend walking and get the hell out of here before the boro wakes up hungry."

75

In the fading afternoon light, Aronsohn peered over Bull's shoulder at the glowing screen of the laptop.

Again, Bull shook his head. "Nup, definitely gone, and it ain't a problem from our end." He was referring to the distress signal they'd lost some minutes ago. "She just stopped, just like that."

Aronsohn frowned. "Dead battery?"

"You're talking forty-eight hours minimum operation time for a standard beacon, but they don't last forever. We don't know how long it's been active."

Aronsohn paused, deep in thought. "What about the helos? How long to extraction?"

"ETA thirty minutes."

Aronsohn checked his watch and motioned to another of his men. "Tag—get back into camp. Give Ms Baxter a hand with her stuff, then get her down here." As Tag melted into the trees, he turned back to the web-enshrouded pyramid.

Grasping his binoculars, Aronsohn wondered again about the signal and why it had died.

Bull seemed to read his mind. "You think somethin's goin' on in there?"

Aronsohn shook his head. "I don't know, Bull, but I can tell you one thing: I got a feeling the show's about to begin."

76

With effort, they got Ed standing.

Luis had woken him while Rebecca had been off with Oliveira. He'd given him some coca leaves for energy. Ed seemed dazed, but lucid enough to make sense of his surroundings.

"Can he talk?" Oliveira asked.

"Give him a moment," Rebecca said. She held her canteen to Ed's lips. Most of the water dribbled out, but he drank eagerly.

As he did, Rebecca noted that Luis had tended Ed's wounds, too. Inspecting them, she observed with relief—and fascination—that the three or four bites Ed had received were already healing. In fact, they looked almost as if they'd been *cleaned*—not by Luis, but seemingly by the swathing-silk itself. Wrapped tightly about him, the gauzy strands had acted as a pseudo-bandage. That there were no signs of infection—which, in this humidity, would occur quickly—seemed to suggest the silk possessed antiseptic properties.

That's how they keep the meat fresh, she thought. They had wanted to preserve him, keep him for later; he may have lasted another day or two before suffering Enrique's fate—

A hand pushed the canteen from Ed's lips, sending water flying.

"Hey!" Rebecca said.

Oliveira lifted Ed's chin to meet his gaze. "Inside the plane... tell me what you saw."

"...sorry?" Ed stammered.

"What did you see inside the plane?"

"...nothing... it was... empty..."

Oliveira pulled his hand away, letting Ed's chin fall. Turning to his men, he issued instructions in Brazilian Portuguese.

Rebecca frowned. Again, Oliveira's behaviour was bizarre. Why was he so intent on interrogating Ed?

"Asensi will assist your friend," Oliveira said to her.

Rebecca didn't argue as Asensi looped his arm around Ed's waist and shifted his weight away from her. Aided so, Ed could likely stumble along. She was happy he was alive and moving, but her thoughts swung to the venom flowing through his veins. While certain the web-builders' toxin was weak, she had no way of knowing if Ed's condition would worsen. She'd monitor him.

Asensi shuffled forward, keen to get going. They'd spent too long in here already.

Quietly, Luis and Costa rolled back the door. As they did, in the corner of her eye, Rebecca caught Oliveira poking through a mound of artefacts. He casually stuffed something into his pack and zipped it tight. Glancing away, she noted that plenty of treasure lay unclaimed, despite the efforts of Oliveira and his men. She wondered why it was here, and concluded it had some sort of religious significance. Jess had told her that the pyramid was probably a religious centre, and by her own reckoning the huge chamber below had been built in reference to the buried sphere. Perhaps this room had served as a priest's quarters, or something similar, and the relics were gifts for the gods.

She'd probably never know for sure.

The men exited, and she hurried after them.

They reached the bottom of the stairs in silence.

Costa looked back with a smile. "We made it." He moved for the opening that led to the main chamber.

Rebecca grasped him by the arm. "No—wait." She pushed past him, and at the doorway turned her gaze to the ceiling. Like before, she was unable to see the high-point of the domed chamber—even with the goggles, the cloak of darkness was impenetrable.

Before anyone could query her, Rebecca put a hand in her pocket and pulled out the heavy rubber case containing the aerial mini-flares she'd retrieved from the floor near Enrique. Fixing one of the cartridges to the tubular launcher, she fired it up to the ceiling.

"What are you d—" Oliveira started, but cut himself off as the flare ascended, arcing with a soft trailing hiss through the domed chamber as though through a night sky. When it reached its peak dozens of feet above them it got stuck in the silk and came to an abrupt halt, throwing out a huge red glow.

Someone gasped. Rebecca thought it may have been her. "*Don't move—do not say a word,*" she whispered.

High above them, suspended from the very top of the ceiling, a huge mass of black—a great, dark *ball*—gently pulsated.

It took Rebecca a moment to come to grips with what it was, and while she did, she could only stare in disbelief, the hairs on the nape of her neck prickling.

They must have been literally in their dozens, all of them huddled together at the top of the dome, all grasping each other, forming the huge, swollen mass—

Dozens of spiders clinging together in a sea of black legs and bodies…

"Oh my God…"

The ball itself seemed to be tens of feet across. It reminded Rebecca of a beard of bees, a seething, organic mass suspended from the ceiling, swelling and contracting rhythmically like a slowly beating heart.

Even so, none of the individuals comprising it were themselves active—despite the gentle pulsing—and Rebecca knew why. "They're roosting together."

A wave of nausea rolled over her. All along, the colony had been sleeping in a giant cluster at the top of the chamber.

And we walked right in underneath them…

As she came to that terrible realisation, standing there watching the pulsing mass in both awe and revulsion, the dark ball began to writhe.

We're out of time…

The spiders were waking up.

· · ·

The first spider dropped from the ball and landed on the floor below with a soft, padded thud. Quickly, it was joined by several more of the creatures, and as others readied to do the same, the ball stretched in the direction of the ground, alive with purpose. It shrank as its members dropped away, and the floor swelled and rippled with movement like the disturbed surface of a pond.

Rooted to the spot, Rebecca could only watch as the spiders—some of them just yards away—disappeared into the funnel in the centre of the floor like liquid down a drain.

They were flooding the passageway below.

No! We should have had more time!

Oliveira's voice was low, urgent. "Come! We have to go back up!"

But Rebecca hardly heard him, and she reached for her temples as the strange intrusion that had earlier invaded her mind gripped her once again. This time, however, it was stronger and more insistent, painful almost.

Close range…

She froze.

It was beside her.

Slowly, Rebecca turned, eyes fluttering shut in resignation, opening again as she came around. It was to her right; at the edge of the doorway, perched on the wall. She saw no detail, just a shadow in the dark.

Barely a foot separated their faces.

They stared at one another, unmoving. Rebecca understood they eyed each other from across worlds—to the thing watching her, she was every bit the alien. But her thoughts weren't really at a conscious level, and as everything slipped into slow motion, she was held motionless by the sight of the jumper's monstrous fangs, dripping and spraying venom as they unsheathed with a slow, menacing hiss.

Rebecca waited for death.

77

There had to be an opening of some kind at the end of the tunnel, something that led outside through which the breeze was passing. It was that knowledge that kept Sanchez lucid, and drove him on.

Some minutes ago, Owen had again fallen silent, probably unconscious. The toxins surging through his own veins threatened Sanchez with a similar fate—with every step his dizziness grew, but still he moved with energy and purpose. He could sense freedom.

Soon, his efforts were rewarded.

Sanchez drew up as the tunnel came to a sudden end, falling away sharply at his feet and widening into a gigantic cavern. This new chamber was much bigger than the one that had housed the spiders' waste, and essentially different for one obvious feature: at its centre was a very large and black pool of water, fed by a narrow stream that disappeared off to his right through several enormous, misshapen boulders. The stream had to be flowing from higher ground…

Sanchez smiled, barely able to contain his excitement as he scampered down the embankment, stumbling to the edge of the subterranean lake.

He'd just found their escape route.

He was about to inform Owen of their success when an abrupt scuttling echoed behind him and caused him to freeze where he stood.

78

The Kalashnikov erupted beside Rebecca's ear. The jumper, illuminated by the muzzle flash, exploded into oblivion.

Rebecca recoiled, stunned and disoriented. Asensi lowered his weapon and mouthed something at her, but she couldn't hear him, just a high-pitched ringing inside her head. Then someone seized her and hauled her bodily sideways, towards the stairs, and as the world tilted crazily, she glimpsed something strange back in the chamber. The image imprinted itself in her mind's eye: a huge, pale grey form, seemingly luminous, still suspended from the chamber's ceiling where the ball had been just seconds before. It was what the spiders had all been clinging to.

And as she replayed that fleeting snapshot, stuck in her silent world, she realised the shape had *moved*.

Then there was a sense of fierce heat beside her and she was fleeing up the stairs, a line of belching flame in her wake…

They hit the landing at the top of the stairs and Rebecca's hearing came rushing back.

"*Move it!*"

She wondered if the blast from the flamethrower had worked, and stole a backwards glance in time to see a giant arachnid burst through the open doorway below—

—with a legion of its companions in tow.

Oh my God...

"*The passageway!*" Oliveira yelled. "*Go!*"

Someone hauled Rebecca to the left, to the sloping passageway rising higher into the pyramid—a better option than the priest's chamber, which was a dead-end. The sound of gunfire echoed off the stone walls, and over the top of it, a thunderous skittering as the creatures—*dozens* of them—fought their way through the bottleneck and up the stairs, barking and scrambling and scratching...

"*Run!*"

The passageway curved to the right. More gunfire, another eruption of flame. At the top of the bend, a dark, empty space.

"*QUICKLY... THIS WAY!*"

They crossed the void. Ahead, another stone door, like the one in the priest's chamber below.

To the rear, from the mouth of the passageway, the first of the spiders emerged, leaping high—

—just as Luis sent a spout of flame back towards them.

The deadly blast engulfed everything in its path. The heat was intense, the flash blinding. Reaching the open doorway, Rebecca dashed through it. Luis, reeling backwards, kept his finger on the trigger, spewing fire even as Costa seized him by the shoulders and towed him into the chamber, and then someone rolled the door shut and it fell into place with a thud—

—and there was silence.

Rebecca whimpered and fixed her gaze on the door, bracing herself for an assault on the huge, cog-like disc.

It didn't happen. No attack, no noise from the other side.

What the hell?

Then Rebecca turned around and saw *why*.

79

Sanchez watched the three spiders emerge from the silk-lined tunnel he'd just exited… and sank lower in the water.

Upon hearing their approach, he'd leapt into the subterranean pool, dragging Owen in with him. Now, with only his eyes peeking above the water's surface, he tracked the jumpers as they moved to within a few feet of the torch he'd dropped to the ground. The three megarachnids were big, each more than a yard across the legs, and they were working in unison, their actions stuttered, twitchy. Sanchez guessed they were searching, pausing to feel for vibrations. One of them came across the cavern's ceiling, the other two across the floor, down the embankment. Then, close on their heels, two more of the creatures darted from the tunnel and at once, all five of them froze.

Sanchez froze, too.

They looked at him and Owen and converged swiftly… only to stop in front of the torch.

Sanchez felt his heart leap into his mouth. The spiders hadn't been looking at them after all, but just in case, he edged closer to the base of some boulders lining the bank, pulling Owen behind him.

The spiders approached the torch, its dancing flame entrapped in the many dark mirrors of their eyes. In that same firelight, he thought the colour of their bodies shifted from jet black to the kind of mottled grey-brown of the embankment on which they had gathered, but he couldn't be certain. They seemed to be inspecting the torch.

With a padded thud, the spider on the ceiling dropped to the floor. At the same time, another of its companions kicked the spear, flicking it through the air.

All of them spun and moved away…

Down to the water's edge.

Sanchez clamped a hand over Owen's mouth and circled the boulders. Fortunately, he was able to walk, the water here shallow.

With the torch-flame reflected in its glassy black eyes and along the velvety hairs of its body, the lead spider touched two of its feet lightly on the surface of the lake.

Sanchez held his breath, muscles tensed.

The creature felt for vibrations.

Sanchez didn't move, prayed that Owen, barely conscious, would remain silent for just a few more moments—

They can't swim, can they?

And with that the jumper did a peculiar thing and Sanchez wished the thought had never entered his mind.

80

Rebecca's breath caught sharply in her throat.

They were everywhere.

Like strange lamps, they dangled from above; white spheres each about the size of a soccer ball, individually suspended on a thread of silk attached to the ceiling.

Eggs.

More accurately, egg *sacs*. The entire chamber was filled with them. There must have been hundreds. "This isn't good," Rebecca murmured.

"Why is it so… *hot*?" Costa's voice trembled.

"To keep the eggs viable," Rebecca said absently, her feet frozen to the spot. She swivelled her head about. "Hive-creatures need high-temperatures, a tropical climate. This is a nuptial chamber. *We have to get out of here.*"

"Where is Luis?"

Rebecca spun. The FH-9 flamethrower—*Luis's flamethrower*—lay discarded on the ground a few feet away… covered in blood.

"Oh, no…"

They were already in here.

The dark shape swooped in from the side, through the air, its legs spread wide. The forelegs collected Asensi in a smothering hug, at the same time the rear legs hit the ground and propelled the creature and its screaming prize back up to the ceiling.

The attack sent Ed sprawling. Reflexively, Costa opened fire, bullets sparking off the stone walls in pursuit as the jumper, defying gravity, twisted gracefully in the air and attached itself to the ceiling with its free legs. Asensi writhed and screamed the whole way, in the process somehow getting his weapon hand free and depressing the trigger.

A deadly stream of bullets rained wildly from Asensi's Kalashnikov as the jumper scurried across the ceiling, hauling its prey towards a large circular hole in the centre of the stonework. Scrambling for cover, Rebecca dived out of the way as bullets pinged around her.

Asensi kept firing until the weapon was torn from his grasp, and then the silenced Kalashnikov fell away, tumbling through the air. It clattered to the ground in front of Rebecca.

She dived for it.

As Asensi was hauled into the black hole, Costa—panicked and still firing—turned his weapon on *her*...

Rebecca snatched up the AK-74 and rolled behind a curtain of silk, bullets sparking in her wake—

"NO!" With a howl, diving sideways, Oliveira slammed into Costa and knocked him off his aim.

His efforts were a fraction too late.

The first of the bullets reached Rebecca—everything now in slow motion—and something incredible happened.

They *stopped*.

Right there, in front of her face. Amazingly, she *saw* the rounds—two of them—come to a sudden halt, stuck in the web.

The silk curtain—a strong, fibrous film weaving through the forest of egg sacs—had caught them. She noticed another bullet had ripped through one of the nearby cocoons, which now oozed fluid. Rebecca thought she saw movement inside the sac, something writhing...

Everything sped up again.

Oliveira and Costa untangled as the second jumper leapt in, seizing Costa in the same manner as the first had snatched Asensi. Kicking and screaming, Costa, too, was dragged to the ceiling.

Oliveira had seen it coming. Ducking, he lunged for the abandoned flamethrower, spinning and firing upwards in the one action. The bright-orange flame blasted the ceiling-hole a millisecond after Costa and his abductor disappeared into it.

The chamber was empty.

Discarding the flamethrower, Oliveira spun with his pistol, targeting Rebecca—

She was already on her feet with her AK-74 trained firmly at his head.

Face to face, neither stood down.

"Thanks for trying to stop him," Rebecca said, her hands trembling on the weapon.

"You are welcome, *senhorita*."

Rebecca gestured to the Beretta in Oliveira's hand. "I need you to drop that."

Unblinking, Oliveira mirrored her tone. "I was going to ask the same of you."

Rebecca had no intention of complying. Neither, it seemed, did he. Barely ten feet apart, weapons pointed at each other's heads, they held their ground, surrounded by the endless clusters of egg sacs. Some of these were still on fire, lighting the chamber and exuding a sickening, sulphurous odour.

"This is neither the time nor the place for an insurgence," Oliveira said. "You know that shortly they will return."

Rebecca held firm but agreed. "What now, then?"

A clicking sound, on Rebecca's right. "That's easy. Drop your weapon, *senhor*."

Out of the corner of her eye, Rebecca saw Ed emerge from the shadows to stand on Oliveira's left. He held an automatic pistol, trained at Oliveira's temple.

Oliveira held his ground. "Where did you get that?"

Ed's voice was hoarse. "The plane. I guess the pilot dropped it. Had it in this vest the whole time." He coughed. "Now, let's do as the lady said, and drop it, nice and slow."

Oliveira turned his head to look at Ed. "I am afraid I cannot."

Ed tightened his grip on the gun and took an unsteady step forward, wheezing and spluttering.

Oliveira had already returned his gaze to Rebecca. "Be careful, *senhor*," he said to Ed. "I don't presume your vision is perfect. You don't want an accident."

Ed held his ground. It was a three-way stand-off.

This isn't good, Rebecca thought. The spiders could reappear at any moment…

Oliveira read her mind. "I am sure they regroup as we speak. We must get out of here."

"What do you propose?"

"We cannot fight each other if any of us hopes to live."

"We don't need you," Ed coughed.

"How can we trust you?" Rebecca said to Oliveira.

"Bec," Ed said, "we're not giving up our weapons."

"Then as a gesture of goodwill," Oliveira said, "I shall give up mine." With that, he dropped his pistol and kicked it across the floor.

Rebecca glanced down as it spun towards her, the Kalashnikov still pointed at Oliveira as the weapon cruised to a stop at her feet. She paused… and then looked up. "Throw me the package."

"What?"

"The package—throw it to me."

Oliveira hesitated.

"We're running out of time," Rebecca said.

Reaching into his vest, Oliveira retrieved the small cloth bundle and hurled it. Rebecca caught it with her left hand. It was heavier than she'd expected, firm yet pliable. She shifted her gaze to look at it. Though intrigued by its contents, the pouch was too firmly tied to open while still holding the Kalashnikov. She looked up at Oliveira…

…and kicked back his gun.

"Bec!"

"He's right," Rebecca said to Ed. "We won't survive this on our own." She turned to Oliveira and jutted her chin at the pistol. "Before you pick that up, you listen to me. I'm going to tell you how this works, and I don't want any more of your shit about striking deals or making demands, okay?"

"I'm listening."

"From now on we work together," Rebecca said. She waved the package at him. "If we manage to get out of here, back into camp, you're going to swap me a sat-phone for this, and you're going to disappear. Got it? I don't care who you are or what you're involved in back in the real world, but we all go our separate ways and pretend we never crossed paths."

Smirking, Oliveira opened his mouth to reply, but no words passed his lips. He looked to the ceiling and his smile faded.

At that moment Rebecca realised the chamber had grown darker—not because the burning egg sacs had extinguished, but because a great shadow descended. Like Oliveira, she turned her gaze upwards.

"Oh *fuck*," she breathed.

It was literally the stuff of nightmares. Rebecca's neck skin crawled.

Impossibly huge, it lowered itself face-first through the ceiling-hole on a silken dragline. Slowly. Deliberately. The size of a large SUV, the superspider was pale, whitish-grey, virtually luminous. Except for two outstretched fore-legs—they must each have been five or six yards in length—its segmented limbs were tucked up beneath it, sprouting from a thorax that seemed comparatively narrow given the improbably huge, round and bloated abdomen that appeared to float in the air above it.

The creature was totally hairless.

Rebecca was reminded of a huge, gnarled hand—the thing appeared to be covered in skin, its knuckled legs looking like bony, human fingers. At the same time, she thought they also resembled the long, almost skeletal appendages of the giant spider crabs that dwelt in the darkness of the Earth's deepest oceans.

Clearly, this was what she'd seen clutching the ceiling in the chamber below—the huge, pale shape around which the ball of spiders had been formed. They'd all been grasping onto *it*.

Delicately and without sound, the creature touched down. For its huge size, this seemed a miraculous feat. Amid the measureless rows of egg sacs, it crouched and took the three of them in curiously.

Unmoving, Rebecca's group returned the creature's gaze. Its huge, pale face sat forward of the shell-like carapace that was its head, and beneath the eight eyes grouped at the front—in three rows, just like those of a jumping spider—two massive, jaw-like chelicerae sheathed unseen fangs.

Rebecca returned her attention to the creature's eyes. The two anterior medians were huge, easily the size of dinner plates. But they were cloudy, milky, as pale as its face and body…

Rebecca sensed movement and swivelled.

Several dark shapes skittered silently from the surrounding silk, encircling them. These megarachnids were dog-sized, more like the jumpers they'd previously encountered. But unlike the jumpers, and like the larger specimen before them, they were hairless. Albino-like.

A flash of understanding struck Rebecca.

With some ant species, the bigger, stronger members assumed positions of leadership. By virtue of its size, this huge, hairless creature was likely the dominant *female* of this colony—the *alpha* female, and in a sense, a kind of pseudo-Queen. The others were possibly nursemaids, assistants that would aid the alpha with her eggs, perhaps tend to her hatchlings and immature spiderlings as surrogate mothers—it wasn't a stretch given cooperative brood care existed amongst social spiders. But it was just as likely her assistants were egg-layers too, all of them—the larger female included—members of some royal or reproductive caste.

Either way, this was bad.

She, Ed, and Oliveira were in a nuptial chamber—full to the brim with eggs—and were now surrounded by a host of *very protective mothers…*

It was suddenly all too clear. This was why they'd been allowed so far—why they'd been able to traverse so deeply into the nest unopposed, why it had felt as though they'd been watched all the way and not confronted.

They'd been surreptitiously *herded*, forced up here into the nuptial chamber, into the clutches of the alpha female.

It had been a trap all along.

81

The air in the room seemed to thin. Rebecca tried to draw more into her lungs but couldn't get enough of it. Fighting panic, she realised she was hyperventilating. The room swam.

With a pop, the Aurora hand-flare burst into life, sizzling as Ed thrust it before him.

The Female hissed and lowered herself, readying to pounce. She didn't, though, and instead, held her ground. The egg-layers that had encircled them retreated a little.

Rebecca knew why. Having spent most of their existence underground, in darkness, the Female and her egg-layers were near-blind—

And the light caused them pain.

She guessed it was precisely what Ed had banked on; like her, he'd probably noted the alpha female's oversized eyes—pale and milky, extremely sensitive.

The light is a weapon…

Oliveira caught on, and at once the two men struck more hand-flares—some red, some white, each of them blazing at a minimum of fifteen thousand candela. They tossed the flares to the ground in a spreading circle.

Agitated, the Female and her egg-layers withdrew, barking and rearing on their hind legs.

"They are calling for help!" Oliveira said. "We have to get out of here!"

On the opposite side of the chamber, barely visible through the hanging egg sacs, was another door. Ed and Oliveira made for it, each waving a flare before them, scattering the egg-layers deeper into the shadows. As they went, Oliveira scooped up the discarded FH-9.

It was only as they reached the door that they suddenly stopped and turned.

"*Senhorita!*"

Rebecca hadn't gone with them.

Panicking, breathing fast, Rebecca searched the mass of spiders for a break in their ranks. She'd missed her chance.

Shit! SHIT!

She was surrounded.

At the blurry edge of the light, no more than a few yards away, the Female and her egg-layers hissed and barked in a tight ring around her, their curved fangs bared and forelegs flailing as they lunged back and forth, seeking an opening.

She'd only hesitated for an instant, but it had been enough. She knew why she'd faltered.

Please, no. Not now…NOT NOW…

A spluttering sound came to her ears, and still hyperventilating, she looked down.

Oh no…

On the ground at her feet, one of the flares spluttered. Then a second, and a third.

Rebecca's heart skipped a beat.

The flares had a burn-time of just sixty seconds.

And now, time was up.

Unable to react, Rebecca watched as darkness pounced from flare to flare, diminishing her protective circle and inviting the enraged Female and her egg-layers ever closer. Her heart pounded, her breath coming in heaving gasps. Soon, she'd be seized and hauled away into the blackness, but try as she might, she remained bound to the spot. She couldn't move.

God no…

And then things got a whole lot worse.

With a rush, a frantic scratching erupted outside the chamber, on the other side of the door through which she and the others had entered. Asensi or maybe Luis had sealed it, but the spiders that had chased them here in their dozens were now clawing at it… trying to get in.

Answering the call of the dominant female.

With that fateful, horrifying sound, Rebecca's last ounce of hope washed away.

This time, there'd be no escape.

82

Oliveira's mind raced. His next move had to count.

Outside, the frenzied clawing intensified, reverberating through the chamber and shaking the walls as the swarm tapped and scratched and heaved against the stonework. Inside, still calling to the horde, the giant spider and its minions hissed and barked at the edge of the failing light, legs raised.

Oliveira's gaze shot down to Rebecca's feet, and the flares beside them.

Only three left…

Two…

One.

It happened very quickly.

Catching Ed's eye, Oliveira nodded—

—and pulled the pin on the canister in his hand, raising it high and tossing it into the centre of the nuptial chamber.

And with that, the world exploded into unimaginable brilliance.

THE
PREY

83

Jessy hunched inside her tent, facing the rear, Priscilla chattering away beside her. Jessy held a finger to her lips. "Shh…"

Then she depressed the radio's talk button.

It was now or never. If she was to get a message to Rebecca, she could wait no longer. She whispered into the mouthpiece. "Hello, Bec? It's me, Jess."

She got only static in reply. She tried again, then changed frequencies and repeated the process. It made no difference.

Jessy heard movement outside and thrust the radio under her pack.

A polite voice called out to her. "Ma'am, you awake in there?"

Jessy unzipped the tent and popped her head out. She looked up with a smile at the young Hispanic soldier standing at the cave mouth. She recognised him: his surname was Hoya, though he went by the name of Tag, his companions nicknaming him after the watch-brand. She'd thought it clever.

"Ma'am, the choppers are on their way. We need to get you down to the EZ. Are you ready?"

No. She needed more time. "Actually… can you give me a few moments… to gather my things?" She put on her best smile.

"Anything I can do to help?"

"No. Thank you. I'll be out shortly."

With that, Jessy slipped back inside the tent, listening for Tag's retreating footsteps before retrieving the radio and depressing the talk button once more.

84

Still dazed, Ed had no more than a split-second to react.

There was no time to question why Oliveira had come so heavily armed—but Ed was glad he had. Recognising the canister Oliveira was about to hurl into the nuptial chamber, he responded accordingly.

If the hand-flares, at fifteen thousand candela, caused the spiders agitation, God only knew what the detonation of the E182 Stun Grenade—or flashbang—would do to them. In the second afforded him, Ed ran back for Rebecca, scattering the spiders with his hand-flare and burying her head in his chest as the flashbang exploded. At 22 million candela, the blast was visible through shut eyes. Fortunately, none of them had been wearing their NVGs, having relied on the flares, glowsticks and the burning egg sacs for light. Had they witnessed the detonation through their goggles, Ed figured they may well have suffered permanent blindness.

As it was, Oliveira had created precisely the diversion they needed.

At 180 decibels, the blast was as deafening as it was blinding, but Ed didn't need his ears to run. Dragging Rebecca, they were through the door quickly, their retreat covered by a suppressing blast of flame that scythed from the FH-9 back into the egg-laden nuptial chamber, followed by another detonation of the E182, three seconds after the first.

Fourteen successive detonations, each as loud and as bright as the last, would follow every three seconds like a relentless, thunderous strobe.

Of course, by the time it ended the three of them would be long gone. And they were.

Flash. Bang.

The booming detonations jarred Rebecca from her stupor. *"What in God's name…?"* she cried, her ears ringing.

"No time to explain!"

They ran down a narrow, silk-lined passageway. His job done, Ed released Rebecca and fell back, lagging.

Rebecca turned. "Here! Let me help you!"

In a torrent, a host of jumpers flooded into the tunnel behind them—likely the same horde that had been clawing at the door. They must have circumvented the nuptial chamber via another passage.

Ed glanced back, then forward to Rebecca. *"Go! Run!"*

Rebecca didn't need to be told twice and took off down the corridor, Ed and Oliveira in tow. A frightful scuttling reverberated underfoot and off the walls. The flamethrower roared. She didn't look back.

Suddenly, the tunnel ended. The group burst into a tiny chamber.

No exits.

"Shit! SHIT!!"

Rebecca spun in a fit of desperation. The chamber was a small recess, enclosed on all sides. She glanced up. The alcove had no ceiling. Instead, a dark, empty shaft rose several storeys to a distant quadrilateral of light.

If they had more time, they could probably climb up to it—

They'd never make it.

"Shit!"

Like a murderous river, the spiders swarmed down the tunnel, nearly upon them—

There had to be something!

Rebecca saw it—not above them, but on the ground.

A deep groove no wider than half an inch separated the floor from the walls of the alcove, running out square from the alcove's corners and cutting across the floor at the point where the passageway ended, and the recess began.

An *edge.*

They stood on a platform of some kind.

A square platform that seemed to run flush with the shaft above them...

Rebecca fell to her knees, searching, spreading the dust with her hands...

In the middle of the platform was a circular indentation, set into a tile in the shape of the sun.

The sun...

"Ed! The disc!"

"What?"

"The disc, the one your grandfather gave you! Give it to me! HURRY!"

The skittering swelled, thunderous now...

"Whatever you are planning, be quick!" Oliveira bellowed, and raised the nozzle of the flamethrower as Ed rifled through his vest—

Too late.

The mass of spiders rounded the corner, gushing towards the alcove—first one, then two, then too many to count, a blur of gnashing fangs surging across the floor and ceiling and walls simultaneously, the legs of all of them spread wide, Rebecca's vision filling with them—

—just as she snatched the disc from Ed's fumbling hands and jammed it into the tile.

A nanosecond later, Oliveira's finger must have depressed the flamethrower's trigger, because in a blinding flash of light, the maw of the tunnel and the tangled mass of spiders pouring out of it exploded in searing orange flame.

Then the light died and there was darkness, as the platform on which Rebecca and her companions stood lifted from the ground and rose into the shaft.

85

Hand clamped over Owen's mouth, Sanchez watched as the spider sprang delicately forward, launching across the water towards them.

Owen had seemed dimly aware of the unfolding situation, and the sight of the jumper wading across the lake was enough to jolt him fully alert.

Sanchez felt him gasp, and he removed his hand. "*Amigo.* Take a deep breath."

Owen did, and together they slipped beneath the surface. In the blackness, Sanchez led Owen by the wrist, moving by touch around the boulders and away from the advancing spider. He could hear the creature's legs propelling it forward—not fast, in fact, ungainly almost, but advancing, nonetheless.

Sanchez hoped it hadn't seen them, but he couldn't be sure. He wished he still had the spear.

Remaining submerged, he pressed Owen against the boulders lining the lake's edge.

The jumper swam forward. Seconds passed. It seemed like forever. A fearful burn came to Sanchez's lungs. He was running out of air. No doubt Owen was, too.

Don't panic.

Another second. More paddling. Owen tapped Sanchez on the wrist. He had to surface.

The paddling stopped.

Hold on, just another second…

Sanchez looked up. He couldn't see anything in the darkness. Had the jumper gone? Perhaps it had paused and was waiting for them to resurface. Maybe it was a trap.

They could stay down no longer. Lungs burning fiercely, Sanchez shot upwards, hoisting Owen with him.

They broke the surface together, ready for an ambush. It never came.

The jumper was gone. So were its companions.

Just like that, all five had simply vanished.

86

Rebecca cast her gaze about as they ascended the shaft, her body throbbing with adrenaline.

The platform was a lift!

She whimpered with relief, thankful her suspicions had proved correct. Fortunately, none of the spiders had made it onto the stone block: the powerful blast of flame from the FH-9 had disintegrated everything in its path. It had been a clean getaway.

She sucked in a calming breath. Despite the lucky escape, she felt as though she might throw up.

Oliveira looked at her. "Close, eh?"

Rebecca said nothing.

"That big one," Ed said, panting. "What the hell was it?"

"An egg-layer," Rebecca said. "They all were. The big one was the alpha female."

Ed nodded and looked about himself in awe. "Man… this is incredible."

It *was* incredible. All around, the air crackled and hummed like buzzing electricity, causing the hairs on Rebecca's arms to stand on end. Beneath her feet, the stone platform shimmered like the moai had yesterday, and the walls of the shaft flickered, although the effect was less physical than optical because she could feel no vibrations. Looking about, it was clear no cables, counterweights, or mechanisms drove the platform upwards, the device apparently powered by no more than the same repulsive energy Ed had yesterday demonstrated. Fortunately, the reaction-time had been faster, maybe because the platform was lighter than the huge statue, or nearer to the source. Whatever the case, there was no escaping it: the lift was rising on air alone.

"'Any sufficiently advanced technology is indistinguishable from magic'," Oliveira whispered.

"Arthur C. Clarke's Third Law," Ed said, coughing.

Magic, indeed. Observing her surroundings, Rebecca felt again that odd sense of detachment, the sensation that something—the platform, the shaft—was somehow uncoupled from reality, not fully in this space. Yesterday, she'd felt the moai had become *untethered*, whatever that meant. Today, the sensation was even stronger. She was part of it.

Above them, the square of light grew larger.

"That must be the temple up there, the one we saw at the top of the pyramid," Rebecca said.

Again, Ed coughed. "So—soon we will be at the *top* of the pyramid, when we need to be at the bottom. We—"

The words died on his lips as the lift bucked beneath their feet. The platform slowed, labouring suddenly. Rebecca shot a nervous glance upwards. They were still several yards from the top of the shaft.

"You think it's *them*?" Ed said. "You think they're doing it?"

"If not, this thing is losing power," Oliveira answered.

Rebecca dropped to her knees to inspect the disc, wondering if the fading afternoon light was causing the repulsive energy to fail, or if the spiders were somehow interfering with the platform. How many had amassed down there, ready to scramble up the shaft after them?

She had little time to ponder. With a jarring shudder, and still eight or nine feet from the top of the chute, the lift jolted to a halt beneath them. There was a pause, and not a second later, the stone platform sank back down the shaft.

No time to hesitate.

Before the lift fell too far, Ed leapt desperately for the ledge above. He caught hold, but only just—one hand slipped off before he consolidated his grip.

For Rebecca, the jump was too high, but lucky for her, Oliveira reacted quickly. Grasping her around the waist with one hand and releasing the grappling hook strapped to his leg with the other, he aimed and fired upwards in the one swift movement.

The steel claw looped over the shaft's lip. Somewhere beyond, it must have found purchase, because there was a sudden, jolting tug. With a sickening lurch, the lift sank from beneath Rebecca's feet, and then she and Oliveira were in mid-air, trailing at the end of the hook's nylon rope and swinging towards the wall. She braced for the impact, but the collision was minor.

Shadows swallowed the platform below.

Rebecca gazed uncertainly at Oliveira. "That's the second time today you've saved me. Thank you."

Oliveira said nothing in reply.

Working his toes into the many cracks in the wall's worn surface, Ed scrambled over the ledge and stretched down to them. "Bec, give me your hand."

Rebecca reached up and Ed hoisted her to the ledge with a loud grunt, grasping her belt to help her over the lip. Once safely topside, Rebecca joined Ed in extending her hand for Oliveira. As she did, she searched the vertical passage for signs of movement. She saw none.

With a united heave, they hauled Oliveira clear of the hole. As soon as he was free, he stood and urged them to take cover. Bringing the FH-9 to bear, he sent a burst of flame back down the shaft.

Nothing emerged from the blackness.

Shifting her attention, Rebecca turned in a circle to take in her new surroundings. They were, as suspected, inside the temple that sat at the top of the pyramid. Two sides of the square-shaped structure—the western and eastern—were totally walled in save for an open doorway in the middle of each, while a series of narrowly spaced columns was all that formed the northern and southern sides. From all four boundaries, steep staircases ran to the base of the pyramid, one each at the foot of both doorways and the other two from between the central columns of the northern and southern sides. Though it was late afternoon and almost dark, Rebecca saw waves of silver-grey silk spreading into the jungle on all sides. What she *couldn't* see—which may or may not have been a good thing—were any of the web's inhabitants.

For the moment, however, her attention was fixed mainly on the temple itself. While the interior was essentially a large and empty space—for some reason, the jungle had not reclaimed it—two features stood out. First, the walls, columns, and ceiling were all a reflective charcoal colour, the same smooth, dark alloy as the sphere beneath the pyramid. The *other* feature to capture Rebecca's eye was not only the temple's most dominant attribute, but perhaps its reason for being.

In the middle of the temple floor, about fifteen feet from the off-centre shaft, stood a large moai. Its arms were not by its sides like other moai, but above its head, holding something high. An object—

—a gift from the gods—

A sphere.

It was like the sphere in the chamber beneath the pyramid, only in miniature, perhaps no more than a foot across. And like its larger cousin, it quivered in the moai's cupped hands. The cycle was identical: every few seconds, the orb would pulse, the smooth, dark alloy intensifying into a ball of glaring orange, its crackling energy sizzling between the crystal rods that protruded from its surface.

It occurred to Rebecca that Ed knew nothing of the larger sphere below. Equally, he knew nothing of her theories about it, and as he caught sight of the object now, his jaw dropped. He stumbled towards the moai, searching for words.

"Oh my God... what...?"

Oliveira, meanwhile, seemed wholly unimpressed by this new discovery. Having shed his pack in favour of the flamethrower, he moved to the open western doorway and squinted into the silk. "We cannot delay," he said to Rebecca, transferring his gaze downwards. "I say we take the northern steps to the base of the pyramid and the plaza out in front. Then we take the tunnel he used"—he jutted his chin at Ed, still mesmerised by the sphere—"to get back to the burrow and crawl the hell out of here."

"Have you forgotten?" Rebecca asked. "They flooded the tunnel. There's no getting through."

Oliveira resumed guard at the shaft. "You have a better idea? We cannot stay here."

Rebecca opened her mouth to reply but cut herself off. At first, the noise sounded like thunder rumbling distantly, but it was too rhythmic, too sustained to be that, and grew steadily in volume.

Whump-whump-whump...

It was more like…

No way! A helicopter! Perhaps even more than one, approaching from the north-west—

With a sudden burst of static, Oliveira's radio—lying on the ground amongst his discarded gear—crackled to life.

Rebecca immediately recognised the female voice at the end of it.

In a flurry of motion, two hands snatched for the radio. Rebecca's was the quickest.

She grasped the handset, lifting it and backing from Oliveira in the one action. He didn't pursue her.

The voice came again.

Rebecca spoke into the mouthpiece. "Hello? Jess, is that you?" *What the hell was Jessy doing with a radio?*

The line was full of static.

"…*Bec? Oh, thank God, finally… I've… trying… some time now… some kind… interference. Look, I shouldn't be on this frequency, and we don't have much time—*"

"Tell me about it," Rebecca said, eyeing Oliveira. "What's with the chopper?"

"…*are…y… okay? …can you talk?… Ed with you?*"

Rebecca glanced at Ed, who was studying the moai intently. "Ed's here. He's fine. We're both fine." She looked back at Oliveira. "And yes, I can talk. Tell me that chopper is for us."

"…*ank God… but tell him… still… my bad books for what he did—*"

"Jess! The chopper?"

"*Sorry—yes… two of them.*" A pause. "*Bec, there's a… goddamned team of Green Berets here…*"

Rebecca's eyes hadn't left Oliveira, who was standing and listening. "What? Say again?"

"*..o time to explain, Bec. But it's all good… tell you the truth, I didn't ex-pect you'd be… one to answer the radio yourself. But I had to put in the call anyway—take that chance… In a matter of minutes, we're out of here.*" Another pause filled with static. "*So… what happened… Oliveira and his men?*"

Again, Rebecca eyed Oliveira, trying to read him before answering. There was something about the way he returned the look, something in his eyes…

"Don't worry about them. It's under control," Rebecca said, her voice even.

"...at's great news, Bec. Thank God." Despite the bad connection, Rebecca could hear the joy in Jessy's voice. "I have to go... one of the choppers will be heading your way shortly... where... you exactly?"

"We're up in the temple. Get the chopper to pick us up there. Oh, and Jess? Tell it to hurry. Things are heating up."

Back at Advance Base Camp, Jessy was beaming. It was almost too good to be true. Ed and Rebecca were alive!

She lifted the radio. "Will do, Bec," she said. "Just hang in there, okay? Can you believe it? This is almost over! Finally, we're going home!"

Still smiling, she released the talk button just as someone burst into the tent behind her, wiping the expression from her face.

87

Rebecca pocketed the radio, glancing sideways at Ed before shifting her gaze back to Oliveira. Her hand crept to the Kalashnikov slung over her shoulder. Tensed, she waited for Oliveira's reaction to the news he'd obviously lost the camp—and his men—in some sort of incursion by a team of *Green Berets*. American soldiers! She hardly knew what to make of it herself.

"They will need to extract you from the roof," Oliveira said. "You should start climbing."

Rebecca looked at him joylessly, relaxing her grip on the weapon. "I can tell them you helped us escape. Better still, that you're one of the hired hands. They don't need to know otherwise."

"Get moving. I will stand guard."

"You can't stay here."

"What? Come with you? Ask for the same mercy they must have showed my men? Go on, get moving."

Rebecca turned to Ed, who looked up from the moai and shrugged.

The sound of the approaching choppers grew louder. Rebecca looked once more at Oliveira, and then moved to the columns of the temple's northern wall to watch for them.

.   .   .

A moment later she turned back and reached into her pocket.

"You gave this up too easily," she said, retrieving the small cloth package and tossing it to Oliveira, who caught it. "I'm guessing it's not the real reason you came here."

"Bec!" Ed said.

Rebecca was unfazed. "We don't need it anymore, Ed, and something tells me it's worthless, in any case."

Oliveira shook his head, half-smirked, then—as if to prove her wrong—unwrapped the cloth bag. Easing open the drawstring, he tipped the contents into his open palm. Like a sparkling waterfall, the load fell glittering through the light of his glowstick.

Diamonds.

Cut diamonds. Lots of them.

Rebecca stared at the gems in Oliveira's cupped hand. They were beautiful. Entrancing, even. "Pretty," she said. "But I know you didn't risk Ed's life, and ours, for a bunch of stones."

"Eight million US dollars' worth of stones," Oliveira said without looking up, careful not to spill the precious load as he returned it to the pouch. "And yes, I did risk you for them."

"Maybe you risked my life and Ed's, even your men's. But you wouldn't risk your own for that. You came here for something else, I know you did. Answers, perhaps? Answers for your employer... or... for *yourself*?" She paused and stared him boldly in the eye. "Why is that plane out there, stuck in the web?"

Again, Oliveira half-smirked, but this time Rebecca sensed the fight had all but fled him.

"You are not unlike her," Oliveira said. "I will give you that. You have courage, *senhorita*."

"Who are you talking about?"

Oliveira held out the pouch. "Two years ago, my employer's brother took these diamonds and that plane and disappeared. But he took more than that. He took his lady as well."

Ed raised an eyebrow. "What... his girlfriend? The guy pinched eight million dollars from his brother, and his *girlfriend*, too?"

"They fell in love."

"And the diamonds were to fund their new life together," Rebecca reasoned. "And so, when you heard about the plane, your boss sent you here to search for the diamonds, but more importantly, for closure. To find out what befell his brother. And his girlfriend." She studied Oliveira. "You knew her, didn't you?"

"She was my sister."

With that, everything fell into place. Now, Rebecca understood Oliveira's erratic behaviour and his persistent interrogation of Ed. This wasn't about diamonds or missing planes or even forbidden love.

Oliveira had been searching for his sibling, pure and simple.

"As I told you earlier... there was no-one inside," Ed said softly. "The plane was empty."

Oliveira nodded and looked back at Rebecca. "Fortunately for you, *senhorita*, it was never my intention to leave you here. There is much about you that reminds me of her—not least your tendency to speak your mind—and it is no habit of mine to abandon a woman to suffering. I was not about to let them... those *things*... take another."

Rebecca wasn't sure how to respond. The sudden sting of tears surprised her, and she turned away, back to the columns. Beyond them, it was near-dark—the horizon smeared only by a faint purple smudge—and off in the direction of the north-western vantage point, twin spotlights bounced over the canopy.

The choppers had arrived.

88

Cartana was nervous.

Never had he felt comfortable in De Sousa's presence; in fact, he'd thought the man nothing short of crazy. This confirmed it.

Hunched low and creeping silently, he followed De Sousa through the darkened jungle. Frogs and insects croaked and chirped all around them.

It had been De Sousa's intention to launch a surprise attack on the camp, but moments ago, upon hearing the radio transmission between the two women, he'd altered the plan. Cartana was glad for it, but he remained uneasy.

He glanced at the yard-long tube slung diagonally across De Sousa's shoulders. The Russian-made RPG-7 rocket launcher, though old, was still a devastating weapon.

De Sousa turned. "Stop lagging. Hurry!"

Not wanting to anger his companion, Cartana scrambled to catch up, juggling the three warheads like a child with bowling-pins.

Some distance north of the pyramid—and east of the place the Americans had dubbed the north-western vantage point—De Sousa found what he was looking for. The position was sufficiently elevated and offered a suitable break in the canopy.

"Perfect," De Sousa said, smiling. He dragged Cartana to his side.

The two men hunkered low and waited.

•   •   •

It was a long time before Sanchez—still up to his neck in water—dared emerge from his hiding place amongst the boulders. When he did, he was deathly quiet, dragging a lucid Owen silently behind him. He moved from the bank where the spiders had been, glancing back at the torch. He considered retrieving it, although it looked virtually spent.

Forget it.

At the edge of the lake, the narrow stream he'd discovered earlier snaked up the bank and into a cluster of boulders.

He and Owen moved towards it.

89

Jessy sat quietly at the north-western vantage point, proverbial tail between her legs. At her feet lay her rucksack. In her arms, a silent Priscilla hid her face against Jessy's chest.

Aronsohn stood off to the left.

Upon catching her transmission, the soldiers guarding Advance Base Camp had burst into her tent and commandeered the radio. Of course, by then the 'damage' had been done, and their only recourse had been to usher her to the exfiltration site. While Aronsohn hadn't personally confronted her about the breach, he'd clearly been displeased by it. Now, he seemed in a rush.

Jessy hated that she'd broken his trust. In many ways, she would have preferred a lambasting to the silent treatment she was getting from him now. Still, she'd done what she'd had to do, and the gamble had paid off. They now knew Ed and Rebecca's exact location.

A heavy, rhythmic thumping caused her to glance up through the canopy.

Skimming the treetops, their twin spotlights cutting through the near-dark, the two choppers cruised into view, sleek and black against the dimming sky. Jessy's heart skipped a beat. Everything had happened so fast. Hell... not only had she discovered that Ed and Rebecca were alive and well, but the rescue choppers, as promised, were *here*. Somehow, they were going to survive this!

She watched the huge machines swing into position, the vegetation above her head convulsing wildly. Aronsohn had chosen the north-western vantage point as the exfiltration site because the trees here weren't as dense, topping out at about eighty feet compared to a hundred and fifty back at Advance Base Camp. Even so, it was too dense for a landing.

A voice crackled over Aronsohn's radio, above the swooshing trees and whumping chopper-blades. *"Echo One—we're coming up on your position now."*

Aronsohn glanced at Hoya and jutted his chin. "Tag, pop it."

With a nod, Tag removed a steel canister from his vest, pulled the pin, and tossed it to the ground. Yellow smoke poured from emission holes at either end of the device, expanding upwards into the rustling canopy. The choppers beat the air in a deafening wave.

"Raven One—you got that?" Aronsohn called above the din.

"Roger that, Echo One. Yellow?"

"That's the one. Listen, the jungle's too dense here. You'll need the Penetrator."

"Roger that, Echo One. How many injured? Just the one civilian?"

Aronsohn glanced at Jessy. "Negative, Raven One. Two injured, three in total."

There was a pause. *"Say again, Echo One? You've now got two injured civilians?"*

Still eyeing Jessy, Aronsohn tossed her a wink. "Just get a Penetrator down here, will you? We've got a short trip to make."

The bright-yellow Forest Penetrator whizzed through the canopy at more than six feet a second. Weighted to pierce the dense vegetation, the three-foot-long cylinder slowed as it neared the forest floor, swaying at the end of the steel cable that dangled from the winch above the UH-60 Black Hawk's starboard door. Aronsohn caught hold of it, and aided by Staff Sergeant Kriedemann and Sergeant Jenkins, released the three narrow seats from their retracted positions and snapped them into place. Once they'd slipped into the webbing safety straps, the three men were hauled topside.

It was imperative Aronsohn appraise the temple situation personally. It was never his intention to abandon the two civilians trapped inside the pyramid, but he wouldn't risk a crew without a first-hand assessment. By Jessy's own admission, her colleague, Rebecca, had been forced into the pyramid against her will, and there was every chance that during their earlier radio conversation, Rebecca had been speaking at gunpoint. He was wary of an ambush.

Even so, once safely aboard, he gave the order and Raven One peeled away, heading in the direction of the pyramid just as Raven Two swung in behind to extract Jessy and the rest of the team.

Standing between the narrowly spaced columns of the temple's northern side, Rebecca fired the aerial mini-flare skyward. The black shape of the chopper grew larger as it nosed to the east and then banked in a looping arc back to the south, towards them, spotlights blazing.

Only seconds ago, she'd thoroughly checked the surrounding barrier web, scanning it on all sides. As best she could tell in the fading light, there were no workers about. The web appeared deserted.

She checked again.

In truth, Jessy didn't require the litter but was given no choice. Strapped on her back into a long and shallow wire basket, she rose through the trees with Sergeant Johansson riding shotgun on the outside. Priscilla, too, was with them, inside a harness attached to Johansson's chest, frightened, but quiet.

Emerging from the bustling treetops beneath the huge body of the hovering Black Hawk, Jessy looked up as Raven Two's crew chief—operating the electrical rescue hoist—leaned out to swing them aboard. It was a practiced movement, and before long he was unhooking the Stokes litter from the harness, preparing to send Raven Two's Forest Penetrator back down for the remaining troops. Johansson moved to help, and as he did, he caught Jessy's eye and smiled, gave her the thumbs up.

Jessy smiled back, for the first time truly revelling in the moment.

Finally.

She was safe.

Something wasn't right.

Rebecca didn't know what, but she was restless.

Come on, get a grip…

The approaching Black Hawk was close now and started to slow. Behind it, the second aircraft hovered like a giant wasp above the north-western vantage point.

What was she worried about? In a matter of minutes, Ed, Jessy and herself would be away from this place, safe at last. She shook her head, trying to clear it.

You're being overcautious.

Maybe so, but the feeling gnawed at her. Somehow, it was all too easy—too good to be true.

And unfortunately, she was right.

Rebecca saw the long white streak emerge from the jungle to the north—and gasped.

Sergeant Diez was on one knee, M16 pressed to his shoulder, staring intently down the sight at the surrounding jungle. Above him, the hovering Raven Two thumped loudly in his ears. All around, leaves shook in its downdraft.

Diez scanned the tangle of dark roots at the base of the tree before him. Just now, his eyes had been drawn back to it, and somehow things looked different to when he'd checked the spot not thirty seconds ago. In what way, he wasn't sure—still a tangle of roots, just *different*. A mass of broad leaves in the undergrowth at the base of the tree obscured his vision, so he slung his rifle and got down on all fours to part the veil with both hands.

His breath caught in his throat. He hadn't been looking at a tangle of roots after all. Not solely, anyway.

Amongst the root system at the base of the tree, not two feet from his face, a large pair of eyes stared back at him curiously.

In the air one hundred feet above Diez, Jessy spurned the order to stay put and freed herself from the litter. Johansson had his back to her, having already moved forward to the flight deck to issue instructions to the pilot. Straining, Jessy pulled herself up to a seat up by the door and strapped herself in. Beside her, the crewman manning the pintle-mounted .50 calibre M2 didn't seem to care, intent as he was on scanning the terrain below. Jessy guessed he couldn't have seen much through the cover of the trees: for the most part, the deep green of the canopy beneath them, shifting and rippling at the mercy of the huge blades thumping powerfully overhead, was impenetrable. Still, she followed his gaze, staring down through the open door of the hovering Black Hawk. From up here, not even the Penetrator was visible, just the thick steel cable to which it was attached sinking into the sea of foliage like a fishing line into dark water. As the cable retracted, the hoist above the door whirred.

Jessy again peered down, watching for the Penetrator to clear the canopy, eagerly anticipating the emergence of the first group of troops.

But her gaze was ripped away.

Through the leaves, at ground level, she caught a flash of orange light. Perplexed, she squinted, searching the swirling green sea beneath her. A quick succession of flashes followed, maybe half a dozen at once, flaring brightly.

Muzzle flashes—

Oh no…

Jessy couldn't see what the soldiers were shooting at, but the bursts of light grew more sustained, coming from all sides. Around her, crewmen shouted, but the thumping of the blades overhead drowned out their voices. A slow panic rose in her, and she sensed it, too, in the men as they swung quickly into action.

We need to get out of here.

The hoist above the door continued to whir, and as the Penetrator finally came clear of the canopy, Jessy screamed.

Rebecca watched the thin white streak rise from the jungle in an unerring straight line, chasing the Black Hawk from behind.

Though she'd never seen one before, except maybe in a movie, she knew the smoke-like stripe was a vapour trail. More importantly, she knew what such a trail *meant*.

Someone had fired a rocket at the chopper nosing towards her and the pyramid's northern face—the chopper that was their only means of escape.

Rebecca watched in horror as the projectile chased down its target and hit its mark.

90

Jessy screamed.

Beneath her, framed by the open doorway of Raven Two and swinging from the empty Penetrator trailing beneath the aircraft, was a single jumper. Having caught the device as it was lifted from the jungle floor, the creature raced up the cable as though it were a thread of silk, the body of the chopper shielding the superspider against the powerful downdraft.

The chopper's crew chief—perhaps unable to believe his eyes—froze momentarily… then hit the cable's brake, bringing it to a jarring halt. But he was too late. The jumper was too close, and the crewman next to Jessy—who had already opened up with the M2—couldn't swing the weapon around low enough.

Unhindered, the jumper leapt straight up through the open doorway, into the cabin of the chopper.

The first of the bullets whizzed past her ear and Rebecca leapt backwards into the temple.

This isn't happening…

The rocket fired from the jungle by parties unknown had nailed the approaching Black Hawk in the tailfin. There'd been an explosion. Now, a volley of bullets slammed into the surrounding columns, causing eruptions of dust and shards of stone to fly in all directions. Rebecca dived to the ground, out of the way of the onslaught, as Ed and Oliveira took cover somewhere behind her.

The bullets were coming from the second Black Hawk, which now hovered erratically in the distance. Obviously, its gunner was firing at *something*, but he seemed to be spraying his shots recklessly, maybe in panic.

Abruptly, the gunfire ended. Rebecca popped her head up.

Somehow, the first Black Hawk had survived the rocket attack, its protective armour presumably designed to withstand impact from small arms. But the tailfin was shot to pieces; the aircraft was crippled. As Rebecca watched, the Black Hawk dipped dramatically, spewing black smoke, before spinning on its axis and plunging through the sky like a loosed missile.

…oh no… God no…

The chopper, totally out of control, dived towards the temple, heading straight for them.

Inside Raven Two it was mayhem.

Jessy hadn't stopped screaming. No sooner had the first jumper cleared the open doorway than a *second* assailed the soldier manning the M2 beside her. Bullets spurted wildly from the weapon's heavy muzzle, spraying through the air above the canopy, the soldier's finger caught on the machine-gun's trigger. The thunder of the spitting rounds hurt Jessy's ears, but it was the least of her concerns. As she watched, the first jumper swept Johansson into its smothering grasp and swatted him out the opposing portside door. In a flash—his face frozen in horror and his arms and legs wriggling in the jumper's grip—Johansson and his abductor dropped from view. Jessy wailed hysterically. Up front, the pilot himself screamed, raising his hands in fright as a third jumper appeared on the windshield. The chopper spun violently, losing altitude, and the terrified pilot struggled for control. He couldn't regain it. The Penetrator, trailing unrestrained at the end of the cable several feet below, snagged in the canopy.

Again, the chopper sank and yawed right, but this time the rotor-blades clipped the trees. It all happened quickly, and Jessy, still screaming, could do little but watch in terror, squeezing shut her eyes as the green of the canopy rushed up through the starboard window.

91

Rebecca watched with dismay as the Black Hawk hurtled towards the temple and straight into the web, metal screaming. Instantly, its fifty-foot titanium and fibreglass rotor-blades entangled and ground to an ear-piercing halt. But the aircraft's momentum was too great, and neither the trees nor the catching-sheet could stand in its way. Squealing in protest, the Black Hawk heaved sideways, rolling laterally on itself and spinning side-on towards the pyramid, wrapping itself in silk like a giant insect.

The web—as its design dictated—was absorbing the crash as opposed to halting the chopper outright, but Rebecca realised it would never do so fast enough. The tumbling Black Hawk grew larger by the millisecond through the columns of the temple, which lay directly in the chopper's path. The huge machine was going to smash into it and take *them* along with it.

Go! Run!

Rebecca snapped out of her daze and turned to flee. She didn't get far.

The huge, pale grey leg appeared out of nowhere, hooking her by the ankle and dragging her to the ground and the open shaft.

It was a single, segmented limb, maybe fifteen feet in length, and then suddenly there was another, shooting out of the shaft with the speed of an angry snake. As she slid across the floor towards the hole, Rebecca saw the second leg swat Oliveira aside, sending him soaring. The flamethrower flew from his hands.

Five or six seconds had passed since the rocket had struck the Black Hawk. His attention most likely drawn to that, Oliveira clearly hadn't noticed the Female climbing the shaft, rising from below. Ed, too, had been caught off-guard, but he was able to dive and grasp Rebecca's outstretched wrist as she slid past screaming. With the gun in his opposing hand, he fired down at the pale, hairless limb as it drew them towards the open hole. With each shot a gush of dark blood jetted high into the air, but still the leg dragged them. The hole yawned. Ed kept firing.

SHIIITTT!!

Barely three feet from the lip of the shaft, the shattered leg finally relented, releasing them. Rebecca skidded to a halt beside Ed, who seized her and rolled her sideways as a third limb appeared, crashing down hard on the spot she'd occupied a second earlier. A fourth and a fifth appendage followed, all thrashing and straining up through the shaft, and before long each of the pale limbs was braced solidly against the temple floor as the creature tried to draw her grotesque, bloated body up through the opening.

Ghostlike, the Female's pale form rose. She was almost free.

Rebecca scrambled to her feet, the sound of gunfire in her ears again. The flamethrower was an irretrievable distance from Oliveira, who was only now drawing upright himself. She shot him a despairing glance. *"ARE YOU COMING?"*

Oliveira nodded. *"I have reconsidered your offer…"*

Trapped between the terrifying image of the emerging Female on one side and the chopper hurtling towards them on the other—crunching through the web and now only yards away—the three of them ran as the Female burst fully out of the shaft behind them—

—and together leapt from the temple out into space, towards the chopper as it in turn hurtled the final few feet to meet them in mid-air.

Rebecca heard a whoosh and a whip-like snap behind her as the enraged Female lunged furiously with her forelegs, evidently unable to squeeze her great bulk through the narrowly spaced columns of the temple. She missed Rebecca by inches. Fortunately, the hurtling chopper reached the end of its run *before* striking the temple, finally surrendering to the strength of the web. Coming to a sudden, weightless halt, it sprang back away from the temple just as Rebecca and her companions reached the peak of their leap and began to fall—

—catching it on the way.

Rebecca hit it hard, the wind driven instantly from her body as she slammed into one of the wheels towards the nose. At the same time, Ed and Oliveira hit the open portside doorway. Bouncing out of the Female's reach, the Black Hawk settled in the damaged web, but Rebecca sensed it sinking, threatening to plunge to the ground. Terrified, covered in silk, she scrambled to get a better handhold. Her fingers were slipping, the force of the rebounding chopper almost too much to bear.

Behind her, the Female hissed, barked madly…

The chopper dropped, sagged. The three of them jolted down with it and almost fell.

"*Ed!*"

"Just hold on!"

"*I'm losing my grip!*"

Again, the chopper sank in the web, lurching, twisting. Metal groaned. Rebecca's knuckles were white. Ed and Oliveira struggled, too. Below them, the steps of the pyramid loomed. They wouldn't survive the fall.

"*No…*"

Another lurch. The Female seemed furious, her legs reaching for them, straining through the columns. Her hissing intensified. Both hands around the wheel, Rebecca tried and failed to swing her legs up. Another lurch and she'd be history…

"*Ed! I can't hold on…*"

Ed opened his mouth, but before he could say anything—and as if to test her—the chopper slipped once more.

As promised, Rebecca lost her grip and fell—

—just as a bloodied hand shot from inside the chopper and snatched her wrist.

Leaning almost fully outside the forward portside window, the soldier tossed her a wink. "Got you," he said, straining through gritted teeth. His face was deeply lacerated. A cloth strip bearing the name 'Aronsohn' was stitched over the right breast of his fatigues. He pulled her up to the opening.

Two more bloodied soldiers scrambled to the doorway. They had Ed and Oliveira halfway inside when one of them glanced towards the temple and paled. "*Shit! Hold on!*"

Half-inside the window, Rebecca turned in time to see the Female—who had pressed her mouthparts between the central columns of the temple—spit a huge thread of silk from the glands behind her fangs. With a resounding thud, it slammed into the Black Hawk, gluing to its side like a thick, taut rope. The other end was still connected in a sticky mess to the Female's open mouth, and she grasped it with her pedipalps and jerked it backwards. The chopper lurched savagely sideways, and *up*, towards the temple, the Female reeling them in like a fish at the end of a line.

Oh shit…

And if that wasn't enough, it was then that several of the Female's fellow egg-layers poured from the yawning shaft behind her, leaping through the air and onto the chopper like a pack of hyenas falling on a carcass…

92

Jessy held on for dear life as Raven Two nosedived through the canopy, punching a gaping hole as it went.

On all sides, branches snapped like match-sticks; others scratched and clawed through the open doors and windows. The scream of twisting metal filled the cabin.

Jessy squeezed shut her eyes. The soldier who'd manned the M2 beside her had vanished, so too the crew chief. She hadn't seen them go. The two remaining jumpers had also disappeared, perhaps brushed free as the Black Hawk fell.

Maybe they escaped, taking the men with them.

Though she wasn't religious, Jessy began to pray, and as she did, the chopper—with a sudden jarring, bone-crunching lurch—came to an abrupt and unexpected halt.

Aronsohn pulled Rebecca through the window and into the chopper as gunfire barked. Rebecca turned and saw one of the egg-layers, at that very same opening, disappear in an explosion of blood.

She jumped to her feet. The floor listed, and she thrust out her arms for balance. The Female, straining against the temple's columns, pulled again on the heavy strand of silk, but the catching-sheet that had ensnared the

Black Hawk resisted, fighting to retain its prize. The tug-of-war tossed the aircraft like a ship in a storm. The floor tilted, and Rebecca fell against Ed, who, along with Oliveira, had joined her and Aronsohn inside. Two more soldiers, and at least one other crew member, stood at the aircraft's various openings, firing into the gloom.

An egg-layer materialized at the portside door, hissing. Legs wide, it leapt onto one of the soldiers who stumbled backwards, screaming and thrashing.

"Jenkins!" Aronsohn yelled, reaching for him as the chopper lurched back towards the pyramid, expelling the younger soldier and his attacker. The remaining occupants hit the deck hard, sliding inexorably for the opening themselves. Screaming, the crew chief, at the top of the pile, disappeared out the door, wide-eyed in terror. Another heave, and the Black Hawk listed in the opposite direction, saving the rest of the group from the crew chief's fate but causing them all to slide back towards the *starboard* door.

On the outside of the Black Hawk, the remaining egg-layers scrambled about like crabs on a tin sheet. One of them appeared with a hiss through the starboard door, companion in tow. The two creatures came for Ed as the floor surged again, Ed sliding back the other way and out of reach. They turned on Oliveira, who had snatched a fire-extinguisher from the wall, but before he could swing at them, he lost his footing and fell. On his back, sliding again, he raised the extinguisher like a shield as the first of the megarachnids leapt voraciously onto his chest. He kept sliding with the huge spider pressed upon him, desperately holding it at bay as he disappeared out the door.

As Oliveira dropped from view, the egg-layer on top of him fanned into a starburst with the speed of a sprung trap. Latching onto the door's threshold—its middle legs on both sides gripping the doorframe, its rear legs grasping the deck of the Black Hawk—it abruptly ceased its forward motion. It must have been incredibly strong, because Rebecca realised its forelegs still gripped Oliveira, who hung just below the opening.

Rebecca hesitated, wondering why the creature hadn't simply exited, just as something—*the second egg-layer*—struck her hard in the back and sent her sprawling to the deck.

· · ·

Jessy jolted forward as Raven Two snagged in the understorey and lurched to a jarring halt.

Hanging from her harness, too scared to move, she carefully shifted her gaze. Leaves and branches poked through the window beside her. Below her feet, through the windshield, the ground, maybe a dozen yards away, beckoned.

She couldn't see the pilot.

Is he gone, too? Am I alone up here?

All around, a faint tick of metal echoed in the stillness. Other than that, silence.

"Hello?"

No answer. Even Priscilla was gone. Had Johansson released her? She couldn't recall.

You're stuck up here by yourself.

A sudden loud groan caused Jessy to jump… but in truth, what really scared her was the horrible tearing sound that followed.

Oh no…

With a faltering lurch, Raven Two broke free of the surrounding foliage.

The ground rushed up through the windshield.

Rebecca's chin crashed into the floor, sparking a lightning-bolt of pain. Ignoring it, bouncing off the deck, she spun onto her back—at the same time whipping up the AK-74 to meet her attacker.

As expected, the second egg-layer was there, its pale three-inch fangs swarming large in her vision, legs rearing in a threat-pose—

Rebecca squeezed the trigger, the sudden report deafening in the confines of the chopper.

The pale-grey carcass stuttered back from her, quivering uncontrollably.

Rebecca whirled back to the doorway and the egg-layer still poised *there*, in time to see the sudden eruption of dark and viscous blood burst from its dorsal surface.

Within an instant of the object entering its cephalothorax—the hard, shell-like region housing its brain—the egg-layer was dead. Rebecca realised the projectile was Oliveira's gas-propelled grappling hook—he'd fired it into the cabin of the Black Hawk, *through the egg-layer.*

With a clang, the hook found purchase on the floor's metal grating. The knotted rope, chasing in blurring loops behind it, tightened as Rebecca scrambled for the doorway. As she went, shots rent the air: Ed and the other soldier firing at the egg-layers still skittering outside, jostling to get in. The chopper rolled again, but Rebecca maintained her footing and pushed past the dead egg-layer still frozen in a starburst at the door's threshold. Fighting to stay upright, Rebecca peered through the opening.

Oliveira dangled below, trailing at the end of the rope.

Rebecca grasped the rope and pulled upwards with all her might.

Aronsohn joined her, and together, they hauled Oliveira to the base of the door. The chopper heaved again, but Rebecca had braced herself tight against the doorframe. Aronsohn had, too, and each of them reached down with a single free hand, seizing Oliveira's wrists. The chopper bucked and swayed like a faulty mechanical bull.

Kicking away the dead egg-layer, Rebecca used the extra space and fell to her belly, straining to reach down. Oliveira swung from the base of the door, gripping the edge fiercely. She grasped him by the collar. As though cresting a wave, the Black Hawk rolled back towards the pyramid, and Rebecca's stomach rolled with it. Behind her, both Ed and the other soldier fired non-stop, the tattoo thunderous. Rebecca looked towards the pyramid. If she could gauge how much time they had before—

Too late.

The spur caught Oliveira without warning, hooking him around the ankle and jerking him backwards. He cried out, and Rebecca and Aronsohn barely held on. Rebecca had been wondering how close the Female had dragged them, and realised they were less than five or six yards from the temple. A claw at the end of one of the Female's feet—normally used for climbing—had snared Oliveira.

The huge Female pressed against the stone columns, still pulling with the appendage that held Oliveira, but at the same time hooking several legs around the chopper.

She had them.

The chopper rocked as she dragged it closer. Another leg appeared and flayed at Oliveira. His collar started to rip.

"*The gun!*" Oliveira yelled to Aronsohn, his gaze darting to the open window and the pintle-mounted M2. "*USE IT!*"

"*If I let you go—*" Aronsohn cried.

"*JUST DO IT!*"

Aronsohn nodded and let go.

"*No!*" Rebecca screamed. She braced against the door with her thigh, half outside the chopper, gripping Oliveira's shirt with both hands. But without Aaronson's assistance, she couldn't hold him for long...

With his left hand, Oliveira let go of the doorway.

Rebecca lunged, fighting to keep hold of him. "*What the hell are you doing?!*"

With his free hand, Oliveira rifled inside his vest. There was something about the way he looked at her...

"Here, take this," he said, holding out his hand.

And with that, he was gone.

93

"*NO!*"

Rebecca watched helplessly as the triumphant Female reefed back her prize with a whip-like snap of her leg. Like a toy doll, Oliveira soared through the air, shooting over the Female's head and into the darkness beyond the temple columns. The huge arachnid didn't turn as he disappeared; she seemed to have no further interest in him.

She wanted *more*.

The M2 opened up with a roar.

Aronsohn strafed the temple point-blank. The assault was withering, the stone columns disappearing behind clouds of dust and shrapnel. The Female shrieked, shrinking from the barrage. Aronsohn didn't relent, sweeping the gun back and forth. Rebecca covered her ears and shut her eyes against the dust.

But as quickly as it had begun, it ended in abrupt silence, and Rebecca opened her eyes again, only to scream.

Lightning-quick, the Female had shot one of her long forelegs through the dust-cloud, right through the open window of the Black Hawk—

And right through Aronsohn's *chest*. She plucked him from the chopper like a cocktail onion on a toothpick.

Rebecca watched in stunned horror, shocked by the gruesome sight, and as the dust dispersed, she saw something that caused her heart to sink even further.

Aronsohn's barrage had done more harm than good. The columns of the temple, centuries-old, had splintered under the assault, and the Female, seemingly unharmed and pressed up against them, had crashed through.

She came for the chopper, but only after dashing Aronsohn against the side of the Black Hawk and waving him in the air like a trophy. Somehow still alive, he struggled in her grip, so the Female reached across and grasped him with three more legs.

Victorious, she quartered him in the air and tossed the four pieces of his battered body to the steps of the pyramid below.

94

The chopper was now the Female's to do with as she wished.

Frenzied, the huge megarachnid dragged it flush against the pyramid, ramming it hard against the temple. The impact, however, forced the pummelled chopper to tip back in the opposite direction, causing the floor to buck away from the structure.

Rebecca lost her balance, as well as her grip on the pouch of diamonds Oliveira had passed her a moment ago. To her dismay, the bag, still tied, dropped to the deck and skated down the slope towards the starboard-side doorway. Reflexively, Rebecca fell to her belly, sliding after the pouch—

—and tipped right out after it, into space.

"*Bec!*" Ed cried.

He'd tried, but failed, to catch her as she slid past—he'd reached for her, but then something had seized him from behind and pulled him in the opposite direction. As he was dragged away, he saw the last remaining soldier grasp Rebecca's wrist, but her momentum had been too great and holding on, the soldier had exited the aircraft with her.

Now, Ed turned. The Female had latched onto his ankle with one of her clawed legs. Shifting the chopper's weight so that its floor angled towards her, she hauled him backwards, towards her open mouth. He slid fast but managed to catch hold of one of the metal seats as he whooshed by. The seat was bolted to the floor and he hooked his arm around it, halting his slide, but howled in pain, suddenly terrified she would tear his leg free of his body.

Pistol out, Ed hit the pale foreleg attached to his ankle with two quick shots before squeezing for a third.

Click.

He was out of ammo.

Rebecca and the soldier fell…

…but not far.

Fortunately, the Black Hawk had been dragged flush against the temple, so the distance to the steps beneath it was short. Had the two of them exited farther from the pyramid, the fall would have been fatal. As it was, they dropped fifteen feet at most, and even then, they were slowed by the barrier web.

Still, it hurt.

Rebecca and the soldier struck the stairs together, bouncing down several steps before coming to a halt and untangling. Dazed, Rebecca leapt to her feet without stopping to brush herself off. She screamed back up at the chopper. *"ED!"*

Shit!

Even if they climbed back to the temple, the Black Hawk was beyond reach. They wouldn't be able to get past the Female.

The soldier who had fallen with her rushed to her side. He was roughly her age, maybe a few years younger, and covered in silk. He placed a bloodied hand on her arm. "Ma'am, my name is Kriedemann. We need to get out of here—"

Rebecca shrugged him off and scrambled up a few steps. *"We're not leaving him!"* Positioned beneath the chopper, she couldn't see through its doors or windows—the aircraft's twisted underside blocked everything, even her view of the temple. She climbed still more steps and grew more frantic. *"ED!"*

Only a few feet above her head, the chopper shuddered against the pyramid. On its other side, the Female barked madly—

Again, a strong hand landed on her arm, this time spinning her around. *"MA'AM!"*

Rebecca glanced up. The chopper's spotlights blazed into the web, and in those powerful beams, she detected movement.

The creatures were built more solidly than the jumpers: hairier, but lighter in colour, not dissimilar in hue to the surrounding silk. And though maybe not as agile, they were still quick.

Very quick.

In scattered groups, they scurried through the barrier web towards her and Kriedemann, at least a dozen of them, on all sides.

Workers—the caste responsible for building and maintaining the web… and attending to captured prey.

Kriedemann's grip tightened on her arm as he pulled her forcefully towards the pyramid's base.

"*RUN!*" he cried.

Ed looked down at the huge, grotesque face framed by the open doorway.

Pressed to the opening, the Female's mouthparts worked feverishly, the rows of tooth-like serrations that surrounded her wide-open jaws exposed to him in all their glory. Her downward-striking fangs clicked and scraped against the chopper. Venom, or some sort of digestive *slobber*, flew everywhere. She seemed rabid, frothing at the mouth, trying desperately to get in, to get at *him*. Enraged, she attempted to drag him back towards her, but Ed managed to keep hold of the seat. At least two more of her legs shot inside the cabin and flailed about, ripping at everything, trying to force the door wider.

Frantically, Ed searched for options. The pilot and co-pilot were gone, probably hauled by the egg-layers through the shattered windshield. He was alone up here.

The Female pulled harder.

Ed screamed. Invisible tongues of flame licked at his ankle, spreading up to his hip. He glanced back at the Female, certain she was going to tear his leg clean off. And she could do it, too, but she had no need for the limb. She wanted everything.

She pressed closer, almost inside the chopper. Slobber from her gaping mouth sprayed across his face. Her huge eyes—now only a few feet away—swarmed large in his vision. They seemed different to how they'd been down in the nuptial chamber. Darker, perhaps. Lifeless.

Oliveira's flashbang had blinded her. She'd used her other senses to locate him.

Rearing, she spat at him.

A spray of silken threads zigzagged towards Ed at one six-hundredth of a second; before he knew she'd even expelled anything, he was spattered head to toe. Clearly, she wanted to pin him there, stop him from escaping—not that he could have. Ed screamed again, the pain in his leg at fever-pitch. Unable to endure it any longer, he moved to let go of the seat, but hesitated as he caught sight of something odd.

Flung back inside the temple, behind the Female, Oliveira had been all but ignored.

Perhaps thinking him dead, or no longer a threat, the creature had willingly exposed her huge, bloated abdomen, and when the M2 had opened up, he'd taken cover on the ground behind it. There, within arm's reach, had been his discarded pack. It contained no weapons, and a scan of the area confirmed the flamethrower was gone, too. But he *had* found something. Unlike his men, who had loaded up with as much treasure as they'd been able to carry, he'd taken this single item from the chamber below, knowing that private collectors paid handsomely for rare and unusual artefacts.

He lifted the object from his pack, and on a shattered left ankle, hobbled for the centre of the temple and the moai with the tiny sphere in its hands.

At the foot of the statue was a slot. Oliveira raised the crystal rod. It was identical to those that protruded from the larger sphere below—and from this sphere, too—except this rod was deep red, and had been grafted at one end to an elongated piece of stone. The fused pieces had been fashioned into a short staff, the stone portion bearing the same grooves and markings as the disc Rebecca had used to power the lift.

If he couldn't attack the Female, he'd *distract* her.

And when he jammed the rod into the slot at the moai's feet, the response was precisely what he'd hoped for.

With a low rumble, the moai began to shake… and rise.

Tears in her eyes, Rebecca fled down the steps. She'd had no choice but to leave Ed. The workers were too close—

She stopped, spun back to the temple.

Trailing behind, Kriedemann didn't notice that she'd halted. He kept running, firing his M16 at the pursuing creatures, and nearly collided with her on the way through. But Rebecca's attention was elsewhere. She looked back up the stairs, unsure as to why she'd stopped and turned, and now unable to believe her eyes.

Enveloping the temple was an orange-gold ring of light. It seemed to be emanating from inside the structure. No, from *above* it—from the sphere cradled in the moai's hands. Somehow, the statue had risen from the floor, in the process lifting the orb and pushing it through the roof of the temple, which had seemingly parted to allow it passage. Blinding lights arced outwards, igniting the near-dark. Pillars of flame—like solar flares, but also like forking electricity—burst forth in every direction.

But to Rebecca, even more incredible was what was happening in the sphere's immediate vicinity—to the objects caught *within* the halo of light.

Objects like the chopper containing Ed.

96

⚡

Ed felt the Female's grip slacken as she turned to the strange light. It was all he needed.

Realising what was happening to his body—and in the split-second afforded him—he pulled himself into the seat, still restricted but not thwarted by the silken spittle. He strapped himself in.

Somehow, he was being *sucked* upwards, towards the door. *What the hell?* All around him, anything that wasn't physically bolted down began levitating and flying out the door, towards the temple. Even the chopper seemed to become weightless and rise. The Female, clearly fighting the effects herself, hadn't let go of him, but she was distracted, and as the chopper bumped up higher to nudge the temple's roofline, she rose with it, too.

At the top of the portside doorway, a gap appeared, affording Ed a narrow view above and across the temple. His eyes went wide.

The sphere! Still cradled by the moai, it had risen through the ceiling, arcing and flaring with the orange-gold light that had initially drawn his attention. Now, everything that had flown from the door of the chopper swirled in a ring around the mysterious sphere.

Ed's mind raced. It was as though the sphere were a tiny black hole—not actually *consuming* things like a black hole, but at least dragging everything towards it.

A black hole.

A black hole was a collapsed star.

A collapsed *sun.*

The power of the sun...

You're kidding me...

The instant he'd laid eyes on the sphere—falling into a stupor of disbelief, awe, and elation—he realised this was the object he'd been searching for all his life. Then everything had gone to hell, forcing him—momentarily, at least—to abandon it, but it hadn't left his thoughts. He'd always assumed the legend of the object, and its fabled ability to harness the 'power of the sun', meant that it could, in some way, channel or exploit the *Earth's* Sun. But now, it dawned on him that he may have misinterpreted the myths—that maybe something had been lost in translation. In fact, he knew that was the case. The myths referred to the tiny *sun* in the moai's hands.

They referred to *its* power...

A loud, alien shriek pierced the air, and as if in pain, the Female reared, swivelling back inside the temple. As she did, Ed saw the cause of her distress—a gaping wound on her swollen abdomen.

Fighting the sphere's pull, the Female wrested a flailing figure from the temple and raised it into the air.

Oliveira! Ed had thought him long gone. In Oliveira's right hand was a foot-long, knifelike shard of stone, likely sheared from the columns by the gunfire. It dripped dark, ichor-like blood.

Enraged, the Female drew Oliveira towards the Black Hawk. He jabbed her leg. With another shriek she dashed him against the chopper—just as she had done earlier to Aronsohn—and the shard tumbled from Oliveira's hands. In retribution, she wrenched Ed again, too. The safety harness bit into his flesh, and he almost slid from under it. Struggling to stay inside, Ed glanced out and locked gazes with Oliveira.

"Behind you!" Oliveira called, blood spraying from his mouth as again, the Female slammed him into the chopper.

Ed turned, craned his neck.

No way...

A khaki-coloured, square pack had shaken loose from its original place of storage to fly across the cabin. Its strap was snagged on the back of the seat beside him, the item straining at the end of it, angled towards the doorway and the sphere trying to suck it out.

A satchel-charge.

"HURRY!"

Twice more the Female slammed Oliveira against the chopper, causing it to reverberate with sickening, hollow thuds. Blood splattered Ed through the window, but still Oliveira writhed.

Clearly, the Female had had enough. Out of the corner of his eye—as he twisted in his seat, straining for the charge—Ed saw her bring the struggling Oliveira to her mouth—

—and impale him through the chest with her yard-long, pickaxe-like fangs.

There was no scream. Oliveira went limp.

The Female crushed her victim between her jaw-like chelicerae. Bones snapped and crunched. She spat the mangled corpse against the chopper and turned to Ed fearsomely, intent on finishing him for good.

Ed fought back bile, but Oliveira had bought him the time he had needed. He had the charge in his hands. Without hesitation, he flicked the switch at the top of the device as the frenzied Female pressed closer.

Inside its canvas satchel, the charge was now armed. Ed raised it.

The blast would be big, of course, and would more than likely take him along with it—but he'd run out of options.

The Female hissed at him, her blood-spattered mouth wide open and ravenous, *hungry* for him. She was only a couple of feet away.

Ed grimaced. "Here then—bite me, *BITCH.*"

Of course, he didn't intend on losing his grip.

Just as he was about to hurl the charge into the Female's wide-open mouth, it flew abruptly from his grasp.

Ed watched in dismay as it swept out the door, *past* the Female—out towards the sphere at the top of the temple.

NO!

It was over. He'd lost his only chance of defeating her. As if sensing this, the Female doubled her efforts, and Ed started to slip beneath the safety harness. She was too strong. He couldn't resist her any more.

Something halted his slide.

Ed stared down the length of his body. He was flat on his back, feet angling towards the door. His *vest*, however, was stuck—too bulky to slip beneath the straps. It was keeping him in his seat, inside the chopper.

And he suddenly knew why...

The X40 strapped to his chest. He'd forgotten about it.

So far, they'd had mixed success with the ultrasonic devices, but at point-blank range…

He reached down and flicked the switch. The effect was instantaneous.

With a high-pitched wail, the Female reared, releasing him and convulsing wildly. Her legs flailed as though in the grip of an electric current, and in pain and apparent surprise she tumbled backwards, across the roof of the temple, towards the sphere—

—*and the satchel-charge.*

And not a second later, it blew.

97

It blew *big*.

The chopper rocked with the shock wave that blasted out from the temple—a huge orange ball of flame billowing into the air and out into the web. The Female was instantly pulverised, bits of her blasting in every direction, splattering Ed through the chopper's open doorway.

She was gone.

But there was no time to celebrate. The blast hadn't just rid Ed of the Female—it had shredded most of the surrounding silk as well. With her grip on the chopper lost, nothing held the stricken aircraft in place.

Not even the sphere's gravitational pull. It too was gone.

The Black Hawk dropped like a stone.

Rebecca saw the chopper fall, impacting wheels-first on the steps of the pyramid's northern face.

Only moments ago, still pursued by the workers, Kriedemann had pulled her from her momentary stupor, transfixed as she was by the strange halo of light. But at the sound of the explosion, she'd again drawn to a halt, snapping around as the chopper was purged from the web. Now, in disbelief, she watched as the aircraft tipped over laterally, rolling sideways, roof to belly, down the steps towards them...

"Oh shit…"

She felt Kriedemann grasp her hand once more… and they *ran*.

The Black Hawk tumbled down the steps, gathering speed.

Hoping to outrun the aircraft, Rebecca and Kriedemann sprinted for the bottom of the stairs, aiming for the plaza at the base of the pyramid. Desperately, they pushed through the barrier-web, the Black Hawk growing larger behind their fleeing forms. Their other pursuers—the few remaining workers that hadn't yet been nailed by Kriedemann—were swamped behind them, crushed and spat out the back as the chopper thundered past, metal screaming and pounding against the stone. Rebecca knew that she and Kriedemann were next.

The plaza beckoned, only a few steps away.

Behind them, the bouncing chopper gathered the web as it tumbled, its spotlights jolting crazily. The roar was deafening.

"GO, GO, GO!"

They weren't going to make it. The Black Hawk was right on their heels, yards away, about to collect them on the way through. They were still several steps from the bottom—

"SHIIITTT!!"

Too late.

The Black Hawk caught them, clipping them on the heels as they leapt—hand in hand—out from the staircase, towards the plaza at the base of the pyramid.

Soaring through the air, nudged by the chopper, Rebecca and Kriedemann plunged into the stone courtyard and skidded across it.

They'd timed their leap to perfection.

The Black Hawk came down behind them with a roar, thundering into the plaza amidst a shower of sparks and slewing across the flagstones. Sensing it on her tail, Rebecca kept rolling, scrambling out of its path, but there was no time. Despite herself, she skidded to a stop, squeezing her eyes shut as ten metric tonnes of metal bore down on her, and she opened her mouth to scream—

—just as the Black Hawk ground finally to a halt—

And was still.

· · ·

One at a time, Rebecca opened her eyes. Bent and twisted and creaking softly, the chopper, on its side, loomed above her.

It had come to rest less than a foot from her nose.

The huge rotor-blades and their mast were gone, torn fully clear of the hub, the mangled remains of which were directly above her head. She faced the roof of the crumpled Black Hawk.

On his back less than ten feet away, Kriedemann lay panting.

Rebecca let out a deep sigh—a sort of self-pitying whimper—then snapped out of it. "*Ed…*"

She got up, groaning, and limped for the door.

The open doorway faced the sky.

Rebecca scrambled up the roof and over the crumpled edge of the chopper's port side. The metal was hot to the touch. She peered down through the opening to find Ed strapped into his seat, pinned by wreckage and covered in blood and silken spittle. He wasn't moving.

"*Ed!*" she cried, swinging into the cabin. She made for him through the surrounding detritus, pulling and pushing at twisted seat frames and loose, hanging cables. "Hang in there, okay, buddy? I'm going to get you out!" When she heard Ed moan weakly in response, she nearly wept tears of joy.

Ed's groan was followed by the sound of Kriedemann scrambling up the roof. The soldier dropped with a thud through the open doorway. "You okay?"

"Yeah… keep an eye out for the spiders, will you?"

"I think they're gone, all of them. Strange, they suddenly just—"

The noise was loud, a terrible shearing sound above them, like a huge piece of fabric tearing in two.

Rebecca jumped in fright. Slowly, almost not wanting to know, she turned her gaze skyward. "*Oh, come on. Give us a break…*"

A short distance from the pyramid's northern face and about two-thirds of the way up, the floatplane hung above them like the Sword of Damocles. The shearing sound, rising again, came from the old silken threads that had held the plane in place for the past two years. One after another, the strands snapped and unravelled.

"Oh, *shit*," Rebecca breathed.

Clearly, the Black Hawk's devastating tumble down the northern stair-case had wreaked havoc on the web, severing most of the support threads. The few that remained seemed unable to bear the plane's weight.

More threads tore, snapped. Directly above them, the plane slipped several feet, sagging in the web, and then slipped again.

Oh, shit!

Rebecca spun back to Ed and tugged at his safety harness. She pulled at the buckle. It was stuck.

"Not now…"

More snapping…

"NOT NOW!" Rebecca wrenched at the harness with all her strength. Kriedemann joined her efforts, but the buckle was jammed. Rebecca pan-icked, fumbling. *"Come on, damn you! COME ON!"*

Above them, there was a final, loud twang, like a bowstring snapping, and the floatplane broke free. Rebecca looked up, a bitter thought rising in her mind as the aircraft nosedived towards them.

Not like this.

She squeezed her eyes shut and cried out, unable to hold back her scream as the plane crashed down on them with a roar.

Then starkly, there was silence.

98

The aft took the brunt of the hit.

For an instant, the plane remained upright—tail in the air, nose firmly buried in the wreckage of the chopper. Then, with a slow, drawn-out creak, the aircraft toppled, picking up speed as it went. The two machines came together like a set of metallic jaws snapping shut on a meal, rocking wildly with the impact before coming to rest. Nose to tail, they lay on their sides, the plane lying fully upon the chopper, lengthways above the ground. Together, they formed a single, tangled mess of machinery.

Inside the cabin, it was dark and still. Metal creaked, settled.

The plane's fuselage blocked the door above, creating a rudimentary ceiling. Rebecca drew a frayed breath. The hit had sounded like an exploding bomb, and the physical impact had been even more frightening. Ed, who remained strapped in his energy-absorbing, crash-resistant seat, had ridden the blow unscathed, but she and Kriedemann had been hurled violently across the cabin. Even so, Rebecca considered the two of them lucky. The Black Hawk, as a combat aircraft, was armour-protected and ballistically tolerant, designed specifically to absorb high-velocity impact. For that reason, the cabin had held its basic shape and form, protecting them. The outcome could have been far worse.

A flashlight came on, its thin but powerful beam cutting a swathe through the blackness. Rebecca blinked, focusing on the dust motes swirling through the glow.

"You okay?" Kriedemann said, moving towards her.

"Yeah, I think so. You?"

"I'll live. Some ride, huh?"

Rebecca didn't answer. She was shaking and needed a moment. Her head swam. She thought she was going to faint.

"You sure you're okay?"

She got it together. "Yeah, a few stars, that's all." She nodded earnestly at Ed.

Kriedemann followed her gaze. "Here, hold this." He passed her the flashlight and she shone it in Ed's direction.

Like before, Ed wasn't moving, but Rebecca could see his chest rising and falling underneath his bloodied shirt.

Sliding a knife from his boot, Kriedemann started sawing through Ed's harness.

"Could have done with that earlier," Rebecca said, directing the flashlight.

"Wouldn't have been time."

He was right: it took several seconds to slice through the toughened material of each shoulder strap.

Once Kriedemann had finished, they left Ed in the seat and examined him thoroughly. Multiple cuts and scratches covered his face and body.

"No sign of any broken bones, no obvious spinal injuries," Kriedemann said. "I think it's safe to move him."

Together, they extricated Ed's listless form from the mass of warped and twisted metal. Groaning with the effort, they pulled him into their section of the cabin, which was more open, and set him down carefully.

"We should tend his wounds before moving him again," Kriedemann said. "In this heat and humidity, cuts turn septic fast." He looked up at the ceiling the floatplane had formed above their heads. "If nothing else, we'll be safe in here for a few minutes. We'll treat our wounds, too."

Grazed and bleeding, Rebecca was already searching for a first-aid kit.

Kriedemann joined her. "I don't think I caught your name."

Rebecca reached out with her right hand and smiled faintly. "Rebecca Riley."

"Nice to meet you."

"And you… Captain?"

"Staff Sergeant."

"And you, Staff Sergeant Kriedemann—though I can't say as much about the circumstances."

"No. Me neither."

The chopper's medical pack was tucked securely inside a closed but unlocked storage compartment. Unzipping it, Rebecca used one of the sterile dressings to wipe the blood from Ed's face, flushing some of the deeper wounds with saline before applying an antiseptic cream. She closed the cuts with suture plaster. A gash above Ed's left eye had to be bandaged firmly.

They patched their own wounds in similar fashion. In addition to cuts to her hands, Rebecca had abrasions on her neck, knees, and face. Blood and silk matted her hair. She was a mess, but she was okay.

Once they were finished, Kriedemann slung the med-pack and glanced about the cabin. "Right, then—what say we find a way out of here?"

99

Jessy moaned and opened her eyes with a flutter. Feeling dizzy, she closed them again.

"Easy, ma'am, you're gonna be okay."

She didn't immediately recognise the voice. Again, she opened her eyes and this time saw the hazy, blurred outline of a figure bending over her. She tried to focus and was assailed by the acrid smell of smoke, maybe from an electrical fire—singed wiring or something. Then there was the sound of a fire extinguisher and the smell was gone.

Her skull pounded, and she moaned once more. "Where am I?"

The figure leaned in close. "Back on the ground, unfortunately."

Then she remembered—Raven Two had fallen from the sky and crashed through the canopy. The impact must have knocked her out.

Her eyes regained focus. Tag smiled down at her as something cold and wet pressed against her forehead. "You got a nice bump there," he said, patting her with the damp cloth.

He turned away, and she followed his gaze to the dark-skinned soldier—she thought the man's name was Bull—standing guard at the door of the felled chopper. It was dark outside, and Bull's M16 was trained on the jungle. Three more, similarly positioned soldiers formed a tight ring around the aircraft, their weapons aimed unflinchingly into the night.

"Bull," Tag said softly. "Anything?"

"Nothing. All's quiet."

Tag nodded. "We better regroup. Let's see if we can't raise Raven One."

100

Lying on her belly, Rebecca poked her head through the shattered cockpit bubble.

Night had fallen.

Slowly, she scanned the plaza with her NVGs. She couldn't see any movement: all the spiders, it seemed, had gone. She glanced at Kriedemann, also prone and searching for threats. He returned her gaze and gave her the all-clear.

They didn't delay. The glass of the windshield was gone, and they squeezed through, dragging Ed—now semiconscious, but still heavily concussed—with them.

Thunder rumbled in the distance.

On the flagstones at the front of the chopper, Rebecca crouched like a wounded animal unwilling to venture from the security of its den. "What now?" she whispered, cradling Ed in her arms.

Kriedemann moved beside her, less fearful, but nonetheless alert. "How did you get in here?"

"There's a tunnel over there," Rebecca said, jutting her chin. "It leads to a burrow down below, which itself leads beyond the web. But it won't be accessible; earlier, dozens of spiders poured into it."

"Perhaps they're gone now."

"Perhaps, but even if they are, we can't get Ed through, not in his state. It's a tight squeeze."

Kriedemann looked at Ed, then up at the dark outline of the temple at the top of the pyramid. "You know, that was a satchel-charge he used." He smiled. "He goddamned *nailed* that bitch."

Static hissed as Kriedemann's radio came alive.

"*...en One..? Any... copy?*"

The connection wasn't good, but Kriedemann answered. "This is Kriedemann. You copy?"

"*...you Sarge? It's Bull... Listen... gotta situation here...*"

"Us too, Bull. What's your sit-rep? You secure at your end?"

"*...for... moment...*"

"Bull, how many of you are... left?"

A pause. "*...six of us... including the girl... crew's gone. And damnit—we lost...*" A long burst of static. "*...how 'bout you?*"

"Me and two civilians."

"*Shit... what about the Cap...?*"

"The Captain's no longer with us, Bull. Is Wit there?"

"*...as I said... Wit's gone, Sarge. Diez... and ...meyer too. We've been... busted up good.*"

"Shit..." Kriedemann said, turning away. "SHIT!"

"*...you're it now, Sarge... you know that? In charge... What do... you want us... do?*"

Kriedemann glanced about, as though trying to take it all in. "Bull, hold the line." He turned to Rebecca. "How long will it take to navigate the burrow?"

Rebecca shrugged. "Maybe an hour, if it was just the two of us. But Ed can't crawl. We need another way out."

"There *is* no other way." Kriedemann turned back, keyed the radio again. "Bull, you there? I want you to sit tight. We're coming to you, but it's gonna be slow. We've got an injured man here. I need you to hold your position. You got that? *Hold your position.* You gotta give us an hour. Maybe more."

There was a long pause. "*Sarge... we may not have... hour. If those things... come back...*"

"Then just give us what you can," Kriedemann said. "Out."

Rebecca listened apprehensively, not keen on heading down to the burrow but knowing there was no other option. She figured Kriedemann was worried the overland route was too exposed, or maybe, in the dark, too hazardous. Both were factors, but there was a more critical issue at play. While the inner barrier-web had been catastrophically damaged, the outer catching-sheet—at least at ground level—was unscathed. That route hadn't been an option this morning, and nothing had changed. They had to go under.

Kriedemann turned to her, his mouth opening just as Bull's voice jumped back on the line.

"*Sarge… you still there…?*"

Kriedemann spun. "Go ahead."

"*Sarge, listen… we may be able to speed things up.*"

Rebecca slipped her left arm around Ed's torso, gripping him firmly by the belt. With Kriedemann on the opposite side and taking the bulk of the weight, they scampered a few short paces with Ed between them.

Rebecca strained with the effort. "I hope this plan of theirs works."

"It will. How far to the burrow?"

"Not far. A few minutes."

"And if there're any of those things down there, this device"—he gestured at the X40 in Ed's vest—"will keep them at bay?"

"That's what I'm hoping."

They shuffled to the chopper's mangled rear and crouched amongst the shadows. Kriedemann jutted his chin at the missing tailfin and rotor: the entire assembly had been blown off.

"Someone hit us with an RPG," he said. "Deliberately took us out. Who would have done that?"

Rebecca recalled the image of the vapour trail and the alarm she'd felt as it emerged from the jungle in an unerring white line. As the truth hit her, so did a familiar wave of unease. She gave Kriedemann a loaded look. "I can hazard a guess."

101

De Sousa slung the rocket launcher and gathered his gear.

"You know, Sandros was there," Cartana whined. "They were going to pick him up."

De Sousa sneered. "That's not what they said. Get the warheads."

For once, there was no further argument from Cartana, and De Sousa watched as the smaller man knelt by the pile of equipment and began scooping it up. As he did, De Sousa walked behind him and drew the foot-long blade of his hunting-knife across his throat.

Cartana made no sound. Wide-eyed, he knelt there for a second—seemingly in surprise—and then toppled to the forest floor.

De Sousa wiped the blade against a tree. Cartana had served his purpose and would only have slowed him. Had he the chance, the weakling might even have betrayed him. He couldn't risk it.

But most of all, he'd had enough of the snivelling.

De Sousa pried the two remaining warheads from the dead man's fingers and slunk into the night, Cartana's body twitching in his wake.

102

Bull watched from the door of the chopper as Heng—Chinese-American, light, lean, and comparatively short—moved to the burrow Jessy had told them about. It had taken some searching even with the infrared binoculars, but several tell-tale tracks around the entrance led them to it. They'd already opened the trapdoor and meticulously checked the tunnel. Nothing lurked inside.

Heng would travel light. A pair of NVGs covered his eyes. A pistol was holstered at his hip. Looped around his shoulders was a nylon webbing rescue strop.

"We got 300 feet of steel cable," Tag said to Bull. "Will that do?"

"It'll have to."

They'd already tested the electrical rescue hoist above the starboard-side door of Raven Two. It still worked.

Kneeling, Heng paused at the entrance to the burrow before dropping down under the watchful eyes of his companions. McGinley let go of Heng's ankles, and as his feet disappeared beneath the rim, the flap of earth that was the trapdoor sprang tightly shut.

Bull keyed his throat-mike. "You there, Sarge? He's on his way."

.   .   .

With Kriedemann's help, Rebecca hoisted Ed, and together they crossed the plaza, this time heading for the tunnel entrance. They'd sheltered at the tail of the chopper for twenty minutes. It would take Heng, at full speed, upwards of half an hour to traverse the burrow, and Kriedemann figured it was better to wait above ground than in the darkness beneath the pyramid. Rebecca had used the time to brief him about De Sousa. She was certain the psycho had fired the rocket. Who else could have?

Paranoid that De Sousa was out there somewhere watching them—watching *her*—she hurried forward, glad to be on the move.

Ed groaned. He'd been drifting in and out of consciousness for several minutes now. He muttered something unintelligible.

"Ed, save your strength," Rebecca whispered. "We've got you."

The tunnel mouth lay at the foot of the pyramid, about forty feet to the left of the large central staircase. The cobbled stone passageway was eerily quiet. They started down, Rebecca's gaze fixed on the gloom ahead. This was the single, long passageway that led to the chamber housing the sphere—the very same chamber the spiders had earlier flooded when they'd dropped from the ceiling.

The burrow entrance was even closer to the surface than she'd hoped. They reached it just as a scraping, shuffling sound echoed off the stonework. Heng's head popped from the narrow hole, and Kriedemann helped him to his feet.

Heng brushed himself off, and there were brief introductions.

"The cable finished up thirty feet short," Heng told them.

"We'll have to drag Ed to it," Rebecca said.

Ed had again roused back to consciousness and interjected groggily. "*I can crawl.*"

"That'll help," Kriedemann said to him, and then turned to Heng. "What about the weight? Can the hoist handle it?"

"We're cutting it close," Heng said. "But we'll take it slow."

Kriedemann nodded. "Okay then. Let's get moving."

To Rebecca's considerable relief, it worked. Strapped by her belt to the retracting cable and with her head and shoulders raised as high as she could manage, she only had to hang on and allow the steel line to winch her and her three companions back through the earthen burrow. Rebecca was at the top of the queue, with Kriedemann aligned somewhere in the darkness beyond her feet and Heng and Ed in turn somewhere beyond his. Ed had the padded collar of the strop around his shoulders, protecting and elevating his head and neck, so he could pretty much lay back and enjoy the scenery. Not that there was anything to see. A continuous rain of dirt marked the journey, and even with the goggles, Rebecca had to squeeze shut her eyes at the barrage. All the while, the cable thrummed in her hands as it transferred through its length the jarring whir of the rescue hoist located somewhere beyond the burrow's entrance, at the door of the felled second chopper.

Careful not to overheat the motor, they kept the mechanism on its slowest setting. Even so, just ten minutes later, all four passengers—with the addition only of a few extra bumps and bruises—were back at the north-western vantage point, safe and sound.

Two soldiers lifted Rebecca from the pitch-blackness of the burrow into the equally dark jungle at its mouth. Immediately, she scanned the area, her gaze falling on the crumpled shape of the second Black Hawk, still hot from the crash and blazing through her NVGs. She and the rest of her group made for it with haste.

Out in front, Heng and Kriedemann each had an arm around Ed, who, though still concussed, was at his most lucid since his tumble down the face of the pyramid. Rebecca trailed a pace or two behind, aided by the soldiers who had lifted her from the hole. As the group hurried to the chopper, Ed looked back at her, over his shoulder.

"Thank you," he mouthed softly.

Rebecca smiled. *You're welcome.*

At that moment a female voice rose from inside the felled Black Hawk, cutting through the night. It was Jessy, calling Ed's name. At that, Ed freed himself, stumbling into a run. As he did, a dark-skinned soldier shot forward from his post outside the chopper and met him midway. Ed shrugged his assistance and burst on unsteady legs past yet another soldier who covered them from the aircraft's window with the pintle-mounted M2. Hastening to catch up, Rebecca scrambled in behind.

She found Jessy sitting upright against one of the chopper's mangled sides and nearly gasped at the sight. The young undergrad—her broken leg splinted and elevated—was a mess: her pigtails had unravelled, and her blond hair was mussed and bloodied, as was her clothing. She held out a pair of bruised, grazed arms. Ed, who was himself bloodied, bandaged and covered in dirt and silk from the burrow, raced forward to embrace her.

"I'm sorry," he blurted in an almost breathless whisper.

Jessy was in tears. "I was so scared."

"I know. Please forgive me."

As they held one another on the chopper's leaf-strewn floor, Rebecca hesitated at the doorway. A rush of raw emotion washed over her, and she realised a decent portion of it was envy. She looked at her feet, trying to collect herself. She wanted to be happy for the two of them, *needed* to be. She lifted her eyes and smiled at Jessy as warmly as she could.

"You did it, Bec," Jessy said over Ed's shoulder. Despite what must have been severe discomfort, she beamed. "You got him back, just as you promised. Thank you."

Rebecca could stand there no longer and hurried over. A moment later all three were sharing a tearful embrace.

They still held one another when a voice interrupted. "Someone else wants a hug, too."

Rebecca turned to the voice, rising to her feet as Priscilla bounded from the arms of a young Hispanic soldier and straight into hers.

"Hello!" Rebecca cried, embracing the tiny monkey, who snuggled in close. "Oh, I missed you!"

Jessy's eyes lit up in surprise and relief. "Tag… where was she?"

The soldier named Tag shrugged. "Found her hiding just now in the bushes outside. She must have leapt free before the chopper went down. She's a survivor."

Kriedemann smiled at the scene. Rebecca beamed back at him before turning to thank Tag. There were introductions all round before the intensity of the reunion subsided and the tone inside the chopper once again grew serious. Rebecca sensed she wasn't alone in feeling they needed a plan, and fast.

"You want me to call for another helo?" Bull asked Kriedemann.

Jessy snapped her head up. "*Please*—no more choppers. I beg you."

"Yeah, same," Ed murmured in agreement.

Kriedemann seemed keen to put both at ease. "No need to worry about that," he said. "While those lunatics with the RPG are running around, we're grounded. I'm not losing another bird."

Tag, on guard now at the window, glanced at Kriedemann. "So, what's the plan?"

"We secure the area and ride out the night here," Kriedemann said. "First light, we'll hunt down those assholes and deal with them. Then—and only then—we'll call for another helo."

It sounded like a reasonable course of action, but Rebecca shook her head. "I don't know if that's wise. That plan, I mean."

Kriedemann turned to her. "Sorry?"

"We need to salvage what we can, get moving, get *out* of here as soon as possible."

Kriedemann nodded. "And that's exactly my intention, but not until we've caught those pricks—and not in the dark."

"But we can't wait for morning. We've got to leave *now*, on foot."

A flicker of impatience washed over Kriedemann's brown and green-streaked features. "Why would we do that?" he said, then reined himself in, tempering his tone. "Bec, listen. I don't like it much myself, but I'm in charge now. You need to trust me—it's too dangerous out there. Here, we can defend ourselves: rig Claymores and flares, cordon off the area, set watches. For now, we need to stay put."

Rebecca listened politely, but at the end of it shook her head, lowering her voice so as not to undermine Kriedemann's authority in front of the other men. "Sergeant, please. There's a reason we have to go. Those creatures... they aren't finished; they're regrouping as we speak. They'll be back, and soon. You need to trust *me*. We don't have much time."

Thunder rumbled in the distance. At its conclusion, Kriedemann sighed softly. "What makes you so sure?"

"I've got some expertise in the area, is all." Rebecca leaned close, her voice almost at a whisper now. "Sergeant, the three of us—Ed, Jessy and I—aren't compelled to follow orders, right? We're free to go? Because we're not hanging around. It's your choice to sit tight, but I strongly urge you not to. You don't want to be caught out here again, just the six of you on your own."

Kriedemann hesitated, his jaw tightening, and Rebecca figured it was less in exasperation than discomfort. Clearly, the pressures of leadership weighed heavy.

"So, what are you suggesting?" Kriedemann asked.

She sensed her chance and took it. "We stirred up the nest—big time. Ed killed the alpha female, and the arachnids will be agitated. In fact, we've done so much damage they'll probably abandon the site altogether, look to start another nest somewhere else. They may be on the move already, and if so, they'll overrun us long before daylight."

Jessy looked at Ed, eyes wide. "You killed *what*?"

"Tell you later," Ed whispered.

Tag threw Kriedemann an uncertain glance. "She might have a point, Sarge. Crews included, we lost *twelve* men out there."

Kriedemann hesitated. "All the more reason to stay till light. You know we don't leave anyone behind."

Leaning close, Bull cleared his throat. "Sarge, listen, we... already checked before you got here. There ain't no bodies out there—not a one. They're gone."

"*All* of them?"

Bull nodded.

"Christ." Kriedemann massaged his jaw, clearly running options and scenarios. At last, he opened his mouth. "For argument's sake... say we move. Where the hell would we go?"

Ed was still groggy but had grown visibly stronger in the past few minutes. "This morning," he said, his voice hoarse, "I talked with Oliveira, and one of his men let slip that they'd arrived here by Zodiac and left it at the ravine. The rain must have flooded the stream. If we head back there and take the Zodiac to the main river, we can radio ahead to a friend of mine who can pick us up in his boat."

Rebecca had forgotten about Chad and the *Tempestade*. It was a good idea.

Kriedemann, however, wasn't convinced. "I don't know that I'm comfortable leading a team into the jungle, at *night*, on the word of some no-good drug runner. You don't have proof there's a boat at this 'ravine', and even if there was, who's to say those lunatics with the RPG haven't bugged out? It could be gone already."

"Maybe, but we still have to get out of here," Rebecca said. "I think it's a good plan. The ravine's not far, just a couple of hours." She scanned the cabin. "You got a map?"

Kriedemann gestured to Chavarre, who produced one. Ed had the ravine's GPS coordinates.

Chart in hand, Bull nudged Kriedemann with his elbow. "Maybe it's not such a bad idea," he whispered. He pointed to a spot. "Just a few hours from rally point Delta. It's on the way." He looked up at Kriedemann, his eyes hopeful. "Boat or no boat, we can pull back to the ravine, regroup, reassess from there. Hell, if she's right and we did poke a stick down the anthill, they're gonna be pissed. And if they do come again, and in more numbers, the six of us don't have the firepower to repel them."

Kriedemann glanced about, taking in the surrounding devastation.

"We could do with your help, Sergeant," Rebecca urged, "and you with ours. Trust me. The Zodiac will be there."

Outside, lightning flashed, followed by a peal of thunder. Rain started to ping on the Black Hawk.

Kriedemann smirked. "You still want to go out?"

"We have to," Rebecca replied, smiling too.

Kriedemann shook his head a final time and then turned to his team. "All right, you heard the lady—let's lock and load. We move in five, people."

They salvaged what they could from the wreckage of Raven Two and assembled in the rain. Rebecca was thankful that Jessy and the soldiers had earlier thought to bring her pack and her laptop down to the exfiltration site. Ed, not surprisingly, appeared to have no concerns about abandoning *his* equipment, just as he wasn't upset about leaving behind Intihuasi and all that it still guarded.

They decided to double-time it. The fittest would pair up and carry Jessy's stretcher between them, interchanging as needed.

As soon as everyone was ready, Kriedemann gave the order, and they moved out.

103

Moments before De Sousa's rocket had blasted from the jungle, impacting with Raven One, Sanchez and Owen had exited the cavern—the scene of their encounter with the five megarachnids—through the clustered boulders over which the shallow stream flowed. They headed through a narrow corridor of rock and were engulfed once more by darkness, although this time, it wasn't absolute.

A pinprick of light shone in the distance.

Supporting Owen, Sanchez wasted no time pressing towards it, sloshing through knee-deep water. Steadily, the pinprick grew wider, spurring him on.

At last, they reached the source of the light: a small opening through which the stream flowed, not much wider than a yard or two. Strung across it was an old plug of silk. Sanchez burst through it, and though it was late afternoon, early evening, the minimal sunlight that seared his eyes was blinding.

They were free…

Sanchez emerged from the muddy water, dragging Owen up the narrow embankment to the treeline, where he finally fell to the ground. He was spent. He still felt dizzy from his envenomation, and the wounds to his head and shoulder throbbed.

He wished he could have kept moving, maybe to a place of greater safety where he could tend their injuries, but he didn't have the strength. The adrenaline that had kept him going all this time was no longer enough.

Sanchez took one last look at Owen, lying barely conscious beside him… and slumped into the mud beside the stream.

He had no idea how long he'd lain unconscious, but as he pulled his face from the soft, wet earth—surprised he hadn't drowned in it—the unchanged light suggested it couldn't have been more than a few minutes. Regardless, he knew he had to get up quickly.

He could hear voices, distant but urgent.

Searching.

The Yuguruppu.

You've got to be kidding…

They couldn't have known he and Owen had escaped, could they? He roused his companion. "*Amigo*, we have to go."

"Robert?" Owen moaned, trying to raise himself from the mud. He seemed more aware—by now, the dose of venom he'd ingested had probably been broken down by stomach acid—but the spear wound appeared to be causing him pain. "Are they back?"

"Yes." Sanchez dragged himself to his feet, and helped Owen up, too. As he did, he saw the leeches, at least a dozen of them gorging on Owen's exposed legs. A similar number fed on his own limbs, but he ignored them. They had to go.

Stumbling through the muck, covered in the parasites, the two men followed the creek upstream. With every step, the mud sucked at their boots.

We're making too much noise, and we're leaving a trail.

Pulling Owen along, Sanchez veered towards the treeline.

The voices were close.

The two men slipped into the thick vegetation bordering the stream, the foliage tearing at their skin and drawing blood. All the while, the pursuing voices grew louder and more urgent. Bodies crashed through the trees behind them. Deviating back towards the water, Sanchez sought to run a different line, and noticed a subtle change in the environment. The muddy bank leading down to the stream had disappeared. Here, the vegetation overhung the water in thick, green waves.

Sanchez drew to a halt, mind racing.

More whooping. The Yuguruppu had heard them and changed course. They were close.

A few feet away Sanchez spied a partially hollowed-out capirona. He pushed Owen towards the trunk. "*Amigo*," he whispered, squeezing him inside and covering him with leaves from the forest floor. "You have to be quiet, once more."

Owen nodded.

And with that, Sanchez turned and slipped into the water as the Yuguruppu burst through the trees behind him.

Sanchez sank low, the water rising to his chin. Pressing himself against the bank, he ducked beneath a small overhang veiled by draping cecropias. He could hear the Yuguruppu above, searching, and tried to steal a glance. As he did, his gaze fell downstream.

About twenty feet away, a large ripple rolled towards him as something enormous slipped from the bank into the water.

The Yuguruppu mustn't have noticed them, because almost immediately they turned and headed back the way they had come. Most likely they'd assumed their quarry had eluded them and changed direction. Their voices trailed into the distance before fading into silence.

But Sanchez had more to worry about now.

Tensing, he slowed his breathing.

Of the countless creatures for which the Amazon and its tributaries are home, few could at this moment have instilled him with greater fear. Of course, attacks on humans were rare, but they were not unknown... and this was a creature that demanded respect.

The animal was a monster.

Hoping it had been startled by his entry into the water and was simply escaping to safety, Sanchez kept deathly still, trying not to draw attention.

At this range, it'll sense your heat.

The creature, he knew, had infrared heat-sensing pits bordering the mouth, beneath the scales. Both the yellow—and its larger cousin, the green—were so equipped.

This one was a green anaconda—the world's largest, heaviest snake.

Unbreathing, Sanchez braced himself as the wave reached him...

…and continued to roll past him, upstream.

He didn't move as it passed, following the huge snake with his gaze as it swam by. All *thirty feet* of it.

Then it was gone.

Sanchez burst out of the water and scurried up the bank.

His clothes dripping, Sanchez hurried to his companion.

"Have they gone?" Owen whispered.

"Yes, *amigo*, they have gone."

Sanchez helped Owen to his feet. Their first course of action was to pick themselves free the leeches, and they did so with vigour. Some of the parasites had gorged themselves to the thickness of Sanchez's thumb. Only when they had finished did the two men slump to the ground and take stock.

"What now?" Owen rasped.

Night had fallen. It started to rain.

Sanchez peered into the blackness. He was tired, hungry, and sore. Worst of all, his feet were killing him. They'd been wet for so long he could feel a rash beneath the socks, the skin no doubt raw and peeling. He tried not to think about it.

"First things first, *amigo*," he said. He slipped Rosenlund's knapsack from his shoulders and retrieved the hip-flask. Offering a sip to Owen, he took one himself before fashioning another torch. Enough whiskey remained to make one for Owen, too.

It was good to have light.

Once finished, Sanchez rifled through the remainder of the pack. He raised one of the rusty food cans.

"Pity we don't have an opener," Owen mused.

Sanchez agreed. He was starving.

There was nothing else of use in the knapsack. Sanchez turned to Owen. "How is your wound, *amigo*?"

Owen lifted his bloodied Hawaiian shirt. He'd redressed the injury while Sanchez been busy with the torches. He'd done a capable job.

Sanchez clapped him on the shoulder. "We should get moving."

"Moving?" Owen asked, surprised.

Scanning the dark, impenetrable jungle, Sanchez nodded. "I know you are tired, *amigo*, but I do not believe we are entirely safe—not yet, anyway. Not here." He was thinking now not of the Yuguruppu, but of the megarachnids.

"We've got nowhere to go," Owen said.

Sanchez reached into his pocket and pulled something out. "Yes, we do."

What he had retrieved was a waterproof, hand-held GPS receiver.

104

Wet leaves brushed Rebecca as she walked—not that she cared. For two hours, they'd slogged through the dark and rain-lashed jungle, and it was all she could do to keep going. But the knowledge they were fast-approaching their destination drove her on. She figured they'd be at the ravine within the hour. What's more, they'd noticed no pursuers, human or otherwise. It had been a clean getaway.

"So, where're you from?" a voice said from behind her.

"Sorry?"

Tag moved forward so that he was level with her. He smiled. "Your accent."

"Oh, that. Australia."

"Really? An Aussie? I like Aussies," Tag said, putting up his hand and brushing aside a broad leaf. "You know, I never got her name." He nodded at the monkey cradled in Rebecca's arms.

Rebecca smiled. "Well then, I'd like you to meet Priscilla."

"Priscilla? Like Elvis's girlfriend?"

"Wife. But yeah, like that."

"Cute."

For the most part, the soldiers remained silent and reserved, but as anxieties eased there came spurts of small talk. Occasionally, like now, Tag would move forward briefly, usually with offers of assistance. He was a friendly young man, polite. Rebecca liked him.

Tag fell back to check on Ed and Jessy, and there was another long period of quiet. Rebecca forced her leaden legs onwards, rain pattering the canopy overhead.

After a while, Kriedemann slipped back level with her, his M16 now resting more casually in his hands. "How are you feeling?"

"Glad to be on the move," Rebecca said. "Thanks for agreeing to this."

Kriedemann nodded. "You know, I keep meaning to ask. What was in the pouch?"

Rebecca hesitated. "Sorry?"

"The cloth bag—you know, the one you dropped when we were inside the chopper."

"Oh, right. Nothing much. Just some personal stuff."

"Must be important, to go diving out a chopper for."

"I slipped." Rebecca didn't like lying to him.

Kriedemann raised an eyebrow and moved forward again. Once more, the group fell silent, only the insects and the rain breaking the stillness around them.

Rebecca watched the sergeant from behind, her eyes fixed to the amber chemlight hanging from his pack. Suddenly, her mind was moving fast. Kriedemann had set her thinking, and after a few moments—no longer able to resist and careful that no-one saw—she furtively moved a hand to a pocket in her shorts.

To her relief, she felt the cloth pouch there, safe and sound.

An hour later, they arrived at the ravine weary and without incident.

Rebecca stood several feet back from the curtain of thick trees shielding their side of the rock face. Even from here, she could hear rushing water below. As suspected, the gorge had flooded.

The soldiers moved quickly, rigging ropes for the descent. Despite the dense vegetation at the top, Rebecca knew there'd be adequate room to manoeuvre; lowering Jessy's stretcher into the Zodiac wouldn't be difficult.

Of course, first things first. They had to *find* it.

.   .   .

Rebecca watched as Heng and Chavarre backed to the ledge and dropped over it.

She figured the Zodiac would be close, probably tethered at the base of the wall. The two soldiers were to move the vessel into place and assist with the group's descent.

Ed had earlier raised Chad on Bull's satellite phone. Fortunately, Chad had been anchored nearby—he could be in the main river in just a few hours. All they had to do was locate the Zodiac and meet him there.

But that, she discovered, was a problem, because the Zodiac was no-where to be found.

Rebecca listened as Kriedemann cupped his earpiece and spoke into his throat-mike. "Roger that. Give it another sweep and then get back up here. Out." He turned to her. "No go. If the boat was here, it's gone now."

Confused, Rebecca said, "Maybe it was dislodged, washed downstream."

"Maybe."

Ed said: "Listen, it doesn't matter, does it? I can get Chad to anchor in the river and bring the tender in. An hour's journey at most... it's not a problem."

Kriedemann glanced at his watch and nodded at Bull, who passed Ed the handset.

"Okay, then," Kriedemann said. "Get to it."

105

The downpour didn't relent—if anything, it got heavier. The surplus ponchos they'd rigged into a crude shelter at the top of the ravine thrummed above Rebecca's head with sleep-inducing rhythms. Indeed, she'd tried to take advantage and get some shuteye, but she was restless, on edge.

Ed must have sensed it. "Hey," he whispered. "We're safe now. Chad's on his way. They can't hurt us anymore. Not here."

Rebecca smiled weakly, reminding herself that Bull and McGinley had secured the area with motion sensors, X40s, flares and trip lines—just to be sure.

Ed jutted his chin. She followed his gaze to the chain she'd slipped around her neck; more accurately, the gold cross at the end of it. She'd been fingering it absently.

"The pendant… was it Enrique's?" Ed asked.

Rebecca nodded. She wasn't sure why she'd put it on, but figured it was out of respect for the young man. She found it comforting.

"'Banish fear and doubt, for remember, the Lord your God is with you wherever you go,'" came a voice across from them. It was Tag. "One of my mother's favourite quotes. She wears a cross like that every day, near to her heart. It gives her strength and direction."

Rebecca looked up at him, understanding perfectly. "Fear is based on association, and so is the reverse. Your mother equates strength and courage—the power of her Lord—with the cross, and in return, that's what she reaps. It's her talisman."

Tag smiled. "Something like that."

Rebecca smiled too, but faintly. *If only it could be that simple*, she thought. She'd never considered herself religious, not overtly so, anyway. Sure, she *hoped* there was more to life than this modest, physical existence, but that was it.

Uneasy, she rubbed her thumb over the pendant.

Ed placed a reassuring hand on her knee. "Get some rest. The boat is on its way."

Rebecca nodded, and prayed for the vessel's swift arrival. The irony of asking for divine intervention was not lost on her.

Maybe it *was* that simple, after all.

It was still dark when, hours later, Rebecca opened her eyes, roused by the low drone of a motor. She hadn't realised she'd drifted off. Straightening, she peered over the ledge. Nosing through the ravine below was a well-lit, soft-hull inflatable Zodiac with a single person on board.

Chad Higgins.

With a squeak, the soles of Rebecca's boots landed on the rubber of the rain-soaked vessel. As the boat settled beneath her, she turned to Chad and they embraced warmly.

"It's good to see you again," Chad said, rain streaming from his Stetson.

"And you, believe me."

Jessy had already been lowered and Ed had followed close behind. As Rebecca broke the hug and took a seat, Ed turned to Chad and raised his voice above the rain. "Any luck getting through to Base Camp?"

"No. You?"

Ed shook his head. "No. No word from Robert?"

"Nothing."

As they spoke, the last of the troops whizzed down the wall and into the boat. It was a tight squeeze.

A burst of lightning zigzagged overhead, illuminating the gorge with retina-searing severity. On its heels, thunder boomed, reverberating off the twin rock faces.

Eager to get moving, Chad hit the throttle and they sped through the rain, heading for the *Tempestade*.

106

Rebecca wasn't just glad to see the *Tempestade* as it appeared through the gloom, sheets of rain slashing through its anchor lights—she felt a sense of homecoming.

In moments, she was climbing up and over the vessel's portside rail, out of the deluge and into the dry beneath the covered aft deck. Behind her, Chavarre commented on the appropriateness of the boat's name. In Portuguese, 'tempestade' meant 'storm'. As if to hammer the point home, thunder cracked so loudly the sky itself may have split in two.

Once the last of them was up, Chad tied off the Zodiac. It trailed out the back, bobbing wildly in the dark. The river resembled a rolling, heaving sea, and whitecaps rode its surface. Rebecca had to fight to keep her balance.

Chad told everyone to make themselves at home. Ponchos were shrugged off, and as Tag assisted Jessy to the forward sleeping accommodation below deck, Rebecca retreated with Ed, Chad and Kriedemann to the relative quiet of the wheelhouse.

"Man, you sure you're okay?" Chad said to Ed. "You look pretty busted up."

"I'm fine," Ed said, though not convincingly. Rebecca had noticed—pretty much from the moment she'd woken to the sound of the approaching Zodiac—that Ed was frequently hunched, and often clutched at his abdomen. He'd declined all assistance. She was worried about him.

Now, he seemed to be steeling himself against more pain as he addressed his friend. "Chad, we don't have much time." He set Chavarre's map on the table and pointed to the spot the soldiers had referred to as rally point 'Delta'. "As I said earlier, we need to get these men here as soon as possible; it's safe, and from there Jessy can be extracted to a hospital. As soon as we drop them off, we ourselves have gotta hightail it to Base Camp and find out why Elson and Martins aren't answering—and to look for Owen and Robert." With that, he straightened a little. "So how soon can you make it happen?"

Chad pursed his lips, blew air through his teeth for what seemed like a very long time. "Listen, I gotta be honest, buddy—I don't know. This storm's worse than I expected. Right now, in the dark, trying to navigate through this kind of shit is dangerous. Visibility's shot, and there's a lot of debris out there, logs—hell, whole trees floating around! The trip in the Zodiac was bad enough."

"What are you saying?"

"What I'm saying," Chad answered after a slight pause, "is that the sensible option is to ride it out, wait until the storm has passed. In fact, it's the only option." He looked up from the map at all three of them in turn before he drew himself upright. "It'll be daylight soon," he said. "Couple of hours, tops. Until then… well, I'm sorry, but we're not going anywhere."

107

An hour later, Rebecca was still in the wheelhouse, sitting in a chair by the window and staring across the bow. Behind her, at the table, Chad and Kriedemann spoke quietly, again poring over the map. Ed and Jessy—both exhausted—were asleep below deck. They'd taken Priscilla with them.

Only now had Rebecca begun to relax, despite the news they'd be anchored for the night. She felt safe here—safe with Chad, safe with Ed and the soldiers, safe on the water. Even so, her head was abuzz, and she had a lot to process. Not now, though—there'd be plenty of time for that later. Right now, she didn't want to think about anything.

She wished Ed was up here with her.

She stared out the window. There wasn't much to see, other than her reflection in the glass, lashed by rain and lightning. It was hypnotic. She realised she'd nodded off when a sound jarred her awake. She listened, and once more heard the muffled banging outside, like something being blown around by the wind.

Chad came over and squinted out the window. "Damn, not again."

Rebecca straightened. "Everything okay?"

"Yeah, just the forward cargo hatch. Latch is loose, must have blown open. I'll go up and secure it. It won't take a second, if you'll both excuse me."

Rebecca got up from her seat. "No, you stay here. I'll go. You two keep at it."

"You sure? It's a simple lever catch. Gets a bit temperamental in the wind, is all."

"Leave it with me," Rebecca said.

And with that, she grabbed her poncho and left.

Kriedemann watched her disappear, glancing at Chad as he came back to the table. Together the two of them returned to the map just as McGinley burst through the door. He seemed on edge.

"Hey," he said, panting, "I think you better come see this."

Hood low, Rebecca edged her way to the bow, hand on the portside rail for support. Her powerful flashlight cut a swathe before her, but even so it was hard to discern detail through the slashing rain. She heard the banging above the downpour, and as she came around the front, she saw the square-shaped hatch set into the deck, flapping back and forth in the wind. She made a beeline for it, fingers reaching through the deluge. Just shy of the latch, her hand stopped. She crouched down.

Beside the hatch were a couple of dark spots, smudges on the deck. She shone her flashlight on them. Small splotches of… *mud?* But they were dissolving quickly in the rain and in moments were gone altogether. She noticed the remnants of others, leading from the portside rail, all washing away in the downpour. She frowned.

They looked like… *footprints.*

Rebecca moved to stand at the same moment she sensed a presence behind her. She heard a loud crack as something struck her on the head and suddenly, she knew no more.

With Chad in tow, Kriedemann trailed the ginger-haired McGinley to the stern. They found Heng and Chavarre at the rail, peering into the storm. Bull and Tag flanked them. At the group's approach, all four soldiers turned, and Chavarre lifted his hand. In it was the frayed end of the rope that had been used to secure the Zodiac to the *Tempestade.*

The Zodiac was gone.

"What happened?" Kriedemann asked as thunder growled.

"We don't know," Chavarre said. "We heard a groaning noise, followed by a loud snap. We came out here to investigate and found this."

Kriedemann examined the rope, but found no sign of wear, or anything to indicate it had been cut. He turned from Chavarre to Chad and then back again. "*Snapped*? How?"

Chavarre seemed at a loss. "You think maybe the boat got snagged on a submerged log, or some rocks or—"

Dark against the sky, it soared through the rain, coming right for them.

The soldiers scattered like pigeons as the object—an indefinable *blob* several feet long and wide—flew in over the top of the stern rail and crashed onto the boards beneath their feet, bouncing and skidding wetly across the deck before slamming up hard against the portside rail.

What the hell?

For an instant, no-one spoke, probably, like Kriedemann, too stunned for words. As a group they stared at the deflated, crumpled mess pressed against the side of the boat.

The *Zodiac*.

The vessel had been ripped to shreds. Its motor was missing.

"Holeeey fuuuck…" McGinley said.

Cautiously, Bull approached the mangled remains and knelt before them. "What could have *done* this?" With his right thumb and forefinger, he lifted a ragged, rain-soaked wedge of rubber.

Off the stern, from somewhere upriver, a loud splash sounded, followed by an explosive, geyser-like spray of water. Kriedemann spun, but the darkness and the rain obscured everything.

"Jesus H. Christ…" McGinley said. "Man, seriously—what the fuck is going on?"

Gripped by a sudden sense of urgency, Kriedemann turned to Chad. "You need to get this tug moving. *Fast.*"

But before Chad could respond, a shadowy, rippling wave, faintly luminescent, rose off the stern.

"What in God's name…" Bull murmured.

There was no time to move the boat. The wave, glowing softly, surged towards them, rolling through the dark and the rain, gaining in speed and momentum and size—

—*Christ, it's going to hit us*—

—and subsided, just shy of the stern.

The *Tempestade* bobbed in its wake, once more at the mercy of the river, which itself seemed in that moment to settle.

Water lapped against the boat, and there was nothing but the rain.

Kriedemann made for the rail and peered over it.

"Fuck me... You ever seen shit like that before?" McGinley said.

"Shh!" Chad hissed, throwing up a hand to quieten him. Slowly, he looked at Kriedemann. "You hear that? There's something underneath us."

Darkness. Something hard but spongy against her cheek, like...

Rubber.

Inflated rubber. She was in a Zodiac.

Lying prone, her head throbbing, Rebecca tried to sit, but her numbed limbs were unresponsive.

"*Ah...* awake, eh?"

She recognised the voice.

Oh my God...

It was De Sousa.

Kriedemann searched the river below, but the water was too dark to penetrate.

McGinley sounded on the verge of panic. "What the hell do you mean, 'there's something underneath us'?"

The deck lurched beneath them, throwing the group towards the stern. Kriedemann almost fell and scrambled for a handhold.

Something had hit them from below.

Something big.

The *Tempestade* steadied, and as it did, a noise resonated from under the hull: a dull but resounding thump, then... scratching.

"What the hell is that?" Heng asked.

Kriedemann had no idea, but the urgent, creeping dread he'd felt a moment ago intensified. It sounded as though the *Tempestade* had been... grasped.

The boat groaned. Huge pressure, it seemed, was being exerted on the hull. Was something trying to pull the vessel *down*? Was that possible? As if in reply, metal whined, and timber creaked as the deck started to angle, the bow lifting.

You've got to be kidding...

In the pelting rain, bodies clambered about in mild panic. Lightning flashed as the bow continued to lift. At the same time, the stern rail lowered. It hit the waterline—

—and went under.

Water flowed onto the boards beneath Kriedemann's feet. The boat's engine revved—Chad must have made it back to the wheelhouse—but it was too late. The trickle became a rush, and the *Tempestade* started to fill with water. The soldiers sought higher ground, but Kriedemann himself didn't move. His attention had been drawn out back, upriver.

No way...

From out of the gloom, through the rain, multiple dark shapes emerged; more than a dozen, maybe more than two.

Superspiders, scrambling across the river towards them.

108

Rebecca rolled over as adrenaline kicked in and the feeling returned to her arms and legs. De Sousa hadn't tied her up.

"Easy, *moca*, you got a bad knock, eh?"

She sat up. A couple of feet away, next to the twin motors at the dinghy's stern, was a black shape.

De Sousa.

No wonder we couldn't find the Zodiac at the ravine. De Sousa beat us to it.

There was no-one else in the boat. Just the two of them.

Rebecca scuttled backwards. "What do you want from me?" she asked, spittle spraying from her lips. Despite her vehemence, her heart thrummed in terror.

De Sousa flicked on a flashlight and shone it in her face. Calmly, he stood, rain falling around him.

"You need to ask, *moca*?"

Half out of his bunk already, Ed leapt to his feet, having jolted awake to the sound of shouting. Immediately, he noticed the cabin floor sloping sharply away from him. Something was wrong… *terribly* wrong.

"What's happening?" Jessy said, gripping her bunk so as not to slip out of it.

Ed tried to answer but was silenced by a stab of pain in his lower right side, the same lightning-spasm that had been troubling him since their escape from Intihuasi. He clutched at it, grimacing.

"Ed? You okay? What's going on?"

Gritting his teeth, he straightened. "Here, put this on." He opened a wall-cabinet marked 'PFD' and retrieved a bright yellow lifejacket. After helping her into it, he slipped into one himself. Again, the hull groaned, the deck angling further. Remembering that Priscilla was sleeping on the floor under the bunk, he reached for her and passed her off to Jessy.

"I'll be back," he said, heading up to the wheelhouse as fast as his legs would carry him.

Kriedemann sloshed through knee-deep water and squinted across the river. The advancing host seemed to be growing in waves. He wondered how the creatures could have tracked them here but didn't hesitate for long.

His men had formed a line beside him. Raising his M16, Kriedemann turned to them and shouted above the downpour. "*Light 'em up!*"

Rebecca scrambled backwards as De Sousa—still grinning—took a step forward, the blade of the hunting-knife in his hand glinting in the beam of the flashlight. She gasped at the sight of it.

"Get away from me!" she screamed, kicking out.

De Sousa lunged and caught her ankle. "Do not fight it, eh?" he said, dragging her towards him.

Rebecca flailed fiercely. De Sousa climbed on top of her, pinning her with his legs.

"Many a woman I have pleasured," he said as she squirmed, lightly brushing the tip of the knife across her cheek and the nape of her neck. "You should feel honoured."

Rebecca thrashed beneath him. De Sousa leaned closer, his foul breath warming her face. She turned away, but he seized her by the throat and forced her to him. He was too strong.

He was reaching for her top when the Zodiac bucked behind him. He turned as the jumper sprang from its perch on the motor, leaping through the rain.

Shoulder to shoulder at the back of the sinking boat, Kriedemann's team opened fire.

Muzzle flashes erupted in the rain-lashed dark, cutting the front line of arachnids to shreds. A new wave replaced them. En masse, the spiders advanced across the river.

There're too many, Kriedemann thought. *We can't hold them off. Not at this rate. Not all of them…*

The first wave of creatures reached the boat, readying to break the line. At close range, Kriedemann realised the spiders leading the charge were different to those behind them. More heavily set, more heavily armoured, with a red crown or carapace on top, and hand-like appendages bordering the mouth that looked like the front legs of a praying mantis, bent and scythe-like. Almost like swords.

As the first of them leapt up from the river, into the boat, Kriedemann understood the nature of these creatures and *why* they were different to the others.

Just like he and his men, these were the soldiers of their species.

The war had begun.

109

Flat on her back, Rebecca screamed as the jumper leapt through the rain and hit De Sousa in the chest. The impact sent him sprawling off her.

Desperate not to waste the opportunity, Rebecca rolled left as De Sousa went right with the huge spider wrapped in a bear hug. How in God's name had it found them here?

She clawed on all fours for the edge of the boat. A hand fell on her, halting her, and she kicked out at it, but again, De Sousa was too strong. Still kicking, she flipped onto her back as De Sousa struggled to his knees—

—and in a flash of lightning, hurled the carcass of the jumper to the floor of the Zodiac.

He killed it… shit… he killed it… stabbed it to death.

De Sousa roared with victory—guttural, animal-like—and lunged for her viciously.

Barely thinking, Rebecca reached for the dead spider. Ignoring the tar-like ichor oozing from its knife-savaged surface, she snatched at the hairs covering the posterior, tearing out a clump and throwing them at De Sousa as she would a handful of dirt.

They struck his eyes and De Sousa howled in agony. Rebecca, too, felt a painful burn in her hand, the hairs—covered in hundreds of microscopic barbs like those deployed defensively by some species of tarantula—stinging her flesh as though she'd plunged her fingers into a nest of fire ants.

Clawing at his face, De Sousa fell back, the hunting-knife tumbling from his grasp.

Rebecca seized it from the floor of the Zodiac and dived into the dark and rain-drenched river.

Rebecca swam hard, hoping to find the riverbank, or at the very least, put as much distance as possible between her and De Sousa. She knew he'd be hot on her tail.

The dark was disorienting. Wind and rain chopped at the river's surface, and waves tossed her about, causing her to swallow water in great gulps. In all the confusion, she couldn't see much of anything—neither bank was visible—so she put her head down and quickened her pace. Within a few yards, she rounded a small bend and realised that after kidnapping her, De Sousa hadn't retreated far. Having emerged from an adjoining creek, she was back now in the main part of the river. What she saw caused her to stop swimming.

Ahead, the lights of the *Tempestade* blazed through the darkness. The vessel was maybe a hundred yards away, though it was difficult to be certain of the exact distance. What concerned her was the angle at which the boat sat upon the river. It was all wrong. The bow of the vessel was *out* of the water, raised about forty-five degrees. The stern was *below* the surface. The boat was sinking.

That, however, wasn't the worst of it.

Unbelievably, the stricken vessel was surrounded by an encroaching army of megarachnids.

Rebecca watched in horror as the horde surged across the river, many of the spiders already swarming the *Tempestade* like ants upon a hapless insect. Standing midship and facing aft, Kriedemann and his men fought back; strobe-like flashes of light flared relentlessly, and the popping sounds of gunfire rose above the storm. But it looked to be a lost cause—there were too many of the creatures. They were everywhere.

Rebecca treaded water, wondering what the hell she should do… when the Zodiac roared around the bend and through the rain towards her.

·   ·   ·

Firing hard, Kriedemann swung his M16... but was too late to stop the rearing red-armoured spider from tracing its sword-like palp through the air—

—and lopping Heng's head clean from his body.

NO!

Heng dropped like a stone, the stump of his neck jetting blood high into the night. Tag spun, and in a flare of lightning that illuminated the young soldier's red-rimmed eyes, obliterated the spider with a prolonged and savage burst from his assault rifle.

Despite the sudden gruesome loss of their comrade, the men held the line.

Even so, Kriedemann knew that to stay put was suicide. At the top of his voice he gave the order to fall back... just as another of the spiders broke the line, thrusting forward its palp and impaling Chavarre through the sternum. The appendage speared out the man's back, between the shoulder blades. Wide-eyed, spurting blood, Chavarre somehow managed to fire off a burst, killing the creature before tumbling into the river still attached to his adversary. A host of frenzied spiders fell upon the corpses as they floated away.

Aghast, but keeping it together, the men fell back as ordered.

The attack didn't wane. More spiders pounced and were cut down, only to be replaced twofold. Fangs and legs were everywhere; scrambling, scratching.

At the same time, the water level kept rising.

Behind them, Chad thrust the door to the saloon wide open. *"Move it!"* he yelled. *"COME ON!"*

Single-file, the men retreated through the angled doorway, covering their withdrawal with sustained bursts of fire. Kriedemann got there last, arriving as the spiders overwhelmed what remained of the deck above the waterline. He barely made it. As his vision filled with a blur of mirrored eyes and venomed fangs, he felt someone, probably Chad, grab him hard by the collar and haul him backwards into the saloon.

As he went, he caught the door and slammed it shut behind him with a resounding clang.

110

Less than a minute earlier, Ed had hit the top of the stairs leading into the saloon, only to be frozen cold in his tracks by the sudden eruption of gunfire coming from the rear deck. He'd abandoned his original plan and about-faced to return to Jessy. With the boat sinking, they couldn't remain below, so he'd helped her and Priscilla up to the saloon, where he'd caught a glimpse of the swarming spiders through the door Chad held wide. Jessy had screamed.

How had the creatures tracked them here?

As Kriedemann backpedalled into the room, Chad bolted the door. Almost instantly, water trickled beneath it.

"This ain't good," McGinley whined, spinning fitfully. "There's no way out—we're *trapped*!"

He was right. The door Kriedemann had slammed shut—steel-framed but otherwise timber and now shuddering with the weight and intent of dozens of enraged, clawing spiders—was the only exit to the outside. Next to Ed were the stairs that led both below deck and up to the wheelhouse, but neither destination bore an option for escape.

More scratching and thumping, louder than before. The door buckled. A loud crack reverberated through the saloon.

The timber won't hold.

The water level continued to rise, faster now.

Again, a lightning-stab of pain flared through Ed's abdomen, and he clutched at it, the involuntary whimper that escaped his lips masked by the horrendous noise outside. He was glad: now wasn't the time to compound Jessy's worries.

Another sharp crack rent the air, and once more, the door bulged inwards.

"What's the goddamned plan?" McGinley cried.

Fearing the door would implode at any moment, Ed shepherded Jessy to the stairs. Underfoot, water sloshed, now ankle-deep. Outside, the stern would be fully submerged.

The scratching stopped.

"What the hell?" Jessy said.

An eerie stillness descended.

"You think they've gone?" McGinley said, stock-still and suddenly hopeful.

Bull's gaze darted. "I wouldn't bet on it."

The *Tempestade* groaned.

"You know, we've slipped anchor," Tag said, his head cocked. "Current's got us. We're on the move."

McGinley looked at him. "Who gives a shit? We need to find a way out of here!"

"I'm just saying!"

Scanning for options, Chad turned to them both. "Quiet!"

Ed could tell by the tone in his friend's voice that Chad was barely holding it together. It was perfectly understandable—hell, on top of everything, all this horror, he'd lost his beloved boat. But as skipper, getting them out of this alive seemed his buddy's priority, and Chad started passing out lifejackets. As he did, he turned to Ed and Kriedemann. "Our best bet is to head up to the wheelhouse. It'll buy us some time, if nothing else."

Ed nodded. The silence from the rear deck reeked of a trap, and he was certain the creatures were capable of such cunning. What's more, there'd be nothing but water on the other side of the door. Kriedemann was obviously of the same opinion; the sergeant was already pointing his men to the stairs.

With an arm around Jessy's waist and one of hers draped across his shoulders, Ed made to move, but hesitated. "Hey—where the hell is *Bec*?"

"She's not below?" Chad asked.

"No," Ed said. "When was the last time you saw her?"

Chad frowned. "She went outside earlier, to close the hatch up front."
"Oh my God…" Jessy said. "Outside? You think they… *got her?*"
"We don't know that," Kriedemann said. "Come on."
They headed up to the wheelhouse.

111

In terror, Rebecca turned and swam hard from the approaching Zodiac.

She never stood a chance.

Rain pelted her as the boat zoomed in. Reaching over the side, De Sousa caught her hair and yanked her violently upwards. Rebecca screamed in agony, fearing her scalp was tearing free of her skull, powerless to resist as De Sousa hoisted her into the boat. Standing, he pulled her to her feet—still by the hair—and struck her across the face with his spare hand. Pain shot through her jaw like a bolt, and she sprayed blood, her teeth loosening with the impact.

Abandoning the throttle and allowing the motor to idle, De Sousa hit her again, chasing her as she flew backwards. She fell hard, and as she landed, something sharp cut her cheek. Groggily, she observed several oars lying against the side of the boat—she'd fallen on one of the blades. Seizing one, she scrambled to her knees and swung the paddle in a wild arc. She got lucky. The blow struck De Sousa square on the temple with a wet-sounding slap, slicing him open.

He staggered, stunned... but kept coming.

Rebecca strove to maintain her balance in the pitching boat, unable to prevent her wild-eyed attacker from snatching the paddle and tearing it from her grip. Blood as black as night streamed down De Sousa's face, emphasising his rage; he was insane with it. Rebecca stumbled backwards, out of his reach, and fell again as the boat lurched underfoot. Dazed and disoriented, she scrambled for the bow on her hands and knees, her mouth awash with the coppery taste of blood, hot tears streaming down her cheeks.

Focus! Don't panic! She was no match for De Sousa and knew she couldn't fight him. She had to escape.

Staggering to her feet, she turned as footsteps thumped behind her.

Through the wet and bloodied hair matting her face, Rebecca saw a crazed De Sousa charging at her with outstretched arms.

112

Ed's group had just hit the top of the stairs when—with a sudden, terrifying roar—the *Tempestade* veered vertically and water rushed up from below to half-flood the wheelhouse. Thrown backwards into the churning torrent, the group was sucked beneath the surface. Ed reached for Jessy and pulled her into a tight hug, and as the boat reached equilibrium, they resurfaced courtesy of their lifejackets, spluttering and treading water in the newly formed pool. Somehow, Jessy had managed to keep hold of Priscilla, the two of them clearly terrified.

"You okay?" Ed asked Jessy.

"I… I think so," Jessy said, coughing. "Please get me out of here."

Ed glanced up. The *Tempestade's* windshield lay a few feet above his head—effectively now the vessel's ceiling—and through the glass he could see the bow pointing skyward into the rain-lashed night. Most of the boat was now directly beneath them, underwater, and he figured that shortly, the remainder would follow.

"We can smash the glass and head out that way," Kriedemann said, reading his mind and scanning the walls in the hope of a way up.

McGinley said, "Are you kidding? They're still out there!"

Chad swam from person to person, passing out chemlights. "Got a better idea? Besides, when did you last hear them? The scratching stopped when the stern went under."

"They've taken off, left us for dead," Jessy said.

Tag looked about. "We're still drifting in the current," he said, but as the words left his mouth, a shattering boom shook the walls and the *Tempestade* pitched fiercely, as though it had crashed into something huge and unyielding. Metal screamed, and so did Jessy, and timber splintered and exploded inwards, showering into the pool. Something hit Ed's shoulder, hard, and he cried out. Overhead, sparks flew as the control panel was crunched and obliterated, and lights flickered and died, and it seemed the wheelhouse was about to shear in two as the hull twisted in opposing directions. But then suddenly everything slowed and settled, and—momentarily, at least—quieted.

Holy shit…

The *Tempestade* had come to a swift and violent stop.

Not knowing what else to do, Rebecca ducked as the Zodiac—still motoring downstream—collided hard with something behind her and lurched to a halt.

De Sousa, still charging, didn't have time to pull up—and flew straight over her head… out of the boat and into the pitch-black river.

Ed shielded Jessy as a jet of water burst through the side of the *Tempestade*, spraying into the pool. The boat must have rammed against a submerged rock, or maybe the riverbank, and was now pressed hard against it: he could hear the water outside rushing against the vessel and holding it in place. They must have been moving fast, because the impact had been colossal—the *Tempestade* was barely holding together.

As the hull moaned and more leaks sprung around them, Ed held out his chemlight and glanced desperately about. The wheelhouse was now almost fully submerged, the water rising as the boat continued its inexorable slide to the riverbed. If running out of time and options hadn't been enough, they were now running out of room, too.

"We've gotta get out before she busts apart!" Ed called to Chad above the din.

A muffled banging from below interrupted them, and Ed peered into the inky depths.

Something was thudding against the boat, under the water…

Kriedemann turned to Chad. "It's back."

"What's back?" Jessy asked.

Kriedemann made no reply. Listening, Ed thought the blows sounded deliberate, as though something was bashing its way in, through the saloon door—

A massive snap reverberated upwards, like wood blown asunder. Even deadened by the water, it was frighteningly loud.

"It's through," Tag breathed.

Unsure as to what the hell was going on, Ed looked down and saw something surfacing beneath them, rising through the dark water. He perceived no detail—only a bright glow, a white luminescence—but panic ensued, and the group scrambled for the edges of the wheelhouse, trying to get away.

Whatever it was, it was quick. With a jerk, McGinley was pulled soundlessly into the depths.

Rebecca was still inside the Zodiac, which—she realised with surprise as she looked around—was pressed up against the bow of the *Tempestade*. The nose of the rapidly sinking vessel was all that remained above the waterline, and the Zodiac had motored directly into it. Obviously, the larger boat had come free of its anchor, drifting in the current to smash into some submerged rocks. Rebecca could see that here the river had tapered, causing a mountain of water to squeeze through a narrow bottleneck. Like a giant plug, the *Tempestade* had further blocked it, forcing the river to rage around either side.

She had a flash of worry for Ed and the rest of the group. Had they gotten free? Had they escaped to the riverbank? She had the Zodiac, and could look for them, but right now, her thoughts jumped back to De Sousa, and she cast her gaze about, searching. To her considerable relief she saw that he was gone, lost in the rain and rushing water. She made unsteadily for the dinghy's stern. The motor droned heartily—ensuring the Zodiac remained jammed in place—but the boat's position was precarious, and she had to move it.

She reached for the throttle just as the water beneath it exploded upwards, and something massive emerged from the depths below.

113

Ed's hands spread desperately at the water, but he could see nothing beneath the pitch-coloured surface.

"I think it's gone!" someone yelled frantically.

"*MAC!*" Bull cried. He too was searching the water, but McGinley had vanished along with the strange luminescence. Except for the chemlights, it was again dark inside the wheelhouse.

Tag sounded on the verge of panic. "What in God's name was that thing? Did anyone see what it was?"

"No, just the goddamned light…" Bull said. "*MAC!*"

"For Christ's sake—he's *gone!*" Jessy screamed at Bull. She was bawling. "Ed, we've got to get out of here! It took him… God, it took him! We've got to go… before it comes back for the rest of us!"

"We're not leaving him behind!" Bull shouted.

Kriedemann grabbed Bull, spun him round. "Hey! She's *right*! He's gone! I need you to focus, Bull—and you too, Tag! We gotta pull together, and we gotta get moving!"

Bull whimpered and slapped the water. "*Shit!*"

Ed looked up. The *Tempestade* was sinking fast, the windshield now less than two feet above them.

Chad was ahead of him. "Cover your eyes!" In his hand was a steel thermos he'd plucked from the floating debris, and he thrust it upwards.

The laminated safety glass shivered, fragments sprinkling into the water. Rain streamed through the newly formed hole. Chad cleared the remnants as Bull's voice came again.

"Hey! There's something coming up!"

Ed turned his gaze back to the water and once more saw a glow rising beneath them, although not as bright as before and not the strange luminescence of moments ago. It wasn't white, either—it was amber.

A chemlight.

"It's Mac!" Bull said, reaching down as the light bobbed to the surface.

It was Mac, all right. His lifejacket had brought him back up. Bull grabbed him and spun him around. Moaning, McGinley's eyes fluttered in recognition.

He was alive!

Gurgling, McGinley stared vacantly at his pal. "Bull... I don't feel so good..." he stuttered, spitting a mouthful of blood.

The colour drained from Bull's face, and Ed's stomach lurched.

McGinley's lower half was missing, gone from the waist down. Bull held no more than a ragged torso.

"Oh no..." Jessy whimpered.

McGinley said nothing more. He was gone. Bull released his friend, his face etched in horror.

"Christ," Kriedemann said.

Jessy burst into a hysterical flood of tears. Ed held her close, turning her from the torso as it bobbed amongst them, entrails afloat. He redirected his gaze to Chad, who had already climbed through the window and was now outside the wheelhouse, reaching down.

"Come on," Ed said, turning to the rest of them. "We have to move."

Just seconds before the wheelhouse glass was smashed—and muffled by the stinging downpour—Rebecca cried out in terror as the monster broke the surface.

It was *enormous.*

The creature reared up from below, seemingly attracted to the droning motor, which it silenced with a pair of huge, horrible fangs that came bursting from the dark. In that same instant, long legs erupted from the river, flailing and dripping. Before Rebecca could properly register it, the creature was rising fast into the air, leaping straight up—

—oh God—

—and into the Zodiac.

The weight was too much.

The boat flipped up like a seesaw, but as it did, Rebecca got a good look at the creature. There was no doubt as to what it was.

Another spider.

Another *massive* megarachnid…

Rebecca was hurled from the Zodiac, into the river.

As she was expelled from the boat, Rebecca's subconscious, working fast, tied the threads together.

Like the Alpha Female, this creature was hairless and pale. Luminous, in fact. It literally *glowed* in the dark, which was why she'd seen it so clearly.

It was, however, with those two features that any similarity with the Female ended. This specimen had a vastly different body shape.

Slightly smaller than the Female, this creature was much sleeker, with a lower centre of gravity and a segmented, cigar-shaped abdomen completely unlike the round and bloated rear of the huge egg-layer. Its exoskeleton, too, appeared more heavily armoured, the 'head' enlarged and more powerfully built. Its weaponry was also more fearsome—a huge pair of downward-striking, paraxial fangs extended from immense, jaw-like chelicerae. Above the mouthparts sat three rows of huge, intelligent but *malicious* eyes. All up, this creature was a much stronger, far more aggressive-looking specimen, its lines sleeker. Built for speed.

Built for killing.

You know what it is, and why it's here.

Earlier, Rebecca had concluded that the specialised caste system of this species was like that of certain *insects*. For most communal insects, the Queen was the only member of the royal caste. *This* species, however, had multiple egg-layers, and therefore multiple members in its royal caste. The strongest royal had been the Alpha Female that had attacked them up in the temple. And with certain insects, like termites, the Queen had a royal partner.

A mate.

A *King*.

And this creature here was, for all intents and purposes, he.

The Alpha Male.

·   ·   ·

416 · WW MORTENSEN

In Rebecca's mind, these elements came together in a nanosecond, with little, if any, conscious thought and no more than a lightning-fast flash of awareness.

She knew that a royal termite couple could survive for years as a partnership. The Queen laid the eggs, the King fertilised her.

For this spider species, the partnership between the Alpha Female and the Alpha Male, as the biggest and strongest individuals of each gender, was probably the same.

Rebecca knew also that with many social insects, the Queen's offspring were typically female, and to ensure her daughters couldn't lay eggs of their own, the Queen would actively *suppress* ovarian development through the secretion of a special pheromone known as the 'Queen Substance'. For as long as she was alive, the substance would permeate the nest, and the females would remain sterile. When the Queen died, the ovaries of the females would develop, and the females would lay eggs of their own.

It was, therefore, the Queen Substance that *confirmed* her presence in the nest. The pheromone was designed to be picked up and transported through the nest by the colony members as they went about their daily routine. Specifically, it was meant to *attach* itself to things.

How and why the Male had tracked them here was obvious.

Not only had both Ed and Rebecca been *inside* the nest, inside the nuptial chamber, but they'd been close to the Female. They would have been exposed firsthand to *her* signature smell. More than that, Ed—who'd been inside the nest for the longest—had been covered in her saliva and spattered with her blood.

Her smell had been on them.

God only knew what they'd touched since, what they'd passed the pheromone onto. It had probably been all over the Zodiac, all over the *Tempestade*. That they'd been protected from the rain by their ponchos had only kept it from washing away.

As such—and through powerful chemoreceptors at the tips of his legs that were designed to respond to airborne chemical stimuli—the Alpha Male had been able to track them here by *scent*, and he'd done so for one simple reason.

He was here for his mate.

He was searching for the Female.

Again, these thoughts were at a subconscious level and formed in an instant. The aspects of Rebecca's brain devoted to logic and science—driven and skewed by years of entomological study—worked independently. But now, as she hit the water, Rebecca's *conscious* thoughts were of one thing only, and that was survival.

Rebecca clawed to the surface and turned in desperation. Through the rain, she saw the Male skitter over the side of the Zodiac, diving into the river after her. In terror, she turned and swam, barely making it two yards before something slid around her waist, dragging her backwards. She struggled, flailing, but he was too strong. Bracing for death, she expected at any moment to be impaled or quartered. She wasn't prepared for what happened next.

The Male dived, plunging beneath the surface and dragging Rebecca into the depths.

Chad had climbed from the wheelhouse a mere second after Rebecca disappeared. He hadn't seen her or the Male. All he noticed was the Zodiac, pressed up against the *Tempestade* in the raging water. He frowned, wondering how it had gotten there, where the hell it had come from. But he wasn't the type to look a gift horse in the mouth. He'd just found their ticket out of there.

Water roared in Rebecca's ears as the Male dragged her deep beneath the surface. As she sank, her pulse quickened, and her muscles tensed—the familiar signs of an impending panic attack.

God no... not now... please not now...

The *Tempestade* was wedged tight against the rocks, its lower two thirds entirely underwater. Dragging her with him, the Male thrust up against the vessel, grasping the vertically aligned and fully submerged roof of the wheelhouse with spread legs. He slammed Rebecca against the roof, pinning her there.

Rebecca couldn't understand. Why would he do that? Why hadn't he killed her outright? He could simply rip her apart or smash her against the boat until she was dead. Was he trying to *drown* her?

As these questions charged through her mind, Rebecca became aware of a kind of *tightening* inside her skull, and she realised the vague, mental intrusion she'd felt in the huge chamber inside the pyramid was happening again, as though something—

—the Male—

—was in there, inside her head, poking around—

—he wants to know what happened to the Female—

—and it wasn't really a deliberate thought but then out of nowhere she was reminded of those species of spider that could stay submerged for hours, *days* even, taking oxygen straight from the water like a fish… and then she was struggling with all her might to get away, but it was no good… she could feel the current rushing against her, pressing her against the roof of the *Tempestade* and swirling all around her like a whirlpool, trying to suck her down, loud in her ears—

Almost out of breath, Rebecca started to fade from consciousness. Oddly, in that instant, her mind cleared, and although she knew she was about to die, she suddenly felt a weight lift—a release—and she calmed, and then she heard her own voice soothing her.

You can let go, Bec.

In one final, almost involuntary attempt to cling to life, she glanced away, resisting, and in the glow of the Male's body, saw debris littering the water all around her. Vegetation, splinters of timber, bits of—

A massive tree barrelled towards her from upriver, rolling laterally, causing white water to froth about. She watched it with a kind of fascination, knowing that without the strength or means to escape she couldn't prevent it from crushing her against the roof of the wheelhouse.

It'll be quick.

As she stared, resigned to her fate and with the blackness of sleep rapidly descending, the tree seemed to snag on something. Then it dislodged and spun, so that its massive base and tangled system of roots faced her, picking up speed in the rushing current, boring head-on through the water.

And it was in that fashion that the giant tree slammed straight into the *Tempestade*, suddenly and powerfully, spearing into it with an incredibly loud crack and smashing straight through the roof of the wheelhouse like a hot knife through butter.

114

The glint had floated into her peripheral vision; a tiny flash of light, gold in colour.

—banish fear and doubt, for remember, the Lord your God is with you wherever you go—

Rebecca had turned, seeking the gleam's source, but she was sinking into an oily blackness that was somehow coming from within and pushing out through her eyes. Already, she'd given in to it and had stopped struggling—

—fear is based on association—

—but then she'd caught the glint again and had drawn her head around to focus on the cross at the end of the chain around her neck.

You know what to do.

Do it.

She still held the hunting-knife. She knew where to aim. She struck hard.

These creatures had no muscles to extend their legs—they had an open circulatory system, and their blood didn't flow through vessels but simply 'filled' their body. It was this pressure that extended the legs, and already, she'd seen what had happened when that pressure had been lost—how in death, their legs had drawn up beneath their body…

There hadn't been time to hack off the limb that held her, but there'd been time to *puncture* it.

The weak point, she knew, lay in the joint *between* the armoured plates separating the two major leg segments.

The blow struck home and blood jetted as though a cork had been sprung, staining the water with a dark cloud. The sudden loss of pressure—and the pain-response—was enough to draw the leg back into the body. *Fast.*

Taking Rebecca with it.

As she went, the massive tree whooshed past her, slamming into the spot she'd been a nanosecond earlier.

Trouble was, she'd created for herself a new problem.

She'd brought herself face to face with the Male.

115

≹

Perhaps it was a propane cylinder or a fuel tank that had ruptured. Whatever it was, the effect was devastating.

Moments after the tree crushed the wheelhouse, an explosion ripped up from below—possibly from the engine room—and blew out the bow in a billowing orange starburst.

Flaming shrapnel blasted in all directions, shooting high into the air and sizzling in the rain. At the same time, tendrils of flame scorched across the river, snaking outwards from the burning wreckage like searching tentacles. The *Tempestade* had obviously been leaking fuel—the fire hot enough to ignite the combustible diesel—and these flames reached high into the night, mocking the downpour from above.

All this came to Rebecca's eyes as she broke the surface of the river, gasping uncontrollably.

She was surrounded by flame.

De Sousa's hunting-knife was no longer in her hand. She'd left it where she'd plunged it: inside the Male's central left eye.

Everything had happened fast. There was the blur of the wide-open mouth, and the fangs, clear in the luminescence of the Male's body, rushing in at her. She'd stabbed out in reflex maybe three or four times, and then there was a release and a thrashing of water and the explosion. The next thing she knew, she was back at the surface, heaving frantically for air.

No time to hesitate.

The Male was still alive, somewhere in the water with her, somewhere near.

He's coming for me.

The surrounding wall of flame towered into the night, its reflection dancing off the river's mirrored surface. Whimpering, expecting at any moment to be grasped from below, Rebecca selected the wall's lowest, weakest point and swam for it as fast as she was able.

She reached the spot she'd been aiming for and dove beneath the roaring orange flame. She resurfaced on the other side, wheezing for breath and sucking in huge gulps of air. It was still raining. The *Tempestade*—all that was left of it—burned behind her.

The Male hadn't yet come for her.

She didn't pause for long. She set her sights now on the riverbank, a short distance away, and started swimming.

Which was precisely when she felt a hand on her shoulder, pulling her back.

"*Bec!*"

More hands, all of them reaching down, and voices both male and female. "What the hell happened? We didn't know where you were! Are you okay?"

Rebecca looked up and saw Ed and Chad leaning over the side of the Zodiac. Both men grabbed hold of her collar and heaved her upwards. Rebecca kicked hard with her legs, desperate to get out of the water.

"He's still alive…" she said, spluttering.

"Who's still alive, Bec?" Ed said. "What are you talking about?"

A loud splash echoed across the water, the sound of something huge breaking the river's surface.

Rebecca slid fully into the boat and rolled to look over at the *Tempestade*. The vessel's bow still stuck out of the water, a blackened skeleton engulfed in flame. But the blaze on the *river* had already begun to die, and beyond it, she could see him.

The Male.

Thrashing at the surface, he appeared to be pinned from below—perhaps by the tree that had blasted through the roof of the wheelhouse. In any case, he'd dragged himself topside and was now lashing about, trying to break free, his long, flailing legs black silhouettes against the flames.

"He's getting loose…" Rebecca breathed. She turned desperately to Chad, who was gazing at the gutted remains of his boat. He held an object in his hands.

Chad raised the RPG-7 and squinted down its length. "Insurance job anyway," he murmured sadly.

Not that he was getting sentimental.

Chad jammed down on the trigger.

Rebecca had a gut feeling this was the weapon De Sousa had used to down the Black Hawk. It must have been in the Zodiac all along, stashed somewhere in the stern.

With a whoosh, the rocket screamed downriver, no more than two or three feet above the surface, trailing a finger of white.

Unerringly, it cut through the dancing flames—

—and careened into the Male and the burning hull of the *Tempestade*, blowing both to smithereens.

116

Seconds after tumbling from the Zodiac and hitting the water, De Sousa had been pulled into the river's depths by the raging current. At its mercy, he was tossed viciously about, end over end. By the time he clawed himself back to the surface, gasping for air, he was already through the bottleneck and into calmer waters downstream.

De Sousa treaded water, taking a moment to get his bearings and catch his breath. By the looks of it, he'd passed around a narrow bend. He couldn't see the Zodiac behind him—just darkness. Rain sprinkled the river.

He weighed his options. As he did, a tingling numbness in his temple came to his attention and he put a hand to it. Blood dripped from his fingers. He thought about caiman and made for the nearest bank.

He saw the spider—one of those jumping ones—come around the bend upriver, skittering across the water towards him.

What the…

De Sousa had seen regular-sized tarantulas walk on water, escaping floodwaters. *But this?* He turned and swam hard for the bank, the spider racing after him. He could hear it behind him, gaining fast. Realising he wasn't going to outpace it, he spun towards it. The creature was closer than he thought, and as it darted towards him, its front legs lifted in a threat-pose, venom glistening at the tips of its fangs…

Shit!

De Sousa raised his hands, opened his mouth to scream—

Water exploded all around him.

Something large and powerful burst out of the river between him and the spider. In an instant, his field of vision filled with a huge set of jaws and pallid triangular teeth... then a flash of gunmetal grey hide as an immense body rolled out of the water in front of him. The thing was huge. Water thrashed ferociously. There was a fin, then a flick of a tail, and then suddenly—

Nothing.

The water settled.

The thing was gone.

Even better...

So too was the spider.

Treading water, De Sousa spun about. Rain fell around him. The spider was nowhere to be seen. He grinned.

No... fucking... way! Of all things, a shark! It was too good to be true. He knew bull sharks lived in the river—and this one had *saved* him.

He hooted, laughing out loud, delirious with excitement. Summoning his strength, he made for the riverbank with a wide smile.

He was still shaking his head in disbelief when suddenly, halfway to the bank, he felt something beneath the surface brush against him. Not a full second passed and it came again, harder this time, jerking him down. He felt no pain, just a heavy tugging sensation, and he was drawn underwater before there was a release and he was back topside again, gasping for air.

He had to get out of the water.

He turned for the riverbank and swam hard, trying to stay calm. But something was wrong: his arms worked vigorously, but his legs weren't responding as they should. He couldn't understand. He flailed, splashing, but he couldn't move fast enough, couldn't get away.

In front of him, the water swirled like a mini-whirlpool, and he stopped thrashing as the bull shark burst out of the river. Time paused. The shark seemed to hang there, jaws wide, and strangely, there was something in its mouth, something long and ragged, covered in cloth and splashed in red, but it didn't make sense—he knew the shape but couldn't fathom how it could be. Then as he watched, feeling a strange detachment, the shark raised its head, opening its jaws wider, muscular body rippling above the water—

—and jerked its head backwards, swallowing the leg whole.

Time sped up again and the shark disappeared with a splash.

Not a moment later, De Sousa felt a runaway train slam into him from the side, under the water.

The jaws of the second shark clamped hard across his chest. The massive fish pulled him beneath the surface, the pressure of the bite squeezing the breath from his lungs. He grabbed at the mouth and tried to wrest it apart. The jaws were huge, engulfing him from waist to chin. Frothing water swirled dark before his eyes. Still he wrestled, punching the shark in the snout, but he could summon no power behind his fist. Churning water roared in his ears, and he thought his eardrums would burst. His strength faded, and he saw stars.

De Sousa knew the shark wouldn't let go.

He knew he would not escape.

He let out a watery scream—

—as his attacker was joined by at least two more sharks, attracted by the commotion.

Insatiable, they rolled and twisted in the blood-bathed water, tearing De Sousa's body limb from limb.

117

Morning.

All was still and calm on the river. It had stopped raining.

The Zodiac drifted quietly downstream. Exhausted, Rebecca glanced at the surrounding jungle. The sun was climbing, dressing the tops of the trees in red, and within their still-darkened lower branches birds and monkeys rose from their slumber in untold, unseen numbers, squawking and chattering abundantly. It was like music to her ears.

The rocket had done its job; the Male was no more. Neither, for that matter, was the *Tempestade*. Following the explosion, the only remains of either had been the odd piece of floating debris, still smoking and burning. Not that Rebecca and the others had hung around. They'd long-since drifted through the bottleneck to leave the devastation behind. The Male's attack on the Zodiac had destroyed both motors, but they had the oars. It was slow going, but Rebecca was unworried. They were safe at last.

She'd told the others what had happened to her, how De Sousa had kidnapped her from the *Tempestade*, and their ensuing struggle. Judging by the horrified stares of her companions as her wounds were tended, she figured she must have looked terrible. For sure, he'd given her a beating, but she was strong—much stronger than she thought. She'd survived. As for De Sousa, she had no idea what had happened once he'd fallen overboard. But

428 · WW MORTENSEN

he didn't bear thinking about anymore. In her heart, she knew he was gone for good.

Rebecca was sitting up the front, with Ed beside her and Jessy in turn beside him. Hugging Priscilla close, Rebecca said, "You know, it was him back in the nest, in the huge chamber above the funnel."

Both Ed and Jessy looked up. "Sorry?" Ed said.

"The Male," Rebecca replied, but she was talking more to herself than anything. "At the top of the dome—I saw something hanging from the ceiling: huge, luminous, at the centre of the ball of spiders. I thought it had been the Female. But it was him. *She'd* been up in the nuptial chamber all along." She looked at Ed. "They knew we were there, probably from the moment we entered the nest. I think they lured us, maybe using a chemical attractant, a pheromone, to drive us up to the nuptial chamber and the Female. I'm sure that's what they used to attract Priscilla, and Enrique, to that trapdoor. Of course, it may have been something more than that, too… a couple of times, I could swear they were… *inside my head*."

For a long while there was silence. Eventually Jessy spoke. "One thing I don't get," she said. "When the *Tempestade* was sinking, we were swamped by jumpers, all trying desperately to get at us. Then just like that, they were gone. What happened to them?"

Rebecca shrugged. "They were dismissed, most likely. The Male wanted you to himself. Being the alpha, he… *gets to eat first*."

Jessy shivered. "But where'd they go?"

"Not far—the surrounding jungle, I imagine. Lucky for us, our escape downstream went unnoticed."

Suddenly a low, droning whir came from behind them, upriver. It sounded out of place in the still morning air. Turning, Rebecca saw another Zodiac approaching with two passengers on board.

You've got to be kidding.

It was Owen and Sanchez.

118

Rebecca held Owen in a tight embrace, barely believing that he and Sanchez were here, alive.

The two men told how they'd used the GPS receiver to guide them back to Base Camp. With no radio or satellite phone to be found, and with no other means of communication, they'd taken the Zodiac—which had still been there, tied up securely—to get help.

Never in a million years had they thought they'd stumble upon their four companions like this, in the middle of the river, in a crippled boat—and with three soldiers in their company to boot.

"Suffice to say, it's a long story," Rebecca said.

"Save it," Owen said with a faint smile. "You can tell me over a beer somewhere far from here."

Another round of hugs. Owen and Sanchez proceeded to share in greater detail their encounter with the Yuguruppu, as well as the fates of both Elson and Martins.

There had been so much death.

After a quick transfer, they headed downriver in Owen and Sanchez's Zodiac, the boat purring through the greenery. Hopefully, they'd pass another vessel before the day was out, hitch a ride, and get some help. Either way, they'd be on the river for some time.

Rebecca leaned against the side of the Zodiac, the sun tingling her skin and the sounds of the jungle lulling her into a sense of peace.

119

Rebecca lost track of time. Her eyelids were getting heavy when Ed's voice came to her softly.

"I gotta thank you again," he said. "For what you did… for coming and getting me, I mean. I won't forget it."

Rebecca straightened, and Ed smiled at her. On his other side, Jessy dozed. Priscilla, too, was asleep, clinging to Rebecca's chest like an infant. She stirred briefly and settled.

"I'm just glad you're alive," Rebecca said.

She appraised him. Alive, yes, but not well. In the full light of day, it was apparent just how sick he was. Sweating profusely and unusually pale, he seemed thinner—the after-effects, she assumed, of his envenomation. Sanchez, too, had been bitten, and Owen had ingested a dose of venom. All three needed medical attention and monitoring. Hell, the whole group did. Still, everyone, including Ed, seemed alert and upbeat, which was all she could hold onto.

After a while she said, "You know, what we saw in there, that object, that *energy*… the implications for humankind—for the future—are enormous."

Ed studied her, as though unsure how to respond. It was some time before he replied. "I said to you once there were things in these rivers better left alone. The jungle is no different."

Rebecca stared into the distance. Maybe she believed that, believed *him*, but she wasn't sure. Something so significant wasn't easily ignored or forgotten.

"The colony," she said quietly. "It'll recover. Now that the Female's gone, the strongest surviving member of the royal caste will take over. Either that or the sterile females will develop ovaries and reproduce." Discreetly, she tossed her head at the three soldiers behind her. Kriedemann was on the satellite phone while Bull and Tag stared vacantly at the jungle. "After what they've seen, this isn't over—it doesn't matter what you or I decide. Their superiors, the powers that be… they'll want answers."

Ed said nothing.

Rebecca braced herself against the side of the Zodiac as Chad steered the boat around a clump of floating debris.

"So earlier," Ed said, "when you told me those things were…*alien*…you weren't pulling my leg, were you?"

Like before, Rebecca kept her voice low. "It's the only scenario that fits."

Ed shook his head. "Who would have thought it—*you* telling *me* something like that? Go figure." He looked pensively at the passing vegetation, as though filling in the blanks. "And the smaller sphere, the one in the temple. You think it might have been a power cell of some description? Removed from the larger sphere in the chamber below?"

"Or severed somehow in the crash—I don't know. Clearly the Intihuasi had handled it—maybe they found a way of opening the larger sphere and removed it. Whatever scenario, I believe it came originally from inside the larger object and was somehow connected—perhaps to its engine, or its heart."

With that, Rebecca remembered something off-topic and reached down, pulled an object from her pocket. To her dismay, the waterlogged pouch had come undone at the top. Gently, she squeezed out the water and peered inside. "This was a little heavier when Oliveira passed it to me back in the chopper," she said to Ed. "Guess I've misplaced a few."

She handed him the pouch. Carefully, he upended the bag into his open palm, and as the sparkling contents spilled forth, Rebecca was relieved to see that a good number of the stones had survived. Ed smiled and shook his head. Replacing the diamonds, he moved to give them back. Rebecca pushed his hand away, closing his fingers over the pouch. "Might be difficult explaining bling of this magnitude to customs," she said. "I was hoping you might pass them on to Enrique's family; Elson's and Martins', too. What do you think?"

Ed smiled warmly. "I think that's a wonderful idea."

He knotted the pouch and placed it in his pocket.

"Hey, that reminds me!" Rebecca said. "One more thing!" Again, she shot a hand into her shorts-pocket. "I can't believe I almost forgot!"

"Forgot *what*?"

Excitedly, Rebecca pulled out the palm-sized, stone disc they'd used to power the lift—the disc Ed's grandfather had given him all those years ago.

Ed's eyes lit up. "How did you get this?"

Rebecca smiled. "When the platform started losing power, I knelt, remember? I wanted to see what was wrong. Just before it receded, and before Oliveira grabbed me around the waist and fired the grappling hook up into the temple, I plucked it out. Then everything went to hell and I totally forgot about it."

Ed hugged her close. "Thank you. Again."

When he pulled back, he had tears in his eyes.

"Hey, you okay?" she asked.

Ed turned the disc in his hands, studying it. He then lifted his eyes to again gaze out the front of the boat. "Yeah, I'm okay."

"You sure? What is it?"

Ed sighed. "I don't know. I guess…" He looked at her, chin quivering. "I wish he could have been there, you know? Seen it himself."

"Your grandfather?"

"It was all he wanted in the end. To see it."

Rebecca placed a hand gently on Ed's knee. "Hey, come on. I'm sure he *did* see it, Ed. I mean, you showed it to him, after all. You found it. He was there, in his own way."

Ed smiled faintly.

The boat droned onwards, and for some time, there was silence between them. Rebecca stared at the jungle. After a while, she turned back. She saw that Jessy had buried her head in Ed's chest. He was holding her hand.

Strangely, Rebecca felt no twinge of jealousy. If anything—and surprisingly—she realised as she looked at the two of them that she was entirely okay with it. At first, she wasn't sure why. Just hours ago, she would have felt differently. Of course, she still had feelings for Ed—strong feelings. She probably even loved him, as she probably always had and probably always would. But as much as she knew that he, too, loved her, she got the feeling that just now, in the clear and rational light of day, he'd made his decision. To her, it seemed the right one—*was* the right one. That she could feel nothing but happiness for him led her to realise that in some deep and profound way, she'd changed. More than that, it dawned on her *when* this change had been triggered: the moment the Male had her underwater, and she'd thought—truly—she was going to die.

In that moment, she'd gained something. Equally, she'd left something behind.

At that, Rebecca smiled, hugged Priscilla close, and tried to get some rest.

EPILOGUE

6 MONTHS EARLIER...

"It's beautiful, isn't it? But I don't understand. How did you get it here, through the jungle?"

Seconds passed as the question was relayed. Nordberg sat cross-legged on the ground and waited for Dominguez to translate the old man's answer.

"He says it walked here of its own accord," Dominguez said. "Just like the others."

Nordberg cast his gaze about the clearing, taking in the numerous statues around him. There were eight in total, set in a circle facing inwards. Each was about ten feet high, except for the individual carving to which they referred. This huge totem was positioned at the circle's northern end and towered a full twenty feet high, dwarfing the others. Like them, it too bore an uncanny resemblance to the moai of Easter Island.

Nordberg frowned, curious. He looked at the old man. Despite his age, the tribal chieftain was taller than expected, and broader, his skin a different tone than most of the indigenous people Nordberg had encountered here in the Amazon. Drawing upon his years in the field—and thinking about it more carefully—it struck him that the old man didn't appear typically indigenous to this region at all, did indeed have a look that was more—*Polynesian* perhaps? For that matter, so did the other members of his tribe, every one of whom sat quietly in a ring around them. That, and the presence of what appeared to be several Easter Island moai seemed suddenly too coincidental. Nordberg's interest had been piqued. He was on to something...

Fortunately, the dialect spoken by the old man bore some of the usual commonalities. Nordberg had brought his assistant Dominguez—himself an anthropologist fluent in several of the local dialects—as well as Tepikan, a member of a neighbouring tribe who knew no English but could converse with the old man. He would translate for Dominguez, who in turn would translate for Nordberg. The process was long and involved, but it worked.

And already, Nordberg had been relayed some amazing stories.

Most exciting of all—particularly in the context of this new revelation—was the one about a tribe of people that had come from over a great expanse of water, and then over the mountains, to settle in a place not far from here. The 'old place'.

The old man and his tribe were descendants of that original tribe.

Now Nordberg wondered: *Could the great expanse of water be the Pacific Ocean? The mountains the Andes, perhaps?*

He could barely contain his excitement. Statues were one thing. *But ancient settlers from Polynesia?*

The old man seemed to sense Nordberg's eagerness. He spoke.

"You are not the first white man he has known," Dominguez translated.

Nordberg nodded. "No, I gathered that." He looked at the old man. "A white man gave you that hat, didn't he?" He gestured to the aged, broad-brimmed fedora atop the man's head, decorated now with several bright macaw feathers.

The old man nodded and smiled. He was missing several teeth.

"Yes," Dominguez said, "But a long time ago, before his last son was born."

"And what was the white man's name?"

"He called himself Ha-Ri."

Suddenly struck by a hunch, Nordberg said, "And this Ha-Ri, he asked about the old place, didn't he? He wanted to go there."

"We warned him not to. We told him there is nothing there but death. It is… cursed. Angry spirits."

"Is that what drove your ancestors away?"

"Yes, from there into the jungle. Never again did they return to the old place. It is lost to our people now."

"But Ha-Ri went, didn't he? Despite your warnings." Nordberg leaned in close. "*Did he find the old place?*"

After a time, the old man nodded. "He found it. Yes." At that, he looked away sadly. "He found it, but he did not return. Just like the other."

Nordberg frowned. "The other?"

"There was another, more recently. The old place is lost to us, but the spirits of our ancestors still speak."

At that, Dominguez paused. There was suddenly much banter between him, Tepikan and the old man. Dominguez appeared to be seeking clarification on something before translating. The old man scribbled in the dirt with a stick.

"What is he saying?" Nordberg asked.

At last Dominguez turned to him, though he appeared uncertain. "He says there are signposts, markers, spread throughout the jungle, all around. They look like these." Dominguez lifted his hand and gestured to the surrounding moai. "When an elder dies the body is taken to one of them for burial. Recently, they found the…" Dominguez paused, searching for the right word, "'paintings', or 'drawings' of this other white man, discarded at one of their markers."

"'Drawings'?"

"Yes, like those of Ha-Ri. That is how they know it must have been another white man."

Again, the old man scratched at the dirt, nodding as he did.

It hit Nordberg. He said excitedly: "Do you think he means a map—or even a notebook or diary, perhaps?"

"Possibly. He doesn't know the name of these things you speak of, but he has them in his possession. He will give them to you."

A map, or a diary, Nordberg thought. If this 'other' man was also searching for the old place, a map or diary would almost certainly contain details of its location, information Nordberg was sure the old man would no longer divulge of his own accord. They might therefore be the only existing record of the place and the only means of locating the site. Nordberg felt a growing excitement. This was getting increasingly intriguing. He was sure his colleagues at FUNAI would be fascinated, too, and would want to examine the items the old man spoke of. Nordberg made a mental note to forward them once he'd finished with them himself.

There was a moment of silence, and the old man stood.

"Come," Dominguez said. "He is hungry now and wishes for you to join him in a meal."

Nordberg nodded, graciously accepting the invitation. He stood also.

"But first he would ask a favour of you," Dominguez said.

The old man removed his hat and offered it to Nordberg.

"Take this, he says. Return it to Ha-Ri's tribe. Ha-Ri was a good friend, an honourable man, but it is not his to keep anymore. This must be done, and he trusts you to do it. He likes you."

The old man pointed to the hat sadly before turning to walk from the clearing.

Nordberg didn't want to offend—but return it? He wondered about this man Ha-Ri, who he was, and what had brought him to the jungle. He studied the hat, turned it over. It was then that he noticed something written neatly by hand on the rim inside. A word. A *name*.

Nordberg smiled, snuffed a laugh.

Well, I'll be...

Not *Ha-Ri*, he realised.

Harry.

Nordberg had a grandfather that went by the name of Harry, though it was just a nickname. Like the former owner of this hat, his real name—the one given him by his parents, and the word written here—was *Henry*.

Nordberg smiled again. If nothing else, it was a start. At least he had a name.

He fell into step behind the old man, and together they followed the path, disappearing quietly into the jungle.

ABOUT THE AUTHOR

WW Mortensen is the international #1 bestselling author of EIGHT and SLITHERS.

He lives in Brisbane, Australia. He has a passion for writing, and devotes his spare time to honing his skills, being with family, and indulging a love of horror movies, adventure stories and action-thrillers.

For more information about the writer and
his books visit wwmortensen.com

He can be contacted at mail@wwmortensen.com

CPSIA information can be obtained
at www.ICGtesting.com
Printed in the USA
LVHW111919140821
695337LV00010B/928